Living WITH Fire

LIVING WITH FIRE

A WITH FIRE NOVEL

TAMARA RENE

Copyright © 2024 Tamara Rene

First paperback edition September 2024

Line Edits by Brenda Mills Bastien

Cover Design by K.B. Barrett Designs

ISBN 978-1-0689047-2-1 (special edition paperback)

ISBN 978-1-0689047-1-4 (ebook)

www.tamararenebooks.com

For Mildred
Thanks for telling me you wanted to burn my book.
I'm never going to stop writing Books My Grandma Wants To
Burn thanks to you.
Burn, Baby, Burn!

AUTHOR NOTE

Hey, Beautiful Reader!

Please note that while we may have a cinnamon roll hero and an adorably sweet heroine, there are some warnings you should take note of before you continue.

- 18+
- Domestic abuse (past experience, not between hero/heroine)
- PTSD
- Violent, graphic scenes
- Explicit sex scenes
- Panic attacks
- Foul language

~Tamara

CHAPTER 1

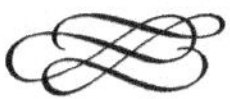

SAVANNA

THERE ARE FEW THINGS MORE EMBARRASSING THAN GETTING caught with your pants around your ankles. Being caught red-handed by a high paying client is probably one of them.

A gasp strangles my throat while my stomach lurches at the sight before me. Standing on the far side of the boardroom I've just stumbled into is my boss, Preston, and his newest intern. Under normal circumstances, that wouldn't be an issue. But when one's pants are dropped and the other's skirt is hiked up to her hips, it can lead to trouble.

"What the hell is going on here?" Mr. Miller bellows from behind me.

Massive trouble.

I turn towards the man in his seventies. His piercing blue eyes are normally sharp and calculating, full of experience that has served him well in his lifetime. I've seen kindness and warmth in them when we've bonded over hockey teams, and annoyance when he needs to deal with someone he's deemed unfit.

I've never seen the rage that's in them now. A look that intensifies as his wife steps from behind him to find out what she's missing. Mr. Miller tries to keep her from seeing, but the woman is fast, despite her age, and darts around him.

"Oh my!" she gasps, a hand coming up to cover lips that are a perfect shade of pink. If her pixie cut hair wasn't already stark white, the shock that radiates from her would turn it so, I'm sure. "Well. This is quite the development."

"I am so sorry you had to see that," I tell them as Mr. Miller takes his wife by the arm and drags her from the room. I'm quick to follow, pulling the door shut with a hard slam, racing down the hall to catch up with them.

My heart feels like it's going to come out of my chest, while heat flushes my entire body. It's not secondhand embarrassment, or our upset clients, that has anger surging through me. It's my own foolishness. Memories of the few dates I've been on with Preston flash through my mind. I knew better than to get involved with anyone, let alone my boss. I hadn't wanted to go out with him. Hell, I'd even turned him down politely at first, declining every advance, ignoring all his blatant flirting.

Loneliness can screw with a person, though, and since I moved to Santa Rosé, California six months ago, I've been lonely. Between the cutthroat nature of my job, and knowing it was best to keep to myself—I couldn't allow anyone to get too close to me—I starved myself of human contact.

Preston caught me during a weak moment one day, asking once more that I join him for dinner. It happened right after I'd caught a couple of my coworkers talking about me in the bathroom. Feeling down and dejected, I'd finally accepted.

The way he lit up when I told him I'd go out with him made me feel special, like I was giving him the only thing he'd ever wanted in his life on Christmas morning. I admit I was pretty dazzled by that. We were planning our fourth date for this Friday, but that's out of the question now.

Mr. Miller stops at the T-intersection of the office and whirls on me. His jaw is clenched, his hand running through his perfectly tousled salt and pepper hair.

"Savanna, this in no way reflects on you, though I question your choice of employer," he states, straining to keep some of the ice out of his tone. "Then again, we've had our money locked in this firm for years, so I question ours as well. No longer. We'll be in touch within the next few days to withdraw everything we invest here."

"I completely understand. Please know I would never have led either of you in there if I'd—"

"We know, dear," Mrs. Miller cuts me off, putting a hand on my arm. "But if that's what goes on in this office, we can no longer be associated with this place."

"Of course," I tell them, nodding my understanding.

I'm pretty sure I can't be associated with it any longer either, but with a million thoughts racing through my mind, it's hard to focus at the moment. One thing I do know is that I won't try to stop them from leaving today, or taking their money out of here.

"I'll walk you to the door," I add.

"No need. We know where it is," Mr. Miller says in a clipped tone. Without another word, he turns and strides down the hall.

Mrs. Miller gives me a pained smile before she follows, leaving me standing at the intersection in the office. One way leads to the elevators, and the other leads to my desk. I can hear a boardroom door open and I'm certain it's from the room we just left. Probably Preston coming to do damage control, but the damage is already done. There's nothing he'll be able to do to save the Miller account. Of that, I'm sure.

People around here don't talk kindly about the Millers. They're known as the "crotchety old people". In my second week as a financial advisor at this wealth management firm, I was thrown onto their account because so many had been kicked off it. The Millers were the type to have their hands on all of their investments. They wanted to know everything that was going on and saw a consultant once every few months. Usually they demanded someone new because no one lived up to their expectations.

Jaws dropped when I walked out of the boardroom with them after our first meeting, the three of us laughing like we were old pals catching up. It bolstered my confidence in my work that the notoriously hard to please couple had taken so well to me.

The downside was being cast as an outsider. I quickly learned the people at this firm weren't here to make friends. They were here to work, compete, and outshine one another. I had outshone many of them without intending to, and while it made Preston, son of one of the owners, extremely happy, it made me a social pariah.

That was okay with me. Mostly. It made for long days and lonely evenings, but when I moved from Denver, Colorado, to this small city southwest of San José, I knew I would need to keep a low profile. What better way to do that than spending your evenings and weekends alone?

"Savanna!" Preston calls my name, and I cringe at the thought of having to deal with him right now.

Putting a hand up, I shake my head, giving him my back

as I walk quickly towards my desk. "Save it, Preston. I don't want to hear it."

"I can explain," he says, causing me to spin around to him.

"You can explain? How exactly do you explain your dick in some other woman?" I sneer, surprising myself. I should know better than to provoke him. I know what can happen when you upset someone, or embarrass them, especially in a public place. Clearly anger is winning over good judgement, though.

"It's not what it looks like," Preston tries again, but even he cringes as the words leave his mouth, knowing how ridiculous they sound. "Okay, it is what it looks like. But it doesn't mean anything. It's not like I've taken her out on a date, like you."

"Wait. Preston, you've taken her out on a date?!" Britney, the intern, says from behind him, causing Preston to jump at the sound of her voice.

"Brit, look, you're fabulous, but…"

Turning on my heel, I make my way briskly to my desk and start tossing my belongings into a pile. In the six months I've been here I've only brought in a few things, but it's enough that I won't be able to carry everything in my hands. I'm not sure if I decided to quit the moment I walked in on Preston and Britney, or if it happened during the short exchange in the hallway, but I know I can't stay.

I'm not happy here, and damn it, I came to California to try and find happiness, or at least get away from unhappiness. I'm an accountant by trade, but when I settled in Santa Rosé this was the first job I could find. Considering that to practice as an accountant in California I would have needed to pass an exam and apply for licensing that would be public record, I opted to find something else. I was told if I were good at advising, it would pay me well. Turns out I am good at it, but the competitive nature, and the people that work here, just don't fit what I want in my life. I've wasted so many years already, and now I've spent six months in a job that I don't like. It's time I confront that and move on.

"Savanna, look, I'm sorry. Tell me what I can do to fix this," Preston says, and I look up from my desk drawer to find him staring at me, an arm slung over the top of the cubicle. He's trying to be smooth and suave, but instead looks slimy.

What did I ever see in him? How did I ever find him attractive? Maybe I didn't. Maybe it's like when you're in a desert and dehydrated. Maybe I was so dehydrated of human contact that I saw Preston as a type of mirage. I envisioned him to look better than he was.

"You can't. I quit."

"What?!" he screeches, and I feel everyone in the office tuning into what's happening. "You can't quit!"

I don't spare him a glance as I open the bottom drawer in my desk and pull out a stash of Sour Patch Kids. "I just did."

"Savanna," Preston hisses, his voice dropping to a near whisper, "You can't quit. You've been putting out all kinds of great numbers. My dad will have my balls if I let you go."

This gets my full attention and I drop a bag of candy back into the drawer and straighten up to my full height. I'm five-six, so I'm not overly tall, but the look on my face must say it all because Preston shrinks away from me.

"Yes, I can quit. And there is not a damn thing you can do to stop me," I tell him, my tone dripping with malice. "Get your disgusting ass out of this cubicle so I can finish packing in peace, or so help me, Preston, the punishment you face with your father will look like a great day at the amusement park."

And there it is. The emotion I knew I could stir up. If he

were someone else, I would be cowering in the corner, terrified of what comes next. The thought creates a wave of adrenaline which hits me like a brick wall. It's all I can do not to reach out and grab hold of the desk to keep me standing straight as Preston belittles me.

"I knew I never should have wasted a minute on you. You have damaged goods and prude written all over you," he seethes at me, the blazing anger in his eyes nearly making me wither on the spot. "You're a waste of fucking breath. Good riddance, Savanna."

It isn't until Preston turns and leaves that I realize I'm holding my breath. It comes out in a harsh whoosh as I sag, my hands coming down hard on the desk to support my weight as my eyes close. Every inch of my body is vibrating, and I know I need to get the hell out of here before I break down and lose any semblance of control I have.

There isn't a single part of me that likes chaos, and I've managed to throw my entire world into it in the span of twenty minutes. This job is the only thing I've got in Santa Rosé. It keeps a roof over my head, food in my belly, gas in the tank; and I've just thrown it away. I *hate* the unknown. Yet here I am, willingly putting myself straight into it.

"Here," a soft voice to my right says, causing me to startle visibly. Turning to the voice, I see Elena, my cubicle neighbor, standing with a box, giving me a small, apologetic smile. "I thought maybe you could use this."

If I could choose one person in the office to be friends with, it would be this woman. We've done the whole small talk thing, chatted here and there, and she's always been friendly enough, but that's as far as it's ever gone between us.

"Thanks."

"You have a couple plants. I thought you'd probably want to make a clean getaway and not have to come back for anything," she explains, tucking a piece of black hair behind her ear.

"I appreciate that. Truly." Taking the box from her, I set it on my desk and start placing my things inside. I almost feel bad that I never made more of an effort to get to know her. Maybe I didn't try hard enough to learn about any of my coworkers. Maybe it was me that was closed off to meeting people and inviting them into my life.

"He tries to date the smart ones, and fucks the ones he deems dumb. I guess after the whole Miller thing, no one warned you. They just wanted to see if you'd sink or swim." Her head cocks to the side and her brown eyes rake up and down the length of my body, making me feel like I'm under a microscope. "After what I just heard, I'm still not sure which one it is."

And maybe I shouldn't have made more of an effort to get to know these people. I don't know what to say, but it seems I don't need to say anything as she turns around and heads back to her own desk, leaving me there feeling more discombobulated than I felt before she appeared.

At least I have a box to use now. I make quick work filling it, double checking all the drawers for anything else that might be mine before I gather everything to head for the elevators just outside of reception. I'm grateful that no one stops me on my way, though I do get a few curious looks and knowing smirks, which seems worse than if someone did say something.

Recognizing I'm making the right decision, I remain as proud as I can with my head up, even if it's making me feel sick every step I take toward the elevators.

My mind is racing with thoughts of my bank account, my savings, and the steps I need to take in order to secure another job, pronto. I don't think to pray that the elevator is deserted so I can ride down to the parking garage alone. Which is probably good since I'm not a prayer kind of person, but maybe it would have helped to throw one up to the big guy, or girl, since it seems I'm having that kind of day.

The doors slide open a second after the bell chimes to signify its arrival, and I'm momentarily frozen in my spot when I see a man already standing inside.

"Shit," I curse under my breath, because I really don't want to do the walk of work shame with anyone to bear witness.

Double shit, since he must have heard me curse, his eyes darting up from his phone to give me a look.

Triple shit when he does a double take at the box in my arms, his eyes moving back to my face for a moment before he sticks an arm out to catch the door before it closes.

"You getting on?" he asks, the rough timbre of his voice sliding down the length of my spine, making me stand taller.

I did not just shiver.

I have no right to shiver over a man's voice. Especially a man I've never met before in my life. Definitely not on the same day I catch a guy I've been dating, fucking another woman.

I also have zero business noticing the insanely gorgeous electric blue eyes that are now staring into mine, or how they're framed by eyelashes that any woman would kill to have. Chocolate brown hair styled in a crew cut, with a little length on top, frames a ruggedly handsome face with a five o'clock shadow, despite it only being ten in the morning. More than anything, though, I know I shouldn't be gawking at the thick biceps and broad shoulders that pull a gray shirt tight across a hard chest.

Slamming my teeth together to keep from saying a word —my mouth can't be trusted at this point—I walk into the elevator. Turning to face the door, I hold my chin high and straighten my back. I hope that the embarrassment of my walk of shame is staying off my face while I pray that he didn't catch me checking him out.

The man drops his arm from the door, stepping back so he's beside me, but I know his eyes followed me inside and are still turned in my direction. It makes me want to melt into the floor. I can feel my cheeks heating, and I'm certain they're tinged a bright pink, but maybe the bad elevator lighting will keep him from noticing.

Please let it keep him from noticing, I send up another silent prayer. *Please make him stop looking at me.*

It's been a rough morning and I do not need some guy, especially one as hot as him, hitting on me.

"I didn't get fired if that's what you're thinking," I tell him, channeling my embarrassment into indignation, turning my nose up. Cutting him off at the knees before he can make a move on me seems like a wise decision.

"Not what I was thinking," he says with mild amusement. "I was—"

"Good," I cut him off pridefully, "Because I'll have you know that I quit. I quit because men are disgusting, filthy pigs, so don't even think about hitting on me while we're in this elevator. I will not take kindly to it."

This is why I was supposed to keep my mouth shut. So I wouldn't say things like this. Though I suppose this is better than telling him he's a hot piece of eye candy.

I can feel his enjoyment for the situation grow as he says, "Is asking what floor you need considered hitting on you? 'Cause that's all I was thinking about."

CHAPTER 2

NATE

THIS OFFICE IS AS SUFFOCATING AS IT IS TINY, NOT ALLOWING A guy to take a single breath without feeling like he's choking on the surrounding air. When I put my gray t-shirt on this morning, it didn't feel quite as tight around my neck as it does now, threatening to strangle the life out of me. And is it hot in here? It feels like I've run into a burning building without any gear for protection.

As a firefighter, temperatures soaring into the hundreds don't usually faze me. I know how to deal with them—drop to the floor where the heat is less dangerous, and crawl your way to safety. Easy. Adrenaline is constant, but it fuels me, pushes me forward, keeps me and my men safe. Fear comes and goes, but dealing with fire and extreme heat has become second nature to me. As a fire lieutenant for the Santa Rosé fire department, I'm expected to handle these things.

I am not equipped to handle the problem before me.

"Did you hear me, Nate?" Larry, my accountant, asks grimly.

Swallowing around the lump that's formed in my throat, I force myself to give the older, balding man a nod. I hear him, I just don't know what I'm going to do about it.

"Everything on that list has to be in my office in the next two weeks," he reiterates what he's already told me, like I didn't hear him the first time. "Invoices, receipts, loans, assets—"

"Income statements, expense records, payroll information," I interrupt, finally finding my voice. "Yeah man, I've got the list." I hold up the piece of paper he shoved in my direction no more than two minutes ago. "I'll get it all together."

"If you need my help…" he starts, trailing off when I raise a hand to silence him.

"I know what you charge an hour, Larry. I'll figure it out." I have no idea how, but I don't have much of a choice.

A week ago, I found out the bar that my sister, Jordan, and I inherited from my uncle on my mom's side, was in trouble with the government. Turns out, Uncle Pete decided not dealing with "Uncle Sam" and the taxes properly wouldn't have any consequences. I didn't truly know how bad it was until twenty minutes ago, when Larry laid it out in no uncertain terms that if I didn't get everything he needed, we would probably be faced with closing the doors.

There's no way I can let that happen.

As bad as Uncle Pete has made this for me—us, since Jordan is technically half owner—I can't lose the one thing that brought my uncle happiness in the last two decades of his life. After he retired from firefighting, 10-42—which means off duty, or ending tour of duty—was his pride and joy, and he turned it into mine.

I've worked in the bar for my uncle since I was sixteen, starting as a dishwasher, and working my way through the ranks. It was what I did before I joined the academy to become a firefighter, it's what I did during my training, and it's what I've done on my days off since.

For the last five years, I've been helping him manage the bar.

At least I thought I had been.

Turns out, I knew nothing about what it really took to make the bar run smoothly. He never taught me how to do much of the paperwork besides orders. Paying employees? Vendors? Utilities? I had to figure that out on my own after he passed.

It's been a stressful six months, but I felt like we'd finally found our footing. Then we discovered the tax situation.

It's beginning to look like Uncle Pete didn't know as much as he let on either.

"Call me if you need me," Larry offers, pushing up from his chair to walk me out.

On my way down to the parking garage, I shove my hand through my brown hair, and sigh as I glance down at the list Larry gave me. Not only is it long, but I need four years' worth of this shit. I think that's the most worrying part of it all. The amount of time I have to go back in history is staggering.

The headache that's starting in the back of my skull tells me the amount of stress I'm feeling right now is in the extreme realm, considering I face stressful situations every day of the week.

Leaning back against the wall of the elevator, I pull my phone out to send a quick text to my sister. Jordan would help more if I let her, but the bar was never her thing. She waitressed when she was younger and in school, but now she's a full-time ER nurse. I know that's demanding on her, so I try to shoulder the load of the bar.

Me: Got a list of things to do from Larry. I'll get to work on it tonight.

I'm headed to the bar now, but I've got a full day of bartending before I can start to look at the stuff for Larry. When my head bartender gets in at six, I'll spend four or five hours dealing with the accounting before heading home for a short night of sleep. I've got to be at the firehouse for an early morning shift tomorrow.

I love our bar. I have a million good memories from it over the years. The thought of losing it makes my chest ache and my throat clog. It will forever be the thing that brought my uncle and me together, the thing that bonded us. He's the reason I became a firefighter in the first place. He was an integral part of me becoming the man I am today. I owe it to the bar, to my uncle, and to myself, to make sure I get this worked out, because I can't imagine not having this place in my life. Not when I can credit it for so much that I have now.

The elevator slows, threatening to bottom out my stomach. I glance up at the number above the door, realizing it's not stopping because we're in the underground parking, but because we're picking up another occupant. The doors open just as my phone vibrates in my hand, pulling my attention to the device.

Jordan: I'm off today, but I've got some stuff to do. I can help after.

"Shit," a soft, feminine voice curses, causing my eyes to shoot up.

The woman standing outside the elevator is breathtakingly gorgeous. Our eyes connect for the briefest of moments before I'm drawn to a box in her arms, which she shifts uncomfortably while her feet stay rooted in place. I'm trying to hide my appreciation for how striking she is when my eyes meet hers again, lingering for a moment.

Beautiful almond-shaped blue eyes are accentuated by high cheekbones in a heart-shaped face. Long, blonde hair falls in waves, curling over her shoulders to sit atop the swell of her breasts—the only part of them I can see thanks to the box in her hands. If I were a betting man, I'd guess they were the perfect size to fit in my palm. Not too big, not too small, just the way I like them.

The doors to the elevator start to close, and instinctively, I throw an arm out to catch them before they shut entirely.

"You getting on?" I ask, watching as her posture shifts to stand taller.

Christ. I don't think I've ever seen anything as beautiful as the way her cheeks turn rosy under my gaze. I hear her teeth audibly come together, steeling herself as she walks onto the elevator with her head held high, looking as though she'd rather be anywhere other than stuck in a tiny space with me.

Dropping my hand from the door, I step back, my eyes doing another sweep of her. If the box wasn't a dead give-away, the air surrounding this woman would tell me that her day may beat mine in the shitty department. It's thick with the type of friction that makes you want to tuck tail and run, but it doesn't scare me. I deal with this type of tension all the time.

"I didn't get fired, if that's what you're thinking," she snaps with irritation, nostrils flaring, before I have a chance to say anything.

My eyebrows raise, and I can't help the upward tilt at the corner of my lips. "Not what I was thinking," I tell her, marginally amused at her presumption. "I was—"

"Good!" she says with disdain, cutting me off. "Because I'll have you know that I quit. I quit because men are disgusting, filthy pigs, so don't even think about hitting on me while we're in this elevator. I will not take kindly to it."

I let her words hang in the air between us for a moment. It feels hazardous to my health to breathe, let alone speak at this point, but there's a pressing question that needs to be answered.

"Is asking what floor you need considered hitting on you?" I hedge, biting back a chuckle for my own safety. "Cause that's all I was thinking about."

Wide, horrified eyes, that I note are more gray than blue, turn to me, and I fight to keep a full-fledged grin from forming. It's obvious this woman has had a rough morning. Normally I'd be sympathetic towards someone walking into an elevator with a box full of their things, but right now, I'm amused.

That might have to do with the fact her face is turning multiple shades of red while she lets my words sink in. Or perhaps it's because I've had my own shitty morning, and this stunning woman is providing a much needed distraction. Either way, I'm having a hard time keeping the enjoyment off my face as I gaze expectantly at the woman gawking at me.

"Oh." Her voice is nothing more than a squeak colored with embarrassment. I have to fight harder to keep from grinning, a battle I'm losing. She glances at the buttons on the wall as she clears her throat. "Same place as you."

"Great," I tell her, taking one last look at her inflamed cheeks before turning to face the door of the elevator.

I'm not the type of guy that would hit on a woman in an elevator in the first place—I leave shit like that up to my best friend, Liam—but if I were, I think I'd pick a woman like this. While she isn't leggy, standing a good five inches shorter than me even in heels, she has nice, toned calves that are shown off in the black skirt that clings to hips that scream she's all woman.

She smells intoxicating. If I could bottle the scent of a woman and take it everywhere with me, it would be whatever this woman is wearing. It's filling the elevator and making my mouth water. It's fruity and sweet, reminding me of a warm summer evening in the backyard, with good friends and great beer. I don't stop myself from taking a deep breath, letting it fill my senses.

When it comes to how a woman smells, it's an aphrodisiac for me. I've always attributed that to spending a lot of time smelling smoke from fires, blood from crash scenes, and cleaners from the firehouse. Being a firefighter for the last twelve years, working my way up from a volunteer to a lieutenant, I've seen a lot, and smelled more. I thoroughly enjoy a nice smelling woman.

"I'm sorry," she says, her voice softer than before, but no less embarrassed. "I shouldn't have assumed anything."

"Rough morning?" I ask with a raise of my brow.

I can feel her look at me from the side of her eye, and in my peripheral vision see her nod. "Yep."

The elevator dings a second later. When the doors open, I stick my hand out to keep it held, gesturing for her to precede me. I'm trying to be a chivalrous gentleman on a bad day for this woman. When I glance at her, however, I'm met with a wary gaze, and I feel my eyebrows shoot up in surprise, given that she just apologized to me.

"Ladies first," I explain tentatively, still holding the doors.

"All due respect," she says with a tight smile, the ire from earlier diminished, "If I get off the elevator before you, I know you're just going to look at my ass and watch me as I walk away, which is the last thing I need right now."

While she's not wrong, I'm not about to tell her that. Any red-blooded male would look—those are just facts—and she's calling me out on them. I must admit, I'm a little disappointed that I'm not going to get a good look at what I'm guessing is a shapely ass, but she isn't moving an inch on this, and I won't be stuck in an elevator with this woman just so I can get an eyeful.

"Suit yourself," I say, shrugging. "But that works both ways. If I can't stare at your ass, you better not be ogling mine."

With a smirk to myself when I hear a gasp of surprise followed by a snort of laughter, I step out of the elevator into the parking garage and start towards my truck. I can hear the woman's heels clicking on the ground behind me, indicating she's walking in the same direction I am.

I can't help it when I give my ass a little shake. Hoping to get another chuckle out of her, I call over my shoulder, "Stop objectifying me. I can feel you checking me out, just like when you got on the elevator."

Laughter from behind has warmth spreading through me. The grin I've been trying to hold back this entire time is now in full-blown breakout mode. When I glance over my shoulder this time, I catch her eyes, amusement dancing in my own. "It's okay. I know I've got a nice ass. It's hard not to stare, but you should really try to refrain."

I'm met with a huff big enough that the box in her arms bounces awkwardly, and though she's trying to keep a straight face, her eyes are livelier than when she got on the elevator.

Turning around to walk backwards the last few feet to my truck, I hear the words coming out of my mouth before I can stop them, "I suppose it's better for you to stare at my ass than my crotch, isn't it?"

My words have the desired effect I wanted. I'm delighted when I see her eyes dart below my waist because she can't help herself. Just as quickly she's looking back up, embarrassment flashing in her beautiful eyes.

"Disgusting. Filthy. Pigs!" she calls out, trying to infuse anger in her tone, but I catch the smile spreading across her lips before she disappears between two cars.

And just like that, my mood has lifted. There's still a cloud hanging over me, but instead of threatening rain, the sun came out to shine.

CHAPTER 3

NATE

"Wait, so after all this, you still didn't get this girl's number?" Liam asks from across the burnt barnwood bar.

Since leaving the accountant's office, I've been bartending the country and western style pub. Liam planted his butt on a black bar stool an hour ago to have some dinner and a couple of beers. I just finished telling him the story about the woman in the elevator, and he's flabbergasted that I did little more than shake my ass.

"Where would that have been appropriate? Before, or after, she called men pigs the first time? Or maybe the second?" I retort, a hip pressed against the bar, my arms folded over my chest.

I shouldn't expect anything more from Liam, but I always do. I love the guy like a brother, but he's the definition of a man whore. There's a constant revolving door of women he finds at the bar to take home with him. Though he's never actually dated a woman for the entire ten years I've known him, I know he's got a lot more to give than he thinks he has. He just doesn't allow himself to see, or think, he's capable of anything other than the playboy bachelor lifestyle.

He picks up his beer and points it at me, concern etched in his sharp facial features and brown eyes. "Dude, the lack of game you have astonishes me. How are we even friends?"

"I have game," I grumble, grabbing a bar rag to wipe down the counter. It doesn't need it, but I know Liam isn't going to let up on my dating life now that I've opened the door. I should have known better than to say anything, but I'm a masochist.

"Really? When was the last time you went out with a woman? Hell dude, when's the last time you got laid?"

"I get laid."

I do. Or I could. I just haven't. Life has been hectic. There's nothing wrong with that. But Liam sits there and stares at me, waiting for me to answer the question. When I don't, he beams in triumph.

"This is my point," he says, leaning over the bar towards me. "You don't get laid. You work too damn much. Dude, you're a thirty-two-year-old bachelor, wasting the best years of your life. You need to live a little. Get out there and meet some ladies, do some fucking, have the time of your life. Stop working all the damn time."

I cock an eyebrow at him, and he does it right back at me. A silent conversation passes between us; me asking what I'm supposed to do about the bar, him suggesting I hire someone else to help out. It's a conversation we've had more times than I can count in the last couple of months, but whatever he sees on my face next has him frowning.

Shrugging, I look down the bar to one of my other customers to see if he needs anything. The guy looks alright, so I turn back to Liam.

"I take it your meeting with the accountant didn't go so well this morning?" he asks, his voice dropping to a whisper.

Besides Jordan, Liam is the only one that really knows what's going on with the bar and the troubles I'm facing, and he doesn't even know the extent of it.

Rubbing a hand up and down the side of my face, I shake my head. The list has been on my mind all day, giving me a headache at the base of my skull.

The stress must be showing on my face because Liam frowns, something he doesn't do a lot. "Shit dude, that's rough. Anything I can do to help?"

I blow out a frustrated sigh. "As much as I appreciate it, I don't even know where to start, so you'd be even more useless than me."

I've been a hard worker my entire life, but for the last six months I've worked harder than ever, which is starting to take its toll. Between my shifts at the firehouse, and all the hours I've been pulling at the bar, I've been burning the candle at both ends. It's chaotic, and I feel like I'm constantly running on a hamster wheel. Usually the firehouse is a reprieve from the bar, and the bar a reprieve from the firehouse, but with this new tax situation, there is zero reprieve from anything. I'm not sure how I'm going to manage everything, but I need to find a way.

There are going to be many sleepless nights in my future. I can feel it. It probably doesn't help that I'm a guy who hates asking for help. A fact that Liam is usually quick to point out.

I gesture to the almost empty plate in front of him, and he nods that he's done. After disposing of it in the kitchen, I check on the guy at the end of the bar, grab him a new beer, then make a couple of drinks for Bryn, my head server, before returning to Liam.

"You should have just been your adorable, charming self

and asked for her number," Liam says with a firm nod. I'm pretty sure he's been thinking about this since I left. "Could have told her you'd show her that not all men are pigs like she thinks. It's true. I mean, I fit that bill, but you? You're an upstanding kind of guy that any girl would be happy to have." He tips his bottle back, but before he takes a drink, he sighs sadly. "Too damn bad you don't have any game."

I don't have a chance to counter before my eyes are diverted to my sister pulling out the barstool next to Liam, sinking into it with a huff. She looks miserable, her brown hair disheveled in a messy bun, her eyes rimmed red. It puts me on edge, wondering whose ass I need to beat.

"What's wrong?" I wince at the bark in my own voice, the protectiveness I feel for my sister showing.

"Tequila. I need a shot of tequila. Please, Nate."

My eyes slide to Liam at the same time his move to mine. I can tell just by looking at him that we're on the same page, both of us ready to kick whoever's ass has made Jordan look like this.

I do as she asks and grab a glass, filling it a quarter of the way before edging it towards her. She takes it, and we both watch as she downs it without a second thought, not even making a face when she's done.

"More," she commands, pushing the glass towards me.

"First, tell me what's wrong," I counter, putting the bottle down to cross my arms, holding firm.

For one long second of hell, I think she might burst into a million tears when I see the shuddering breath that she releases. I'm certain Liam feels the same because he stiffens in my periphery. The moment comes and goes with no tears falling, but eyes the color of mine are full of them before she looks down at the bar.

Her voice is barely above a whisper when she says, "I think Paul is cheating on me."

"Douchebag Paul?" Liam asks, beating me to the punch of questioning her. "I thought you broke up with him a couple of months ago."

Jordan's arms slam down on the counter, and she falls forward dramatically, wailing loud enough for both of us to hear, despite her face being muffled by the bar and her arms. "I did!"

If my sister weren't about to lose it in the bar, I would burst out laughing at the panicked look on Liam's face as his eyes bounce from Jordan to me, floundering with what to do. His hand is outstretched, ready to touch her shoulder, but I can tell he's not sure of himself, so I give him a nod to comfort her.

"They got back together," I tell him quietly as he tentatively pats her upper back.

I wasn't happy when she reconciled with the asshole, but it's not my life, and as much as I hate it, I can't tell Jordan who she should and shouldn't date. For the most part. She and I have an understanding that she doesn't date my friends, something that we decided a long time ago when we were still kids.

"He left his phone open on the coffee table when he went to the bathroom, and a text came up," she says, lifting her head from the counter. I'm surprised to see no tears have fallen, though they're still there, threatening. "I saw the message come across the screen asking if something was sexy and then I couldn't help myself. I know I shouldn't have looked, but I did, and… and…"

"Deep breath," Liam says with a calmness he didn't appear capable of a moment ago.

I raise an eyebrow, surprised at the softness in his tone.

The guy isn't as emotionally unequipped as he thinks he is, when he stops letting his brain get in the way. Either that, or his firefighting training is kicking in and he's treating her more like a patient than a woman on the verge of a breakdown.

He confirms the latter when he takes in a deep breath, showing her how to do it, and lets it out slowly. Jordan follows him the second time and then she nods, closing her eyes for a moment. When they open again, she gestures towards the tequila bottle, and this time I fill her glass.

"Whoever this woman is," she says, picking up the fresh drink. "She's been sending Paul all kinds of pictures in her underwear. And he's been sending shirtless pics back. God, why am I such an idiot?"

"I'm going to kick his ass," I say, my jaw ticking as anger floods my veins. The only time in my life I've gotten into a fight was when a different jerk hurt her—apparently I'm not above making this a thing.

"I'm in, let's go," Liam seconds, already moving to stand from his barstool.

"No!" Jordan exclaims, flailing her hands at the two of us. "No, please, don't. I don't want extra drama, and you both know you can't do that. You're firefighters. You can't just go beating people up."

Liam snorts. "We'll wear masks."

Jordan levels him with a glare, and he puts both hands up in surrender, slowly sliding back into his seat, but not before he shoots me a look as if to say we can go later when Jordan isn't around. I ignore him and pour her another small shot of tequila before grabbing a glass to fill with water.

"If you're drinking that much tequila, you need to follow it with some water."

Giving me a brief nod, she looks to Liam, her eyes pleading. "Drink with me? I don't want to drink alone, but God, I need to drink. I just want to forget."

Liam grimaces. "Uh…"

"Jor, we're on shift in the morning. Liam can't drink hard al—" I stop mid-sentence to watch my best friend reach over the bar to grab a glass, then the bar gun. He fills it with water then nods to her glass for me to fill.

"I can't drink tequila with you, but I'll still drink with you," he says, lifting his glass to her. "Fuck the disgusting, filthy pig."

"Exactly," she says, clinking her glass against his, happy enough that he's putting up the pretense of drinking with her, even if he's not going to get wasted like she is. "Never be those guys, guys."

Liam chokes on his drink with Jordan being none-the-wiser of how direct her comment is in regard to my day. I roll my eyes, already sensing what's coming. Liam is about to open his big mouth and tell her all about the woman in the elevator. I don't want any part of it, so I leave them and wander down the bar.

After checking on my other patron, I make sure Bryn doesn't need anything. Then I say hello to Martin, my head bartender, when he walks in. We talk for a few minutes about the day before he goes about setting himself up for his shift while I stroll back down the bar.

The sound of my sister's laughter makes me hopeful that her crisis has been diverted.

It has, for the time being, but it's at my expense, just as I thought. It's obvious that Liam has told her, and she turns to look at me while she says to Liam, "Let me guess—he's trying to claim that he has game."

"You know it," he confirms with a smirk.

"Because I do!" I say, jumping to my own defense. "I can

get a date just fine."

"Then why don't you, brother?"

"Been a little busy, if neither of you have noticed." It's the answer I give to everyone. I'm not opposed to dating, or love —hell, I'd welcome it with open arms—but firefighting and the bar come first for me, and I don't know how to find someone who will accept that long term.

"You don't even try. Do you know how many women around here look you up and down, giving you the eye? Have you ever realized how many women would love it if you just asked one of them out, or bought them a drink?" Jordan asks, eyebrow raised.

"I leave that up to Liam," I say dryly.

Jordan tsks with disapproval. "You're wasting your life away by working so much. I know things haven't been easy, but Nate, you're not getting any younger. I worry about you."

Liam nods his agreement. "I've tried telling him the same thing."

"I could say the same thing about you," I turn on him, trying to take some of the heat off myself.

He shakes his head this time. "Nope. I don't want a relationship. Not made for 'em. You, however, are. You've always been the relationship guy out of the two of us, dude."

"At least go out and get laid, Nate," Jordan says, filling her own glass this time.

"I do," I grit out through my teeth.

The only reason I'm entertaining any of this right now is because it's taking Jordan's mind off what happened with Paul, and if I can do that, it's worth it. I think.

"Really? When's the last time?" she asks.

I throw my hands up in frustration. "Do you two compare notes before you gang up on me? Why do you both have such an interest in my sex life?"

Jordan looks at Liam and frowns. "Is he this grumpy at work too?"

"Getting worse by the day," Liam confirms with pursed lips and a nod.

They both look at me again, and I glare back. I know Liam is teasing with his comment, but I'm becoming irritated by the two of them. They both know how hard it's been the last few months. They know where my priorities lie. I won't let Uncle Pete down. Or any of my staff. Closing down would mean jobs lost, and I won't have that on my conscience.

Jordan smirks. "This is why we have an interest. You get kind of testy when you're not getting any action."

"Five finger action doesn't count," Liam adds with a snort.

"Besides, do you really want to go to Mom's birthday next week without a story to tell all the aunts? I'm not the only one who worries about you," Jordan says, swishing the tequila around in her glass. "They're going to be all over you like vultures on a dead carcass if you don't tell them you're dating someone. Hell, without proof they'll be all over you anyway."

Christ. Our aunts.

We have a great family, but every one of my aunts—my mother included—is far too interested in when we're planning on settling down with someone. They bug all the cousins, but so many have now gotten married, and had kids, that the spotlight is on those of us who are single. In their minds a person isn't happy unless they're married with a couple of kids, and a white picket fence. I know they mean well, but they can be a lot at times.

"I can handle them," I tell her confidently. "I always do." I point a finger between the two of them. "Now stay out of my damn sex life."

SAVANNA

Drinking my problems away sounded like a really good idea in the moment. This morning? Not so much. It's been a rough one since I woke up; not even a shower helped. I went a little overboard last night after the day I'd had, hoping that all my problems would magically disappear. I was sorely disappointed when I found the box I'd packed at the office had followed me home.

"Savanna," the barista calls out, placing a large cup of hot heaven on the counter.

Snagging the caramel macchiato goodness I splurged on, I head back into the blinding sunlight of the late August morning, tipping my sunglasses over my eyes. I'm headed to the one place where I've found sanctuary since the moment I set foot in Santa Rosé six months ago. The beach.

God, that feels like both yesterday and a lifetime ago.

The weight of the world feels crushing at the moment,

making me feel older than my twenty-nine years. Yet, as the beach comes into view, and the pier stands out in the distance, it feels like just yesterday when I drove into town, running for my life.

As I gaze at the pier, I remember the cool night at the end of February when I ended up in Santa Rosé. I had no idea where I would end up after leaving Denver, letting fate decide on the flip of a coin, between the west or east coast. When the coin landed on tails I headed west, my final destination being the coastline in whatever state was closest. I had never seen the ocean, let alone touched it. It was the only thing I knew I wanted in the new life I was going to carve out for myself.

It had taken me three days to get here as I hadn't dared travel the major interstates, worried that my ex, Vincent, might be looking for me. There was only a slim chance he would contact law enforcement, but I was trying to be as safe as possible, so I zig-zagged my way across the country, taking in all the sights that I came across.

I was freer than I'd been in years, a feeling that I held onto as tightly as possible.

Like a moth to a flame, I stumbled upon Santa Rosé, the pier, and the ocean, falling in love immediately. I can still feel the tears that sprang to my eyes when I took in the ocean breeze for the first time, tasting the saltiness in the air.

It was the taste of freedom.

That night, a fisherman stood on the pier, with a line cast over the side, while a few people walked along the wooden boards. I heard laughter in the air, the hum of endless possibilities and new opportunities, and inhaled the smell of a fresh outlook on the ocean kissed wind. The pier was exactly as I had always imagined one to be, with a multitude of buildings selling souvenirs and trinkets, and restaurants over the water. I took my time as I walked along, gratefully absorbing it all, and incredulous that I had made it.

I had found my new home.

Something about this little city called to me. It wasn't something I understood, but it wasn't something I was going to question.

Walking across the sand until I'm closer to the water, but not close enough to get splashed by the waves, I sigh as I plop my butt down. Kicking my flip-flops off, I bury my feet in the sand, wrapping both hands around my coffee cup as I look out over the water.

There have been a lot of moments when I've felt homesick in the last six months. When I left, I cut off all communication so that no one would know where I was. I didn't delete my social media, but I haven't logged in since I left. There isn't one person from back home that I've spoken to, and while I've felt the weight of that decision, today it feels extraordinarily heavy.

A familiar prickle behind my eyes forces me to take a deep breath, my heart aching within my chest.

I wish I could talk to my best friend, Maddie. I miss her so much. If she'd heard about what happened yesterday, I know she would have flown all the way here just to give Preston a piece of her mind. Then, knowing Maddie, she'd track down the hot guy from the elevator, with his fine bubble butt of an ass, and demand he take me on a date.

Laughing at the audacity of my made-up story quickly turns into my chin trembling as tears threaten to fall. I take a quick sip of my coffee to distract myself, whimpering as the hot liquid scalds first my mouth, then my throat.

Putting the cup down, I sink my feet deeper, leaning back

until my hands are propping me up by pressing into the sand. If I could talk to Maddie right now, she would tell me everything was going to be okay, just like she did before I left Denver.

She was the only one that knew I was leaving. The only person that knew some of the abuse I was suffering at the hands of my ex. The last time I talked to her, I hadn't made it to Santa Rosé yet, but she knew I was headed west, and my final destination would be along the coast. It was all I was willing to tell her, though her instructions were to tell everyone I went east. The less anyone back home knew, the safer I felt they would be.

The safer I felt I would be.

But every single day it kills me a little more inside not to hear my dad's voice. Not to hear my brothers bickering over who gets the last chicken breast at family dinner. It hurts so damn much not to be part of their laughter around the table. I wonder if they still laugh, even though I'm not there. I wonder if Maddie joins them like she used to when I was home.

The ache in my chest deepens as a lone tear slides down my cheek. Until yesterday, things had been going smoothly, and I was clinging to the faith that this city was right for me. I got a job right away, though I question Preston's motives for hiring me now, and I even lucked out and found an apartment pretty quickly. Mind you, it's a bit run down, but the neighborhood seemed okay, and it's within walking distance to the beach, which was the biggest draw.

Now I'm questioning whether coming out here was the wrong decision. I could have told one or both of my brothers, but I always felt they'd murder Vincent if they knew what he had done to me. I could have gone to the cops, but unless Vincent stayed behind bars, I had no doubt he would come after me for turning him in. He never would have let me out from under his thumb.

Running seemed like the only option, but now I'm wondering if I should pack my stuff and head home. My stomach churns at the thought, while a full body shudder shakes me from head to toe.

That would be a no from the body.

The ache in my heart says screw what my body thinks. With no job it won't be long before I can't keep a roof over my head, and going home to my family would dull the hurt.

Vincent's face pops into my mind, and I already know if I were to go back, he would make me pay. While my heart may miss home enough to go back, I know, logically, it isn't in the cards.

Which means one thing. I need to find a new job, and I need to do it quickly. I have a small amount saved, but not a lot. Trying to furnish my apartment as well as build up savings means I haven't grown the safety net as big as I'd like. I'm kicking myself for that now, but it was also important to have some comfort at home, especially given all the free time I spend there.

Sitting forward, I push my feet through the sand, watching it fall around my legs as my feet pop up from beneath the small granules.

God, I love it here. I've sat on this mesmerizing beach for countless hours since I moved here, watching the tides roll in and out, listening to the surf. From watching kids take their first steps into the water, to paddleboarders, windsurfers, and kayakers, the entertainment the beach provides for free has kept me captivated from the start. I dream of learning some of the things I've seen when I've got the extra cash.

There's no way I could leave all this behind. Even though I miss home, and as much as I want to turn tail and run away from the situation I've found myself in, I've fallen in love with Santa Rosé. My time here hasn't come to an end.

Picking up my coffee, I nod to myself, decision made. Tomorrow I'll find a new job. Today? Today I nurse this hangover, and maybe do the other thing that brings me calm and solace—cleaning.

CHAPTER 5

SAVANNA

Dropping a bag of trash at my feet, I survey my apartment. It's cleaner today than it was the day I moved in, though that isn't totally surprising. The apartment itself was worse than the rundown building, but at the time it was what I could afford. It just needed a little TLC.

I spent every spare moment making it a home, scrubbing it from top to bottom. I even got permission to paint, turning the place into my own little oasis, and as I look around, there's a calmness and serenity that washes over me.

When I got to Santa Rosé, I didn't have anything but the clothes in my suitcase, yet I've managed to make my space comfortable, and my own. There's a white reading chair I love to spend my evenings in, a brown couch I can sink into after a long day, and a window nook that houses a myriad of plants to bring life and color inside.

After all my unnecessary cleaning, I've got a small trash bag ready to take out before I hit the shower and sit down to relax with a good book for the rest of the night. It sounds like a little slice of heaven before the job search begins tomorrow, and I've been looking forward to it since I started cleaning earlier.

Slipping on a pair of flip-flops, I grab the trash and open the door to step into the hall. Sniffing the air, my nose wrinkles. Someone burned their dinner somewhere because it smells, and not in the mouthwatering delicious kind of way.

Hustling to escape the stench, I head to the garbage room to toss my bag in the chute, annoyed when I get there and find the doorstop across the room.

My landlord explained when I moved in that the door was faulty, and if the door closed on me, I'd be stuck until someone let me out. Unfortunately, in the six months I've lived here, he still hasn't been by to fix it, despite my reminders to him. This isn't the first time I've found the wedge across the room, which I don't understand since everyone on this floor knows the deal.

Maybe I should just leave the bag inside the door and say screw the chute.

"You aren't that person, Sav," I tell myself.

Setting the garbage bag against the door, I eye it, ensuring it doesn't move for at least a minute before gathering the courage to dart across the room for the little safety device. I'm halfway back to standing when a scrape causes me to look up, my eyes widening as I see the door slowly start to slide closed.

"No, no, no," I yell, lunging towards the door.

In my haste, I manage to get tangled in my flip-flops, and stumble. Reaching out to break my fall, I catch the door, but the momentum of my body crashes into it, and with a sickening thud, it slams shut, ensuring that I'm stuck in this god forsaken room that reeks like trash.

"No!" I shout, banging my hand against it. "Shit!"

I know it's pointless, but I grab the handle and jiggle it, then pull with all my might, like I might be able to get somewhere with it. The landlord demonstrated all of this by locking himself in the day I met him, trusting that I would let him out. I'd freed him, but I'm suddenly wishing I hadn't.

Pounding my fist on the door, I scream as loud as I can, "Help! Someone help!"

There are two other occupied apartments close to mine. The rest are either vacant, or on the other side of the building. I'm praying that one of my neighbors is home and awake, or at least doesn't sleep like the dead.

But beating, kicking, and yelling until my throat hurts and my hands feel like they're bruised, is all in vain. No one comes to my rescue, and with each passing moment, I'm feeling a little more frantic.

I can't be stuck here all night. Five minutes is five minutes too long, let alone hours upon hours. I hate small places. I hate enclosed spaces. I hate being locked away.

The panic comes on strong and fast once my thoughts are triggered by being confined with no escape. My breathing quickens and grows shallow while terror floods my body, making me feel dizzy and lightheaded. It's enough to make me stop wailing on the door, though I think I preferred bruising my hands to this.

I need to breathe. I need to relax. I need to stop thinking about the worst case scenario, or that this is like before, but it's hard not to be sucked into things that I remember so vividly.

Trapped in a basement, the only light coming from under the door if it was nighttime. Hours spent clawing at the door, desperate to get out, begging to be set free, promising I would do better, act better, be better.

"No," I gasp to myself, sucking in a deep breath. "No!"

I will not allow my past to dictate my future. This isn't the same. I'm not in the same place. No one has locked me in this room against my will—unless you count the useless landlord who refused to fix the door.

Turning my back to the door, I slide down to the floor, resting my head between my knees, counting to four as I breathe in, repeating the process as I let the breath out. It takes seven rounds before my lungs aren't screaming and my head feels clearer and capable of actual thought.

I can figure this out. I'm a smart woman. I've gotten myself this far in life, I can get myself out of this situation. I just need to figure out how.

Looking around the room, I frown. It's empty. Bare. Not even my trash bag is inside with me because the damn door knocked it back into the hallway. I glance at the hinges on the door. I could try to knock the pegs out and open it that way. The problem is I don't have anything to hit them with and I'm fairly sure my flip-flop isn't going to cut it.

My eyes land on the garbage chute next, causing me to cringe. Eyeing the little door that opens, I wonder if I would fit, and if I did, would I survive falling down it and into the bin? That's probably a bad idea, but I'm not sure if the alternative is any better. Being stuck in this room is going to screw with my mind, and I've worked hard in the last few months to get myself in a healthier mindset.

I'm about to get up and take a better look at the garbage chute, if for no other reason than to assess the situation, when I freeze and sniff the air. This room doesn't smell great; I've witnessed many abandoned bags of garbage in here when dropping off my trash. Some people can't be bothered to take the few extra seconds to open the chute and toss their bags in, which creates quite the stench, especially in the California summer heat.

As I sniff again, I can smell the garbage, but there's something else that's beginning to overpower it. A second passes before I realize what it is. The same odor that was in the hallway is now seeping into the room, but I was wrong earlier. It isn't someone's burnt dinner. Something is burning. Something is on fire.

The shrill sound of the fire alarm goes off, startling me so badly that I slam my hands over my ears and tuck my head down, shoulders raising as the noise assaults me. It's got to be one of the worst things I've heard in my life. It's so loud that I'm positive it would wake the deepest of sleepers, which I suppose is the point.

Jumping up, I start pounding on the door again, screaming to anyone who might hear. The elevators are in the middle of the building with a set of stairs at either end, and the garbage chute is next to the stairs closest to my apartment. If my neighbors are home, they should go right by, and maybe one of them will hear me screaming. If they aren't home, or they don't hear me, I really hope I'm not totally screwed. I have no idea where the fire is, but if the smell of smoke is any indication, it's too close for comfort.

I'm still banging relentlessly when I notice a little puff of black smoke come under the door. "No!" I shriek, hitting the door with all my might. "No, no, no. Someone hear me! Please! Help! I'm trapped!"

Another larger cloud wafts in and I know I'm about to be extremely screwed if someone doesn't hear me, or I don't do something drastic soon. I glance at the garbage chute again, taking a break from beating on the door. Maybe it won't be so bad. I can probably fit. It's better than dying of smoke inhalation, or burning alive, right?

Dashing to the chute, I wrench on the door to open it, crying out when it only lifts halfway to its full height.

"What?" I gasp, tugging harder.

Panic seizes my heart when it doesn't move even after I start to jump up while jerking on it. Throwing my body weight into it, hoping it'll knock it loose, I scream as anger drowns out the fear when it doesn't budge an inch.

If I ever get out of here and see my landlord, I'm going to murder him for not fixing everything that is wrong with this damn building. I'm facing a potential life or death situation, and I might not make it because of his negligence.

I might die in a garbage room.

The thought has me giving up on the chute. Turning back to the door, I ready myself to resume my assault on it when I realize I need to do something about the smoke coming in from under the door. I don't stand a chance of surviving if smoke fills this room before someone can find me.

Acting on instinct, I strip down to my bra and panties, using my yoga pants and t-shirt as a barrier at the bottom of the door, stuffing them into the crack. It only takes a second to see that the smoke isn't billowing its way under the door anymore causing me to pump my fist in the air in victory.

Score one for Savanna. Now if I can just get someone to open the door.

As if the universe heard my thoughts, a voice bellows from the other side of the door, "Fire department! Call out!"

"In here! I'm trapped! Help!" I cry, relief flooding me as I slam my hands against the door with such fierceness I'm sure they'll be bruised if I get out of this.

"I hear you," someone shouts, banging on the door. "Stand back!"

I'm so thankful I'm shocked that I don't sag to the ground and start crying. Thank God for adrenaline and survival instincts because I do what I'm told instead of what I want to do, backing away from the door.

I have no idea if the firefighter can hear me, but I yell anyway, "Okay, I'm ready!"

Not ten seconds later the door opens and my hero stands before me in full firefighter gear, complete with a mask that obscures his face. I launch myself at him, throwing myself into his arms—I'll look back on this moment later and realize that I didn't form a coherent thought beforehand. I'm just so grateful that I'm out and I'm not going to die.

Despite not being able to see his face, I'm certain he's male. He's tall, at least six feet, and I smash myself into him. There is no comfort of a soft chest against me. Only a body that feels solid as a wall. That might have something to do with all his gear, though.

"It's okay, I got you. You're going to be okay," he says, grabbing onto my upper arms to steady me. "But we need to get out of here."

I nod. If he thinks I want to stay in this building a second longer than necessary, he's got another thing coming.

"James, King," he says, pressing a button on the radio attached to his jacket. "I'm taking one out. Finish the sweep of this floor then you're out." Dropping his hand back to my arm, he looks down at me and for the first time since he opened the door, I see shining blue eyes staring back at me through his mask. "Let's go."

An arm is around my waist then and he's leading me out of the room. As we get into the hallway, there's a loud bang that causes me to flinch so hard I nearly fall to my knees. The only thing that keeps me upright is the man beside me, and suddenly I'm in the air, being swung into powerful arms that hold me to his body like I weigh nothing. I don't question it, allowing him to pick me up, my arms automatically going around his neck. I bury myself into him, seeking a comfort and safety that a few minutes ago I wasn't sure I would live to see.

The next few minutes are a blur. He's down five flights of stairs and out the door with me before I know what's happening. Without a word he drops me off with the paramedics who wrap me in a blanket, take my vitals, and throw an oxygen mask on me.

I can't stop watching the scene before me. The flurry of firefighters working on the fire, another ambulance, and a couple more paramedics. There are people who live in the building, neighbors from around it, and police ensuring no one except the firefighters get too close. There's so much going on that it's impossible to follow it all. It's like I'm in a dream, seeing it all unfold without being there in my body.

I can't believe I was stuck in the building that I'm now watching burn. The firefighters look like they're doing a good job at knocking it down, but it's not like I know anything about fighting a fire, so I could be terribly wrong. All I know is there seems to be a lot less orange now.

"Miss?"

Tearing my gaze from the building, I shake my head and blink a couple of times, focusing on the copper-haired paramedic in front of me. I'm sitting at the end of an ambulance, the blanket she gave me pulled tight around my shoulders. I realize she's waiting for an answer that I don't have.

"Sorry?"

"Just wondering if you're ready to go. You should really have your lungs checked out. Lieutenant Miller said you were trapped."

I haven't seen the firefighter—Lieutenant—since he left me with the paramedics, but that doesn't stop my eyes from looking over the men in uniforms again. Is it customary to thank someone for saving your life before you go to the hospital? Because I'd like to, though I understand that he's probably pretty busy. I'm not sure I would even know which one he is with all the others running around, though I'm certain if I saw those eyes again, I would know them.

My search for him is halted when I spot my landlord. In a flash, my blood is back to boiling and I'm on my feet, ripping the oxygen mask off my face. The blanket falls from around my shoulders as I stalk towards him without thinking it through.

"You son of a bitch!" I scream in fury. My voice is hoarse, and my throat feels like it's on fire, but I refuse to let it stop me. "You son of a bitch! I could have died in there!"

The man turns towards me, his eyes filled with surprise, but I see the moment recognition dawns. Both hands come up in defense, his eyes darting around for an escape as his head shakes. From what I know after our brief encounters, the man doesn't live far from here, something I'm grateful for so I have a chance to give him a piece of my mind.

Words are forming on his lips, but I don't let him get a single one out.

"I've told you over and over again about that door," I shriek, getting in his personal space, my hands clenching and unclenching at my sides. I really want to hit him, and it's taking everything in me not to do so. "But you wouldn't fix it. You never fix anything! I was trapped because of you. I could have burned alive because of you!"

"It's not my fault," he stammers.

I see red. My arm is halfway back to hit the guy when strong arms wrap around me from behind, pulling me away from him. I don't care. I want this man's blood on my hands for everything I've gone through tonight, and for claiming it isn't his fault.

As I'm pulled away, I kick, struggle, and scream at my landlord who stands there looking frightened.

"You gotta calm down," the voice of whomever is holding me says.

That's a big ask of me right now because calming down is the last thing I want to do. I want to kick my landlord's ass from here to hell and back. I want him to feel one tenth of the fear I felt in that room. Fear I don't think I've even begun to comprehend. Fear that will settle deep within my bones once all the adrenaline is gone, and I'm left picking up the pieces.

"Breathe," the voice says, and I recognize it as male as I'm carried behind a fire engine, away from prying eyes. "In, one, two, three, four. Out, four, three, two, one."

That gets my attention because it's the same way I calm myself down when I'm panicking. It's the technique I used when I first freaked out being trapped in that room.

It takes another cycle of him repeating it before I'm following what he tells me, and then I'm doing it on my own without any coaching. It's another minute before his arms are fully relaxing instead of securing me to his body. Then, with his hand on my arm to steady me, he moves to face me.

I'm shocked to my core when I see the blue eyes that stared down at me in the garbage room. I think somewhere between me screaming at my landlord, and being told to breathe, I realized it was the same man that rescued me, but that's not what has me stunned.

This man, the one who saved me, is the same man from the elevator yesterday.

"You," I whisper, my throat unable to handle much more.

He gives me a toothy grin, like he's as amused with himself as he was when he shook his butt at me. Before he can say a word, he's turning serious again, and I'm pretty sure I know why.

I can feel the blood draining from my face as I stare at him, my gaze getting hazy around the edges as I start to turn away. "I think I'm gonna—"

The words don't make it out of my mouth before I'm heaving my dinner all over the sidewalk beside his beautiful red fire engine.

CHAPTER 6

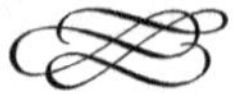

NATE

"Wʜᴀᴛ ᴀʀᴇ ʏᴏᴜ ᴅᴏɪɴɢ ʜᴇʀᴇ?"

I grin at my baby sister, hands shoved into the pockets of my Santa Rosé firefighter jacket as I walk towards her. She's come to a stop in the middle of a hallway in the ER of Santa Rosé General.

I shrug nonchalantly, hoping she doesn't see right through me. "Can't a guy come and visit his sister at work?"

Jordan looks at me like I've gone mad. "No." Her arms cross over her chest, and she repeats her initial question. "What are you doing here?"

She has a point. I don't tend to drop by without reason, and this isn't any different. Having a sister that works in the ER can be beneficial occasionally, especially as a firefighter who sometimes wants an update on patients that come in after being in my care. Not that I'd ever ask Jordan to violate privacy laws, nor would she consider doing so, but we manage to get around those kinds of things without getting either of us into trouble.

I'm simultaneously hoping she'll help her brother out while also questioning my own sanity. Breakfast should be the first thing on my mind, followed by a nap before I head to the bar to work on things for the accountant, but I couldn't get the woman from the fire out of my mind.

Elevator girl.

The one who had deemed men disgusting, filthy pigs.

I hadn't recognized her to begin with. My blood was pumping, and I was focused, strictly in first responder mode with the intention of getting a civilian to safety. As lieutenant I have to be on my game at all times while I'm on shift, but especially in dangerous situations.

When she slammed into me with fear filled, grateful gray eyes, recognition dawned. I'd met this woman somewhere, but I couldn't quite place her despite the gnawing feeling in my mind. Unfortunately, the fire didn't afford me the time to figure it out.

It wasn't until I was talking to my captain later on that everything clicked into place. I caught sight of the mostly naked woman stalking down the sidewalk, a murderous look on her face. I'd seen that ire before. Hell, I'd been subjected to it before her embarrassment had taken over.

I couldn't believe my eyes. I stood there for longer than I probably should have, gawking as she strode up to a man and started giving him hell. The shouting spurred me into action, pulling her away from the man while she kicked and screamed against me. I'll give her credit. She calmed down a lot faster than I thought she would, considering how much she fought against me.

"Hailey and Quinn brought in a girl last night from the fire down on Birch," I explain, forcing myself to keep my hands rooted in my pockets so I don't fidget. "I wanted to check in and see how she was doing."

"Nate," Jordan says, exasperated. "You know I can't just give you information on a patient."

"Not technically," I hedge, glancing from left to right and over my shoulder before I look back at her. "But you wouldn't be breaching anything if you had permission from said patient."

"Let me get this straight," she says, her hands resting on her hips, her long ponytail swinging over her shoulder as she cocks her head to the side. "You want me to go to a patient's room, if she's still here, and ask if she—what?—minds if I tell a firefighter from last night that she's still here because he wants to visit?"

Now she's busting my balls, and I fight to keep from frowning at her. I was really hoping she would give this to me easily, but it seems Jordan wants to take the hard road this morning. My sister can be such a pain in the ass at times.

"Jor, c'mon. I pulled her out of that building last night, and I kind of know her. I want to make sure she's okay."

The sass erodes from her face, her hands falling off her hips as she grabs me by the arm, concern etched in her features. "Jesus, Nate, you know her?"

Things are always harder when you know the person you're working on, or rescuing from a scene, something that Jordan knows firsthand working in the ER. Santa Rosé is small enough that it's inevitable we help people that we know sometimes. It's not easy, but if I had to choose, I'd rather it be me helping than someone else. Feeling helpless is not one of my fortes.

It's just that I don't really know the woman from the fire. I've met her before, so while I'm not exactly lying, I'm not being entirely forthcoming.

"Sort of."

Suspicion fills Jordan's narrowing eyes and I clench my jaw, preparing for what's about to come.

"How do you know her?" She crosses her arms again. "What's her name?"

Damn it. Jordan had to go and make this difficult. I really don't want to spill how I know this woman, especially not when Jordan knows the story. But I know the look in my sister's eye, and she isn't going to give me anything until I tell her the truth.

"She's the woman from the elevator," I mumble with the hope she won't catch it.

I'm not sure if she does or not when she enunciates very clearly, "Pardon?"

Scrubbing a hand over my face, knowing it's heating up despite the fact that I'm trying to remain cool and collected, I look anywhere but at my sister. I wish she could have made this easy on me. But she won't, and doesn't, standing there staring at me while I go through numerous levels of discomfort.

Finally I pull in a breath and meet her eyes, speaking quietly but clearly, "She's the woman from the elevator."

"The girl you pulled from the fire is the same girl from the elevator? The girl that Liam was telling me about?" she asks, a smirk slowly spreading across her face.

I can see the gears turning in her head as she thinks about this, causing me to groan inwardly. It was the one thing I didn't want to tell her. Premonitions of conversations between us later are already flashing through my head. She's going to want to know every detail.

I give her one slow nod of confirmation, shoving my hand back into the pocket of my jacket.

"Nate, why didn't you just tell me that?" Jordan gives me a

light punch on my shoulder, beaming with far too much enthusiasm. "Let me go see if she's still around, or if she's been discharged."

Rolling my eyes, I drop my body weight against the nearest wall as she spins and skips down the hall as though I've put a pep in her step. Given how she's been poking into my love life lately, like everyone else, I imagine I have given her a boost by showing up to ask about a beautiful woman.

She's going to turn into our aunts one day. One day soon, if she isn't careful. Maybe that's why she's so eager to ignore some of the possible red tape.

Honestly, this is the most interest I've shown in a woman in a long time. At least that anyone in my life has seen. When I need to scratch an itch I'm a lot more subtle about it than Liam is, usually finding a woman through a dating app that knows the score. Drinks, maybe dinner, and then heating the sheets. No strings attached, no having to explain that I'm a workaholic. Just a night of fun.

Not that I've had one of those nights in a while. Christ. The last time I did that was well before Uncle Pete passed away. I don't see that changing any time soon, either. Coming to the hospital to check up on a victim is just that. I'm being a good guy to someone who has had a couple of rough days. I'd do it for anyone.

Keep telling yourself that, buddy.

"Nate," Jordan's voice pulls me out of my thoughts, causing my head to lift. She wears a triumphant grin and gives a nod behind her. "C'mon."

Pushing off the wall, I can't help but chuckle at her enthusiasm, the bounce still in her step as she leads me down the hall, past a multitude of curtained rooms in the ER. I was feeling pretty relaxed while I waited, but the further down the hall we get, the more nervous I become. All I'm doing is a good deed. There's no reason for my palms to suddenly be sweating or my mouth to go dry, but here I am.

Jordan pulls the curtain back on one of the rooms, stepping inside. "The firefighter I was telling you about," she says as I step around the curtain to see the blonde haired woman sitting in a bed. "If he gives you any trouble, or you want me to kick him out, just yell. I won't be far."

I glance at Jordan as she steps by me, not missing the "good luck" that she murmurs for my ears only before pulling the drape shut again.

"You," the woman says, and I look back to her, finding her eyes full of curiosity.

I flash her a grin. "Me."

"What are you doing here?"

Taking a couple of steps further into the small, draped room, I stand toward the end of her bed, shrugging a shoulder as casually as possible. "Well, considering I saved your life, I figured I'd come by and see how you were doing."

I can already tell how different she is now than the other times I've seen her. She's reserved, almost shy, but full of inquisitiveness, like she wants to know everything, but doesn't know how to ask. It's so opposite of the woman in the elevator who laid it all out for me, gave me her story without so much as a word from me.

The only similarity I can see so far is her cheeks turning a beautiful shade of pink, enhancing her already gorgeous features. I didn't notice in the elevator, or last night, but in the light of the hospital room, and the moment of peace and quiet, I realize she has this pouty bottom lip that looks so kissable I can't help but lick my own lips.

I'm not here to hit on her, though, so I need to keep my focus, and my eyes, away from her lips and curves.

Curves that I damn well noticed last night, especially

when I had her pulled against my body, not once, but twice. Curves that caught my eye as she walked across the sidewalk to give that man a piece of her mind. Curves that are now hidden by a hospital gown, though I'm well aware they're there. I accused her of checking me out the other day, but the truth is I was just as guilty. Much like now.

"Right. I guess I should say thank you. I was starting to think I wasn't going to get out of that room," she says, bringing me back to her eyes. The one and only place that I should be looking.

"I wasn't talking about the fire," I tell her with a smirk. "I'm talking about interrupting the murder you were ready to commit on that guy."

For a moment she's silent, stunned I think, and then she throws her head back and laughs. The sound of it shoots pleasure straight down my spine, and I break into a wide grin. I don't think I've ever heard laughter so intrinsically pure and joyous, and I'm certain I've never been the cause of it.

"Well then, forget you saving me from the building—thank you for saving me from myself," she says, her laughter dying off, though the smile remains.

I'm glad it stays because it's stunning, and I like that it's turned on me. Caused by me.

"You're welcome," I tell her before glancing briefly over my shoulder to the curtain. "Did they tell you when you might be able to bust out of here?"

"The nurse—"

"Jordan," I interrupt.

She looks surprised, then nods slowly, her smile fading a touch. "Right. Jordan. She said the doctor should be around within the next half hour and would probably discharge me then."

"Want some company until then?"

The woman's gray eyes narrow slightly, and she tilts her head to the side, appraising me. I'm pretty sure I've just crossed an invisible line, probably the same one that had her telling me not to hit on her in the elevator. I'm about to apologize when she tries to cut to the chase.

"Not to be rude, but—"

I hold my hands up in resignation. "Say no more. I probably shouldn't have come to check on you, but I know you had a couple of tough days and wanted to make sure you were doing okay. I should have realized that you wouldn't want some strange guy coming around, though, especially after the whole elevator incident."

I run a hand through my hair, the nerves that I was doing a good job at hiding coming out in a rather pronounced, blabbering way. "But you should know that I'm not some strange guy. I mean, I am, to you, but I know lots of people, and most of them don't think I'm strange. They'd definitely all tell you I'm not a disgusting, filthy pig."

Fuck. Liam's right. I have no game.

"I was just going to say that I don't even know your name."

"Oh shit."

The grin on her face gets wider, and I can tell it's taking a lot for her not to laugh at me right now.

"Wow, I am so sorry," I apologize, my face heating all the way down to my neck as I move to the side of the bed and hold my hand out for her to shake. "Nate Miller."

Jesus. It's like the heat of every California summer night shoots through me when she slides her hand into mine. I feel electricity sizzle around us as our hands are connected, our eyes locked on one another. I'm sure she can feel it too. Surprise flashes in her eyes, and I know mine are a mirror of hers as we stare at each other, lost in the moment together.

Her voice is throaty when she breathes her name out to me, "Savanna Walsh."

"Savanna," I repeat, committing the feeling of her smaller, delicate hand in mine to memory. "It's a pleasure to officially meet you."

Slowly I let her hand go, and the moment we're no longer joined I miss the warmth, but I force myself to glance at the chair beside the bed. This woman has made it extremely clear that she doesn't want anyone hitting on her, and I'm not about to do that. Besides, I just proved to myself, and showed her, that I don't have game. "Mind if I sit for a while? I promise I won't hit on you."

I thought it would get a laugh out of her, referencing the elevator, but instead she looks sad for a fraction of a second before it fades and she nods. "Sure. I'd like that."

Taking a seat, I cross an ankle over my knee, leaning back in the chair. It's not the most comfortable, but we're in a hospital, and I'm pretty sure they don't make any part of these places comfortable. "So, no permanent damage from the fire?"

"Nope. All thanks to you. I don't know what I would have done if you hadn't come along," she tells me, picking at her fingernails. I wonder if it's a nervous habit.

I shrug like it's no big deal, because to me, it isn't. It's my job to pull people out of burning buildings, wrecked cars, or a multitude of other scenarios that I come across in my daily life as a firefighter.

"Liam or Brody would have found you if I hadn't," I say, referencing my two best friends, both of whom are under my command at the firehouse.

"I guess I'm extra lucky then," she tells me with a smile, and damn if that doesn't warm me from the inside out.

"You are," I nod affirmatively. "Liam would have tried hitting on you before you were out of the room, and Brody, well, he would have acted like me, but he's not as good looking."

Jesus Nate, take a bite of some humble pie.

I find myself grinning when she gives a small giggle, despite my thoughts. "Seriously, though, you are really lucky. How'd you end up in there, anyway?"

Groaning, she brings her hands up to her face to give it a good rub, almost like she can't believe what she's about to tell me. As I hear the story, I find myself growing increasingly angry with her landlord. It's no wonder she looked like she wanted to murder the guy.

"I'm almost regretting pulling you away from him now," I tell her honestly.

Savanna is quick to shake her head. "No, you were right to do it. I shouldn't have made a scene, but I wasn't thinking. I was just reacting. I was coming down from all the adrenaline, but seeing him had it rushing back, and I just…"

"Reacted," I finish with understanding, nodding. "Believe me, I get it. I'm trained in using those adrenaline dumps to my advantage, so I can only imagine how it was for you, someone who isn't used to them."

I don't understand the frown that pulls her lips down and makes her eyebrows furrow, as if she disagrees with me, while her words contradict the look. "Exactly. I'm not used to them, so it was a lot to handle."

"I do have one question," I say to her, my foot dropping to the ground as I lean forward and place my elbows on my knees. My voice is low as I ask, "Why were you taking the trash out in your underwear?"

This is further proof I don't have game. The second the words are out of my mouth I wish I could take them back, but they're out there, and they've caused Savanna's mouth to pop open, her eyes bugging out in horror. Based on her reaction I'd say she forgot that I saw her practically naked, along with everyone else at the scene.

When her cheeks flame, I almost take back wishing the words away. I can't help but think how becoming the blush looks on her, causing her gray eyes to stand out from the rest of her.

"I'm sorry," I say, cringing at her embarrassment, and that I'm the cause of it. "I shouldn't have said anything. It's not my business to be asking that anyway. Forget I said anything."

"I had clothes on," she grits out, and I'm pretty sure she's warring with herself on whether or not she wants to tell me to get out. "But there was smoke coming up under the door, so I took them off and used them to stop it."

It's my turn to look shocked. Sitting up straight, I stare at her, totally enraptured by this woman who isn't just beautiful, but is also smart as a whip. For her to have the insight, even in a dire situation, to keep the smoke out the way she did, impresses the hell out of me.

"You're a firefighter's goddamn wet dream," I tell her without any thought to how that sounds.

Once again, her mouth is dropping open, and that beautiful color is returning to her cheeks as she looks away from me and down at her lap. Christ, I promised I wouldn't hit on her, but I'm not doing a very good job.

I'm saved before I stick my foot any farther into my mouth when the curtain is pulled open and Jordan steps in the room, closing the drape behind her again.

I can feel her eyes dart back and forth between Savanna and me before she says, "Do I need to kick him out?"

I'd be offended if I hadn't just spoken about wet dreams.

"No," Savanna says hurriedly, shaking her head. "No, it's been nice to talk with someone. Helps pass the time until I can get out of here."

"Which won't be much longer," Jordan tells her. "Dr. Verdeem is two patients away from coming to see you." Her eyes flicker to me for a moment before looking back to Savanna. "Do you have someone you can call to come pick you up?"

"Oh. I, uhm, don't have my phone with me. Everything is still back in my apartment," she says with a frown, and I notice that she's back to picking her fingernails.

"Here," I say, pulling my phone out of my pocket. "You can use mine."

"There's also a phone at the nurse's station that I can bring you," Jordan says quickly, giving me a reproving look. "In case you're not comfortable using Nate's."

There's a long silence from Savanna as she looks back and forth between Jordan and me, and I can see her trying to decide if she's comfortable using my phone. I can't blame her if she's not, and I finally mumble, "Sorry. I was just trying to be helpful. I didn't think how that might make you feel."

"It's okay," Savanna says after another beat of hesitation just as I'm about to shove my phone back into my pocket. "I don't mind using yours. If you don't mind."

It's not like I'm about to get her phone number, so I'm not sure why I suddenly feel like puffing out my chest like a damn caveman. Maybe it's because my sister is standing there watching the exchange, and she was on Liam's side the other night. Maybe this will be the proof to convince them both I'm not totally useless when it comes to the opposite sex.

"Not at all," I say, handing Savanna the phone after unlocking it for her and she smiles her thanks at me.

"Nate, why don't you give her some privacy to make her call?" Jordan suggests, but I know it isn't really a suggestion. "And Savanna, feel free to delete whatever number you call afterwards."

I watch as Savanna's face falls completely, and she nods like she understands something I'm completely missing. "I will."

"I'll be right back," I assure her as I get to my feet, hoping that the smile comes back to her face. It doesn't, and for some reason that irritates me.

Or maybe it irritates me that she's going to delete whoever she's going to call from my phone, and I won't have any way of contacting her after this is all said and done. Because I'm not going to ask for her phone number; I promised I wouldn't hit on her, and I'm going to keep that promise—despite the wet dream comment.

Jordan crooks her finger to follow her when we step outside the room. She leads me to the nurse's station and stops in front of a small pile of clothes sitting there. I look from it to her and raise an eyebrow as she picks it up and shoves it in my direction.

"I could easily go back in there and give these to her, but I feel like they might mean more coming from you," she tells me, and when I stare at her in confusion, she rolls her eyes. "Nate, she's about to be discharged and the only thing she had to wear when she came in was underwear. I'm certain she isn't going to want to walk around in a hospital gown, so I ran down to my locker and got these. I think we're close to the same size, except I've got more boob going on than she does."

I wrinkle my nose at the last comment, not wanting to

think about my sister's tits, but take the pile of clothes that she hands me, now recognizing them as scrubs, as well as a pair of flip-flops. "You do this for all your patients?"

"My bonehead brother doesn't have a crush on all my patients, so no, I don't," she tells me before whacking me in the arm. "You had to go and offer her your phone, didn't you?"

I stare at her dumbfounded. "I was being helpful!"

"And I was trying to set you up so you could take her out for a coffee, but you had to jump in there like the hero you always are," Jordan says, shaking her head at me like I'm the biggest imbecile out there. "We tried to get her to call someone she knew earlier, but she said there was no one she wanted to bother."

Well shit. Who knew that my need to help would come back to bite me in the ass like that? Now Savanna is in there calling someone to pick her up when I could have been the one to… what? What exactly would I have done with her? She didn't want to be hit on, and if I offered her a ride some-where, would she have thought I was hitting on her? Taking her for coffee would seem a lot like a date, and wouldn't that be a step above hitting on her?

Suddenly I'm irritated with my sister for trying to pry, not only in my life, but in Savanna's. "She doesn't want someone picking her up, Jor. She doesn't want to be taken out for coffee. She's just had a couple of really horrible days, so while I'm sure you mean well in your meddling, leave Savanna alone, and stay out of my damn love life."

Turning around, I head back for Savanna's room. Despite my warning to Jordan, I keep the scrubs, because the hell if I'm letting that beautiful woman walk out of here in her underwear, or a hospital gown.

CHAPTER 7

SAVANNA

I'M NOT SNOOPING, PER SE, BUT I AM STARING AT THE background picture on Nate's phone. I find myself surprised that it's not of him and his girlfriend, but one of him, and what I'm assuming to be his parents. I can see the family resemblance in the picture, and for some reason it feels familiar to me, but I'm guessing that's because I've been staring at Nate for the past half hour.

It's hard not to. He's one of the hottest, if not *the* hottest man, I've ever seen. He screams pure, unadulterated male to me. Just being in his presence has my body buzzing in a way I don't know I've ever felt. It was all I could do not to climb out of this bed and into his lap, something I've never found myself wanting to do.

It's a tad unnerving. Sure, I've felt an instant attraction to men before, my ex being one of them. But a zing to my hand? Or the way he's a magnet for my eyes? Never.

Too bad he has a girlfriend. A really nice, super beautiful girlfriend.

At first, I thought he was here to see me, but then I realized he must have been at the hospital visiting her, and I was an afterthought to him. It was pretty obvious that they knew each other intimately when she touched his arm on her way out of the room when he first got here. Then the way she told me to delete whoever I called solidified that she was putting her mark on her territory. If that wasn't enough, he's been very upfront that he's not hitting on me.

That hasn't stopped me from ogling him, much like I did the first time I saw him in the elevator. He might be even sexier now, even though I can't see that wide expanse of a chest very well with his jacket that declares he's a firefighter.

I've noticed other things, though. Like how he runs his fingers through his hair a lot, and how his neck turns redder than his cheeks when he's said something, and then a second later, realizes what he's said. It's adorable.

I also may have taken another peek at his backside when he got up and left, and let me just say, it's obvious the man works out because his ass is stellar the way it fills out his jeans. I'd be lying if I said I hadn't checked it out when he was walking out of the elevator the other day, but damn it, that was his fault for bringing it up.

"Get a hold of someone?"

His voice comes out of nowhere and startles me so badly I drop his phone in my lap, my head snapping up. I wonder how long he's been standing there staring at me. Long enough that the drapes are closed, and not swaying, which causes a flush of heat to tinge my cheeks red.

"Yeah, I—" I'm about to offer an explanation, but then stop myself with a bite to my lip before repeating, "Yeah."

When lying, it's better to stick to the simplest of answers rather than offer anything needing to be remembered in the future. The truth is, I didn't make a single phone call. I was going to call my own phone and just listen to it ring until my voicemail picked up, but when I saw Nate and Jordan's feet disappear from under the curtain, I didn't bother. It didn't matter because I told her I would delete the number from Nate's phone anyway.

There was no number to delete because there was no one for me to call.

I could call home. I considered it earlier. God, did I consider it. I thought about calling my older brother Devin because he'd know what to do in this situation. The responsible one out of my two brothers, Devin would have made fast work of finding me a place to go, ensuring I had a roof over my head until I could get into my apartment.

But then I thought about all the questions that would come with calling him. The disappointment I would no doubt hear in his voice. The hurt and the pain. And I know once I open the door of calling home, there's no going back. There's no more protecting my family from the dangers of my ex.

So I decided I was better off figuring things out on my own.

"Good," Nate nods, reminding me of his presence. It only takes him a couple of strides before he's at my side. It's then I notice he's got something in his hand that he holds out to me. "These are from Jordan. She thought maybe this would be better than anything else for you. The two of you are about the same size."

I blink a few times, staring at the articles in his hand, recognizing he's holding clothes and a pair of shoes. Hesitantly I take them, my face turning up towards his, his blue eyes peering down at me with warmth that makes me want to melt.

"Your girlfriend is really nice. She didn't need to do this," I smile, trying to be grateful instead of disappointed.

Nate rears back like I hit him, his mouth opening and closing like a dying fish.

"My—my gir-girlfriend?" he stutters, clearly appalled which causes me to flush again. "Jordan? God, no! Jordan is my sister. I don't have a girlfriend, and if I did, it definitely wouldn't be my sister."

Oh boy. Evidently, I got that wrong. Even though Nate looks disgusted by my interpretation of their relationship, I can't help the relief that washes over me, though it's short-lived when I remember that he still didn't want to hit on me. It shouldn't bum me out that he doesn't want to flirt, because I have no business wanting a guy to like me, but it does. It probably hurts worse to know that he's just not interested.

"This is awkward," I say with a small laugh. "You two looked like you knew each other, and I just assumed. She seemed a bit protective when you offered your phone."

"Of you," he tells me, and I know I look confused when he adds, "She's your nurse and doesn't want you to feel uncomfortable, even if she knows me, and knows I'm harmless. While you're in this bed, you're her first priority."

I never thought of it like that, but it makes sense and I nod. "Is that also why she gave me clothes?"

He laughs and runs his fingers through his hair before reclaiming his spot in the chair beside the bed. "I think that was actually more for my benefit. But I ruined all her plans of playing matchmaker when I offered you my phone."

"Pardon?" I ask, tilting my head to the side.

"She thought if you didn't have anyone to call, I would swoop in and ask you out for coffee or something," he says, an amused smile dancing on his lips. "But don't worry, I set her straight."

He doesn't elaborate, and I don't ask because I don't want to be embarrassed or let down any more than I already am by him not wanting to hit on me, so I just nod. "Thanks."

It's then that the opening to the curtain is pushed to one side and a man in a white coat steps in. "Ready to get out of here?" he asks, and I nod my head at Dr. Verdeem. He takes notice of Nate and smiles. "Nate! How you doin'?"

"Good," Nate says, standing up.

The two of them shake hands and exchange a couple more pleasantries before Nate turns back to me and smiles, though it doesn't quite reach his eyes. The swirling blue looks sad, and I wonder if it's for the same reason I'm feeling it. Our time together has come to an end.

"It was nice talking to you, Savanna. I'm glad you're okay." He pauses and then adds, "Maybe I'll see you around."

"Yeah, maybe," I say, offering a smile, but I don't for a second believe it.

There's an awkward moment where we both just look at each other, and I don't think either one of us wants this to be goodbye. Maybe that's just on my end because he finally gives another nod and turns to leave while I look down at my lap.

"Nate?" I say and he turns, perking up hopefully. "Your phone."

"Right. Thanks. Wouldn't want to forget that."

He's back to the side of the bed a second later, and I hold the phone out to him, our fingers brushing as he takes it from me. There's a crackle between us, and I see in his eyes that he feels it like I do, the heat spreading from my fingers all the way to my lower belly. It's another moment before he blinks rapidly, as if to clear his mind, and then he's gone, leaving me with the doctor.

~

I didn't see Nate again, but I saw Jordan on my way out of the hospital. I thanked her for the scrubs and flip flops, promising to return them, but she waved me off, telling me not to worry about it. When I looked at her that last time, I realized I was an idiot for not seeing the family resemblance between them from the start. They have the exact same eyes, noses, and their smiles are practically identical, especially when it reaches their eyes.

It didn't matter, though, because knowing they were siblings didn't change the fact that Nate didn't want to hit on me. I have to remember that's a good thing, not bad.

Taking a breath of fresh air, I close my eyes and savor the feeling as it travels down my sore throat and into my rough lungs. Between the smoke and the hospital air, I'll never take fresh air for granted again.

Wearily, I glance around at my surroundings and heave a sigh, watching a few cars travel by on the road in front of me. I realized after being discharged that I probably should have hung out as long as I could in the hospital because I have no idea what I'm going to do with myself now that I'm out. Deciding to figure things out on my own would have been swell if I'd actually come up with a plan while I was sitting in the hospital bed.

My eyes are heavy and my body sags with exhaustion after being up all night and having all the adrenaline wrung from it. Though I dozed a little in the hospital bed, there was always something going on, or someone checking on me, that didn't allow me to sleep.

Now, sitting on a bench in a park across from the hospital, I force myself not to lay down and close my eyes right here. Wrapping my arms around my knees, I turn my head to the side and rest my cheek against it, sucking in my bottom lip.

Not only do I not know if I can get into my apartment, but I also have no phone, no money, no identification, no clothes, no car, no nothing. Even if I had my car, I don't have my keys to get into it, which really sucks because I have a few things stored in there in case I ever need to bail on short notice. I suppose I could break into it, though short of breaking a window I haven't a clue how to do that effectively.

But running through my options, I'm certain I'm going to need to do something I don't want to do if I can't get into my apartment. And geez, that's assuming I even have an apartment to get into. I have no idea how bad the fire got or whether it reached my place. Shit. If it got into my place and all my stuff is destroyed, what the hell am I going to do?

I've been in bad situations before, but the more I think about this, the more screwed I realize I could be.

It has the threat of tears stinging the backs of my eyes. Maybe I should call Devin. Or I could try Connor, my other brother. While Devin is the more responsible one, Connor is the one that'll offer less judgement. Besides Maddie, he's always been my secret keeper.

Thinking of the three of them back home has a tear sliding down my cheek. My heart aches with how much I miss them right now. There would be so much comfort in a phone call to them. Probably for both sides. I can only imagine that they're worried about me, and after the last couple of days, that worry would be more warranted than ever.

Besides, what else am I going to do with nothing but the clothes on my back that don't even belong to me?

"Your ride not show up?" A deep voice calls, and I look up to see a silver truck stopped, the man inside leaning over so he can see out the passenger window.

Nate.

Seeing his face makes it hard to keep the dam behind my eyes from breaking wide open, and I suck my bottom lip between my teeth to try to stop it as I shake my head.

"Get in," he says, and I must look at him like he's lost his mind because he reaches over and pushes the door open. "Get in the truck, Savanna."

I have very few options right now, but I don't know if getting into a vehicle with a virtual stranger is the best idea. Sure, I've met his sister now, and I know he's a firefighter who saved me from being burned alive, but that's all a lot different than getting into his personal truck to go God knows where, to do God knows what.

Sucking in a deep breath, I glance down the road, considering my alternatives.

Calling either one of my brothers is at the top of that list. But Vincent dances through my vision, and I'm reminded of why I didn't call them from the hospital in the first place. Protecting them is number one. It's why I left. Making that phone call home has to be my last resort.

Walking to my apartment is an idea, which will take me a couple of hours I'm guessing, and that's only if I can figure out how to get there. In the six months I've been in Santa Rosé, it's not like I've been to a lot of places and know the lay of the land. I realize now how much of an oversight that was on my part.

Finding the beach and hanging out there is another option; I could camp out there in the sand. It's still warm enough outside at night that maybe I could sleep there. It's not really a long-term solution, though.

Or I could just get in the truck with Nate. I could ask him if I'd be able to get into my apartment today or not, and if I can't, maybe he could drop me off at the beach and save me from figuring it out on my own. Or maybe he'd let me use his cell phone again, and I'd truly make a call I'm dreading.

I think my decision was made before I thought it all through, because I'm on my feet walking towards his truck before realizing that I made the choice to get in with him.

Sliding into his passenger seat, I close the door and grab the seatbelt, taking in my surroundings. There aren't any weapons visible that look like they'll harm me, so that's a plus. Nate doesn't seem the type that could hurt a fly, though you can never quite be sure about someone. Even when you know them. I have firsthand knowledge when it comes to that.

Vincent never seemed like he could hurt me. Not at first, anyway. He was kind, caring, considerate. When we started dating he would look at me with this warmth in his eyes that made me feel like the only girl on his radar. He would drop everything to pick me up from work, or if I had to stay late, he'd drop off dinner. Flowers came regularly, and coffee showed up even more frequently.

He knew exactly what he was doing to lure me into a false sense of security. I never saw the abuse coming.

"You hungry?" Nate asks, pulling me from my thoughts as he pulls away from the curb.

I turn to look at him, surprised by the question. I want to say no, but it's been a long time since I last ate, and now that he's brought it up, my stomach rumbles in protest at not being fed.

I know he hears it when he says with amusement, "I'll take that as a yes."

"I don't have any money for food," I tell him quietly, embarrassment coloring my cheeks. Not that I can help it, and I know he knows that, but that doesn't make it any better.

"Well, I'm starving and planned on going for breakfast. I'm not about to eat by myself in front of you, so you might as well let me buy you breakfast," he says, glancing in my direction with a grin. "You ever been to the Windmill Diner?"

"No," I tell him, shaking my head. "I haven't really been to many places around town."

"You're not from around here, I'm guessing?"

While I don't make a habit of telling strangers that I'm not from here, I find myself telling Nate before I can think about it. "No. I've only been here for six months."

He stops at a red light and looks over at me, curiosity filling his stunning blue eyes. I'm pretty sure that I could get lost in them if I looked long enough. I've never met someone with such an intense, brilliant blue, and he has these amazing eyelashes that frame them, making them stand out even more.

"Where you from?"

"Colorado," I tell him honestly, again without hesitation.

"Ah," he says, nodding as if this makes sense. "From the mountains to the ocean."

I smile, my thoughts drifting to that first time I got to see the ocean. "I'd never seen the ocean before I moved here."

"It boggles my brain when people tell me that," he says with a laugh. "I've been in Santa Rosé my entire life, so I can't imagine not being near the ocean."

"I can't imagine it anymore," I respond with a content

sigh. "I haven't been able to stay away from it all summer. There's so much to see, and it's as relaxing as the mountains used to make me feel. The beach has been my second home."

"Hence why you haven't gotten to know all the other local amenities," he teases, and I can't help but laugh. "There's a lot more to Santa Rosé than the beach, you know."

"I figured I'd check those things out when the weather wasn't so great, but does that actually happen here? I don't think I've seen a day that isn't nice."

"It'll start getting chillier," he promises, eyes darting in my direction. "You can already tell in the evenings that it's getting cooler. With any luck, we'll get a ton of rain in the next few months."

"And that's when I'll start exploring things that aren't the beach," I tell him, and I'm rewarded with laughter that has me staring at him from across the truck. It's hearty and happy, and I like the way it makes his face light up, making him even more handsome.

Before the light turns green he holds my eyes and grins. "Your exploration starts now."

CHAPTER 8

SAVANNA

When Nate pulls into a parking lot, I lean forward to look out the windshield. The building in front of us has a main level where I'm guessing the diner is. There's another part of the building that rises above it with a few windows placed here and there throughout. But what really captures my attention is the windmill sticking out of the roof on the higher part of the structure. It's white, just like the rest of the building, but given that it's so close to the roof, which is black, it stands out very distinctly.

I'm immediately charmed by this place. With trees, shrubs, and a multitude of different flowers surrounding the building, it feels like it's being hidden, adding to the magic.

"This is adorable," I tell him as we both open our doors and get out.

"Wait until you see the inside. It's even better," he says as I meet him around the front of the truck before he leads me to the door.

He wasn't kidding. The inside is just as cute and quaint as the outside. The walls are painted bright, cheerful oranges and yellows, fun knick-knacks and pictures cover every available space, and fairy lights decorate the windows and the ceiling. There are tables and chairs spread around the space, and double French doors lead to a patio that features more tables and umbrellas.

My favorite part may be the counter at the front filled with all kinds of delicious looking treats. Muffins, cakes, cookies, pies… my mouth waters at all the things I see in front of me, and I'm licking my lips, grateful that Nate brought me here and won't let me just watch him eat.

"Nathan!" A cheery voice to my right says, and I turn to find a woman, who must be in her fifties, with an apron around her waist lighting up at the sight of Nate beside me. She has blonde, shaggy hair that stops at her chin, and warm, affectionate blue eyes that are bouncing between Nate and me.

"Hi, mom," Nate greets her, arms spread wide for her to step into. Once they part, Nate turns to me and introduces us. "Savanna, this is Elizabeth. Mom, this is Savanna, a friend of mine."

"A friend, huh?" she asks with a wink at Nate before turning to me, hand extended. "Lovely to meet you."

I'm a tad surprised that Nate took me somewhere his mom works, but then I remind myself this isn't a date.

Shaking Elizabeth's hand, I smile. "Likewise, but don't let him fool you. I'm just some girl he picked up on the side of the road."

Nate snorts because he knows it's true, but Elizabeth laughs with delight. "Well, that would be like Nathan. This boy would help everyone in need if he could."

I glance at Nate, wondering if he's ever done this before,

but before I can ask, or allude to such a thing, he's holding his hands up in surrender. "Okay, okay. No need to divulge all my secrets."

"It's not a secret," Elizabeth interrupts, and I can't help but giggle at Nate's expense.

He ignores her. "Do you happen to have a table, or should I take Savanna elsewhere?"

"You wouldn't dare," she chides, grabbing two menus before leading us to a table outside.

I have a sneaking suspicion that Nate enjoys sitting out here because she didn't bother asking if we wanted to sit inside or out, and I'm okay with that. I'd much rather sit outside and enjoy the heat of the late morning sun, even if I don't have sunglasses to shield my eyes.

"You want your usual, honey?"

"You know it," Nate says to her, then looks to me. "A chocolate milkshake is my usual. You haven't had a milkshake until you've had a milkshake made by my mom. Best milkshake I've ever had in my life."

"That sounds hard to resist. I love all things ice cream," I tell them. "I'll have a vanilla milkshake."

"I'll be right back with those," she tells us, and then she's gone with a twinkle in her eye.

"Can I ask you a question?" Nate asks, and I look up from the menu, catching him as he runs his fingers through his hair. His menu is still to the side, making me guess he doesn't need to look in order to know what he wants. When I nod, he leans forward, and with quiet intensity says, "The other day you seemed to have a considerable dislike towards men, and someone must have made you feel that way. Today no one showed up at the hospital. Did you call the disgusting, filthy pig to pick you up?"

I bark out a surprised laugh and slap a hand to my mouth.

That's the second time he's brought that up, and I have a feeling it's not the last time I'll hear about it.

"No," I tell him, shaking my head as my smile dies away. I breathe out a sigh and look down at my menu again, not wanting to look at him as I confess. "I didn't actually call anyone. I don't really know anyone in Santa Rosé."

He's silent for a moment, and I think he's either contemplating whether to let the subject go or not. I hope he does, but I'm not that lucky.

"Why didn't you just say that?"

Looking at him, I shake my head in bewilderment. A guy like this wouldn't get it. A guy like a firefighter, a lieutenant, someone who I'm told helps all kinds of people because that's who he is, wouldn't understand. I hate that I have to explain it, my cheeks heating underneath his stare. "Because it sounds pathetic. Would you want it to be public knowledge that you have no one to call, and nowhere to go?"

"I would have offered to take you out for breakfast if you'd just told me the truth," he says, his eyes narrowed with disapproval that I lied to him.

It makes me feel a little defensive, and my tone is sharper than I intend when I fire back with, "You set your sister straight, remember?"

He has the sense to look abashed, but that doesn't stop him from saying, "You made it pretty clear the first time we met that I wasn't supposed to hit on you."

I close my menu, my temper spiking marginally. "Is that what you're doing now? Is that why you stopped and picked me up? You wanted to hit on me?"

"No. Yes. I mean—Jesus, I don't know what I mean," he says, scrubbing his hands over his face. I can see the telltale sign of his neck turning red. He's flustered, and I almost laugh. Almost.

"No, I'm not trying to hit on you, and no, it's not why I picked you up. Did I want to hit on you?" His eyes roll. "That's a dumb question, of course I want to hit on you, but I'm not going to because you've had a few really shitty days from what I can tell, and I don't want you thinking I'm some disgusting, filthy pig."

I knew I hadn't heard the last of that.

I also think that's one of the sweetest things a guy has ever said to me. If that doesn't say something about the quality of men I've been around, I'm not sure what does.

"I'm sorry I didn't tell you the truth," I say quietly, and despite wanting to look down, I keep my gaze trained on his. I may not owe Nate an apology for trying to protect myself, but his kindness and earnestness make me want to give it to him.

"Apology accepted," he says, and smiles at me. "I think I'm just relieved you didn't call whoever that douche is."

After a moment of hesitation to decide how much I want to embarrass myself, and how much information I should give a man I don't know, I sigh and lean back in my chair.

"That douche would be my ex-boss," I tell him, picking at the corner of my menu, refusing to look up at Nate. "I foolishly went out with him a couple of times, and just before our elevator encounter, I caught him screwing an intern in one of the boardrooms."

Nate whistles low, shaking his head. "No wonder you quit."

"Here we go," Elizabeth says, appearing beside the table with two shakes. She sets them down in front of us. "Have you two decided what you'd like to eat?"

"Oh dear, I haven't even looked. Nate keeps interrupting me each time I start," I tell her with a laugh. "What's good?"

"California Burger," they say in unison, causing me to look between the two with a grin.

"Well then," I laugh. "I'll have that."

Nate orders the same, and when Elizabeth is gone, I tell him about Preston. He sits there, listening attentively, watching me with those blue eyes so intent that it makes my stomach flutter in ways that Preston never did. I have to admit to myself that I'm a little dazzled by Nate. I know I'm still lacking in the human interactions, but I think if I had a full social calendar, I would still be dazzled by this man sitting across from me. That's a little scary because I've been in that situation once before and it ended with me leaving the only home I'd ever known.

"How's that milkshake?" Elizabeth asks as she stops by to check on us, her eyes keen and full of interest as they dart between the two of us before staying on me.

"Delicious!" I reply, having just taken a sip of the thick and creamy drink, notes of true vanilla flavor coming through, none of the fake stuff. "Honestly the best I think I've ever had. Nate was right."

She laughs. "Don't tell him that. The man will get a big head." She glances at Nate with affection, and he looks back at her with a smirk. "So," she turns her attention back to me. "Do you work at the hospital?"

I'm a little confused until she looks at my shirt pointedly and I clue in as to why she would think that. The scrubs.

"Oh, heavens no! These aren't mine, they're Jordan's. She let me borrow them because all I had was my underwear." Nate, who is in the middle of taking a sip from his milkshake, chokes and starts coughing, making me realize how that must have sounded, so I try to explain further. "Because that's how Nate found me! I had to take my clothes off—"

"I pulled her out of the burning building on Birch last

night," Nate interrupts, talking over me. "She'd been using her clothes to keep the smoke from getting in."

Elizabeth, who looked half concerned and half delighted, gasps and presses a hand over her chest. "I heard about that. It sounded awful."

"It was, but Nate jumped in and saved my life."

"Whoa, whoa. Calm down," he says, gesturing in a calm down fashion. "Let's not be dramatic."

I raise an eyebrow at him then rephrase. "Nate is my hero and rescued me?"

He rolls his eyes and shakes his head, clearly not liking the whole hero idea.

It must be something he shies away from regularly because Elizabeth gives him a knowing look. "Always so humble, Nathan. We all know you're just doing your job, but you have the job of a hero, and you might as well accept that."

Nate swirls his straw in his milkshake, evidently not entertaining this conversation any longer. It seems to be clear to Elizabeth that he isn't going to budge an inch on this because she changes the subject. "You're still off next Sunday?"

"Of course," he smiles warmly at his mom, the indifference vanishing. "I wouldn't miss it for the world."

"Good." Elizabeth looks from Nate to me and then back again. "You should bring Savanna." Her eyes land on me once more. "It's my birthday and I would be delighted if you joined Nathan at my birthday barbecue. You can tell me more about how he rescued you. I love hearing firsthand stories about my boy."

My mouth is unattractively hanging open, unsure of what to say. I don't even know Nate, not well anyway, and his mom is inviting me over for a barbecue. This isn't weird at all. "I, uh… I mean…"

"Mom," Nate says, and I hear a warning in his tone. "Savanna and I don't know each other that well. Let's not make her uncomfortable."

"What better way to get to know someone than to bring her to a barbecue?" Elizabeth says, paying no attention to the warning. "In fact, if you don't bring her, maybe you shouldn't show up. I would be sorely disappointed, as would your aunts." The woman beams at the two of us as if she didn't just utter a threat to her son. "Now let me go check on your burgers, I'll bet they're ready."

I stare at Nate, my eyes wide, unsure of what to say. He just sighs and shakes his head, running a hand through his hair. "If you hadn't picked up on it, my family likes to meddle, and their favorite thing to meddle in is my love life. Ignore them."

"Was she serious about you not showing up without me?" I ask, stunned that the woman who seemed so sweet and nice would say such a thing. Nate shrugs and my eyes grow larger. That's definitely not a no, and he won't meet my eyes which makes me believe he's not entirely sure. "But… but… she seemed so normal!"

At this, Nate laughs, but what he finds amusing is beyond me. "My mom is amazing, and I love her, but she's definitely meddlesome like the rest of the women in my family."

I know I look a little freaked out because he leans forward and waves a hand. "The older generation of females in our family tend to harp on the younger, single generation. What my mom is telling me, without telling you, is that she's going to blab about you and me being here together, and if I don't show up with you, I'm going to be met with a lot of questions."

Oh. I see. His laughter wasn't amusement, it was resignation. Something I hear clearly in his voice now.

"Why would you bring me here then?" I implore, eyebrows furrowed until my face smooths out, my eyes widening. "Unless... Was this part of your not hitting on me plan?"

This time his laughter is genuine. "Not at all. I stop here most days when I get off shift and have a bite to eat before I go home and crash. I wasn't really thinking about my mom, and what she might think about you and me being here, until I saw her. By then it was too late to do anything about it."

"And now you're going to be subjected to the third degree if I don't come with you?" I ask hesitantly, and he nods. "Why do they meddle?"

He shrugs through a long, low sigh. "What can I say? They love *love*. They think happiness means having a partner, a family, all that stuff. So considering I've been single for a while, that must mean I'm miserable."

"Are you?" I question before I can think better of it.

Nate chuckles, flashing me a wide grin. "Far from it. I'm too busy to be miserable."

"Is that why you're single?" I ask, and when he shrugs noncommittally, I raise an eyebrow. Maybe I shouldn't be curious, but I am.

"Lately it's definitely been because I'm busy, but it's a combination of that and not finding the right woman," he explains, making me wonder what's been happening lately.

Twirling my straw in the thick milkshake, I eye it for a moment while chewing on my lip. Nate seemed serious that he would be bombarded with questions, and based on his reaction, it doesn't sound like a pleasant time. I hate to think that I'd be the reason for that. "I don't like knowing I'm going to be the cause of grief for you after you've been nothing but generous with me."

"It's okay. Honestly. I'll explain the situation, and while they might be disappointed, they'll understand," he tells me with a confident nod of his head.

When I give him a dubious look, he smiles sincerely and reaches over, laying his hand on mine, creating that same electricity that ran through me before. I watch his Adam's apple bob as he swallows hard, obviously feeling the same thing I am.

I don't think it's my imagination that his voice is an octave deeper when he says, "Let's just worry about getting through today before we start talking about barbecues, okay?"

Right. Today. I've been enjoying Nate's company so much that I haven't given another thought to the rest of the day, and while it was a nice break, I need to think about where I go from here.

I chew on my bottom lip for a moment before asking, "Do you think I'll be able to get into my apartment today?"

Nate frowns, and I see the answer in his eyes before he says it out loud while giving my hand a squeeze. "Unfortunately not. It might be a while before you can get back in there. Do you have renter's insurance?"

I pride myself in being a smart woman, but I'll admit that not getting insurance was not one of my smarter choices. I sigh, shaking my head as I look down at my milkshake.

"The last time I thought about it was when I moved in, and I didn't have a single thing to my name besides my clothes, an air mattress, and some bedding." I lean forward, my head dropping into my free hand. "It didn't seem important at the time."

"Hey, it's okay," he says, his voice warm and soft, gently caressing over me like a cozy blanket.

He continues to hold my hand and the comfort I find in that is immeasurable. After trying to survive for so long, looking after myself and ensuring I'm safe, having this man ease my worries, even if just with words, is a lifeline I didn't know I needed.

"We'll figure it out."

My head pops up, shaking at him. "You've done plenty. Taking me out and buying me a meal is more than you needed to do. If you could just drop me off at the beach after this, I'll figure it out."

"There's a difference between need and want, Sav," Nate says gently, and I can't help the warmth that spreads through me when he shortens my name. "I can't in good conscience drop you off at the beach and have you fend for yourself. You don't have anything with you. No phone, no ID, no money, no clothes."

I want to snap, "thanks for the reminder", but I refrain, instead pulling my hand out from under his, severing the connection. I miss it instantly and my gut says to grab on and hold tight until he's the one to let go, but I ignore it.

"What would you propose I do then? Find a bench and sleep on it?"

I can tell he wants to laugh, but he has the good sense to keep it hidden as he slides his hand back to his side of the table and grabs his milkshake, giving it a stir with the spoon in it.

"I suppose that's one option, but it's not what I was thinking," he says, amusement dancing in his eyes before the blue depths turn serious. "Hear me out before you say no. I have a guest bedroom—"

"Nate, no," I cut him off, my hand coming up to silence him. "You don't even know me, I don't know—"

He grabs my hand, and talks louder, overpowering my voice. "Hear me out. Just hear me out, that's all I'm asking."

His eyes are pleading with me, and honestly I'm defenseless against them. The way they look at me with such hope, imploring me to just listen and not shut him down right away. Releasing a sigh, I nod in agreement, pulling our hands back down to the table.

"Thank you," he says, giving me a smile that lights up his eyes. "I know we don't know each other, apart from today, but you wouldn't know anyone at the beach if you slept there, either. Jordan and I live together, so she would be there as well. It wouldn't just be the two of us. You can get a good sleep, and in the meantime, I'll try to reach out and see if I can get you into your apartment to at least get some of your things."

Well shit. I know I'm staring at him skeptically, but inside I think he makes a solid case. If I slept on the beach, we both know it wouldn't be pleasant. It would probably be downright terrifying, if I'm being honest, and I wouldn't get much sleep. That he lives with Jordan, another woman that I've already met in a professional setting, does help ease some of the fear I have about staying with a man I don't know. Even if I feel deep in my bones that Nate is a good man.

But what really does it for me is his willingness to try and help me get into my place for some of my things if I can't stay there. I would at least have some money and I could stay in a hotel while figuring out my next move. Staying with Nate eases a weight from my shoulders, knowing the rest of the day and evening, I'm taken care of. That I don't have to figure out what to do before I figure out what to do.

Plus, I think I'm going to crash the second we're finished

eating, if not before. It's been a whirlwind twenty-four hours, and I haven't slept in what feels like forever.

"What do you think?" Nate asks hesitantly, running his free hand through his hair.

Taking in a deep breath, I let it out slowly. If Nate weren't holding my hand, I'd be picking at a cuticle right now, a nervous habit I've had since I was a little girl. "I think… even though I love the beach, maybe a bed does sound better than the sand."

Triumph erupts on his face, and he looks so jubilant I've said yes that I laugh, sharing in his happiness. "I knew I could win you over. You realize how much better I'll sleep tonight knowing you're not on the streets, right?"

"Oh, so this was all for your benefit, then?" I ask, laughing.

"Yep. You just happen to be getting something out of it as well," he tells me with a wink.

Elizabeth shows up then with our lunch, and eyes the two of us, pointedly looking at our hands still joined on the table.

"Just friends my ass," she mumbles, and Nate and I look at each other with grins.

I can only imagine what will be said if his family finds out I'm spending the night at his place.

NATE

Looking up from my tablet when I hear footsteps shuffling across the hardwood floor in the hallway, I listen as a door shuts. A glance at the microwave from my spot at the island tells me it's not even six o'clock in the evening. I'm surprised that Savanna's already awake, but Jordan isn't home from work yet, so there's no one else it could be.

We were both wiped when we got back to my house this morning, and after a quick tour we took showers and went to bed. I was tired after the long shift, but I know my fatigue didn't compare to Savanna's.

Despite my exhaustion, sleep eluded me. My mind wouldn't shut down, replaying the last few hours over and over.

Anyone who knows me knows that I'll help anyone in need. It's part of my DNA. That doesn't generally include asking a stranger to stay in my guest bedroom, though. I couldn't help but wonder what the hell had gotten into me, but there was no stopping the words that came from my mouth. Am I crazy? No. I'm usually pretty level-headed. I have to be. But something about Savanna stirs an instinct deeper inside of me than just wanting to be helpful. It isn't about wanting to help. I *need* to help.

Savanna couldn't say no fast enough. I appreciated that I had to convince her. She's independent and wants to take care of herself, but she also wasn't closed off to accepting the help once the logic was laid out for her.

I like that.

Not needing more than the six hours of sleep I managed to finally get, I woke up a half hour ago. I'll be dog tired again by midnight, but between now and then, I have a few boxes I want to get through for the accountant. If Savanna goes right back to bed like I suspect she will, I'll be gone and back home, and she'll be none the wiser.

But when the bathroom door opens again, I don't hear her door close. Instead, footsteps pad down the hall, and a second later she appears in the entryway to the kitchen, bleary eyed and disheveled in a borrowed pair of my sister's pajamas.

And holy hell, she takes my breath away as she gives me a sleepy smile, rubbing one of her eyes with the back of her hand.

The blue checkered pants hang low on her hips, revealing an inch of her stomach which looks just as tanned as the rest of her. The black t-shirt is so worn it should probably be thrown in the garbage considering I can tell she's not wearing a bra. How could she be? I know for a fact her underwear are in the wash along with some of my clothes and the scrubs she wore from the hospital.

The blonde beauty in her sleepy state looks perfect in her rumpled condition.

It's not the first time I've had to say "down boy" to my cock. When Savanna and I touched earlier, the heat between us shot straight to my dick and made him want to come out and play. Unfortunately for him, once we got home, the only thing he got was some five-finger action in the shower.

"Is it six in the morning, or six at night? I feel so disoriented," she says, her voice raspy, the product of smoke and sleep.

The sound goes down my spine, doing nothing to help the situation in my pants. I can't help but lick my lips, forcing my eyes to stay locked on her face rather than travel to her breasts like they want to. The blonde braid that falls over her shoulder is like an arrow to the succulent peaks.

"Evening," I tell her, clearing my throat. "Why don't you go back to bed? No reason you need to get up yet."

"If I keep sleeping now, I'll be up in the middle of the night, and it'll be a horrible cycle," she says, turning to eye the coffee pot. "Besides, there's coffee, and it smells amazing."

"Help yourself. Cups are by the sink."

She turns to look at me, eyebrows furrowed, then looks at the cupboard near the sink before looking back at the coffee pot. "Why do you have the cups way over there?" she asks, walking over to grab one.

I shrug. "Used to keep the coffee maker over there, but switched it around a while ago."

"You should really switch your mugs then."

"That's a lot of work."

"But at least it would make sense and be organized."

"And then I would be so confused when I got up in the morning, went to that cupboard to get a mug, and it wouldn't be there," I say, pinning her with a mock serious look. "Then I'd have to blame you, and I just don't think I can have that."

That earns me a roll of her eyes along with a chuckle as she pours herself a cup, making herself at home as she finds the sugar above the coffee and the milk in the fridge. I watch with interest as she meanders through my kitchen, locating a spoon to stir, not once asking for help. It's like she belongs here, and I would be lying if I said I didn't like it, which seems ridiculous given we've just met and nothing is going on between us.

But man, I'd like it to be.

"So," she starts, leaning over the counter towards me with her cup of coffee in both hands.

She takes a moment to sip the warm liquid, and the look that comes over her is seductive, though I don't think she intends it to be. My imagination runs wild, though, picturing the way she looks when she comes, and it looks damn similar to her expression thanks to that coffee. I swallow hard to keep from drooling all over the counter, reminding my cock that now is not the time.

"Oh god, that's so good. So freaking good," she mumbles, taking another sip, and Jesus, I don't know if I'm going to survive while she makes love to her coffee, especially when her tongue peaks out and runs along her upper lip.

"So," I prompt, and as if this couldn't get worse, I swear to God my voice cracks like a teenager. I clear my throat, but when Savanna's eyes pop open and she gives me a perplexed look, I know she heard it. She must see something on my face that tells her exactly what's going on because she suddenly straightens and puts the mug down, clearing her own throat.

"Sorry. You make really good coffee, and I needed a caffeine fix," she explains, but her cheeks are flushing as she says it. If there was any doubt that she was clueless as to where my mind was, it's gone now. "So, I was, uh, going to ask what your plans were for the evening."

That's a much safer topic than where my head is currently, and I'm grateful for the change.

"I'm headed to the bar," I tell her casually, bringing my own coffee mug to my lips.

Her voice shifts a couple of octaves higher when she replies, appalled, "The bar?"

I nearly spit the lukewarm liquid all over the place at the wide eyed, gaping mouth look she's giving me. Shock and dismay meet my eyes, like she can't quite believe I would be headed to a bar. Or maybe can't believe it because I've got her here in my kitchen, staying in my guest bedroom.

I can't help it, I laugh. "It's not what you think," I tell her, putting my cup down. "I'm not only a firefighter. I work in a bar as well. Own, I guess."

"You guess?" she asks, the pitch of her voice still high with bewilderment.

"I'm still getting used to that part. Jordan and I inherited it from our uncle about six months ago," I explain, gazing at her across the counter.

She hasn't leaned over again like before, but she's pressed against the hard surface of the island, making that tanned piece of skin on her stomach stand out. I'm finding it increasingly hard not to look at, but damn it, I am not Liam. I have restraint.

"I've worked there since I was a teenager, but it's different now that it's mine. And Jordan is more of a silent partner, so most of it falls on my shoulders."

"Oh." Savanna nods in understanding, bringing her cup to her lips to take a sip. There aren't any moans or closed eyes this time, but I can tell she enjoys it just as much as the first drink she had, and it makes me want to puff my chest out for my stellar coffee making skills.

"If you plan on staying awake, why don't you join me? We can grab a bite to eat."

"Don't you need to work?" she asks, eyes narrowing skeptically.

I shrug. If I'm being completely honest, the answer would be yes, I definitely do. With each day that passes I have less and less time to get things organized for the accountant. I've already wasted most of today, and if Savanna is joining me at the bar tonight, I can pretty much kiss that time goodbye as well.

Yet, I can't find it in myself to care because I'd really love to spend the rest of this evening getting to know the woman standing across from me. It isn't that I'm trying to shirk my responsibilities, or that I'm overwhelmed by the massive amount of work—at least that's what I'm telling myself. It has to do with this intriguing woman, and the pull that I feel towards her.

Her gorgeous gray eyes are guarded, but inquisitive. She's logical, but willing to go with the flow, though she hasn't had much choice. There are things beneath the surface that I want to know more about, if she'll tell me. Like why she's been in Santa Rosé for six months and doesn't know anyone enough to call them for a ride from the hospital.

It isn't as though she's unfriendly, or not personable. She's sweet, adorable, and a little feisty when she's worked up. All good qualities in my book.

"Nate..."

I hear the question in her tone. I haven't committed to an answer, and she wants one before accepting my offer. I don't want to lie, but I don't want her to say no on account of me having things to do.

I settle somewhere between the two. "If it looks like they need help, I'll leave you sitting at the bar and jump in."

"You've already done so much for me, I can't interrupt what you need to do," she says hesitantly, but I can tell I'm coaxing her towards saying yes.

"You aren't, I promise. I can take care of the things I need to do tomorrow," I say, shaking my head. "And I swear I will help them if they need it."

"I'm getting the impression you would help them out even if they didn't need it," Savanna says with a laugh, setting her mug down on the counter. "Okay. If you're sure, then I think that sounds lovely. It'll be nice to get out."

"Because you don't do that often," I remark, and she sticks her tongue out, causing me to laugh.

After a quick back and forth on wearing Jordan's clothes, I head to my sister's dresser to grab something for Savanna to wear. This time I steer clear of the top right drawer—no brother should know about the things in that drawer when it comes to his sister.

Once I pick out a sky blue tank top with yellow writing that says 'Sunshine and Coffee' which seems to suit her, I meet her back in the hallway.

"Love it. That color is gorgeous," she says with genuine pleasure over my pick. Taking it from my hands, she gives me a smile that has a shy quality to it. "Thank you, Nate. For everything. I don't know how I'll ever repay you."

My hand is moving before I give it permission to do so, and I tuck a piece of hair that's strayed from her braid behind her ear. "The only thing I ask is that if you come across someone that needs help, you do what you can." My eyes are soft as I gaze down at her, the pads of my fingers slowly running along the length of her jaw. I feel her shiver beneath my touch. "Everyone needs a hand once in a while."

"Even you?" she whispers, her eyes locked on mine.

Help isn't something that I take very often, from anyone, and it drives my friends and family nuts. I'm the guy that helps everyone else, and I hate to come across looking like I need it, let alone want it.

"Let's get the rest of your clothes and we can both get ready. Then I'll let you help me look good by having dinner with me when we get to the bar," I tell her, not giving her a direct answer.

My suggestion has the desired effect though. Savanna gives me the same laugh she gave me in the hospital. The one that warmed me from the inside out and filled me with an amount of pride I didn't know was possible.

CHAPTER 10

NATE

"I hope you like the inside as much as you like the outside," I mutter as I pull into the alley leading to the back of the bar.

I drove Savanna around the front to show her what it looked like, and she seemed rather enthralled. I'm curious to know what she'll think of the inside.

My uncle styled the bar country and western. I always appreciated the rich brown mahogany floors, burnt barnwood bar, and booths and tables that match the bar, complete with black chairs and stools. The place always felt homey and comfortable to me; somewhere to come and kick back with friends to relax, or drown troubles with strangers.

"I'm almost positive I will," Savanna says, quick to unbuckle and open her door to jump out. "I love the outside with all the wooden beams and the wooden sidewalk out front. It reminds me of an old western saloon. I've never been to a place like that, not even back home."

I laugh as I meet her around the front of the truck and lead her to the back door. I let us inside where we're quickly assaulted with laughter and shouts from the boys in the back of house.

When the door closes behind us, three of my employees turn, a hush falling over the room. I know it's my presence. The same thing can happen at the firehouse, even though I'm friends with all the guys on my watch.

"Boss man!" Jeremy, my sous chef, says, breaking the silence after an awkward beat. "What's up, bro?"

"Don't let me kill the party, guys," I say with a smile, leading Savanna further into the kitchen.

I turn towards her and make the introductions. As I suspected, Savanna is gracious and sweet, taking it all in with wide, curious eyes. After a quick update from Jeremy about the day's events, I feel pretty good about taking it easy, though I'll make my final decision on whether I'm leaving Savanna at the bar alone once I talk to my head waitress and bartender.

"Come on, I'll show you the bar," I murmur to Savanna, taking her hand. The same shock runs up my arm causing me to shiver and glance in her direction. Her round eyes are larger than before, taking me in, and I know she felt it too, but I keep my mouth shut as I lead her towards the swinging doors to the pub.

We make it a few feet when I feel resistance against my hand and turn to find her attention pulled towards my office, looking aghast.

"Nate…" she says, appalled. "That's… that's… this explains why your cupboards are all a mess. I think it might also explain the disaster in your dining room."

I glance inside and cringe. It is pretty bad, with files, paper, and boxes all over the place. In the last few weeks a bunch of it has migrated from the bar to my house and has taken up residence in my dining room. Despite her assessment of my coffee cup situation, I'm a relatively organized guy. I like things neat and orderly, in their own place.

My office is the furthest thing from that. My face flushes and my hand is clammy in Savanna's. For some reason, I don't want her to see this side of things. Brushing the boxes and paperwork off at home had been easy given Savanna's exhausted state earlier today, but she's wide awake now.

"It's not that bad," I say, running a hand brusquely through my hair.

It is that bad, and she gives me a look that says as much.

"You know, I'm really good at organizing… if you wanted, I could help you out," she suggests with hope.

"I know it looks like a disorganized disaster, but it's like my kitchen. If you touched it, it would screw me up for days and I wouldn't be able to find a mug in the morning. But I appreciate the offer," I tell her, offering as much of a smile as I can muster. "Now c'mon. I'm starving."

The mountain of work can wait. The responsible side of me says it can't. I should be getting it more organized because the clock is ticking. Putting it off is stress inducing, but I shove the feeling down. Tonight is about getting to know this beautiful woman that intrigues me more than any other in years. As much as I know the work needs to be done, maybe Jordan and Liam are right—maybe I do need to have some fun. Even if the only place it can lead is learning a little more about Savanna.

Tomorrow. The work can wait until tomorrow.

Tugging Savanna towards the swinging doors, I push the right side open before coming to a dead stop in the middle of the doorway. Liam and Brody are both sitting at the bar, something I should have thought about prior to this moment. Normally I would have, but I'm distracted by a certain blonde currently running right into my back.

She bounces off me, her surprised gasp hitting my ears as I quickly turn, grabbing her by the elbows to keep her righted.

"Shit! I'm sorry!" I say at the same time she says, "What the heck, Nate?"

A second later, with both of us just inside the kitchen, the door swings open and hits me in the back. There's a yip of alarm, and then a crash of dishes hits the floor.

"Fuck! Nate, what the hell? Why are you standing right there?" Bryn, my head server curses again as she sets down a stack of dishes on one of the counters.

The crash turns out to be one broken plate. I'm not sure how she managed it, but it's one of the reasons I love her so much and rely on her as the glue that keeps this place together. When she finishes school in a few months and goes to work as a massage therapist I'm going to be lost without her.

Bryn is shaking her head, her chin length brown hair swaying around her face while she picks up some of the larger pieces of the broken dish. Savanna is kneeling beside her a second later, helping, and I'm torn between making an introduction and grabbing a broom for the rest of the mess. I'm a firefighter at heart, though, and getting hazards out of the way takes priority over niceties, so I go for the broom, returning a moment later to find the two women making their own introductions.

Bryn slides her eyes over to me when I return, an eyebrow cocked in question. I choose to ignore it, sweeping up the leftover bits of plate instead.

"I'll finish that if you tell me why the hell you were standing there in the first place," Bryn says.

"Yeah, I'd kind of like to know why you stopped so abruptly," Savanna chimes.

Christ, now they're ganging up on me.

If I tell them the truth, Bryn will laugh her way back to Liam and Brody and tell them all about this. At the same time, I do want to warn Savanna about my friends before we head into the bar. They're like brothers to me, but they can be a handful, especially together.

Actually, it's Liam. I'm worried about Liam.

Brody is a beast of a man who half rocks the surfer look—only the top half of his hair is long because of regulations at work—which is fitting considering he's a surfer. He's a quiet soul. A year younger than I am, but in many ways older. Losing a wife can do that to a person. A couple years ago Heather was killed in a car accident. It was crushing for him, and for a while I wasn't sure he would make it to the other side, but these days he's doing better. A part of him didn't make it out, though, and I don't know if he'll ever truly be able to move on.

Liam, on the other hand, requires a warning before meeting. While he's the most loyal person I've ever met, and is the one I'd call on to help bury a body, the guy is a shameless flirt. He'll pry into what's going on the second he sees Savanna and me together. If I let her walk out there without a word of caution, it would be like sending her into the lion's den.

"It's fine, I can finish this. Go deal with your tables," I tell Bryn, nodding over my shoulder towards the pub.

I can feel her hazel eyes on me, and I clench my jaw to keep from looking up. Bryn has worked here for years and knows me well. She's also perceptive as hell, and I don't need to give her any insight into what I'm thinking.

"Okay," she says with a shrug. "Suit yourself. Savanna, it

was nice meeting you. Next time just shove him through the door."

"He's like a brick wall," Savanna laughs. "I'm not sure how I'm supposed to do that."

"You could try slapping his ass. I know that always makes me move," Bryn smirks before disappearing through the door separating the kitchen and the pub.

I choose to ignore Bryn, instead focusing on the mess, depositing it into the garbage. "See? I told you I'd help out if needed."

Savanna tries hard to contain a snicker, but she isn't doing a great job, and my comment causes her to give me a full-blown laugh. "You caused this! You deserve to clean it up!"

Only when I'm done with everything do I turn fully to her and explain. "I didn't want to send you out there without proper warning," I say, ominously.

She steps closer to me, eyebrows furrowing as she stares intently. She's so close I can feel the heat from her body, and see little flecks of brown around her pupil that I hadn't noticed before.

"The guys are sitting at the bar. Liam and Brody."

"The ones I'm lucky didn't rescue me," she says so seriously that I bark out a laugh.

"Yeah, those ones," I concur, giving her a toothy grin. "They're going to recognize you, and they're going to be really curious." Turning solemn, my eyes dart towards the door. "They probably won't be able to help themselves, and there'll be questions. And when I say they, I actually mean Liam. Brody will be interested, but he's more the strong silent type. Liam, on the other hand, is outspoken. But they're family. With everything we go through together, he's become a brother to me. They both have, so I put up with them."

Giving me a firm nod, Savanna gestures towards the doors that lead out front. "I got this. Lead the way."

Her confidence gives me confidence, and I hope to hell she's right. It takes a strong woman to take on the two men I'm about to introduce to her.

"Well, well, well, look who finally decided to grace us with his presence!" Liam bellows over the music as we walk through the swinging door.

Savanna is right behind me and judging by the look on both Liam and Brody's faces, they haven't spotted her yet.

The two of them are sitting at the end of the bar closest to the kitchen doors, and there are a couple of barstools available beside Liam. I'm still trying to decide if that's a good or bad thing when Liam elbows Brody and I know they've both noticed Savanna, who has stepped out from around me.

"I know, I know. I'm a little late," I start, and then immediately recognize my mistake as I come to stand at the end of the bar.

Savanna joins me to my right, standing close to where Brody is sitting. I'm damn thankful that it's Brody sitting at the end and not Liam, but then again, the open seat is next to Liam, so I'm not entirely sure how thankful I should be.

Liam's grin lights up his face and he leans over a little further so he can see around Brody's large frame. I swear I can see smoke coming out of his ears as the gears turn in his brain at the woman standing beside me. "And we can see why. Your reason is more than acceptable, dude."

"You must be Brody," Savanna says, her attention on the closer man, and Christ, I could kiss her for it. I don't know how she knows to play it off like Liam isn't even there, but it's the best thing she could do.

Brody, in all his tiny man-bun glory, swings his head towards her, surprise flashing in his brown eyes that she voiced his name over the man sitting next to him. His eyes dart to me before he looks back to her and gives her a slow smile, extending a hand to her. "That's me."

Savanna returns the expression and takes his hand, giving it a shake. I'm positive she's winning points with the large man. "Savanna. I hope you don't mind me joining Nate for dinner."

Shaking his head, Brody releases her hand, his grin growing the longer Savanna ignores Liam. He's getting as much pleasure out of this as I am, and even though Savanna doesn't know either of them very well, I'm certain she's almost as amused as we are.

Liam is sitting there, his jaw on the bar, staring at the interaction going on like it's the most baffling thing he's ever witnessed. And for Liam it might be.

The guy commands the attention of females with his good looks and buoyant personality. Women fawn over him, wanting to know his name, be on his arm, have his attention on them. None of us shame him for it, or hold it against him. That's how he is, and we wouldn't change him for the world, but it must be a humbling experience for me to show up with a woman, and for her to introduce herself to Brody without giving Liam a second look.

Finally, she puts him out of his misery. I watch as she tilts her head to the side and looks at Liam on the other side of Brody, giving him an appraising look. "Which makes you Liam."

Now that he's not floundering from being ignored, he

pulls out the signature Liam charm, giving her a smile that has melted countless panties in this bar.

"The one and only," he says, leaning towards us as he extends a hand across Brody.

Savanna takes it, but instead of a handshake, he takes her hand in his, his index finger resting beneath her palm.

"If I didn't have the big lug between us, I'd be inclined to sweep my lips right here," he says, and I don't need to look at their hands to tell his thumb is running along her skin.

Rather than answer him, Savanna turns her head to me, forehead crinkled, gray eyes deadpan. "You made him seem like a ladies man. Do these moves actually work on most women?"

Brody damn near spits out his beer, and I crack up with laughter, while Liam looks too stunned to form an actual sentence. I'm thrilled Savanna is more than holding her own with my brothers, vanquishing all the worries I had about sitting with these two. Every layer that gets peeled back from her only encourages me to like her more.

"Girl got jokes," he finally says, and nods with appreciation as he lets go of her hand. "Okay. I see you there."

Savanna finally laughs, her forehead smoothing while her eyes light up as she looks between the three of us. "I'm sorry, I couldn't help it. Nate hasn't told me a lot, but he's told me enough."

"That's one sided. He hasn't told us a thing about you," Liam says, eyeing me. I can feel Brody's eyes land on me as well, both wanting to know what's going on.

"Why don't you take a seat," I say to Savanna, nodding towards the space next to Liam. "I'll get us a drink."

She does as I suggest, and I move behind the bar. As I do, my head bartender, Martin, makes his way over to me. We have a brief chat about the evening and how it's going—

steady for a Thursday night, but not so busy that he can't handle it by himself for the time being—and then he's gone, back to the other end of the bar.

I hear Liam mention Savanna's shirt looks like something he'd seen Jordan wear; why the hell he remembers that, when he can hardly remember a girl from the night before, I don't understand. I don't question it, though. Mostly because I don't want to know, but also because I trust the guy wholly.

"So," I interrupt Liam and Savanna. "What can I get you to drink?"

"Uhm," Savanna hums, chewing on the inside of her lip, drawing my attention to them. I'd rather it be me nibbling on that full bottom lip, but if all I can do is watch her do it, I won't say no.

"Oh," Liam pipes up in a calculating tone, "Something hard. He loves that."

Sliding my gaze to his, I find a devious glint staring back at me. Christ. This bastard. My eyes narrow at him, and I have the sudden urge to punch him in the face. The guy loves to ride my ass about finding a date, but the second I show interest in a woman he's all about trying to embarrass me.

Savanna doesn't seem to catch Liam's innuendo, her excitement evident as she asks, "Do you have something special you make? Something hard?"

I can see in her face that the only thing she's thinking about is a drink, but Brody and Liam erupt in laughter before I have a chance to say a word. It's only then that Savanna realizes what she said, and what Liam must have meant, and I watch as her face turns twenty shades of red right before my eyes. It's fucking gorgeous on her, and despite her embarrassment, I might be a tad happy over Liam's annoying behavior.

"To drink! I mean do you have some kind of special hard

drink! You know, like bartenders make signature things!" she explains, gesturing with her hands wildly as the two men beside her continue to crack up.

"Savanna, ignore these two. Their brains stopped developing at the same time their dicks did when they were twelve. You two are cut off," I tell them, turning towards Martin at the other end of the bar. "Liam and Brody are cut off!"

I get groans from both of them, but it does what it's intended and sobers them up.

Liam turns on his stool towards Savanna, an apology etched into his facial features. "Savanna, I sincerely apologize. It's just that, well, you see… the last time our friend Nate, here, brought a girl into a bar, it was six years ago."

"Screw you, it was not."

"Oh, so you bring girls into the bar often then?" he shoots back, eyebrows raised at me.

"No! Jesus. Savanna, I'm sorry, he gets carried away," I say, turning to look strictly at her, ignoring the look of triumph Liam is sporting.

"You don't need to apologize, Nate," she says, chuckling. "You told me they were like family. Brothers. I have two of my own, so I know what it's like."

Then she leans across the bar towards me, arms folded in front of her, her breasts resting on top of them. The sweetest, most innocent smile blinds me as she practically hums, "So, do you have something hard for me?"

CHAPTER 11

SAVANNA

"Sᴡᴇᴇᴛ ᴏʀ sᴘɪᴄʏ?"

Something about the way that Nate is looking at me has my stomach flipping with excitement. It's been forever since I've flirted with a man. Flirting with Preston felt forced instead of playful, so I never reciprocated, or gave him much attention. By the time I left Vincent and Colorado, it had been years since we'd flirted. When I was with him I didn't dare do anything that resembled flirting with another man for fear of him finding out. If he even thought I was looking at someone else I would pay for it later.

So it's been a while. And I find that I really want to flirt with Nate. There's something about him, something about the way all three of these men are interacting with each other that makes me feel safe enough to be bold. It could be my lack of human interaction talking, but I really think it's more than that. I can see the brotherly bond between them, and it reminds me of home, and of a familiarity that I haven't felt in half a year.

In the dim light I can see that Nate's eyes have darkened, their focus intently on me, watching my every move. It's exhilarating, and I can feel the energy bouncing between us across the bar.

I lick my lips, keenly aware of his eyes darting down to follow the move. "What if I want a little bit of both?"

His eyes shoot back to mine, his nostrils flaring. I wonder if his heart is beating as fiercely as mine.

"It would be a pleasure to give you exactly what you want," Nate tells me, his voice low and gravelly, the sound of it reverberating in my lower belly. My eyebrows raise in challenge, our eyes locked in a heated exchange that has my pulse fluttering out of control.

"You guys keep eye fucking each other like that, I'm gonna need to take my shirt off with how hot it's getting in here," Liam says from my left.

"Shut up, Liam," Nate says, his eyes never leaving mine.

"I'm just saying, you could cut the sexual tension with a spoon right now. I feel like I'm about to watch live porn."

I finally break our staring match to look at Liam, a grin spread wide across my face. "I hate to disappoint, but I'm not that kind of girl."

"The porn kind?" Liam asks, pointing his bottle at me before turning it towards Nate. "That's a good thing cause Nate wouldn't go for a porn star."

"That's more Liam's style," Brody says from the other side of Liam, and we all laugh.

I might not know these guys beyond this exchange, but I already like them. Nate felt he had to warn me, and I'm glad he did, but I didn't need it. They remind me of my own brothers, Connor and Devin, and how they would poke fun at each other, and at me, whenever they had the chance. It makes a pang of longing go through my chest and my jubilant mood dives for a second before I push the feelings away to focus on the present.

Liam shrugs, flashing an impish grin, not denying Brody's claim, which makes me giggle. I wonder if he would actually go for a porn star, but I don't ask. Heck, for all I know, he's already had one.

"What kind of girl would Nate go for then?" I ask curiously, doing a double take when I glance at Nate.

He's closing a cocktail shaker, his eyes trained on what he's doing, but I can tell he's listening closely to the conversation between Liam and me. I'm not sure what he's making, or how he did it without me realizing, but I'm a little disappointed that I missed him in action up until now.

His hands are nimble and swift as he opens the shaker after his concoction is mixed and pours the liquid into a two-ounce shot glass rimmed with salt, or sugar, I can't tell which. He looks skilled at what he's doing, and it's kind of hot.

Once the orange-colored shot is in front of me, his eyes meet mine, and his smile is sinfully sexy and mischievous. Slowly his eyebrows raise in challenge.

I want to ask him what's in it, but I don't because I feel like it would give him some kind of satisfaction, and I don't want him to have that just yet. We've challenged each other, and now we're in this dance that's fun and suggestive. Admitting I wasn't paying attention at a crucial moment feels like it would have the bubble bursting.

Taking the shot glass, I lift it towards my lips. First, I take in the smell. The tequila hits me immediately, but a second later the fruitiness of mango touches my nose, followed by something that makes it tickle. Sticking my tongue out, I taste the rim of the glass, sweetness exploding across my tongue.

I'm about to throw it back when Nate stops me. He bends down behind the bar and when he pops back up, he sets a beer in front of me. With a smirk, he explains, "In case you need a chaser."

My eyes narrow before I throw my head back, my eyes never leaving him as the liquid enters my mouth. Sweetness slides down my throat, but there's a heat right behind it that makes my mouth tingle in the most delicious way.

"Mmm," I murmur, my tongue sliding along my lips as I set the shot glass down. "Just the way I like it. Screw the chaser."

I can feel all three pairs of male eyes on me. Under most circumstances I would feel apprehensive about that, but with these guys I don't, and I'm not sure why. They're all insanely strong, I'm sure, given that they're firefighters. I know first-hand how strong Nate is, which means they could all crush me without a second thought.

Instead, I feel safe. I've just done a shot, something that will no doubt knock down a few inhibitions and defenses, and I'm not even breaking a sweat over it. I'm not worried about what could happen. I'm not worried about saying or doing the wrong thing, or how someone might react to it. It's been a long time since I've felt at ease around people that aren't my family, and it feels better than I can describe.

"You." Liam's voice pulls me out of my thoughts, and I glance at him, the burning in my mouth slowly starting to subside. I must look confused because he elaborates, "You're the type of girl Nate would go for."

I give a short burst of laughter, looking between Liam and Nate. "Nate doesn't even know me," I tell Liam, feeling the slightest bit of unease.

I can't be the type of girl that Nate goes for. I have way too much baggage. Between not having a job, not having a place to live at the moment, and of course the biggest problem of running from my ex, my life is a mess. The man has already been so good to me that even if I really, really want to be his type, I need to look out for both of us. Even if he didn't care about the job or housing situation, I couldn't put him in a position where he might be in danger if Vincent were to find me. It's why I've isolated myself for so long, and it's why I need to continue to remain on my own.

"And yet," I hear Nate say. I look to him and find him looking pensive, and I know he's thinking about how we went for brunch this morning, how he's invited me to stay the night in his home, and how he's feeding me once again.

I give him a warm, grateful smile. And yet I find myself not wanting to do anything on my own while this man is around. "And yet he knows more about me than anyone else in this city."

"There's a story there," I hear Liam murmur to Brody.

At least I think it's to Brody. I'm not entirely sure since I'm too busy looking at Nate who is studying me curiously, questions in those bright blue eyes. I told him I didn't really know anyone in Santa Rosé, and I'm sure he's remembering that part of our earlier conversation.

"Why don't we all order dinner, grab a booth, and you guys can tell us all about it," Liam suggests.

Nate's eyes shift to him for a second, and then back to me, asking me silently if I'm okay with that idea. He doesn't want to pressure me into having dinner with his friends, something I'm thankful for, but I'm enjoying their company, and I think it'll give me more insight into who Nate is. Despite the fact that I shouldn't be interested—I have no business liking a man right now, and I don't want to lead

Nate on—I want to get to know him better. Besides, I'm going to be staying in his house tonight, and I should probably know a little about him for me to do that.

At least it seems like a good justification.

"Sure. What's good?" I ask, and the four of us order dinner before we grab one of the booths that line the same wall as the main door of the place.

I squeeze in on one side with Liam across from me, Brody beside him, and Nate taking up space beside me. We took one of the extra-long booths, one that can fit six but comfortably seats three firefighters and me, and I can still feel the heat coming off Nate's body beside mine. The air between us feels charged, like it's ready to snap and crackle the second one of us looks at the other, or gets too close, threatening to touch.

"So, how did this all come about?" Liam asks, gesturing between Nate and me. "And don't tell me that Nate pulls you out of a burning building and asks you out to dinner because I won't believe it."

I turn to look at Nate at the same time he's glancing in my direction. His eyes tell me that he's just as aware of me sitting next to him as I am of him, and I need to suck in a deep breath to keep my thoughts clear of things like moving closer to him, touching him, or wanting to kiss him.

He's got fantastic lips, the bottom one just a tad fuller than the top one, and I'm pretty sure they would feel incredibly sweet and soft if they were on mine, just like the man himself. Or maybe they would be hard and commanding, more like the man I met at the fire, ordering his men around, determined to get me out of the building safely. Then I realize I think he would be both, remembering the shot he made me, which causes me to lick my lips while I'm still staring at his.

Shit. I shouldn't stare. My eyes pop back up to his and I can see his have darkened again as he watches me. I'm pretty sure all the guys are waiting for me to say something, but my ability to think like a rational human seemed to go out the window the second I looked at Nate's lips. Distraction can be a bitch.

"Please tell me you're seeing this," Liam says.

"I'm not blind, dude," Brody replies, "Just not as vocal as you."

It's enough for me to pull my eyes away from Nate, shaking my head to clear the thoughts of lips, kisses, and wanton eyes. "What was the question?"

Brody snorts and Liam smirks, gesturing once again between Nate and me, this time with his beer bottle. "You two. How'd you hook up?"

"We haven't hooked up," Nate corrects quickly, his tone hard and unyielding, a clear warning to Liam.

He's taken the ribbing that Liam has been feeding him since we got here, but I can tell by his tone that he's drawing a line. It makes butterflies erupt in my stomach, making me feel safe and respected, a feeling I haven't felt with many men besides my brothers and dad. I realize that since the first time I met him he's made me feel at ease, though I didn't recognize it in the elevator the other day. I was far too irritated with men in general to see much of anything.

"And we didn't meet at the fire," I tell the two men across from us. "We actually met the day before in an elevator."

Liam chokes on the beer he's currently drinking, and I know I'm damn lucky I'm not wearing it when he covers his mouth with a hand, liquid sliding out from under it. His eyes dart between Nate and me, wide with what I think is shock. Brody whistles low between his teeth, his eyes focused on Nate, subdued surprise etched in his features. Based on their reactions, I'm gathering Nate told them about our interaction.

"You're elevator girl?" Liam says, incredulous, his eyes settling on me while grabbing a napkin.

I feel my cheeks heat, and dare a glance at Nate, making sure I don't look at his mouth. "You told them about that?"

Nate shrugs, his neck redder than his face. "I didn't think I would see you again," he says by way of explanation. "And I only told him," he adds, pointing to Liam. "He just has a big mouth."

"You say that like you wouldn't have told Brods," Liam says, slinging an arm around the other man. "Don't leave the big lug out like that. It'll hurt his feelings. Right, Brods?"

For such a quiet, reserved guy, he sure has expressive eyes. They turn on Nate, and I nearly "aww" at the puppy dog look in them, like he's truly hurt that Nate wouldn't tell him about our interaction. I suddenly wonder if Nate should have warned me more about Brody than Liam. It's always the quiet ones you need to watch out for, and I feel like Brody is proving that right now. The two of them are probably a lethal combination for the ladies.

"Jesus, you two," Nate mutters, scrubbing his hands over his face and then through his hair.

His clear irritation makes me giggle and I throw a shoulder into his side to tell him it's okay. It's the wrong move because I'm suddenly acutely aware of him, even more than before, and how solid and hot his body is. An image of him moving above me flashes in my mind and I press my thighs together instinctively, need washing over me.

I can feel his eyes on me again, watching, and I chance a glance up at him, inhaling sharply at the look I see in his eyes. The same need I feel is reflected back to me, and if we were anywhere but in a very public place with his two best friends watching us, I would say to hell with all my baggage and fling myself at him to find out exactly what those lips would do.

I don't understand what it is about him that's making me react to him like this. Sure, I've lacked in the personal relationships department for the last six months, but that doesn't explain this reaction. I was lacking when I accepted a date with Preston, and I never behaved like this or had thoughts of wanting to throw myself at him.

Nate is different. I don't know why, but he is. My body's reaction to him is proof enough of that, even if I don't understand it.

Damn it. I know by the end of tonight I'm going to want to call Maddie to tell her all about this. There've only been a few instances since moving to Santa Rosé that I've desperately felt the need to call her and gush about an experience— something I've probably subconsciously set up for myself— and this is definitely going to be one of them. She would help me understand exactly what's going on, and why I want to throw all caution to the wind and mold myself to this sexy as hell firefighter.

"Okay, before you two go eye fucking each other further —Savanna is the girl from the elevator? The one that thinks men are filthy, disgusting pigs?" Liam says, recovered from the initial shock of this information.

And damn it, I knew I hadn't heard the last of that line. Groaning, I pull my eyes away from Nate and pick up my beer, taking a pull from it.

"If you'd just walked in on someone you'd gone on a few dates with screwing the newest intern while you were with clients, you'd think the same thing," I tell him, and he cringes. "Especially when that someone is your boss."

"Oh shit," Brody mutters, and I cringe, nodding, telling them the same story I told Nate earlier today about Preston.

I end up telling them a bit about working at a wealth management firm, and how my summer was spent at the beach. They have me opening up in a way I haven't with anyone in this city. I share that I'm from Colorado and when they ask about the mountains, I tell them how magical they are, especially after a fresh snowfall, but how the ocean is better, and that I couldn't imagine not living near it again.

Liam asks why I left home in the first place, but all I say is I needed a change. I don't tell them I left one day without telling a soul besides my best friend, or that I left because I was finally done putting up with abuse.

Even though I don't share those details, I talk and share more of myself with these men than I have with anyone in the last six months, and the more I say, the lighter I feel until it seems like I'm floating on cloud nine. This is the connection I've been missing. The human interaction that I've craved so badly. It helps that these three are attentive listeners, and ask questions.

The longer I sit with them, the more I'm reminded of my own family. There's a genuineness about them that I haven't encountered since the last time I had family dinner. It makes my heart both ache and rejoice at the same time. A feeling of homesickness and belonging washing over me time and again in their company.

"Orders up, Nate," Bryn says, suddenly appearing next to the table. She's balancing a tray of full glasses, on her way to a table with them.

Nate nods and starts slipping out of the booth from beside me and I'm quick to follow suit. "I'll come help."

"I can handle it," he says, turning to look at me.

"Nate, please." I give him a chastising look. "You're

feeding me and giving me a place to stay, this is the least I can do."

"Whoa, what?" Brody pipes up from across the table, and my head snaps in his direction, catching sight of Liam as well.

Shit.

They both look bewildered at this new development. I hadn't considered them when it came out of my mouth, and I toss Nate an apologetic look. I didn't want to say anything if he didn't want to, but he's looking at me with a smirk that says, "You got yourself into this mess, get yourself out."

"Or you can stay and explain that," he suggests with a laugh.

"You should do that," Liam says, followed by Brody who adds, "I agree."

"Not a chance." I leave them both hanging, scrambling the rest of the way out of the booth to follow Nate to the kitchen. "I am so sorry. I didn't even think before I said that."

"Nothing to be sorry about," he says, holding the swinging door open for me to follow him through. "They'd find out eventually, anyway. I didn't want to tell them anything you weren't comfortable with, though. Figured I'd follow your lead on all this."

"Oh." I stop at the pass where our four plates are sitting. "Well I think everyone should know how generous you are, so I don't mind telling them I'm staying with you tonight."

"Liam will take it wrong," Nate replies distractedly, his eyes taking in the chaos of the kitchen.

"Then we'll just have to set him straight," I respond, laying a hand on Nate's arm to draw his attention back to me, his warmth seeping into my fingertips. "Why don't you let me take care of our food, and you take care of that." I nod towards the two cooks who look extremely busy.

"I can handle it," he tells me again, and I smile simply at him.

"I'm sure you can, but why not let me help so you can deal with your business? Remember the whole 'I'll jump in if they need me' thing? It looks like they could use your help." I spot a serving tray on another counter behind us and grab it, bringing it over to the pass to load up our plates. I can feel Nate's eyes on me, suspicious as he watches what I'm doing, and I laugh. "Relax. I served all through college. I'm a pro at this."

"Leave mine," he tells me before I can pick it up. "I'll leave it under the heating lamps until I can make it back to the table. You sure you're going to be okay?"

I don't think he's talking about the plates of food I'm about to lift, and I give him an encouraging smile that I hope doesn't show any of the uneasiness I'm feeling. Liam and Brody have made me feel comfortable, but I'm about to go in there with them wanting answers to questions for which I have no answers. I don't want them to think I'm using Nate, or taking advantage of him. Or worse, leading him on when I can't give him anything more than friendship.

Despite the growing attraction that seems to be reciprocated.

"I got this."

Lifting the tray, I give him one last smile before I'm headed back to the table where the two men sit, nursing their beers. Liam's the first to spot me, which doesn't surprise me, and he elbows Brody who turns to look my way.

I set the tray down and pick up the first plate, handing it to Liam.

"Dinner is served, guys," I say because they're both too silent for my liking.

"He giving you a job too?" Liam asks, and my eyes snap to his, certain I'll see contempt in the brown depths.

There's none there, though; he's just looking at me inquisitively, trying to figure it all out, and when I look at Brody, he's wearing a similar expression. Neither of them look like they're judging me, or that they're worried I'm taking advantage of their friend, and I could sag with relief over that.

"No," I say softly, dishing out Brody's plate and then mine. I slide back into the booth. "They just got kind of busy in there so he's helping out for a few minutes."

I drop the serving tray to the bench beside me and take a deep breath, eying them both with resolve. It's better to get the questions out of the way before I dig into my dinner. They both got distracted earlier, asking me about Preston, and then Colorado, and my time in Santa Rosé over the summer. Now I take the opportunity to fill them in on the day Nate and I have had.

When I'm finished, I'm filled with relief that neither of them is looking at me any differently. There's no disdain in their eyes, no suspicion narrowing their gazes. Nothing but the same two friendly faces that I've been looking at all evening.

But my relief is short-lived.

"He likes you," Liam says, in the most serious tone I've heard since I met him.

I shake my head, picking up my burger. I had one at brunch, but I have a thing for burgers and fries. They're my number one comfort food, and after the last couple of days I'm definitely seeking comfort. "He doesn't know me."

"You haven't been sitting where we're sitting all night," Brody says, and I look up in surprise to see him wiping his hands with his napkin, his dark eyes focused on what he's doing. For him to voice an opinion before Liam can jump in is astonishing, which makes me want to pay close attention.

"There are varying degrees of like, Savanna. Just because he doesn't know you well doesn't mean he doesn't know to like you. Sometimes it's a feeling you don't understand, but you know is true." His eyes slowly rise to look at me and I swallow hard at the honesty in them. "What I know to be true is that I haven't seen Nate look at a woman the way he looks at you in a very long time."

"If ever," Liam adds in a mutter.

"Why are you guys telling me this?" I ask, slightly irritated that they're divulging Nate's secrets and what it's doing to me, and my resolve about not leading him on. I can't get involved with this man. I don't even know him.

I set my burger—the one I haven't even taken a bite out of —back down on my plate with a frown of frustration. Continuing, my voice rises with each word, "As his friends aren't you supposed to keep stuff like that close to the chest? It's not like we've even been on a date. It's not like we can go on a date. I don't know him. I just got out of something. And even if I hadn't, my life is a mess right now. I have no job, no apartment, hell, I don't even have my own clothes!"

"Douchebag bosses don't count as getting out of something," Liam scoffs, and I wish that's what I had meant when I said that, but I don't correct him. He nudges Brody with his elbow. "I think she likes him back."

I huff when Brody nods his agreement, and then nearly jump out of my skin when Nate slides into the booth next to me asking, "Who likes who back?"

My eyes plead to both of them to keep their mouths shut, and I nearly lunge across the table at Liam when I see his eyes fill with mischievousness, taunting me from where he sits. I suddenly understand the warning that Nate gave me when we first got here. I thought I could handle Liam, but I haven't even known him for a few hours and I'm contemplating murder if he opens his mouth.

"The couple at the bar," Brody says casually and my eyes dart to him, gratitude evident. "We were debating if she's falling for whatever he's saying."

When Nate looks in that direction, Brody shoots me a wink and I grin at him. I think being the strong, silent type offers Brody the perspective of observing everything going on around him and he picks up on things that most of us don't. That's definitely working in my favor right now as the big man comes to my rescue.

Glancing at Liam, I stick my tongue out in victory, and he rewards me with a laugh.

The rest of dinner goes by with the guys asking me more questions, some of which I answer, some of which I dodge, and me asking some in return, most of which involve firefighting. We laugh and talk like we've all been friends for years, which I learn the three of them have been, so I'm the odd duck out, but they don't make me feel like it at all. I don't remember the last time I felt so included in a social situation that didn't involve my brothers and Maddie back home.

"Let me get those," I tell Nate as he starts piling the dishes to clear them from the table.

He gives me a quick shake of his head. "I've got it."

"I need to use the bathroom anyway. I'll drop them off when I go by," I tell him, pushing my body against his to get him out of the way, ignoring the heat that rushes through me at the contact. "Besides, it's your turn in the hot seat with Riggs and Murtaugh."

"Boo! Hiss!" Liam glowers at me. "We're firemen, not donut loving glory hunters!"

I walk away with the dishes, laughing all the way to the kitchen over the three scowling men I leave behind. My belly is full, and my mind feels hazy, thanks to a shooter and a couple of good beers, and better company. My soul feels like it's had a dose of medicine that I didn't know it needed.

For the first time since I moved to Santa Rosé I have a sense of belonging, which baffles me a little. It's not like I know these guys very well, but they've made me feel right at home. Maybe it's easy for me to get swept away in those feelings because it's been so long since I've felt them, and maybe I'm letting my guard down a little bit because of it, but it feels so good that I can't help myself.

At least not for tonight.

For tonight I'm just going to count my blessings, that despite being out of a job, and out of my home, I have somewhere to go, and someone who cares that I'm okay.

When I get back to the table, Nate slides over to where I was sitting, and I slide in next to him. The three of them are quiet, all eyes turned on me, and I look down to make sure I haven't spilled something on my top, forgotten to pull my pants up, or something else ridiculous like that.

"What? Why are you all looking at me like that?" I ask, picking my cuticle self-consciously.

Nate levels me with a serious look, lips pursed in thought, his fingers tapping on the side of his beer bottle. I feel like whatever he's about to say is going to carry a great deal of weight, and I'm not wrong when he asks, "How would you like to come work for me?"

CHAPTER 12

NATE

"Morning brother," Jordan greets me as she walks into the kitchen, ready for work in a pair of blue scrubs. She grabs a coffee mug from the cupboard as I grunt a "morning" and go back to reading the news on my tablet. "I see you're in a great mood."

It's not that I'm in a bad mood, I'm just in a mood where I don't want to talk to my sister. I made a rash decision last night, something that isn't like me, and I know she's going to question me on it. Christ, I'm surprised she's not questioning me on a lot of choices I've made in the last twenty-four hours. Then again, she probably sees the decisions as part of my love life, and she wouldn't dare negatively question that. It's the only reason I think I might get through this conversation without her having a heart attack.

"I thought you'd be all smiles this morning given that we have a house guest," she muses, leaning against the counter as she sips on her coffee, studying me. "Then again, it looks like said house guest slept in the guest bedroom, so maybe that's why you still look grumpy."

"I'm not Liam."

"Clearly."

I swipe down to the next story on the news, picking my mug up to take a sip of my own coffee, ignoring my sister, although I need to talk to her. I may run the majority of the bar, but Jordan is still part owner, and I gave Savanna a job without consulting her. I'm pretty sure there are rules against that, or at the very least it's frowned upon, especially when you're facing a world of unknowns where finances are concerned. The bar does well, but given the tax situation, I don't know where we stand and I won't know for a few weeks, something that Jordan is well aware of after the meeting with the accountant.

I sigh and push my tablet away, looking up to find her still watching me. Damn her perceptive eyes and knowing me so well. It's like she's been standing there waiting for me to spill whatever is on my mind.

Deciding to get it over with, I sigh. "I hired Savanna as a server last night."

"What? Nate!" Jordan hisses, eyes bugging out of her head.

I don't mention that it took Liam and I some convincing to get Savanna to agree. Brody was useless, sitting there minding his own business the entire time. After Savanna left the table, Liam was on me like white on rice, bringing up the fact that she didn't have a job, and if I had more help I could take more time off.

It didn't take long to persuade me because the thought had already been on my mind when I watched her walk out of the kitchen with that serving tray held like she had done it all her life. But after everything I had already done for her,

Savanna wasn't as inclined to take the offer until I told her it didn't need to be anything long term if she didn't want it to be. Which was stupid as shit of me because it's pointless to train someone only for them to leave shortly after.

I think I was feeling a little desperate to keep her in my life somehow because, despite our flirting—super hot, leave me semi-hard all-night flirting—I get the sense that Savanna is skittish when it comes to men and dating. It's nothing that she's said specifically, minus the whole thing with her boss, but more what she hasn't said. There were times last night when Liam or I would ask her a question about her life prior to moving here and she would avoid answering, usually by asking a question of her own.

"I know, I'm sorry. I should have consulted you," I apologize, meeting Jordan's eyes.

She's moved to lean against the island instead of the back counter, her cup set down in front of her. She looks pissed and I can't say I blame her. I'd be angry if the situation was reversed.

"I thought you liked this girl?"

"What? I do. What's that got to do with anything?" Except I already know, and I was hoping to hell that Jordan wouldn't call me on it.

My sister's eyes narrow at me, and she already knows that I know what she's going to say, but she says it anyway. "You and I own the bar. Do you really think it's appropriate to be dating someone who works for us?"

"We aren't dating," I point out. "Besides, we're the owners. Don't we get to make the rules? Is this really what you're questioning me on? My love life? I thought I told you to stay out of it."

Jordan snorts. "Since when do I do what you tell me?"

Hardly ever. I sigh and run a hand through my hair.

"Look, I know what you're saying, but we'll cross that bridge if we ever come to it. In the meantime, I'm trying to help her out. She's had a shitty time since she moved here, and I can do something to make it better."

"My brother, the hero," Jordan says with a roll of her eyes, but I know she wouldn't try to change me. "Okay, fine. On to the other problem—can we afford it?"

"I'll make it work," I tell her, firm and confident. "I don't know if she'll stick around long or not, but if she does, I think she'd be an asset. You should have seen her last night."

In my time working at the bar, I've seen my fair share of servers come and go. I've learned to observe someone carrying a stack of dishes, both plated and dirty, to tell if they'll be good or bad at the job. Savanna passed a test that she didn't even know I had with flying colors.

"Bryn is going to be cutting her hours, we're going to need someone…"

"But you don't know if Savanna will even stick around," Jordan points out what I just told her. "You met her in an elevator of some professional building, Nate. What was she doing there? Don't you think she'll want to go back to that?"

I'll admit I didn't think about this when I offered Savanna a job last night. That was the impulsive side of me not looking at all the angles, and one of the reasons I was up so late thinking about everything. But I kept coming back to the fact that when she finally accepted my offer, she lit up like it was the best thing that had happened to her in her whole life, and she couldn't wait to get started.

Her smile had been damn near blinding, and the rest of the night she glowed, which had me staring at her, captivated by how beautiful she was. I've never met someone as gorgeous as her. The more time I spend with her, the more I'm attracted to her on every level. I'm just hoping that's not going to be a problem now that she's working for me and I'm going to be her boss. Especially after what happened with her last boss.

Christ. Not that anything is happening between us.

"I'm not sure," I say, picking up my mug to hide my cringe behind it. "She was pretty damn happy when she accepted, so maybe not."

Jordan rolls her eyes, her frustration with me glaringly obvious. "It's like I don't even know you anymore, and yet you're being exactly who I know you to be." Pinching the bridge of her nose, she lets out a deep sigh. "My brother isn't usually one to offer his guest room up to a stranger, and he's definitely not one to make decisions about the bar without talking to me about it."

"But," she continues, waving her hand in the air. "He is the guy that would give the shirt off his back to someone who needed it, even if it were below zero in a snowstorm." Her hands come to rest on her hips. "I just don't know what to make of you right now, Nate. The only conclusion I can come up with is that you like her. A lot. Which I think might surprise me the most."

I frown at her, my eyebrows furrowing. "Why? I do like women, you know."

"Thank you, Captain Obvious. Yes, I know."

I should really start playing a game with myself when I'm talking to her. The rules would be pretty simple: guess how many times in one conversation I can make Jordan roll her eyes.

She picks up her coffee mug. "You guys just met the other day, though, and you're not the kind of guy that rushes into anything."

"I haven't rushed into anything except offering her a job,"

I point out, and then amend, "And offering her a place to stay."

"Just be careful. I don't want to see you hurt," Jordan says, her voice and eyes soft with affection. "Speaking of the bar, though… have you made any progress on the stuff for the accountant?"

"Not yet. Yesterday was a write off. Going to get working on it today." I down the last bit of my coffee and shove my mug towards Jordan for her to refill it since the coffee maker is behind her.

"I can try to help when I get off later. Or tomorrow. I have the day off," she offers, pouring me another cup.

"It's okay, Jor. I've got it handled. I can always call Larry if I need help."

That's a bold-faced lie. I don't have anything managed and I have no idea where to start. But I know my sister could use a day off without worrying about work, especially after her breakup with Paul. I'd rather see her relax and process things in her own life than worry about the bar. Even though I know she's willing to help.

"Nate…"

I shake my head while she slides my mug across the counter. "Once I get things organized you can help. Let me get a handle on the office today and tomorrow. You just take care of yourself, okay? That'll help me more."

While her eyes don't roll—they're focused on something interesting on the floor—a loud sigh expelling from her lungs has her shoulders sagging. Pure exhaustion rolls off of her in waves in that moment, and I know I've made a good decision in staving her off from helping. Giving her permission to look after herself made an invisible wall come down, and she finally nods her agreement. When her eyes meet mine again, I can see a shine in them that wasn't there before. It makes me want to find Paul and kick his ass all over again.

"Thanks," she whispers appreciatively. "It's been a rough week. I could use a day to decompress. Plus I need to get my stuff from Paul's and drop his crap off."

"I can go with you," I offer.

Jordan's head is shaking before the words are out of my mouth. "It's okay. I can handle it."

"Morning," a sleepy voice says from the doorway, and we both turn to find Savanna standing there.

It's like déjà vu the way she takes my breath away, and I find myself instantly sporting a semi. Around Savanna it seems like I'm in a constant state of arousal. Her blonde hair is pulled into a high ponytail this morning, the length of it wavy from the braid she had it in, and she looks deliciously disheveled in the same pair of pants and t-shirt as yesterday. I could really get used to her being around looking like this every morning.

It's not only that she's stunning, or that I know she has a bit of feistiness lurking beneath. It's the way she handles herself in every situation I've seen her in. Nothing has been too big for her to deal with. The job, the fire, the apartment, my best friends last night at the bar. Christ, she was brilliant with them. Fit in perfectly without missing a beat.

"Coffee?" Jordan asks, already headed for a mug. She's a much better hostess than I am host.

"Please," Savanna says, smiling.

Once she has a coffee poured and doctored, Savanna joins me at the island, letting out a sigh of pure bliss that goes straight to my cock and has me gritting my teeth. It's made worse because she's so close to me today, not standing across the island where I can't feel the heat coming off her body.

"Sleep okay?" I ask by way of distraction, but I choose a horrible topic. All it does is make me picture her in my guest bed, sprawled out with her hair splayed across the pillow. The things I would love to do to her in that bed… or in mine.

Savanna nods before taking another sip of her coffee, that blissful smile on her face as she looks over at me. "That bed is heavenly. I don't think I've ever felt so rested."

The things I'm picturing doing to her would make her the opposite of rested.

"So, Savanna," Jordan pipes up from across the counter and we both look to her. I can tell by the expression on my sister's face that she's going fishing, and I'm a little apprehensive that I might be in trouble. "Nate says you're coming to work for us at the bar."

Savanna perks right up, and when she speaks, excitement laces her words. "Yeah! It took some convincing on Nate's part, but I'm honestly thrilled about it. It might sound weird, but I loved serving in college."

Fuck.

"Oh really?" Jordan turns her eyes to me, a penetrating look in their blue depths.

Savanna ratted me out and doesn't even realize it. I know I'm going to need to answer to the fact that I had to convince her to come work at the bar, but I'm saved by the vibration of my phone before anyone can utter another word.

It's Tina, the fire investigator that I reached out to yesterday, returning my call about Savanna's apartment. Tina and I came up together in the academy, but a few years in, she decided to switch directions with her career and go into investigations. She's worked her way up high enough that if anyone I know is going to get me clearance into Savanna's building, it's her.

"This is about your apartment," I tell Savanna who swings

her entire body towards me, eyes wide as I swipe 'answer' on my phone. "Tina! How are you?"

We exchange pleasantries, doing a quick catch up, during which time Jordan packs her lunch into her bag, waves, and takes off to work. I'm relieved that for the time being I'm saved from her wrath. But I saw the look she gave me before she left, and I know this is just a reprieve until I see her next.

"You said something about the fire on Birch in your message," Tina says, finally getting to the reason for our chat.

I glance at Savanna who has gone back to her coffee, but is definitely keeping tabs on the conversation, judging by the side eye I'm getting from her. "Yeah, was wondering if you had any idea when people would be let back in the building."

"Oh jeez, Nate. That whole place is a disaster," she says, and I can hear the frown in her voice. "I was out there yesterday to take a look, and it's going to be a few weeks at least. The whole sprinkler system needs replacing."

"Shit," I mutter, watching Savanna deflate right in front of me. But I'm not giving up. I had a feeling this might be the case and I'm hoping Tina will do me a solid. I hold up a finger to tell Savanna not to lose all hope yet. "What are the chances you'll let me in?"

There's a pause before Tina asks, "For what?"

"A friend of mine lives there, and she's got nothing with her. No purse, no phone, nothing. I was hoping you'd give me the okay and we could go in and get some of her things," I say, watching as Savanna sits up, her hands coming together in a prayer fashion, almond eyes wide with optimism.

"Ah, Nate…"

"I know. It's a big ask, but I wouldn't ask if it wasn't important. She didn't have a chance to get anything when we pulled her out," I say, my tone hedging on pleading.

"This is the woman you pulled out of the building?" she asks, sounding a little stunned.

"Yeah."

"Oh, Nate. I didn't realize… gosh, that must have been tough."

I don't correct Tina's assumption that we were friends prior to the fire because I can tell I've struck a chord. While it might not be the most straightforward I've ever been, I'm going to take advantage.

There's another long pause before she sucks in a deep breath, and I can hear it whoosh out of her on the other end of the line. "I'll tell you what—I'll let you go in there, but you gear up, and you take someone with you. Brody, Liam, one of the other guys, I don't care."

I give Savanna a thumbs up and grin when she pumps her fists in the air.

"But she doesn't go in, Nate. I don't want her anywhere near the inside of that building. If she isn't okay with you getting her things, tough shit. Understood?"

"Shouldn't be a problem," I tell her.

At least I don't think it will be. Savanna might not get everything she wants out of her apartment, but at the very least we can go in and get her purse and phone. If she's comfortable enough, we'll grab some of her other things.

Tina and I talk for another couple of minutes, and when we finally hang up, Savanna launches herself off her stool and into my arms, nearly knocking both of us onto the floor. It's reminiscent of the night of the fire, though I was more prepared for it that night, and I wasn't nearly as attracted to her as I am now.

"You are the best, Nate!" she says, hugging me fiercely, her body pressed as flush to mine as she can get, given that I'm still sitting and she's now standing between my legs.

I squeeze her back, but the closeness has my cock thinking it's time to come out and play as it gets harder by the second. I grab onto her hips to hold her back, so she doesn't feel what she's doing to me. I don't need that complication right now, especially after the conversation Jordan and I had this morning.

Holding her hips has consequences of its own. With her pajama pants so low, and the worn out t-shirt riding up with her arms high, my hands find purchase along her skin. She's warm and pliable beneath my touch, and I know I should remove myself from her body, but fuck, I've wondered about this little piece of skin since yesterday morning, and I'm having trouble not committing it to memory while this moment is here within my grasp.

Savanna releases her hold around my neck and leans away from me, but her hands remain on my shoulders, her face lit up in excitement. "Seriously, I think you're the best thing that's happened to me in a really long time."

I can feel the heat rising in my cheeks at her praise, so I shake my head and her compliment away, even though my chest wants to puff out in pride. "Not a big deal. Just helping where I can."

"Does that often get you into trouble?" she asks, her tone a little more subdued.

I know she's referring to Jordan, and I give a sigh, fighting the urge to run my hand through my hair because I really don't want to stop touching her. "You caught that, huh?"

"She didn't sound very happy, Nate. Are you sure it's a good idea for me to work for you guys?"

I can feel her fingertips playing with the neckline of my shirt, and I swallow hard, commanding my eyes to stay locked on hers and not drop down to her breasts that only moments ago were pressed against me.

"Let me worry about Jordan," I tell her, forcing myself not to smooth my thumb over the skin at her hip. "In the meantime, let's focus on your stuff." I'm rewarded when the tiny frown that had formed dissolves into a smile for me. "There's a catch to getting your stuff. Tina won't let you in the building."

Savanna's face falls just an inch. "But… you can go in?"

"As long as one of the guys comes with me, yeah. If you trust me, I'll go in and get your stuff." Something clouds her eyes, but it's so fleeting I wonder if I imagined it. Before I can think better of it, I give her hips a slight squeeze, my tone soft as I add, "It'll be better than nothing, because I'm pretty sure you're not getting in there for at least a few weeks."

I watch as she drops her eyes between us, her lip pulling between her teeth. I wonder if she wasn't busy fiddling with my shirt if she would be picking at her nails like I've seen her do so often.

"I trust you," she finally says quietly, her eyes lifting to meet mine. This close I can see the brown flecks around her pupils, but today they look more gold than brown. "After everything you've done for me, how could I not?"

My hand has a mind of its own as it slowly travels from her hip to her waist, giving her a slight tug to pull her body closer to mine again. Trust is one of the most sacred things I believe a human can give to another, and her words touch me in a way I haven't felt in a long time.

I like this woman. I like her a lot, which I know is crazy since we've only known each other for a few days, but Christ, she just does something to me, and I haven't even kissed her. I plan on rectifying that situation, though, my other hand finally leaving her hip to come to her jaw, her skin smooth beneath my touch.

Our eyes are searching each other's and I can sense her anticipation as much as I can feel my own as I tilt her head towards me. My heart is beating wildly in my chest, and though I want to claim her mouth and devour her, I want to take my time and savor every second of this moment.

I wait too damn long. When I'm inches away from her, so close that I can feel her breath against my lips, my phone vibrates violently on the island beside us. The noise is so unexpected that we both jump, the magic of the moment vanishing as we pull away from each other in surprise.

Of all the times to get a fucking call, it has to be now. To make it even more ironic, it's the one person who probably wants to see me get laid more than I do. Liam.

"I should answer that," I tell Savanna, releasing my hold on her waist.. "I'll need someone to come along, and he's the most likely candidate."

"Of course," she says with a small smile, suddenly looking shyer than I've seen her. It doesn't stop her from leaning in to press a kiss to my cheek, though. "I'm going to go get ready for the day."

"Okay," I say, then pick up my phone and answer it. "Hold on," I tell Liam, and throw him on mute. "Savanna?"

She's already halfway across the kitchen and turns to look at me.

"That bedroom is yours for as long as you need it." Before she can answer me, I take Liam off mute and greet him with a "hey asshole", watching Savanna with serious eyes as she just looks at me, stunned, before turning around to go get ready.

CHAPTER 13

NATE

"Does she realize how lucky she was?" Liam asks as we stare down the hallway on Savanna's floor.

He met us here fifteen minutes ago after Savanna and I stopped at the firehouse to grab some gear. Once we got dressed, we headed into the building right away, with a list and location of everything Savanna needed.

"I don't know," I say hesitantly, my eyes glued to the door that I kicked open. It's charred black now from smoke and flames, and it makes me sick to think that she had been stuck in that room. If we hadn't found her when we did… "But I'm not going to tell her."

Liam nods his agreement, his mood sober for once. "Probably for the best."

Not wanting to stand there and think about the "what if's" any longer than I have to, we head towards Savanna's door which has definitely sustained some damage from the smoke and heat. It's black just like the other door. This one, however, opens when we try it, just like Savanna said it should.

We both take a moment to peer inside, taking in the extent of the destruction. Overall, it's not bad. There's definitely some smoke damage that will need to be cleaned up by restoration, but everything looks salvageable from first glance. It's one good thing about these apartment doors. They can be good in a fire. Unlike the piece of crap door for the trash room.

"C'mon, let's go," I tell Liam, just wanting to get in and out.

"Tell me where to start, boss. I'm not opposed to the underwear drawer," Liam says, punching me in the shoulder as he strolls across the threshold into Savanna's apartment like he owns the place.

I grit my teeth together to keep from punching him back. "You won't be going near her underwear drawer," I growl at him.

It's something I've already thought about, and I figure it's safer if I take care of the clothes on the list and he can deal with everything else.

"Pfft, dude, I'll be way better at picking out the good stuff. You should let me do this for you. This way you can be surprised when you finally land the girl," he says, taunting me.

He's a smart fucker because he stays out of my reach as I move into the apartment, the need to hit him growing stronger by the second. I don't generally condone violence, and I'm usually pretty level-headed, but Savanna seems to be bringing things out in me that I'm not used to. I feel protective over her. While that's not necessarily out of the norm for me with any human, there's a drive inside me that seems hardwired to protect her.

"You're on cell phone, laptop, and purse duty," I tell him, choosing to ignore his teasing. Instead I take a more thorough look around the place, taking in my surroundings instead of the damage.

Everything I see shouts "Savanna" at me. The couch looks big and comfortable, but the chair is what really catches my attention. I can picture Savanna lounging in it, maybe curled up with a book on a quiet evening or watching a hockey game during the season. Both things she mentioned she liked to do last night at dinner.

Plants are scattered around the apartment, most noticeably within a nook at the window, and I smile at all the life that she has within the place. "Maybe see if you can find a box for the plants too. I doubt they'll survive if we leave them. Hell, some of them might not survive anyway with the smoke damage."

"Roger that, Lieutenant."

I roll my eyes and head for the bedroom, finding more of Savanna in here. A lot more. I overlooked it in the kitchen just inside the apartment door, and then again in the living room, but her neatness can't be ignored in her bedroom. Everything has a place.

She's got some jewelry stands on her dresser along with a host of lotions and perfumes. A lamp and book sit on her nightstand. A light gray and pink comforter is crisp on her bed, not a dent in the material, the pillows perfectly placed at the top. The place is feminine, organized, and seems like her.

I head for the closet where she told me a suitcase would be and get to work pulling things out, folding them haphazardly and stuffing them in her luggage. She's probably going to kill me for it, but I'll cross that bridge when I get there. Once I've checked off everything from the closet, I move to the dresser, pulling out everything except for her underwear.

I'm avoiding that for as long as I can, but it's inevitable that I'm going to get there.

Honestly, I've been simultaneously looking forward to it, and dreading it. The number of times I've thought about Savanna in her underwear from the night of the fire is probably reprehensible—I try to be a gentleman, but I'm still a guy—and going through her underwear drawer is only going to add to that mental image. I really don't want to be a creep, though, so I've been trying to psych myself up for it.

I can't put it off any longer. I've got everything that needs to go into the suitcase besides her bras and panties, and toiletries from the bathroom. I could go do those first, but if I have to spend more time in her bedroom afterwards, Liam is going to question me.

Christ, he's probably going to question me anyway.

I'd rather only go through that once, so I suck it up and pull the drawer open, letting out a low "fuck" the second I see the contents.

This woman.

Everything is arranged by color and material. There's definitely some obsession with organization there, but I don't mind it.

Jesus, I think I kind of like it.

My eyes are feasting on an array of lace, satin, and cotton in every color under the sun. I can just picture her in her business getup like she had on the first time we met with a pair of bright coral lace panties beneath that pencil skirt, something only she would know, and it's hot. Really fucking hot.

"Attaboy," Liam says from behind me, and I slam the drawer shut, whirling around on him.

"The fuck, man?" I bark at him. He's standing in the door-way, leaning against the frame with his arms crossed over his chest, a smirk the size of Texas on his face. "Shouldn't you be finding a box for the plants?"

"Done. I also did Savanna a solid and cleaned out her fridge. Then I decided to check on your progress. I see it's going well," he says, barely containing his laughter.

I know I'm the color of a tomato right now which is probably more obvious in our yellow gear, so I point out the door. "Go be useful and start packing up her bathroom stuff."

Now he does laugh but heads for the bathroom, calling over his shoulder, "Okay, but don't jizz in your pants, dude. It won't be a good look for you."

Cursing him beneath my breath, I get back to what I was doing. One good thing about being interrupted is I feel more capable of dealing with the underwear drawer. Though by capable I mean I'm just grabbing handfuls of lace and satin and shoving them into the suitcase, paying no attention to what I'm picking up or where it's going in the bag.

By the time I'm done, I've got most of the drawer emptied, and I'm a little concerned that I look even creepier by bringing along so much of her underwear. Maybe I'll just explain that I didn't know what to bring, so I took every-thing. Or maybe I won't say anything at all. I'm not entirely sure what sounds less like a disgusting, filthy pig.

"Dude," Liam says from behind me, but this time his voice is full of apprehension instead of amusement. "What the hell is this?"

I turn around to find my best friend holding a velvet bag in one hand, and a mini plastic cup in the other, and I can't help it, I burst into a fit of laughter.

"That," I gasp between snickers, "is karma."

The horrified look on his face has me doubling over.

"What is it?!" he virtually screeches, sounding very un-Liam-like. A second later he's flinging the cup out of his hand. It hits the bed and bounces to the ground, ending up right back at his feet. The way he dances out of the way like it's a piece of molten rock has me grasping my sides as I howl even harder. "Dude! What is it?!"

"It's," I try to pull in a breath to tell him what it is. "It's a," another breath, "a period cup."

The color drains from his face. Liam, the guy who has never had a relationship in his life, is currently facing something he probably doesn't even know exists. I have to wonder if he's ever seen a real tampon in his life, let alone a cup.

"Why on fucking earth do you know what a fucking… fucking peri… why do you know what that is?" he sputters, repulsed.

This might be the funniest shit I've ever seen in my life. I've never seen him so horrified, and we've encountered some nasty shit in our days as firefighters.

Sucking in a deep breath of air, I try to get a hold on myself. "Christ man. Because I've got a sister who lives with me, and she leaves her shit all over the place. Not to mention, I have actual relationships with women, I don't just fuck them."

"That is some fucked up shit right there," he tells me, watching with a grimace as I cross the room and pick up the cup that he tossed along with the bag that also ended up on the floor.

"You do realize where you stick your dick, right?"

Liam scowls at me. "If you ruin sex for me, I will fuck you up. Not another word!"

The guy is going to be a bachelor forever.

He chooses to stand by the door to wait with the things he got together while I finish up the rest of the packing. I think maybe I've scarred him for life, and I look forward to the times I'll have the opportunity to bring this up in the future. The prospect of that makes me gleeful. As much shit as I get from everyone about not having a woman, Liam gets it just as bad for being a player.

Once we're finished, we make our way back downstairs and out of the building to where Savanna is standing beside my truck waiting for us to return. She perks up when she sees us, jogging over to relieve Liam of her purse and laptop bag.

"You brought my plants?" she asks, looking from them to me.

I shrug casually like it's no big deal, but I can tell by the gleam in her eyes that it is. "Figured they'd survive better if they were taken care of properly."

"They weren't even on the list," she says, her voice thick with gratitude. "Thank you. Both of you."

Liam grunts, setting the box on the edge of the tailgate to my truck, clearly not over what happened upstairs. "All I have to say is, you owe me." He shudders so hard and dramatically I think he might tip the plants over.

Savanna looks to me for an explanation and I pull the little velvet bag out of my pocket and hold it out to her. "You know how they say curiosity killed the cat? Well, curiosity bit Liam in the ass."

Then, like me, she bursts into laughter, though she tries to cover her mouth and contain it better than I did.

"I definitely want to hear all about this," she says.

"Screw you both. My part in this is done." Opening the backdoor to the truck, he sticks the box inside and then shuts the door, hardly giving us another look as he turns to walk to his vehicle. "You both owe me a beer later!"

We look at each other and grin. "I'll tell you all about it," I tell her, hoisting her bag into the back of the truck bed. "I should probably also tell you about your underwear drawer…"

CHAPTER 14

SAVANNA

IT'S OFFICIAL. I'M STAYING WITH NATE.

Until my apartment is ready, or he kicks me out, I'm staying.

I'll admit, it took some convincing on his part. It wasn't unlike when he offered me a job, if I'm being perfectly honest. Already he's done so much for me that taking more of his generosity seemed imbalanced. I argued with him for a bit on it, but the man is good at persuasion, and when it came down to it, I wanted to stay.

I find myself craving his presence. His home. His comfort. I've spent so much time in a constant state of fight or flight. Watching. Waiting. Ever ready for any sign of Vincent.

Before the fire, I checked the locks on every window and every door three times before I went to bed every night. I slept with a baseball bat beside my bed. Multiple times a week I would wake up in a cold sweat, terrified by the nightmares my subconscious dredged up. Nightmares that I once lived.

It's only been a few days, I know, but I've had exactly one nightmare since staying with Nate. And it was…different from all the rest. It wasn't the bone chilling nightmares of my past. I was stuck in a dark expanse of nothingness. Smoke billowed around me, threatening to choke the life from my lungs. The only light came from a fire that burned so hot in a ring around me that if I moved a muscle in any direction, I felt the hot singe of it on my skin.

When I startled myself awake, heart pounding, and face flaming with heat, I took a few gasping breaths before I got my bearings. Nate's house. I was in the guest bedroom at Nate's house. He was on the other side of the far wall, in his bedroom, asleep. If I screamed, he would hear me, and he would come running. I knew he would.

That was it. I came down from the nightmare and fell right back to sleep. There was no getting up to check on every entrance to the house. There was no creeping through the dark of the night to ensure there were no monsters lurking in closets, or under the bed.

I haven't slept this well in years. I wake feeling more rested than I can remember in recent times, and I'm certain it has nothing to do with a nice mattress or comfortable bedding, though both are true. Nate makes me feel safe. It could have something to do with the fact that he literally saved my life, but I'd like to think it's deeper than that.

"Go," Bryn hisses at me with a playful swat to the middle of my back. She's urging me to handle the table of four men, all Nate's size, that walked in a few minutes ago. "You can do it. Make me proud."

I shoot her a narrow eyed glance over my shoulder then grin. It's only my second day, a Saturday no less, but it's still early—well before the dinnertime rush—and she thought it would be a good idea to test the waters on my own before it got busy.

Grabbing four menus and pulling my writing pad out from the pocket of my apron, I head towards the table, still thinking of the man I've hardly seen all day.

It's the intensity of his stare each time I answer a question he's asked. Like he's committing everything I tell him to the best places in his memory.

It's the way his calloused hands caught me in the kitchen and held me with a gentle touch. Like he somehow knows all my darkest secrets and wouldn't dare touch me with anything but the soft fingers that ran along my skin.

It's how he deals with the other women in his life—Jordan, Bryn, the other servers—always treating them with the utmost respect. And the way he laughs and has fun with the cooks in the kitchen. And all the interactions he has with his chosen brothers.

It's everything about him, and I've only known him for a handful of days.

"Hey guys," I greet the table of four, handing each of them a menu. "Can I get you all started with a drink?"

Nate started the training process yesterday, once we got back here from picking up my things. When Bryn got in later in the afternoon, she took over while Nate snuck off to his office.

Probably to work on the stuff for the accountant.

I didn't say anything to him, but I overheard him and Jordan talking yesterday morning when she asked if he'd made progress on things. I don't know what exactly she was referring to, but I know that he wanted to get working on it.

He stayed cooped up in the office the rest of the day until we left at ten, and the second we got in this afternoon he went straight there. He's hardly come up for air. It makes me hopeful that he's gotten somewhere, but the state of the office when we left last night was chaos, so my optimism is low.

He was stressed and exhausted. The whole way to his place he kept pushing a hand through his hair, hardly speaking a word. The tension radiated off his shoulders in waves. I hated seeing him like that, but it didn't seem like the time or place to ask him about it. He pushed Jordan away from helping, and she's part owner of this place. Why wouldn't he do the same thing to a nobody like me?

Except he doesn't know what I truly am. When we talked about my previous job, we only talked about the wealth management firm. The financial advising. I've kept my accounting degree to myself since coming to Santa Rosé. At least from everyone except for Preston, and that was only because I had to tell him in order to get a job in the first place.

My plan is to talk to Nate about it today. I thought maybe it would be a good idea to let him flounder by himself for a few hours, though. It might make him more inclined to allow someone to assist him. When he told me before that everyone needs help sometimes, and I questioned him, he deflected his answer. I allowed it because his answer was sweet, and I was hungry, but I tucked the little tidbit of information into the back of my mind for safe keeping. Help doesn't seem like something he likes taking.

"Haven't seen you around before," one of the guys, a blonde-haired one closest to me, says once I've taken everyone's drink orders.

My eyes flit up to him while I'm writing the last of the drinks down on my pad. I ask distractedly, "How often do you come?"

Without missing a beat, the guy next to him responds, "Probably once a day," and the entire table, minus the blonde, erupts in laughter.

A patient smile is plastered on my face, my eyes darting to the man making the joke. Younger than the first. One thing I learned in the early days of serving was never to let customers know they were getting under your skin.

"Feel free to drop a beer in his lap by accident," the blonde says, redirecting my attention to him. "We only let him out in public a couple times a month. Usually to come here."

"Thanks for the warning," I muse to the man, before adding in jest, "I'm more of a fan of spitting in beer versus having someone wear it, though."

Now everyone at the table, besides the younger one, roars with laughter. It feels good to be able to joke and laugh with people. My smile becomes more genuine, and I tap my pen to the paper in my hands. "I'll get those beers started for you guys."

As I step away from the table, I look towards the bar, nearly stopping in my tracks. Vivid blue eyes, which seem brighter than usual thanks to his sky blue t-shirt, are watching me intently from across the bar. My breath catches in my throat, cheeks heating at the way he tracks my movements as I head in his direction.

The way he stares makes me think of our almost kiss yesterday. He had me so heated that I thought I might explode into a million little pieces just from his close proximity and the slight touch of his fingers at my hips, waist, and then face. It didn't help that, even though he tried to hide it, I felt the telltale evidence of his arousal against my belly before he moved me to a safe distance.

I was disappointed that we were interrupted. I'm disappointed that he hasn't tried to make another move. I'm also a little relieved. Even if I want him to kiss the breath out of me, it would be a complication since I'm not only staying at his place, but he's now also my boss. I don't know if I want to complicate things for myself at work. What would all my coworkers think? They've all been really cool about my circumstances, but if I were suddenly sleeping with the boss, would their opinions change?

Then again, who am I kidding—they probably already think I'm sleeping with him.

I left Colorado for a fresh start. Okay, I left Colorado to get away from a bad situation, and go somewhere no one could find me. But it was also for a fresh start. Somewhere that no one knew who I was, or what had happened to me.

It's taken me six months, but I finally feel like I belong somewhere, and I don't want to give up on that feeling. I feel like I could actually make friends here, maybe even move on from everything horrible that happened. From Colorado to the fire in my apartment. I'm starting over for the second time since coming to Santa Rosé, and it's a lot. I only have Nate and Liam's account on what survived and didn't survive in my apartment. And I have little clue what kind of money I'll be making working at the bar.

If I stay at the bar. If Nate will even want me to stick around.

I don't know that starting something with Nate in the midst of all that is something I'm capable of. Nor do I know if it would be fair to him.

A smooth, easy smile slides across Nate's face and touches the corners of his eyes. The glass of water he's holding touches the bar as he greets me. "Getting on okay?"

As I start pressing buttons on the point-of-sale, keying in

the drink order from the four men, I nod. "Bryn has been great. I forgot how much I enjoyed serving."

Nate hums low in his throat, peering over my shoulder at what I'm doing. He's standing close enough that I can feel the heat from his body, but not close enough that I could lean back and touch him. "You say that now. Wait until you've experienced a crazy Saturday night."

"Bring it on. I can handle it." I glance back at him. From this distance I can see the fatigue in his eyes, even as his lips twitch upward. "Did you finish whatever you were working on? You've been at it for two days now."

The curve of his lips flattens, and he runs a hand through his hair. A deep sigh has his shoulders sagging, causing me to turn towards him. "I think I'll be working on it for a few weeks." As quickly as his smile faltered, it's back again. His eyes scan my entire face, drinking me in like I'm the glass of water he set down on the bar. "Just needed a break from all the paper. The change of scenery has been nice."

I'm the change of scenery. The way he looks at me, he might as well have spoken the words aloud.

While my face tinges red, I realize that one of my "ifs" has an answer. Nate wants me to stick around. He feels this thing between us just as much as I do, and he's as curious as I am. I think he's equally hesitant, though, which is slightly annoying. It would be less attractive of him, and easier for me, if I had to fend off blatant advances.

"I should get back to it," he murmurs softly, his hand raising halfway to my face before he thinks better of it and drops it to his side.

I tuck a strand of hair behind my ear. Something I think he wanted to do. "Okay."

His gaze lingers on me for another second before he turns to head back to the office, leaving me biting my bottom lip. Even though I don't think it's a wise idea to get involved with Nate, things with him feel different.

When Vincent and I started dating, I'd always thought something was a little off, but I was young, and loved the attention he gave me, so I ignored it. Looking back there were warning signs. Even in the honeymoon stage. With Preston, I was lonely and in need of connection. Prior to saying yes to his advances, I turned him down over and over again.

It's not like that with Nate. Besides living and working with him, there are no blaring alarms going off in my head. There aren't even any little red flags that I've found—I've looked. And I definitely don't want to put him off. Not if I'm being honest with myself. It's just what's best for both of us. For so many reasons.

Vincent's face creeps into my mind. The biggest reason I should steer clear of Nate.

While we may both be curious about this thing between us, I know that all I can offer Nate is my friendship. My friendship, and expertise. With those two things I'll get rid of those tired circles beneath his eyes.

If I can do nothing else for the man who has given me so much, I can do that.

CHAPTER 15

SAVANNA

An hour later I'm standing at the doorway to the office. Nate hasn't noticed me yet, his head buried in a box with his back to me. I take a moment to appreciate the way his shoulder blades flex and move beneath his t-shirt as he rifles through the box, looking for god knows what. My eyes, of their own accord, drift lower to his jeans, and I take a deep but quiet breath. Whatever he does in the gym, he needs to keep doing it.

Just because I know nothing should happen between us doesn't mean I can't enjoy the view.

"Objectifying me?"

The sound of his voice startles me, a yelp of surprise flying from my lips. My eyes dart upwards to see his neck craned, head twisted to look over his shoulder. Embarrassment colors my cheeks, our conversation from the elevator replaying in my mind.

"No," I squeak, but it's a lie, and we both know it. He caught me red handed.

His eyebrow raises as he turns to face me, arms crossing over his broad chest. It takes everything in me not to look down at the corded muscles of his forearms that I've looked at one too many times.

"I wasn't objectifying," I double down, clearing my throat. Lifting my head high, I add, "I was appreciating."

Nate barks out a surprised laugh, his arms dropping from in front of him. He moves to sit on the edge of his desk in the one place paper doesn't touch. "Something I could also be accused of."

My stomach does a somersault as his eyes rove over me. It's not the first time I've felt the warmth of his gaze. The bar's dress code is denim bottoms with black tops and it's our choice in whatever that looks like. Today I went with a pair of light wash jeans and a black camisole with lace along the neckline that runs into a deep V between my breasts. It's a little racy, but not racy enough that I couldn't wear it to work. It caught Nate's eye before we left, just like it does now.

When his eyes meet mine again, he smiles then glances at the clock. "How's it going out there? You guys need some help?"

It's only five. The bar isn't too bad yet, but the dinner rush will start showing up soon. It was much worse at this time yesterday when the after work crowd came in, but today I'd be willing to bet we don't get slammed for another hour.

I shake my head, dropping my shoulder against the frame of the door where I still stand. "Nope. We're good. Bryn just sent me to take a break before the dinner rush comes in." Pausing, I take a second to glance around the room at all the boxes piled up and then at Nate's desk. It's a disaster in here. "I was hoping you had a minute to talk."

Nate raises an eyebrow at me. "That sounds serious."

"Not serious in an ominous way," I tell him with ease. "But first, are you hungry? Because I'm famished and I could use a bite to eat while we talk. I told Bryn I needed to see you, and she said to take my time."

"Starving." Nate's eyes slide down to the V in my shirt, his tongue darting out to wet his lips. He shakes his head a second later, clearing his mind of whatever was going through it. "A break would be good."

My stomach is full of butterflies by the time he gets to his feet. It seems like every time I remind myself that I cannot get involved with him, he does, or says, something that makes me waver. It's as though there's some kind of force beyond my control that keeps pulling me towards him.

We head out to the front of house, and I show off all that I've learned in the past two days by keying in our meals. Once I'm done, Nate fills a couple of glasses with sodas.

"Nate! How you doin', man?"

We both look across the counter to see the man who gave me permission to drop a beer in his friend's lap standing there. I've learned that the entire table was filled with fire-fighters from a different house. This guy, Tyson I think his name is, has been particularly flirty. When he catches my eye now, he flashes me a smile.

"Tyson Saxe." Nate reaches across and shakes Tyson's hand. "Saw you guys sitting over there earlier and was going to come by and say hi in a bit."

"Beat you to it. Thought I'd come over and tell you how good your new girl is," Tyson says, his eyes slipping back to me. I feel my face heat instantly and Nate tenses imperceptibly beside me. "She's had us all laughing since we sat down."

"Just doing my job," I murmur, dread filling my stomach.

I wonder what Nate is going to think about this. It's not like we've gone on a date, but there's been clear interest on both of our parts, despite what I try to tell myself, and the way Tyson is looking at me in appreciation, I have little doubt that he'd ask me out given the chance.

The last time something like that happened to me, I ended up with a black eye and a lost job. Vincent had been sitting at the bar when I was working one night and one of the regulars was flirting with me, which wasn't unusual. Vincent hadn't taken kindly to it. The second my shift was over and we were in the car, he started screaming at me, demanding I quit. When I tried to stand my ground and tell him no, he hit me.

But Nate isn't Vincent, and maybe he foresaw men hitting on me because he remains calm and collected despite being stiff as a board beside me.

"Guess I found the right woman for the job."

I turn at his tone of voice, looking up to see him gazing at me with candor, a hint of affection in the blue depths of his eyes. It warms me from the inside out, melting away the dread that had turned my blood icy.

"Sorry to say that I'm stealing her for dinner, though," he adds to Tyson, not sounding sorry at all.

Tyson obviously sees whatever has passed between Nate and me because he takes a step back from the bar, nodding his head in understanding. "Good to know, man. Just thought you'd want to know your girl is doing a good job."

"Appreciate it. I'll pop over to the table in a bit if you guys are still around." Nate glances over to the table where the group is sitting, catching the eye of another guy, and lifts his hand in greeting.

After Tyson says goodbye, I pick at my nails as Nate leads

me back to the kitchen. Our dinner isn't ready yet, so we head back to his office, where we both stop just inside the door.

"Did you… I mean, were you…" I stumble, biting down on my lip. I want to know if what I just witnessed was him staking a claim on me, or something else, but I don't know how to ask.

"Tyson can be a lot like Liam. He likes to date a woman for a couple weeks, maybe a couple months, and then it's on to the next best thing," Nate supplies.

"So you were just looking out for me?"

The same fire from yesterday is darkening his blue eyes. When he takes a step closer to me, I can feel the heat radiating off him in waves. My pulse quickens, anticipation filling my belly.

"Something like that."

I don't know exactly what that means, but words fail me when his hand comes up and he tucks a piece of hair that's fallen out of my braid behind my ear. When it's out of his way, his fingertips graze the skin of my jaw causing a puff of air to expel from my lungs.

There is nothing in this moment that I want more than for him to kiss me. The only problem, besides the one where I shouldn't want it, is we're at work. Anyone could come barreling around the corner into the office and catch us. That might not bother him, but it would bother me, so I blurt out, "We need to talk."

It's enough to send his hand dropping to his side, his eyes blinking rapidly as if to clear the thoughts from his head.

"Right," he says, clearing his throat and taking a step back, putting some much-needed distance between us. "You wanted to talk to me about something."

Stifling a sigh of resignation, I nod and grab the door, swinging it shut. "I do."

"Whoa, this is a closed-door meeting? I'm not sure if I should be scared or excited." When I turn wide eyes onto him, he grimaces. "Maybe I should have kept that thought to myself."

At this I laugh, taking his arm to spin him around, pointing at his office chair. "It's not going to be anything that you could guess, so refrain from being either."

Once we're both seated, I take a deep breath and let it out, but I don't say anything. I take another moment to look around at all the paper he's got stacked everywhere, along with boxes that contain more of the stuff. It makes me wonder just how bad he's floundering with whatever problem he's facing.

"Sorry," he says, misinterpreting my silence and inspection of the room. "I know it's a disaster. I also know you like things orderly. This is mass chaos. I can clear some space on the desk so we can eat."

Nate starts trying to pick up piles of papers to stack on top of each other, but I reach out and put a hand over his for a brief moment, shaking my head. "Don't. It's fine. I'm more curious about what all of it is. You're drowning in paperwork."

Running a hand through his hair, he leans back in his chair and lets out a sigh. I can tell by that one action that he's exhausted and overwhelmed. "Nothing to worry about. Just trying to get some stuff together for my accountant. This is all shit from my uncle that I'm trying to sift through."

Now it makes sense. Though I gave Nate shit over his kitchen, he doesn't strike me as the chaotic type of guy, and I realize it's because he isn't. This isn't his mess; it's his uncle's, and he's been left to pick up the pieces. I've seen it before.

"What kind of stuff?" I ask, even though I have a good idea.

Nate's eyebrows raise in surprise over my question, and I can tell he's not sure if he wants to answer it. A battle wages in his eyes over how much he wants to tell me because I think he knows the more he spills, the more danger he's in of looking like he's struggling.

The thing is, I already know he's struggling.

"Just... bills, vendor invoices, expenses... business crap," he finally says, trying for nonchalant. To the untrained eye, he might get away with it, but I know better.

"I'm going to help you." I say it matter-of-factly, confidence ringing in my tone even though he's fighting me before the words are fully out of my mouth.

"Sav, I appreciate it, but you can't help me," he says, and I watch him sag in his chair, giving up the charade of pretending to have it all together. "I can't even help myself here, and if I can't do that, there's not much point in you trying to help."

"How far have you gotten in the two days you've been at this?" I ask.

Nate eyes me warily, then looks at the stacks of paperwork in front of him on the desk. "Not very," he admits. "I'm trying to make sense of it, but I never handled this side of things when Uncle Pete was around, and I'm not sure he really did either."

I nod in understanding but push forward. "What is your stress level right now?"

"Through the roof," he says, this time without hesitation. The words seemed to spill out, and now that they're in the open, he cringes and runs a hand through his hair, embarrassment taking over. He doesn't like to look weak, I get that, but asking for help isn't a sign of weakness. I'm just not sure anyone has told him that. "I'll figure it out, though. I always do."

I don't acknowledge either statement, instead forging ahead in my line of questioning. "How much easier do you think it would be if you had an accountant in here helping you?"

Nate laughs humorlessly, and shakes his head, his eyes locking on mine. "Finding an accountant who doesn't cost an arm and a leg is impossible. But in a perfect world? I think I'd see it as a miracle."

"Awww, that's sweet," I say, pressing a hand over my chest with an affectionate pout of my lips, though there's a hint of teasing in my eyes. "You'd think of me as a miracle? That might be the nicest thing anyone's ever said to me."

I can see the change in him instantly. Sitting up a little straighter, his eyes narrow as the gears turn and he starts to put everything together. "Wait." He holds up his hands for me to wait, then points a finger at me. "You're an accountant? I thought you were a financial advisor."

All I can do is beam at him. "Financial advising was a blip. I graduated third in my class six years ago, and I've been licensed in Colorado as a chartered accountant for the last four." My lips lift with pride at the dumbfounded look he's wearing, so I press on. "I'm not licensed in California, but I can do all the work and you can take it to your accountant for him to finish." I gesture to the paper, the boxes. "I know this looks like a disaster to you, but it looks like a fun puzzle to me."

Nate doesn't move. He doesn't even blink. I'm not sure if it's because he doesn't believe me, or doesn't believe his luck.

Leaning forward, I persevere, determined to have him accept my help. "I've done this before, Nate. It's what I spent the last six years doing."

The dumbfounded look is still there, but I can see he's starting to process this, and what it could potentially mean for him. "Christ. You're a fucking accountant."

"I am. I, uhm—" I pause, my smile faltering, my stomach twisting uneasily as I consider something I hadn't thought of.

I was about to offer him references, but if he were to call and inquire about me, people back home would know I was in California. Not something I want.

"If you want a reference, I could maybe try and get one for you, but… I, uh, I don't really talk to anyone from back home," I admit, dropping my eyes down to the desk. It's the first time I've admitted that out loud to anyone.

A pang of homesickness hits me square in the chest and I have to take a steadying breath to keep myself composed as a wave of emotion I wasn't expecting washes over me. Maddie's face floats in front of my eyes and then my brothers. Connor, Devin. My dad. I miss them all so much.

"You in some kind of trouble?"

My head snaps back up, shock evident in the stare I give him. "What? No!"

I'm not entirely sure what kind of trouble he means, though. My first inclination is trouble with the authorities, but trouble can mean so many different things. Am I in trouble with Vincent? Well, if he found me I would be.

In a less indignant tone, I amend carefully, "I'm not running from the cops, if that's what you mean."

Nate regards me meticulously, turning my words over in his mind. My stomach takes a deep dive to my feet as he does, and I fight not to squirm under his watchful gaze. He knows something is off. Something I'm not telling him. I can feel it.

I can see the questions in his eyes as he nods slowly as if

figuring it out. "But… you are running from something? Or someone?"

I'm taken back to the moment when I told him yesterday that I trusted him, and I know it's as true now as it was then. There aren't a lot of things that I trust these days, but Nate is one thing I think I can, even if I can't explain why. I could probably tell him every sordid detail of my life from the last few years and face no judgment from him. In fact, I could picture him vowing to keep me safe and protected from Vincent.

The problem with telling him any of it, however, is that it opens things up for him to get hurt should Vincent ever find me. Getting involved with Nate in any capacity puts him in harm's way, something I'd be smart to remember in those moments when I want him to kiss me.

I wouldn't put it past Vincent to try and assault Nate if he saw some of the looks we've shared in the past few days. Vincent would be livid. Thinking about it, I have little doubt that Nate wouldn't feel his wrath. I can't put Nate in that kind of situation. I can't put him in that kind of danger. I can't risk it. Especially after everything the man has done for me.

"Sav?" he says quietly, his blue eyes soft and patient.

I break out of my speculations with a heavy breath, mustering up a sad smile. "I'd rather we didn't talk about it, if that's okay with you."

It's confirmation enough for him, and he nods, allowing the conversation to drop, though I'm not foolish enough to think it's the last time it'll be brought up. For now he's giving me this reprieve.

"I don't know if I can pay you what you're worth," he says, bringing the subject back to the issue at hand. "I'm guessing I should be paying you at least what my accountant charges me, but there's a reason I'm sitting here trying to do this and he isn't."

"Nate, I wouldn't dream of charging you something," I say, laughing. "You do recall the fact that you're letting me stay in your home, right? And that you've fed me the last couple of days?"

He snaps his fingers like he's just figured out the solution to the world's biggest problem. "Free meals. Christ, you can drink for free too. And I'll up your wage from the serving position, obviously."

"Why don't you see how I do first? Let me prove myself to you," I caution. I have the utmost faith in myself, and I know I can figure this all out for him, but I'd like him to see that for himself.

He's already shaking his head. "You won't be making tips if you're not serving."

"I wouldn't mind still serving some of the time," I tell him with a small frown. I didn't realize it was going to be one or the other. "It's been nice to be around people."

"Sav," he says, leaning forward across the desk, his facial expression conveying how serious this is. "The government has threatened to shut me down in less than five weeks because the taxes haven't been done in years. My accountant gave me two weeks to get everything sorted. From there, he gets to figure the math out. I have ten days left."

He lets out a long, exhausted sigh that sounds like he's been holding in for days. He curses right after, scrubbing his hands over his face.

"I haven't told anyone that. Haven't even spoken the words out loud to myself." He surveys the disaster in his office and for a man who has been nothing but ready to take on and conquer the world for everyone else, he looks posi- tively defeated by this, and what it could mean for him. He slumps back into his chair, his eyes finding a spot on his desk that seems fascinating, and adds quietly, "Even if I manage to get all this stuff to the accountant, and he gets it in before the deadline… if we owe a lot of money, I stand to lose the bar."

My heart aches for him, with him, in that moment. The stress, exhaustion, and lack of knowledge have done a number on him. I feel for him. I know exactly what it's like to bear a secret so big that it can destroy not only you, but those around you. I know how heavy that is. And I know what it's like to keep it to yourself to protect those you love the most.

I look around at the mess in the office. It's going to be more work than I thought, but I've faced tighter deadlines than this. And I think I can work even more magic than Nate's prepared for.

Doing some quick math, I work it out in my head. He has less than five weeks, so I narrow that down to four. The accountant will want a few days with my reports and numbers, though I'm confident in myself. I know my shit. Three days should be enough for him. That gives me twenty-five days with this mess. Though, I should narrow my own deadline down to twenty-one and give myself a couple of days leeway. Just in case.

"Nate?" I murmur his name, bringing my eyes back to him. It takes him a moment to lift his to mine and I have to fight not to frown, instead giving him a reassuring smile once I see the crushing weight of the world in the blue depths. "Call your accountant and tell him he'll have it within twenty-five days. It'll all be prepared so perfectly for him that all he'll need to do is look it over and submit it."

Nate stares at me for a long time, his eyes assessing, weighing if he thinks I can do what I'm promising. I know I can, so I sit confidently and allow him the time he needs to figure it out. I know there's a lot riding on this, and it can make or break his business, so if he needed a day or so to think about it, I wouldn't fault him.

But instead, he says, "Okay. I trust you."

I'm pretty sure those three words just melted me into a puddle of goo that he's going to need to mop up from his office floor. Yesterday I gave him my trust, and today he's giving me his. Given that I don't believe he allows anyone to help him often, I feel honored. This place means a lot to him, and I don't want to let him down.

He smiles at me, some of the burden easing from his eyes, and I swear my heart stutters as he adds, "You start tomorrow. Tonight, we eat."

CHAPTER 16

NATE

It's been six days since Savanna told me she was an accountant, five since she started working in the office to get all the financial documents up to date. In those six days, I've worked two shifts at the firehouse, the rest of my days and evenings behind the bar.

The first day I came back after a shift at the house was the day after she started, and I was astonished to see how much she had gotten done in the office over the course of a twenty-four hour period. She had everything organized into neat piles and there seemed to be some order to the chaos.

For the first time since I found out about the tax situation, I took an entire breath. The fear that I wouldn't admit to, the one that was sitting not only on my shoulders, but on my chest, weighing on my heart, eased. I had hope. Hope that I wouldn't lose the bar. Hope that my employees would keep their jobs. Savanna had given me so much hope.

I couldn't believe my luck when she sat me down to talk

to me that night. I'd be lying if I said I hadn't hoped her "needing to talk" had something to do with the two of us, but I can't say I was disappointed when I found out what it was really about.

I learned a lot that evening over sandwiches and fries.

She opened up to me about the job she quit, and what it had been like to work with people who seemed to hate her. I learned how she ended up in Santa Rosé by flipping a coin, and how her first stop was the pier where she fell in love immediately. There were stories of her dad and her brothers, and I found out that her mother passed away when she was giving birth to Savanna, but that her family did a great job at making her feel like she knew her mom growing up.

The most interesting pieces of information were the ones she wouldn't share with me.

Since the day we met in the elevator, I've never seen Savanna as someone who has a hard time talking with people or making friends. Everyone that has encountered her in my presence has been nearly as taken with her as I am, and yet that day in the hospital, she didn't have anyone to call to pick her up. I've always thought that was strange, but I never pried because I figured if she wanted to tell me, she would.

The pieces started to come together last week when I point blank asked her if she was in trouble. It took me a minute to figure out her answer, and since then I've had a lot of time to think it through.

Based on the disgusting, filthy pigs comment, coupled with how affectionate and happy she looked when she talked about her family, I've deduced that it has to be an ex. That or she's a gambling addict and hasn't paid her debts. If I find her with a couple of broken legs, I'll know it was my second theory.

I haven't seen her in over twenty-four hours. In fact, I

think we're closer to the forty-eight-hour mark, and I've determined it's far too long for my liking, even if we've exchanged a few texts and a couple of work-related phone calls.

Savanna had left this morning before I got home from my shift at the firehouse. I'd even forgone my usual breakfast with my mom just so I could see Savanna before she went in, so I was more than a little disappointed to find her up and gone. I don't think she's put in less than ten hours of work a day since she started last Sunday, but now it's Friday evening and I'm cutting her off for the weekend. The last thing I need is for her to burn out.

There might also be a couple of selfish reasons I don't want her to work all weekend.

Entering through the back, I'm whistling a tune as I nod at the guys working the kitchen tonight, and head straight for the office where I'm sure I'm going to find a beautiful blonde haired, gray eyed woman for whom I have a question. Not one of the guys says a word to me, though I feel their eyes following as I stride by.

I'm not wearing my usual faded jeans with a t-shirt tonight, so I'm sure that's raising some eyebrows. Tonight I decided I needed to look my best if I wanted the best, so I threw on my darker denim jeans and a crisp black button down that I've been told makes my eyes stand out.

I'm not generally the type of guy that will dress up for much, preferring jeans and a t-shirt to anything, but I can clean up when it's appropriate. I'm not ashamed to admit that Jordan and Bryn previously approved this outfit for a night out.

I feel alive. Exhilarated. The hope in my chest has grown over the last few days. I've found myself smiling and laughing more. I even put up with everyone poking at me about Savanna while I was at the firehouse. Liam even slapped me on the back and gave me a grin that said, "Hey man, glad to see you happy."

I round the corner to the office and stop dead in my tracks. Savanna's there, and while I know she'll take my breath away the moment I give her my full attention, I'm floored by the state of my office.

I haven't seen the desk or the floor in months, and both are currently devoid of anything. Against the far wall, boxes are stacked, and they're all neatly labeled in Savanna's flowy lettering, organized by the year and contents.

The filing cabinet doesn't look like it has a speck of dust on it. In fact, nothing in the office does. There are also a couple of plants on top of the cabinet, and one sitting on the desk beside the computer monitor.

The place has been completely transformed since I saw it two nights ago, and I'm blown away. It looks amazing, but it's not just the paperwork being organized and sorted, it's that Savanna has walked in here and made it her own, which has warmth spreading from my chest outward.

"Wow," I say, incredulous. It's not enough to describe what I'm feeling, but I'm not sure there are words to do that.

My eyes land on the beautiful woman at the desk just in time to see her start at the sound of my voice. I smile as she brings her hand to her chest, her eyes darting to me, and I'm right—she does take my breath away.

Her blonde hair isn't curled today, but lays straight and falls over her shoulders, touching the swell of her breasts where my eyes are drawn by the flutter of her hand. She's wearing a black flowing top with tiny cutouts all along the neckline, right down to the top of her cleavage, her skin playing peek-a-boo through those little holes.

The top does what I'm sure it's meant to, draw the eye

there, and Christ, I'd love to stand here and stare for the rest of the night.

But I'm a man on a mission so I force my eyes back to hers as she laughs.

"You scared me," she admits, tucking a piece of hair behind her ear.

I'm pleased when I see her eyes slide down the length of my body, taking in my choice of attire. It's the same way she looked at me in the elevator, and the other night when I caught her staring. Full of appreciation, and it makes my dick twitch.

Crossing my arms over my chest, I lean against the doorframe and grin at her. "Couldn't help it. I'm a little in awe right now. Where did my office go?"

Now she gives me a full laugh. My pulse races at the sound, my stomach clenching with anticipation. I've never heard such a beautiful sound. I'm really hoping I'll hear a lot more of it tonight, and the rest of the weekend.

"Don't let the organization fool you. It might look better, but there is still so much to do." Savanna glances at the wall full of boxes. "I'm only three boxes into all the data, and I need to be a lot further than that, but I couldn't work in the chaos anymore so I may have gone a little overboard in cleaning yesterday."

"No, not at all. This place looks amazing, Sav. It looks like you," I tell her, my eyes dancing along her face. Warm, inviting, beautiful. Effortlessly beautiful. I've never seen her with much makeup on, but she doesn't need it, and I like that about her. I like a low-maintenance kind of woman, and Savanna is definitely that. "I like the plant addition, but you don't think they're going to die in here? That window doesn't offer a lot of sunlight."

"Oh, Nate," she giggles, shaking her head at me, and damn

it if I can't help but grin wider at her. "So much to learn. You've got to pick plants that don't need sunlight."

She points at one of the plants on the filing cabinet. I think she's referring to the one that looks viny and has big green and yellow leaves attached to it. It's pretty nice and looks good with the vines hanging over the side. "That's a devil's ivy. It doesn't need much sunlight. The one beside it is a snake plant, doesn't need a bunch of light, and it purifies the air."

"Then this guy," she says, pointing to the one on the desk, and I realize there's actually more than one plant in the big bowl that it's in and looks more like a miniature garden than a plant, "is a succulent. Or a few different succulents all mixed together, and they're okay without the light. I like him on the desk because it adds some life to it."

She glances at the big round pot on the desk then lifts her gray eyes to me, looking like she's about to frown. Instead she starts picking at her nail. "You don't mind they're here, do you?"

"Not at all. I think they're perfect." Pushing off the doorframe, I move to take a seat at the visitor's chair across from her. To see her talking about the plants, watching her eyes light up as she explained each of them to me, makes me light up inside. She loves her plants far more than I realized, and I'm glad that Liam and I saved them from her apartment. "I like that you're making it your own in here. Maybe I'll get lucky and you'll want to stick around once all of this is done."

Savanna grins back at me. "You haven't scared me off yet."

Leaning back in the chair, I cross an ankle over one knee and clasp my hands in front of my stomach, quietly studying her for a moment. Her skin is kissed by the California summer with all the time she spent at the beach over the last few months. It looks silky smooth, and it's not the first time I've noticed. There have been more than a few nights this week that we've sat on the couch together, watching movies or just talking, her at one end and me at the other, her legs sprawled out for my eyes to enjoy. I try not to stare, I swear, but I've got a thing for a set of toned legs and hers are as perfect as those beautiful breasts.

"Nate?"

"Hmm?" I mumble, lazily looking back up to her face.

"You're staring."

I jolt upright, realizing she's right, my neck and face immediately heating. "Sorry. You just look nice today. Your hair is different."

Savanna smirks and I feel my face redden further. "You weren't looking at my hair, Nate."

"Sure I was," I say, gesturing towards the ends of her hair where they tickle the tops of her breasts and grin. "I was looking at where your hair is."

And thinking about how nice it would be to touch you there.

It's her turn to blush. I love the way her cheeks tinge pink, and that I caused it. I've realized it's not hard to do, and it makes my chest swell with pride.

"Well, you look nice too," she states, waving a hand at me. "Hot date?" I don't miss the cringe before she adds, "Sorry, that's none of my business."

Dropping my foot from my knee, I lean forward in the chair and cross my arms over the desk. A week ago I wouldn't be taking the step I'm about to take, but I've had a lot of time to think about how this might work, or not work. After weighing the pros and cons, I've decided I need to go for it. I know Savanna is my employee, but I just don't give a damn anymore.

I want to take her out. I want to kiss her. I want to touch

all that gorgeous skin. I want to be able to pull her across the couch when we're laying at opposite ends and have her body rest on top of mine while we make out for a while.

I want a hell of a lot more than that, but I'll take what I can get to begin with. If she'll let me.

"I'm giving you tomorrow off," I say instead of answering her. "And Sunday."

Savanna balks at me. "What? Nate, no! I can't take tomorrow off, let alone Sunday too. I have so much to do here."

"Are you saying that if you took the next two days off you wouldn't be done by your deadline?"

She glances at the computer screen then narrows her eyes at me. "I would make sure I'm done."

That's what I was counting on. "Then as your boss, I'm giving you tomorrow and Sunday off, Savanna. You've been working non-stop the last week; I don't need you burning yourself out. You can come back on Monday refreshed and ready to keep going."

Sitting back in her chair, she crosses her arms over her chest. I swear to god she does it just to taunt me because her breasts rise higher and I'm finding it almost impossible not to look. But this is about work and if I'm going to do this, if we're going to do this, we need to keep things separate.

"And what would you propose I do with two days off?"

"I was hoping you'd ask that," I say, pushing away from the desk, though my gaze doesn't lose its intensity as I watch her. "I have two questions for you."

When she raises a questioning brow, I continue, starting with the first, easier, question.

"Some of the crew from the firehouse are coming to the bar tonight. In fact," I glance at my watch, "I suspect some of them are here or they'll be here shortly."

"Liam."

It's not a question, it's a statement. Savanna has learned in the week she's been around that Liam is a constant fixture at the bar when we're not on shift. It's not like he gets wasted when he's here, nor does he always find a woman to pick up. He hates cooking, I give him a discount, and more than that, I think he gets lonely though he'd never admit it. There's no doubt in my mind that he'll be the first one to show up tonight.

I grin at her, nodding. "Yeah, if he's not out there already, he will be soon. Brody's coming too, but there'll be a few others that you haven't officially met yet. Shawn is coming, Mac will be there with his wife Lynn. Hailey thought she'd show up, and Quinn too. Hailey and Quinn were the paramedics that took you to the hospital."

"Hailey and Quinn… isn't that a movie?"

I bark out a laugh. "It's Harley Quinn, but don't ever bring it up around them. Especially Hailey. I can't tell you the number of calls they go on and she comes back fuming that she got called Harley the whole time." I shrug with a smirk. "I don't think it's a big deal, but we all know better than to say anything around them."

Savanna nods in acknowledgement. "Got it. No Harley Quinn comments." Dropping her arms onto the desk, she leans toward me, an eyebrow raised expectantly. "You haven't asked me a question yet."

"Right," I say, mimicking her by leaning across the desk again. I swear she's close enough now that I can feel her heat, but maybe that's just in my mind. "Will you join us for dinner? The rest of the crew wants to meet you."

"Oh." She chews on her bottom lip and glances towards the computer then at the boxes against the wall. "Well, I don't want to intrude, and I really do have so much to do."

"You aren't intruding, and you need to eat. You've been working all day. Time for a break."

"You've been talking about me?" she asks, her voice quiet.

My dick twitches as she peers at me through her long eyelashes, hopeful and innocent.

There's no denying it, though my first instinct is to say that Liam and Brody talk about her, but that's not completely truthful.

Liam definitely brings her up a lot, but it's because he's been encouraging me to ask her out all week. Brody just sits there and silently eggs him on. Quinn has gotten into it now as well, while Hailey throws in a comment or two, but she tries to stay out of it to a certain extent, along with Shawn. Mac is old enough that he knows to keep his mouth shut, but I see the supportive looks he gives them, and the pointed looks he gives to me as if to say, "You're not getting any younger, son."

"I'll answer that if you agree to dinner," I finally respond.

"What's your second question?" she asks, instead of agreeing to dinner.

I should have seen that coming. I've realized that when Savanna isn't ready to give an answer she changes the subject, but if I wait her out she'll usually circle back. I'm guessing this won't be any different, though it makes my palms suddenly sweaty while my heart begins to race thinking about the second question.

"I, uh… well, I was… kind of thinking… maybe…"

Jesus. I've been doing so well around her the last week, but suddenly the thought of asking her out on an official date makes me feel like a teenage boy asking his crush to prom. The confidence I've been walking around with since I got home from the firehouse vanishes into thin air. I convinced myself that the only answer she would give me was yes, but now that we've arrived at the moment, I feel unsure. Awkward. What if she says no? She's living in my house. Working in my bar.

I run my hand through my hair and take in a deep breath, blowing it out. My heart is thundering in my chest so hard that I can hear it in my ears. It's not like this is the first time I've asked a woman out, but Christ, it feels like the most important. I like Savanna. A lot. Rejection will be crushing.

The way she's looking at me now, amusement lighting up her face, isn't helping, and she's not even trying to contain it.

I rake my hand through my hair a couple more times, and then sit back, hoping that putting more space between us will help my nerves. "Tomorrow... I was thinking that maybe... you'd like to go out... with me."

The amusement is still there, but the grin morphs into one that I can only describe as pure elation. It's becoming on her, and my heart races faster as I take it in.

"Like a date?" she questions.

My stomach nosedives when she doesn't immediately say yes, but I nod. "Like a date."

An eyebrow arches, but her smile remains. "You're asking me out on a date?"

Christ. Maybe this was a bad move. I'm trying not to panic here, because that look makes me think she was going to say yes, but her questions are making me think the opposite. "I am."

"You're my boss," she says, and I can hear the hesitation in her voice, even though her expression hasn't changed.

"I won't be tomorrow. As your boss I'm giving you the weekend off, remember?" I blow out a breath, some of the nerves gone now that I've gotten the question out, though the rest will remain until she answers me.

"Look, I know the working thing complicates it a bit, but

I get to make the rules, and there's no rule that says we can't go on a date. Maybe more than one if things go the way I hope." I lean back across the desk, my gaze intent on her. "I like you, Savanna. I want to take you out. I want to keep getting to know you. If you'll let me."

She's picking at her fingers again, casting her eyes down to the desk where her hands lay. The smile has faded some, and I can feel real concern trickling out of her. "I don't want anyone treating me differently here."

I can understand her apprehension. It's something I thought about. When I went through the list of my employees, there isn't one that I could see being upset about this, or who would change the way they treat her. My uncle never hired those kinds of people, and neither do I.

Reaching a hand out, I take one of hers and run my thumb over the back of it reassuringly. "They won't. I know them, Sav. They wouldn't do that."

I don't bother adding that if they did all she would need to do is tell me, because I know she wouldn't. It would make her feel like a bigger outcast if she were to do that.

When her gray eyes lift back to me, I can see my answer, and I can't help the grin that starts to spread across my face. I think she knows I'm right about everyone at work, but she had to say it out loud and get the confirmation before she said yes to my date.

"Well then, to my boss Nate, I'm letting you know that I will be taking the weekend off."

My grin widens. "And to the Nate who asked you on a date?"

"I was starting to think you'd never ask," she says with a cheeky smirk.

I can't help laughing, giving her hand a squeeze before I link our fingers, enjoying the way that our hands fit together.

"Believe me, I've wanted to ask for days, but I wasn't sure if you'd say yes for the very reason you brought up."

Her expression slowly falls and she turns pensive, releasing a sigh as if she's just let go of a weight she was carrying. "I wasn't sure either. I mean, I would have wanted to say yes even if I'd told you no. But with staying at your place, and now working for you, I didn't know if it was a great idea."

Slipping her fingers from mine, she turns my hand over so my palm is facing up, and runs a fingertip in a circle along my skin, making me shiver. "But I feel this," she says in a whisper. "I've felt it since you introduced yourself to me in the hospital. Maybe even before that."

I know exactly what she's talking about, and right now, I want nothing more than to pull her straight across the desk and into my lap so I can kiss the hell out of her. The electricity that crackles around us every time we touch is nothing short of magic. I can only imagine what it might be like to put my lips on hers.

It's not just when we're touching, either. I can feel the hum of it whenever she's near, and it drives me crazy in a way I didn't know I could like. It might be a miracle that we've both been able to ignore it for this long.

"I feel it too," I tell her, gazing at her as she watches her finger trace patterns along my palm.

With each stroke of her finger, I find it harder to resist dragging her across the desk to me. I take a deep breath to try and help keep my mind clear of fantasies I've dreamt up over the last week. I'm fighting a losing battle, though, my eyes dropping down to watch what she's doing on my palm. Makes me wonder what else she can do with those fingers. I'd love to feel them running down my chest, my stomach, straight down to my cock where they could stroke me. And Christ, if she added that pretty little mouth of hers to it…

Fuck, I need to stop. I'm getting hard sitting here while she runs a finger over my palm. A finger! When did a single finger become sexual enough to get me going?

"Savanna?" Bryn's unexpected voice sends both of us flying in our seats.

I whip around in my chair to look at her, knowing my neck is turning red as hell as her eyes dart back and forth between us. The smirk on her face tells me she knows she walked in on something.

"What's up?" Savanna says, clearing her throat. She withdrew her hand when we both jumped. I know she has no intention of giving it back, so I pull my hand away, fighting the urge to reach down and adjust the semi I'm sporting.

I'm half turned in my seat so I can see both women when Bryn says, "There's some guy asking for you at the bar."

I glance at Savanna and watch the color drain from her face. It puts me on edge, and I turn back to Bryn, the conversation about Savanna running from someone flickering in the back of my mind.

"Who is it?" I ask sharply.

Bryn rolls her eyes, oblivious to Savanna's anxiety. "He told me not to say, but his name might start with an L and end with an M."

Liam. Christ. Sometimes I feel like punching him, and right now is one of those times. Not because he did anything wrong, but my protective instincts are flying high after seeing the petrified look on Savanna's face.

"Tell him we'll be there shortly," I tell her. When she nods and leaves, I turn back to Savanna and reach out to take the hand that she's picking at nervously. "You okay?"

The way her body relaxes almost immediately when I

take her hand brings my own uneasiness down. Her lips still form a thin, tight line, but she nods. I'm not sure if she's trying to convince me, or herself. "I'm good. I just don't like surprise visits."

I give her hand a squeeze, tucking that information, and her reaction to the situation, into my mind for later analysis. In the meantime, it sounds like the crew is arriving.

"So, dinner with the gang?"

"Yeah," she says, her smile a little forced, but I can tell she's glad for the change of subject. "As long as I'm not intruding on firehouse time, I'm game."

"You're not," I retort, rolling my eyes as I release her hand and get to my feet. "I spend enough time with the knuckle-heads. I'll be happy for you to be a distraction."

As she gets to her feet, I whistle low when I catch sight of her legs in a pair of jean shorts. Her ass doesn't hang out of them, but they don't cover more than an inch, two at best, of her thigh. "Very, very happy."

She just laughs and comes around the desk, giving me a glimpse of those toned calves before pushing me towards the door. "C'mon, let's go. Can't keep Liam waiting, you know."

Oh, we could. We definitely could. Lucky for Liam I'm too much of a gentleman.

CHAPTER 17

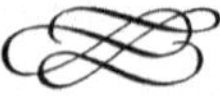

SAVANNA

"They're alive!"

Nate and I both look across the restaurant to see Liam sitting at a table, grinning at us, his hands up in the air like he's just scored a touchdown.

Beside him sits a woman I recognize from the night of the fire, but I'm not sure if she's Hailey or Quinn. Whoever she is, she's stunning. Despite still being behind the bar where Nate is getting us both a beer before we join the table, it's easy to see her beauty.

She has jet black voluminous hair cut with shaggy attitude just past her shoulders. Wisps of hair frame her face, the style saying she doesn't try too hard, but still makes it look damn good. A sharp jawline, high cheekbones, and pale skin make her standout. With the curves I can see from here, it wouldn't surprise me if every pair of eyes in the place follow her whenever she moves.

"Remember when you met Liam and Brody, and I warned

you about them?" Nate says, drawing my attention back to him. I nod and he continues as he hands me one of the beers, "This might be worse than that."

I laugh at his sudden apprehension. "I did just fine that night. Don't worry, I got this too."

As if to prove my point, I grab his hand and pull him away from the bar, heading towards the table where Liam and the girl sit. The second we're in their sight, I see the girl elbow Liam in the side, and I know they're both zeroing in on our linked hands.

"Oh shit. This just got serious. They're holding hands," Liam says in a mock whisper loud enough for us to hear. Leave it to him to call us out on it.

"Has this ever happened before?" The woman asks, and I glance at her, awestruck by the color of her eyes. They're a shade of violet that can't be anything besides contacts, but they make her striking features stand out even more.

He shakes his head. "Not that I've witnessed."

"Okay, okay. Enough out of the two of you," Nate says, releasing my hand to pull the chair across from the girl out for me. Someone has put three tables together for all of us and Liam and the woman have chosen the middle table to sit down at. "Can we please not scare her off?"

"Oh!" The woman gasps, turning to Liam as I sit down. "Is this it?"

I'm not sure what she's talking about, but Liam narrows his eyes and glances between Nate and me before leaning back in his seat to shake his head. "Nah. Not his M.O. He'd do something spectacular, and this isn't it."

I look to Nate for some kind of explanation. He raises his beer to his lips, I think to hide a smirk, and doesn't meet my eyes. Nate would do something spectacular? For what?

Turning back to Liam and the woman, I raise my eyebrows. "I don't suppose one of you wants to fill me in?"

"You'll find out soon enough," Liam supplies cheekily.

The woman adds with a finger in the air, "But when Nate asks you a question, you should definitely say yes."

My head snaps towards Nate, and I break into a full grin. Nate's already asked me a question. Two, in fact. I'd bet that Liam means Nate would plan something spectacular for our first date.

My stomach assaults me with butterflies. They've been swirling around in there ever since Nate stuttered his way through asking me out. He was so adorable. I've seen his neck and face redden before, but they've never been the shade of crimson they were when he was trying to get the words out.

With the nerves so obvious, I was pretty sure I knew what was coming. Though I might have looked more composed than Nate, my heart was racing, and my hands were shaking. I've thought about Nate a lot over the last week, and I decided that if he were to make a move, I wouldn't stop him. I don't think I could, even if I wanted to. There's this connection between us that is so strong, it's been near impossible to keep myself from jumping him at times, especially in the moments when we touch accidentally.

Oh hell, even when it isn't accidental.

I got sprayed with bacon grease the morning before his last shift when we were cooking breakfast, and he went all fireman on me, taking my arm to inspect it and rinse it under cool water. It wasn't bad at all, probably didn't even need to be run under water, but Nate was determined so I let him take care of me. It was sweet and innocent until our eyes met and I'm pretty sure if Jordan had walked in thirty seconds later, she would have caught us all over each other.

Maybe tomorrow on our date we'll get to act on the tension that has been building all week. I would really love it if we did. My thighs have never had such a workout with all the clenching they've done around Nate this past week—and at times when he isn't around. I didn't know it was possible to drench a pair of panties without someone even touching you, but I've found out firsthand that it is.

"Oh shit," Liam says, surprise evident in his tone. "You actually did it, didn't you?"

I glance at him and he's staring at Nate, amusement and pride mixed in his expression. A quick glance at the woman next to him and I see she's staring at Nate with eyes that are wide and hopeful.

Turning my attention back to Nate, my grin is permanently in place while his eyes dance in amusement, silently asking me if we should tell them, or let them continue to guess. The giggle I give in return is enough to tell him we should let them steep in misery for a while longer, even if it's obvious.

"What have I missed?" Asks a voice from behind me.

I crane my neck and find a woman with stick straight copper hair cut to her collarbones, parted deeply to the side, side swept bangs covering her forehead. Murky green eyes look around the table expectantly before landing on me.

"Savanna," she says in greeting, and I suddenly recognize her as the paramedic that was in the back of the ambulance with me. "I'm not sure you remember me, but I'm Hailey."

"Whoops," says the woman across from me, who must be Quinn. "Been too focused on whether Nate asked her out, or if they're on a date right now, to think about introducing myself."

This perks Hailey up as she takes the chair next to me,

her body angled my way. "Did he? Oh, please tell me he did. We've all been urging him to do it."

"Yeah, Nate, did you?" Quinn asks, then her eyes move to me. "I'm Quinn, by the way."

I nod in acknowledgement, but turn to Nate, my head tilted to the side. "So you have been talking about me," I say, amusement lacing my tone.

His neck is turning red and it's all the confirmation I need. Before he can confirm or deny it, Brody shows up and the noise he makes as he falls into the chair next to Quinn is enough that we're all turning to look at him.

Brody is a giant of a man, and since the day we met I've been impressed by the gracefulness of his movements. A stealth that you wouldn't expect from such a large guy. This is neither of those things, though, and he looks to be in extreme pain as he adjusts in his seat, trying to find a comfortable way to sit.

"What the hell happened to you?" Liam asks, leaning forward to look around Quinn.

"Bailed at Slab," he says with a groan. "I need alcohol."

"Slab is a surfing spot in town," Nate whispers in my ear before I can ask. I realize he's a lot closer than I thought he was, a jolt of awareness pumping through my body. "There's a bunch of rocks and if you fall in the wrong spot, you can get caught up in the churning water. This is what happens. Or worse."

"Let's see it," Quinn says beside him.

As Brody leans forward and turns so his shoulder is facing us, he tries to grab his shirt to pull it up, but it's obviously painful so she helps him out. It's her that hisses as the scrapes and cuts are shown, deep red and angry, parts of it still bloodied. I can see from my spot that there's already purple and blue bruises forming.

"You get this looked at?" she asks.

His head shakes minutely. "I'm good. A friend helped clean it out."

It doesn't stop her from checking it over, glancing at Hailey every so often as she does. I can feel Nate leaning over the table into me to get a better look at what's going on. Liam is doing the same to Quinn, though it's harder for him given she's got her back turned to him while inspecting Brody.

"I don't know why you have to surf there, Brody," Hailey says from beside me, frowning deeply. I'm guessing this has been a topic of conversation prior to today. "It's so dangerous. Why can't you surf at one of the other spots?"

Brody grunts when Quinn touches the skin that isn't scraped, gently prodding and poking him, and I can imagine that it doesn't feel good the way he cringes away from her.

He manages to turn his head to look at Hailey, even giving her a grin. "You'd understand if you'd come surfing with me."

"That will never happen," she retorts, throwing her red hair over her shoulder, but it's too short so it falls right back to where it was.

Quinn smirks from her seat, but doesn't look up from what she's doing. "You know Hailey doesn't do anything remotely dangerous, why would you even try?"

"I ride with you every shift," Hailey retorts, garnering a laugh from everyone around the table.

Brody's laughter turns into a groan.

Quinn looks up now and blows her a kiss. "And you love it because it's the most thrilling thing you ever do."

"I would imagine your job comes with a lot of dangerous situations," I muse. "I mean, maybe you don't run into burning buildings like these crazy guys, but I can't imagine everyone you deal with is of sound mind. That can't always be safe."

"Oh, I like you so much already," Hailey says, leaning back in her chair to give me an admiring look.

"Yeah, I might be a little in love with her," Quinn says appreciatively from the other side of the table, and I catch her looking me up and down with a demure smile. "I do enjoy a beautiful woman, especially one who's intelligent."

"Quinn is a shameless flirt," Liam says from his seat, where he's been unusually quiet so far. "She'll flirt with anyone."

"Pot meet kettle," she tells him, rolling her eyes as she pulls Brody's shirt down. He turns back to the table with a groan, and she's quick to add, "You might have a couple broken ribs. You should really get checked out."

Brody shakes his head and lifts the hand opposite his hurt side, trying to get the attention of whoever is serving us. I haven't noticed who it is, but the place isn't too busy, so I'm surprised no one has been by. Unless Nate was planning on doing it all, and just hasn't gotten up yet because of Brody's arrival. I don't like the thought of him having to do it, especially since he just came off shift at the firehouse this morning and has been working more than I have.

I push up from my chair. "What would you like, Brody? I'll get it. And Hailey, I'll grab you something too." Liam and Quinn already have drinks from when they got here, neither looking ready for another.

"Sit," Nate says firmly from beside me as he stands. "You've been working all day."

I smile at him. "It's fine, I don't mind. You worked all night."

"Nate, the boss, says sit," he tells me. Then he raises a hand and brushes a lock of hair behind my ear as he leans in and whispers, "And Nate, the guy you're going on a date with tomorrow, says enjoy tonight."

My eyes fall closed as his fingertips gently move down the column of my neck, skirting across the bare skin above my collarbone to my shoulder. It's innocent, but sensual at the same time. I'm a puddle of mush that can only give a nod of my head.

I feel a little dazed as I open my eyes to find him watching me intently, heat filling his own blue depths. I'm positive if we weren't standing in the middle of the bar with everyone watching, he would be kissing me right now. Part of me wishes he'd just say screw it and do it anyway.

There's a throaty quality to my voice when I murmur, "Okay."

Nate's eyes flash hotter with that simple word, his nostrils flaring, and I'm certain he's in the same boat as me. The heat between us keeps intensifying, and if we don't do something about it soon, I think we may both spontaneously combust.

Thankfully, he has some sense of self-preservation in front of everyone because he steps away from me and quickly gathers orders. I can do nothing but sink back into my chair, still feeling a little incoherent and dreamy from our shared moment.

It takes me a moment or two to realize that everyone is staring at me and not saying a word after Nate leaves. "What?"

"You got it bad," Liam says, and I know everyone is trying to hold back snickers as my already rosy cheeks, courtesy of Nate, turn scarlet.

Quinn nudges Liam. "She's totally going to say yes."

"She already has."

Liam's amused gaze watches me over the table. He's

confident in his assessment, and my eyes twinkle with silent confirmation as I lift my beer to hide my smile. I know from some of the conversations I've had with both Nate, and Liam, that Nate has had way too much on his plate to even think about dating. To know I'm the one changing that has the butterflies living in my stomach swirling in the most delicious way.

"Whether she has or not, I'm just glad that she's here tonight," Hailey says to my right, and I glance over at her with appreciation. "I feel like I've heard so much about you, we're already friends. I'd hoped Nate wouldn't keep you hidden away."

My face must show my surprise—or horror, Vincent flashing before my eyes—because Quinn quickly adds, "She doesn't mean that he's going to tie you up in a dungeon with whips and chains and keep you to himself. He's not into that." She pauses for a moment and looks to Brody like he might have an idea, thinks better of it, and turns to Liam. "Is he? I can't see it, but it's always the ones you least suspect."

"Why are you asking me?" Liam asks, incensed.

Quinn scoffs, as if the answer should be apparent. "You're his best friend. If anyone knows, it's you. Brods would never ask, but you… you would."

He grimaces, shaking his head. "We do not discuss fetishes. I don't know what he does with his dick, or what he likes having done to it, other than he hasn't been using it, and really needs to."

If my bottle had made it to my lips already, Quinn would be covered in beer. I gape at Liam, eyes wide. There seem to be no secrets among this group, a far cry from what I'm used to. Or maybe it's that there are no secrets when it comes to Liam. He just puts it all out there for anyone to hear.

I don't hate knowing the information, though. Nate has

priorities. Responsibilities. I've witnessed him take those very seriously with my own eyes, and it's only been two weeks. It makes me wonder how long it's been since he's really had any fun. Or done anything besides work. Contemplating it makes me even happier that I said yes to a date.

Brody leans over the table, his hand covering his eyes like he can't believe what he's hearing. That or he's just in so much pain he's not paying attention. Hailey is sitting beside me, and I can see in my peripherals that she's shaking her head at both Quinn and Liam. The two of them are amusing to me, feeding off one another. I wonder if there's something going on between them, or if there ever was.

"I'm sure Nate already told you this, but ignore both of them. They're bad enough on their own, but when they get together it's next level absurdity," Hailey says, obviously trying to come to my rescue, but I'm not offended, or concerned in the slightest.

I might not know what Nate likes, or what to expect with him in the bedroom department, but instinct tells me he would never do anything I, or any other woman for that matter, wouldn't want to do. He's been far too much of a gentleman for that. Sure, we've exchanged looks, and there've been a few intimate touches, but he's had plenty of opportunity to take advantage of me and hasn't. He always backs off instead of pushing forward.

"This is one reason I worried he'd keep you to himself. But I suppose you'd already met Liam, so throwing the rest of us into the mix wasn't too unfeasible," she adds.

Despite my previous thoughts, Hailey bringing up Nate keeping me to himself for the second time makes my hands tremble. Surely, he's not that kind of guy. He had me meet his two best friends the first night I knew him, and almost two weeks in I'm meeting everyone else from the firehouse.

That has to mean he's not the type of guy that will prevent me from seeing people, right?

"Believe me, he warned me about what I was getting into," I say, giving her as much of a reassuring chuckle as I can muster.

Vincent managed to isolate me from nearly everyone, though it didn't happen until later. It's why I only had my brothers and Maddie by the time I left Colorado. All my other friends slipped away after getting fed up when I declined invitation after invitation to hang out. But with my brothers and Maddie, Vincent knew not to screw with my relationship with them. Much good it did, since I ended up losing them in the end anyway.

My heart aches with sudden homesickness thinking about them. I haven't spoken with my brothers since before I left. At our last call, Maddie begged me to call her when I got somewhere, but I whispered it was for her own good not to know. For the good of Devin and Connor and my dad. For my safety.

She'd gotten angry. Cursed me up and down, and swore my brothers wouldn't care what my letters said, or that she was supposed to lie to them about me going east. They'd look for me all over the country, so I was better off calling. I'd considered it. I knew it was a risk, but it wasn't one I was willing to take.

It was Maddie's last desperate attempt to stop me from severing all contact. She knew I needed to leave and get out from under Vincent's thumb. She didn't know the extent of what was going on between us, but she knew enough.

Far more than either of my brothers, who would have killed him, I'm sure. I made Maddie promise that she wouldn't let either of them hurt him, if only so Connor and Devin didn't end up in jail. The same went for my dad, but I know if I start letting my thoughts meander to him, I'll end up crying.

This isn't the time or place to be losing myself to tears.

"Nate!" Quinn calls, pulling me back to the present. He's back from the bar and setting a shot in front of Brody, along with a beer, and a glass of wine for Hailey. "Are you a chains and whips kind of guy?"

Hailey's wine almost topples over as Nate fumbles from the question.

"Jesus! Are you shitting me right now?" he exclaims, righting the glass just before it ends up in her lap. His eyes are a little wild as they dart around the table, glaring at everyone before landing on me, apology overriding the annoyance.

"Oh fuck," Liam mutters, leaning into Quinn. "Maybe he is. Just when you think you know a guy."

Nate flips him the bird, taking his seat beside me, pulling his chair closer to mine before he leans in. "I am so sorry about them. I won't leave you alone again, I swear."

I can tell his imagination is running away with ideas of things that might have been said in his absence, so I cover his hand with mine and shake my head. "I'm fine. I told you, I got this."

Lacing our fingers together, he brings my hand up to his lips and kisses the back of it, his eyes never leaving mine. It has my stomach swirling with heat, my heart taking off in a race. His lips are warm against my cool hands, probably a product of my memories. This—him—washes the rest of them away, and warmth embraces me.

But I can feel the anxiety rolling off him, so I try and ease his worries with a squeeze of his hand.

I know it doesn't work when he mutters, "All the same, part of me wishes I'd kept you locked in the back office."

The blood drains from my face, the cold slipping right back into my hands, though this time it's for a different reason. A wave of nausea hits me at the thought of being locked up anywhere, especially in a small, enclosed space where I can't escape.

It's not the memory of the fire, or being stuck in the garbage room, that has my world spinning. It's the memory of being locked in the basement.

The first time Vincent did it, I don't think he realized how it would break me. After all was said and done that night, he knew it was the worst kind of punishment he could dole out. I remember that first night so vividly, it's as if it's happening to me now.

I'd made plans with friends to go out, but when I told him that afternoon, he'd become furious with me. How dare I make plans without speaking to him first. He'd already accepted an invitation to a friend's party, and we were both expected to be there. The look in his eye told me I was treading in deep water, but I hadn't seen one of my friends in over a year since she'd moved away.

I pushed. Even after he told me not to. The next thing I knew he was slamming me against the wall, my head hitting it so hard that the drywall caved. Then I was shoved through the doorway leading to the basement. Somehow I managed to catch myself before I fell down all the stairs, but the resulting bruises didn't feel very good.

They were nothing compared to the psychological scars inflicted on me that night.

Vincent had gone to the garage where the electrical panel was, and flipped off the lights, so I had no way of seeing. I'd never been a fan of basements, this one in particular, something he was all too aware of. He kept me locked in until the early hours of the morning while he went to the party without me. The same party he'd said I had to be at.

I spent the first hour screaming at him to let me out, shouldering the door to try and get it open, clawing at the bottom to try and rip part of it away and make a hole big enough to fit through. I didn't even make a dent, only ending up with bruises up and down my arm, my fingertips and nails shredded. It was the most degrading thing he'd ever done to me, making me feel like a dog trying to get out.

More than that, I was scared beyond comprehension. I spent the entire evening crying, though how tears kept coming, I'm not sure. To make things worse, by the time he let me out I was so out of my mind I dove into his waiting arms, begging him to make me feel better.

"Sav," Nate's gentle, calm voice breaks through my thoughts, and I feel his hand touch my cheek, making me flinch. "Whoa, hey, it's okay."

Focusing on him, I see the concern etched in his face. I try for a smile, but I'm positive it comes across as more of a grimace than anything. The remnants of my lunch from hours ago are churning in my stomach. It's not often I allow myself to go to that place, never in public, and I can feel the shame creeping through me until my face is so colored I'm surprised Nate isn't checking my temperature or blood pressure.

"Sorry," I mutter, dropping my eyes between us. "Spaced out."

Nate isn't normally one to pry, something I've learned to appreciate about him, but I don't think I've given him a choice this time. His voice is so quiet that I know I'm the only one that can hear him when he asks, "Where did you go?"

I'm keenly aware that more than one set of eyes is on us,

and that the table has fallen quiet, adding to my sudden discomfort. I don't want to make a scene. Sucking in a deep breath, and summoning every bit of strength I can gather, I raise my eyes back to Nate's and flash him a reassuring smile, this time managing to make it look half decent.

"Locked offices might remind me of burning buildings," I say, nudging him with my shoulder, and adding a laugh so he knows there's no harm done by his comment.

It doesn't work.

His incredibly gorgeous face falls, and he looks stricken as he puts it all together. I can't help but cringe because I put that look there; it's better than the alternative. He doesn't want to know the other horrors I've endured, especially in front of a bunch of people.

Dismayed blue eyes stare at me, his fingers gripping my hand tighter as I'm sure the memory flashes through his mind. "Fuck, Savanna, I didn't—"

"Don't," I cut him off, swiping my other hand through the air gently. "You didn't know. You didn't do it intentionally."

As the words leave my mouth, I know how true they are. I know Nate would never do anything to hurt me if he could help it. The devastation in his eyes tells me as much. That's not something you can fake or hide. It's killing him to think he put me back into the nightmare of the fire.

"Hey, I'm okay. Because of you," I say quietly. "Because of you, I've got a roof over my head, a job to go to every day, and people that I'm really enjoying spending time with."

He doesn't look convinced. I can see the war going on within him. One side saying he should beat himself up for causing me anguish. The other wanting to listen to my words and take them at face value. To trust me.

"I'm sorry," he croaks, and I watch his Adam's apple bob harshly.

Reaching up, I press my free hand against the side of his face. I wish I could take a moment to savor how the whiskers of his five-o-clock shadow scratch my palm, but I don't. Instead, I lean in and press my cheek against his other, my lips at his ear.

"I'm here because of *you*," I say, emphasizing that it's because of him. "Don't beat yourself up for something you didn't know. I'm here. Be here with me too."

I can feel him breathing in deeply, breathing me in, taking in the words that I tell him, and slowly he starts to relax. Part of me wishes I had told him the truth, but another says it would have made him feel even worse.

Maybe I should have told a different lie, but I was on the verge of panic when he pulled me out of my memories, and it was the first thing I could think of that would make sense.

But fuck, I wish I hadn't made him feel like he feels now.

Nate might act like he has everything together all the time, like he never needs help, but I've seen the cracks in that armor. He hates looking like he has a weakness, but he has them, and I'm almost positive that I'm quickly becoming one. I'd do well to remember that the next time I'm triggered by an old memory.

Because there will be a next time. I'm sure of it.

CHAPTER 18

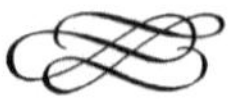

NATE

I FEEL LIKE A STEAMING PILE OF SHIT THAT'S JUST BEEN RUN over by a fire engine. I can't believe I was so careless in my choice of words, eliciting such horrible memories for Savanna. She's wrong; I should have known better; I should have thought my words through more wisely.

When I got back to the table and Quinn asked that asinine question about chains and whips, I was worried that whatever happened in my absence had made Savanna uncomfortable. The first thing I thought was maybe I shouldn't have invited her for dinner, or hell, maybe I shouldn't have asked everyone to come out tonight for dinner. It had been my idea this morning when we were getting off shift.

The thing is, I want her to meet my friends. Not just Liam and Brody, but everyone who is a big part of my life. Plus, I know she could use friends of her own, and I think she'll get along great with Hailey and Quinn. If they don't scare her off first.

She's trying so hard to make me feel better, and while her words are soothing, it's truly the scent of her that seems to be calming me more than her voice. Hints of citrus and vanilla have been lingering around me since we sat in the office. Side by side at the table it's wafted my way occasionally. Multiple times I've had to stop myself from leaning in to take a big breath of it.

Now that she's up in my space, with her face pressed against my cheek, I don't need to lean in. It's all around me. I inhale deeply, once, twice, a third time, completely under the spell of the sweetness that is Savanna, and Christ, all I want to do is stay right here in this moment and keep breathing her in.

"I'm here," I whisper to her.

Her cheek lifts against mine, and I know I put a smile on her face, which has my own lips curving. As much as I would love not to move from this spot, I have to remember we have an audience.

I force myself to slowly pull back from her, realizing my mistake the moment our eyes meet. The tenderness I see there as she continues to hold my face in her small hand settles in my chest. She's so close that it wouldn't take much to tilt my head and capture her lips. An opportunity that Savanna recognizes as well if her soft intake of breath is any indication.

We both want it. My heart is pounding in my chest, and I'm half a second from claiming her mouth when the empty chair next to mine scrapes across the wood floor, screeching in a way no chair should screech. It causes both Savanna and me to pull away from each other, our attention diverting to the intrusion.

"Dude!" Liam groans in complaint, and I must say for once I agree with his tone.

"I know, I know, we're late," Mac says as he drops down beside me. "Have you guys ordered yet?"

Quinn, exasperated, sighs as she falls back against her chair. "No, but you just interrupted everyone's movie."

My head turns to the opposite end of the table where I find Shawn sitting next to Brody. His deep brown eyes are filled with amusement, but dart to the man next to him when I pin him with a glare. I wonder when the hell he got here, and how long Savanna and I were in our own little world.

Then I realize the movie Quinn's talking about was probably Savanna and me. I run a hand through my hair and grit my teeth, trying not to be irritated with my friends. We were providing the show after all, but these assholes can be so nosy.

Mac snorts and knocks an elbow into me. "You can thank me later!"

Shaking my head and blowing out a breath, I make introductions for Savanna to the newest members of the table, which include Mac, his wife Lynn, and Shawn with his girlfriend Lisa.

Mac is pushing into his fifties and has been with the firehouse since his early twenties. He's been talking about retirement for ages now but loves the job so much he can't imagine not doing it. Honestly, I can't imagine walking in for a shift and not seeing his surly face waiting for all of us, but I know the day is coming, sooner rather than later. It'll be a sad day, but I'll also be happy for him, and for Lynn, because I know she has big plans for him when he finally hangs his coat up.

Shawn, on the other hand, is a young buck. He's the newest member on our team, and he fits in like he's been there for years. He lives outside of the city in one of the smaller towns up the mountain, and I know he'd love to get on with one of the little departments closer to home. Those positions are few and far between since a lot of them are filled with volunteers versus paid permanent spots. Still, I've written him a good letter of recommendation, and I hope one day he'll get what he's looking for. Even if it will leave a hole in my team.

Mac's been chatting Savanna's ear off since he sat down. I've hardly paid attention to whatever he's talking about, instead choosing to focus on Savanna's soft hand inside of mine, and the sweet scent of her that keeps washing over me.

I still feel like an asshole, but with each minute that passes, I let a bit more of my carelessness go. It was hard to watch the way she paled so suddenly, her eyes glazing over like her memory was right in front of her, though I suppose it was. It was reminiscent of her in the office earlier when Bryn came in and said someone was looking for her.

No, not someone. Some guy. It's a thought that has me gritting my teeth and squeezing her hand a little tighter. Raw instinct swells inside of me, protectiveness over the woman to my right building like a storm with the power to lash an entire city. Whoever put that fearful look in her eye better hope he never meets me. He'll regret it, and this time, unlike with Jordan, being a firefighter won't stop me.

"I'm going to use the restroom," Savanna says, breaking into my thoughts, and as I focus my eyes on her, she gives me a smile.

Reluctantly I let go of her hand and give a nod, watching as she gets up and walks away from the table. The restrooms are in my line of sight, which means I get a nice look at her ass in those shorts. It's the reprieve I need from my thoughts, and I can't help the grin that forms as I follow her with my eyes. I might be a gentleman, but Christ, I have some ungentlemanlike thoughts when it comes to that ass.

"How many fantasies do you think are running through his head right now?" I hear Quinn say, and look over to find her and Liam staring at me.

"All of them. Definitely all of them," Liam quips.

I point a finger at both of them, then look to Hailey and Brody, and hell, just for good measure I include Shawn in my glare. The only one that gets a pass is Mac, and that's because he's mostly kept his mouth shut.

"Every one of you leave her alone. I'm not asking anymore, I'm telling. Best behavior. If any of you fuck this up for me, I will make every single one of you pay."

I'm met with silence from them, each of their faces looking a little sheepish. Except Brody. Brody just looks like he's in pain, something that concerns me as his lieutenant, and worries me as his friend, but I'm not dealing with him tonight. If he doesn't think he needs to get checked out, I'm not going to force him. I'll have a chat with him before next shift, and I'll force him as his leader if I have to.

"Aye, aye, Captain! I mean, Lieutenant," Quinn says, saluting me, the sheepishness gone, replaced by a failed attempt to hide a smirk.

I love Quinn like a sister, but she can be just as annoying as my own sister with some of her defiance and antics. Between her and Liam, there are days when I want to pull my hair out.

"It might calm these two down if they knew if you asked her out," Hailey muses quietly from the other side of Savanna's chair.

She's right. Part of this is my fault because I was feeding the beast while we were on shift yesterday. While everyone has been hounding me all week to ask Savanna out, I expressed my nerves about it. Mostly to Liam, but he has a big mouth, so it's not like it was kept a secret at the house.

Since my uncle died I haven't had a single thought about dating. Unless you count those that were forced on me. It's been on the bottom of my priority list. And before Uncle Pete passed nothing, and no one, had truly sparked any kind of interest in me. I was always too busy with my career, too busy with the bar. So it's been a while since I asked a woman out. Even longer since I asked one out in person and not over some impersonal dating app. As much as I hate to admit it, Liam and Jordan are right—I don't have game. Something that everyone else has been quick to point out this week.

And… no one has ever been like Savanna. Fascinating and kind. Hesitant and a little unsure. But confident and feisty when she needs to be. She's a combination of sweet and spicy, just like the shot I made her on the first night.

"Okay, okay," I say, putting my hands up in surrender to all of them. I look around the table and every pair of eyes is focused on me, including Brody. "I asked her out."

"Oh, thank God!" Jordan exclaims from behind me, causing me to nearly jump out of my chair. "Does this mean you guys are going to stop making kissy faces on the couch and go actually fuck? Because the tension in the house is seriously starting to kill me."

My sister has impeccable timing, and her comment has everyone roaring with laughter. I'd almost forgotten I invited her tonight, so of course she would choose now to show up.

"You could always get your own place," I retort, my eyes rolling as she moves around the table to drop down next to Liam.

"Why, when you're so much cheaper than anyone else?" she replies with a sickening sweet tone. "So, what did she say? Where is she, anyway?"

"There's no way she didn't say yes with all the eye fucking they've been doing at the table," Liam tells her, a smirk pulling his lips up.

"Perfect. This calls for a round of shots since I'm not going to have to live with this angst anymore. Bryn!" Jordan calls as she walks by. "Can you grab a round for the table? On me."

"Jor?" Liam says, his tone amused. "I think you might be forgetting one thing."

Frowning, Jordan looks at him, her eyebrows furrowed. "What?"

"The angst is there because they aren't fucking. If they start, you're the one that shares a wall with your brother," he reminds her to everyone's laughter, except Jordan's.

I don't blame her when she balks, grimaces, and then scowls at Liam.

"Hey Bryn!" he yells out to her. "Make Jordan's a double! She's gonna need it."

CHAPTER 19

NATE

It's just after two in the morning and the bar is officially closed. Most of our table left a couple hours ago, but Liam and Quinn are both still sitting across from Savanna and me, downing the last of their beers so they can get out of here and let us finish closing.

"Well, beautiful, what say you?" Liam says to Quinn. "Wanna take a walk?"

She glances over at him and grins. "Take me home, handsome."

I can feel the question in Savanna's gaze as she gives me a sideways look. I smirk. I'm used to these two, but this is the first time Savanna has ever seen them together, so it's no wonder she's confused.

They flirt with each other on a regular basis, but it's harmless, and completely platonic. Has been since the day they met. I think there's some kind of unwritten agreement between them that says they can flirt endlessly, but it'll never go further than that. Neither one of them dates, both of them choosing to play the field to have fun instead, and they often play each other's wing person at the bar. While I know that Liam doesn't think he's capable of a relationship, I don't actually know the reasoning behind Quinn not dating.

"You two," Liam points between Savanna and me as he pushes out of his seat. "Have a fabulous night. Do everything I would do when picking a girl up at the bar. Which includes using protection."

I didn't notice it, but he must have grabbed something from his pocket because he's tossing it at me now. It hits the table and bounces once before stopping right beside my hand resting on the table, and I realize it's a condom.

"You're welcome." He holds out his arm to Quinn who is full of drunken giggles. "Come on, beautiful. Let's take a walk."

"I'm sure I'll see you again soon, Savanna," she says, looping her arm through Liam's. "Unless Nate deems us unfit for company, but he shouldn't because we're fun."

Savanna, though blushing exquisitely, laughs. "All of you were a hoot. I enjoyed myself thoroughly."

It takes them a couple more minutes, but when they're finally out the door and I've locked it behind them, I find Savanna starting to clear the table. I don't bother telling her I can handle it because I know she won't listen. Instead, I go to work moving the tables and chairs back and getting them in order before I grab what she couldn't and follow her into the kitchen.

I'm two steps from the swinging door when there's a loud crash and the sound of shattering glass. I'm inside the kitchen in a flash, finding Savanna already on her knees, trying to pick up what she can. Glass is everywhere, and I cringe, setting my dishes down on the counter before I kneel to help her.

"You okay?" I ask, her sandy blonde hair wrapping around her like a shield. Unable to see her, I'm unsure if she's cut herself, or if something serious made her drop things in the first place.

"I'm sorry. I didn't mean to, it was an accident," she says hurriedly, and the tone in her voice makes my stomach twist with knots. She shrinks into herself with each word. "You can take it off my pay. I know things are expensive. I shouldn't have been so reckless. I shouldn't have had that last drink. I'm sorry, Nate. Please don't be upset, I won't let it happen again."

There are a few things ringing every alarm bell for me at this moment, and none of them are the actual broken glass on the floor.

I've never heard her sound so small and distressed, like breaking a glass will be the end of her world. It sets my blood to a boil to think of someone hurting her over something as silly as this. I think back to her running from someone, and I'm more convinced than ever the someone is an ex, and he was abusive towards her.

I reach out to touch Savanna's hand so that she'll look at me, something she has yet to do, but when I'm about to touch her, she recoils from me so sharply, one would swear I slapped her across the face. The jerking motion has her hair moving from her face while her gray eyes dart up to mine, making it impossible for her to hide the tears pooling.

Every muscle in my body is screaming to grab her and pull her into me, but I have the sense I need to tread carefully, and rather than allow that raw emotion to kick in, I slip into my training as a firefighter. Savanna reminds me of a wounded animal, ready to take flight if I move too quickly or say the wrong thing. I want to tell her it's okay, that I'll protect her from whatever is haunting her, but I'm certain it would send her fleeing.

I may have pried earlier when she went to some other place in her mind, but I won't this time.

"I promise I'm not upset," I tell her in my calmest voice, the one I use for victims at work. "Why don't you let me clean this up, and you go see if Bryn, or Martin, need help with their cash out?"

She's shaking her head before the words are out of my mouth. Her voice cracks when she responds with, "It's my mess. I need to clean it up."

"Sav," I say gently, glancing down at her hands which are trembling so ferociously that I fear she's going to do more damage if she keeps trying to clean up. "I need you to go take some deep breaths and try to calm down a little. I don't want you to cut yourself."

Following my eyes, she looks down at her hands and sucks in a sharp breath. I don't know if she realized how badly she was shaking until that moment. It's enough for her to rise to her feet, dropping the pieces she had in her hands into the trash before disappearing through the swinging doors into the bar without a word.

A big part of me wants to go after her, to make sure she doesn't run out the front door and out of my life. I fear she thinks I've seen too much. She's been opening up to me little by little over the last week, but there have been a few things tonight that she's let me see, or hasn't been able to hide, and I have this feeling she's reached her limit with what she wants me to know.

I work quickly to get everything cleaned up, but Bryn and Martin are quicker. They come through the doors together, carrying everything for their cash out. I glance up as they come into the kitchen without Savanna, and an icy feeling of dread rushes through me.

"Where's Savanna?"

"She was just coming out of the bathroom," Bryn says, and I can see the question in her eyes. I doubt Savanna said anything when she went by, but Bryn is perceptive. "I left a glass of water on the bar for her."

"Thanks."

"You need anything else?" Martin asks casually, but his head turns a fraction towards the bar and I know he saw whatever Bryn did.

I shake my head. "Nah, you guys go ahead. I'll finish up. Have a good night."

I drop the contents of the dustpan in the garbage, give my hands a quick wash, then head back into the bar, worried I won't find Savanna anywhere.

My fear is unjustified, however, because she's sitting on a bar stool, the water glass between her hands, her head bowed. She looks just as small as she sounded a few minutes ago, making my insides churn.

I don't go to her at first, even though that's what my body and heart are telling me to do. The analytical side, the one trained to assess, calculate, and plan, needs a moment. And I wouldn't doubt that Savanna needs one as well.

I head behind the bar to get a glass of water for myself, letting her feel my presence before I try to talk to her. Once I've got my water in hand, I come around the bar and slide the stool out beside her, remaining quiet as I settle in, facing the bar. Trying to convey that she's the one in charge of how this conversation is going to go.

"The first time I dropped a glass," she starts after a moment, her voice barely above a whisper, "he yelled at me. I told myself it wasn't a big deal; he'd had a bad day, and sometimes after a bad day he'd get snappy with me over stupid stuff. We all get snappy at stupid stuff sometimes."

Savanna pauses and lifts her glass to her lips, taking a small drink before setting it back on the counter. I slide my eyes to the side, letting them rest on her hands that are once again on the bar in front of her. They aren't shaking as badly as they were, but there's still a tremble in them. It's not her hands that bother me as much anymore—not with the threat of cutting herself gone. It's the way she caves in on herself, making herself small. As though somehow by balling herself up she can protect herself.

Protect the vital, most vulnerable parts of her.

I want to reach out and touch her, but I force myself to remain motionless. Already I can tell that I'm not going to like where this is going, but I need to do my best at remaining cool and collected so she can voice whatever she needs without my feelings interrupting her.

"The second time I broke something, it was a plate. Nothing special like his grandmother's china or anything, but it still set him off. I was kneeling down to clean it up and I remember him grabbing me by the throat and hauling me up until I was on my tiptoes." Savanna blows out a heavy breath as I take a slow, deep one into my lungs, resisting the urge to curl my fingers around my glass until it shatters.

If I ever meet this douchebag, he's going to wish he'd never laid a hand on her.

"There were plenty of times in between where he'd yell. The bad days often outweighed the good ones. But I was young, and I thought I was in love." She pauses, taking a moment to collect her thoughts, to think about the story she's laying out for me.

My head turns faintly, just enough that I can do a sweep of her face. The same look from earlier is back. Eyes unfocused and droopy, mouth pulled downward, skin the color of ash. Haunted. The ghosts of the past resurfacing to plague her again.

"Pretty soon I didn't have to break anything for him to lift me to my toes. And soon after that, lifting me to my tiptoes wasn't enough for him. My reaction wasn't enough. God, I'd gotten so used to it that when I didn't react it made him angrier." The entirety of her body releases a shudder as though it too is remembering what it was like. What the horror was like. "I didn't always dent the drywall, but when I didn't, his fist would."

"He'd scream at me. I can still hear him, 'What the fuck, Savanna? You're so goddamn useless, you can't do anything right! You know things cost money! Do you think I'm made of money? Do you think I had a good day?' Do you think, do you think, do you think…" Her voice is louder, bitter, but her tone is lower, mimicking that of a man.

I clench my jaw, grinding my teeth back and forth. I knew I wasn't going to like this, but this is…gut wrenching. My instinct to protect and help those around me has always been strong, but there's a stirring in my chest where that instinct seems to bury deeper in a part of me that says I need to protect her at all cost.

Savanna laughs, the sound humorless. I hate it. I hate the sound of this laughter because it's nothing like the one she usually gives me. The real one. I swear to myself in that moment that I will do everything I can to always hear that kind of laughter from her. Not this cold, dead sounding noise full of apathy and pain.

"I tried to be so careful. Not that it mattered; he always found something to berate me about. There was always another reason to throw me into a wall. But I learned to handle those things." Another laugh sends a shiver slicing down my back at how flat and lifeless it sounds. "Wow. How pathetic you must think I am right now."

"No," I say sharply, my head whipping in her direction. I didn't intend on saying a word until she was finished, but I couldn't help myself. I need her to know that I don't think she's pathetic at all. "Nothing about you is pathetic, least of all this."

Sucking in a breath, I let it out, pushing my water away from me. It feels dangerous to have it in my hands for a question I'm not sure I want answered. "Were there things you didn't learn to handle?"

At my question, Savanna slowly turns to look at me for the first time. Fresh tears are brimming in eyes that are already red rimmed.

I've never known restraint before this moment. Every shift I have to practice restraint at the firehouse. The bar can be the same way. Dealing with panicked people in the worst moments of their lives. Corralling drunk people having the time of theirs.

But looking at this woman who has become a fixture in my life so quickly, all I want to do is wrap her in my arms and make everything bad that's ever happened disappear forever. And when a tear falls, and she gives one small nod, I know I'd do anything in my power to take away the look of pain and fear from those beautiful gray eyes.

"What happened?" I ask, my voice as quiet as hers was when she first began to tell me her story.

"By the time I broke the next glass," she says, voice thick with the emotion I see reflected in her eyes, "he'd learned what really broke me."

I don't want to know. I really fucking don't.

But I need to. I need to know the worst. I need to know how badly this asshole hurt her, and how badly I'm going to fuck him up if I ever meet him. Not that it matters right now.

The only thing that matters is Savanna, and how hard this all must be for her. Despite what this guy did to her, she's opening up to me, letting me in, and I'm grateful to her for it. The vulnerability she's showing me has my chest squeezing with tenderness for her. She's trusting in me not to take any of this information and use it against her.

Every day I have to go out and trust my brothers with my life while they put their trust in me. Trust is sacred to me, and I would do nothing to break it intentionally.

I turn on my stool and reach out, hesitantly at first, but when she doesn't flinch away, I run my thumb along her cheek, brushing away another tear that falls. "What did he do?"

Her lip trembles, almost making me regret pushing her for the answer. She angles towards me, our knees brushing, mine on the outside of hers. It's making it harder to stay on my stool and not envelop her in my arms, especially when she can no longer meet my eyes, casting hers down between us.

There's a long moment of hesitation, then, barely audible, she whispers, "Locked me in the basement."

"Fuck." The word is a harsh exhale whooshing from my lungs like I've just been gut punched. Squeezing my eyes shut, I recall how just a few hours ago I commented about locking her in the office. The way she looked at me after, white as a ghost, had little to do with the fire, though I don't doubt the little room I found her in did her any favors.

Fuck. Fuck. Fuck. I triggered her. I put her right back into the moment with her ex. Me. I did that. By telling her a part of me should have kept her locked in the office. How does that make me any better than her fucking ex?

Hands are suddenly at my face, pressing against my cheeks. As though she can read my mind she says, "You are not him."

My eyes flash open and I grit my teeth together, ready to argue with her. I should be the one comforting her right now, not the other way around. But she sees my protest before I can say a word.

"Nate, you are not him." Her voice is unexpectedly confident, full of life that had been sucked dry while she told her story. Warmth is pressing in close to me, and I realize that she's standing between my legs, having come off her stool.

Christ, I need this. Need her close. Need to know she's okay, that she's still here with me. Which is asinine considering all she went through, and I only had to witness it through her eyes. But I need to know I didn't do irreparable damage with my comment earlier.

"You are kind, and good, and thoughtful," Savanna says to me, her fingertips fluttering along both sides of my jaw.

My hands rest on my thighs, but at the brush of her fingers on my face, they slide over my jeans until they're gently grasping her hips. "Stop."

"No," she whispers, her hair dancing along her collarbones and shoulders as her head shakes. "You gave me everything when I had nothing. You've been my hope, and my joy. In the last week you've made me feel safer and more protected than I've felt in years."

Her gray eyes, now clear of old memories, peer up at me, imploring me to believe what she's saying. "You've made me realize that there are still good people in this world, and you've surrounded me with them. You've opened your world up to me and made me want things I didn't think I had any business wanting again."

Snaking my hands around her, I press them into the small

of her back, pulling her flush to my body. My pulse, which quickened with every word she spoke, is now hammering in my veins. She's making it extremely difficult to keep my control because I suddenly find myself in a position I've been in before—on the verge of kissing this woman.

My voice is gruff when I ask, "What do you want?"

"You, Nate," she breathes, the pads of her fingers pressing into my jaw. "I want you."

Perhaps I should think of why this moment is happening. Maybe I should consider if it's because I'm the only one that has offered her comfort. But I can't.

Her words are my undoing. The thin thread I had on my control snaps with her admission, and before I can think about it, my mouth is on hers.

Soft and warm, her lips are pliable beneath mine. My kiss isn't rough, but I'm not gentle either. And when that first little gasp of a moan slips past her lips to mine, I know only one thing.

Nothing is ever again going to be the same in my world.

CHAPTER 20

Nᴀᴛᴇ's ʟɪᴘs ᴀʀᴇ ᴍᴏᴠɪɴɢ ᴀɢᴀɪɴsᴛ ᴍɪɴᴇ ᴡɪᴛʜ ᴀ ɴᴇᴇᴅ ᴛʜᴀᴛ I feel deep in my bones. My body is full of butterflies, swarming so hard my head is dizzy with them. I'm positive if Nate were to put a hand between my legs right now, he would feel the wetness through my jean shorts. He's taken me from zero to sixty in three seconds flat, solely from his kiss.

Sexual tension has been building between us all week. Tonight alone we've been ready to attack each other more than once. But I wouldn't have imagined I'd be primed and ready after the conversation we just had.

He was so sweet. So gentle and undemanding. Allowing me to tell him in my own time, and in my own way. I hadn't meant to give him all the sordid details, but when the words started to come out, I was helpless to stop them. They've been bottled up for so long. The weight of them pressing into me, some days making it hard to breathe.

Nate took some of that weight tonight. Eased my burden, and for the first time in such a long time, I felt my lungs expand in a way I had forgotten they could. And now, with his lips to mine, I feel light and airy, my body buzzing with that hum of energy that I've started to become accustomed to being in Nate's presence.

He tilts my head with soft, firm fingers, and when I open to him, his tongue sweeps through my mouth. The taste of him makes me moan. Fresh and minty, and I recall the pack of mints someone pulled out that went around the table tonight. Perhaps for an occasion such as this.

Suddenly his kiss turns more aggressive, the sound I made propelling him to claim more of me. His hand slips into my hair, holding me against him as our tongues dance and twine together. I've wanted this since I met him, and now that I've gotten his kiss, I want so much more. I won't be satisfied without it.

My hands travel down his neck, over his pecs and abs until they land at the waistband of his pants. While I'm not going straight for the prize, I can feel him pressing against the fly of his pants as my fingers search for the end of his shirt. All I want is to feel some skin while he's kissing the breath from me, but I quickly realize he must think I'm going for gold because one of his large hands stills both of mine. Then he's breaking our kiss, leaving us both panting.

"Sav," he rasps, pressing his forehead against mine.

Tilting my head to find his lips again, I murmur, "Don't stop."

There's a muted chuckle from him, and while he kisses me back, it's not the same frenzied pace as before.

He also hasn't let go of my hands; he's moved them further up his body, pressing them into his stomach. That's when I remember he's not wearing his usual t-shirt, he's wearing a button down. I groan that I went so low and interrupted the heated kiss when I could have just gone for anywhere on his torso if I wanted a sliver of his warm skin.

"Sav," Nate murmurs into my mouth. It's a gentle request, not a moan. Not that it would take much to get him to do the latter.

Pulling back enough that I can look at him, my eyes are full of questions. Releasing my hands, he moves his to my face, gently skimming his fingers along my jawline which has my eyes half closing, a delicious shiver running down my spine.

"We don't need to rush anything," he tells me, and I nearly whine. I know it hasn't been that long, but after living under his roof this entire time, working in his bar, it sure as hell doesn't feel like we're rushing anything at this point. "I haven't even taken you on a date."

I blink at him. One of Nate's best qualities is that he doesn't push me into anything—for the most part. Under other circumstances, I like that about him, but right now I might go out of my mind because of it. "You're taking me on a date tomorrow."

"I know," he says, pushing a lock of hair behind my ear. "All the more reason to slow down tonight. It's late, and it's been a long night for both of us. Getting some sleep after everything isn't a bad thing."

Everything? I can't help but wonder if he means the drinks with friends—that one beer he nursed all night before switching to water, and my two beers and two shots I finished hours ago—or our chat. My confession.

Maybe he's right. Maybe it is better to get some sleep. I want him, badly, but going through my history wrung out a lot of emotions I've been holding onto. My body and hormones don't agree, but it would probably do me some good to get a good night's rest.

Dropping my head to his shoulder, I sigh. "Why do you have so much self-restraint? It's kind of annoying."

That earns me a deep rumbling laugh that I feel vibrate through me which makes my lips curve upward.

"Trust me," he murmurs into my ear. "It's not because I don't want to. I've spent most of the evening picturing you bent over a bar stool, laid out on a table, or riding me on the pool table. Those shorts have been driving me insane."

As if for emphasis, his hand drops, and he tugs on the hem of my shorts. The brush of fingers on my thigh, and the fantasies he's putting in my own mind, aren't helping the wetness pooling in my panties.

"I put them on this morning thinking about you," I confess, and I'm rewarded with a groan. If he's going to put thoughts into my head, I'm going to do it right back. "Don't think I haven't noticed you staring at my legs when we've sat on the couch."

My hands slowly slide up his body to his chest, my fingers curling ever so slightly as I press my hips into him. I drawl, "Or my ass when I'm wearing yoga pants. Or my boobs, especially when I'm not wearing a bra. Which I now do on purpose."

Another groan has my center throbbing.

"Drives me fucking insane," he mutters.

As if he can't help himself, his hands are wandering, both coming to my ribs, thumbs grazing the underside of my breasts. My nipples tighten, the sensitive peaks straining against my bra, and I can't help my moan. I know he wants it just as badly as I do. He needs to say screw being a gentleman for once, but I say nothing. I don't want to push him after everything he heard tonight.

I knew I had to tell him the truth after breaking that glass. The way I reacted, jerking away from him when he was trying to help, and then the tears I know he saw. I didn't have a choice. He deserved the truth, and he got it, even the parts that were hard to tell.

I was so sure he would think I was pathetic. Positive that if I looked at him, all I'd see was pity. But I didn't. That abrupt "no" he gave me, the words that followed. The burning rage I saw in his eyes that he tried to hide when I finally turned his way. It gave me the strength I needed to tell him the rest. It made me feel less alone than I've felt in months. Maybe years.

"Will you take me back to the house?" I ask, lifting my head off his shoulder. "We can pick up my car tomorrow after our date."

Nate's thumbs run along the side of my breasts again, and I can see the thoughts warring in his mind. The man is caught between fondling me and being the wholesome gentleman that he is.

Putting him out of his misery, I step back, my hands dropping from him, and his from me. Tomorrow after our date isn't that far away, considering it's the middle of the night now. Hopefully then he'll be more inclined to touch me in all the ways I've been wanting him to.

Taking his hand, I lead him back into the kitchen where we dump our water glasses, and quietly finish cleaning up before securing the safe. Neither one of us says anything, though we catch each other's eye more than once.

I know he's thinking about that kiss as much as I am. My lips are still tingling, and I wonder if he'll allow himself to kiss me again tonight, or if that would be tempting fate too much.

We don't say a word to each other the entire way to his

place, the silence thick with sexual tension pulsing between us. It's enough to make me ache between my legs, which has my knees bouncing with energy I won't get to expend tonight.

I don't want to wait. I don't want him to be so respectful. I want him to let go of his control and have his way with me, and I want that to happen tonight.

I have this feeling that it's not just him being a gentleman and wanting to take me on a date before he gets me in bed. He wants me to be sure of what I'm doing, and after the information I shared tonight, doesn't think I can make that choice soundly. I respect it, but I don't necessarily like it. I'm already positive about this and have been for longer than this evening. I just don't know how to make him see that.

The chance is lost when he parks his truck and we get out, his hand finding mine when we meet around the vehicle. Without a peep from either of us, he leads me into the house, taking me straight to my bedroom door. I think we both know where this will end up if we linger anywhere in the house together. When he turns to me, I have confirmation of that. The battle is still warring in his eyes, unwilling to lose the fight, though I don't think he knows which side he's really on.

I wish I could throw myself at him, or make myself start stripping right here so that desire would make the decision for him, but since we've met, he's always given me everything I need, allowing me to come to terms with things on my own. I want to do the same thing for him. If that means waiting until tomorrow, so be it. Even if it seems like it'll kill me.

"If I kiss you, I won't stop," he murmurs quietly, eyes searching mine.

He's still holding onto my hand, his fingers gently moving

along mine, like he's nervous. I can feel the uncertainty radiating off him; he wants me to tell him it's okay, not to kiss me, but I think he also wants me to give him permission to do so.

I give him neither. "I know."

Nate groans in response, his forehead bowing until it's touching mine, eyes falling closed. "I don't want the reason we do this tonight to be because of what some asshole did to you, that I then joked about."

My mouth opens to respond to him, then snaps shut quickly. It would be so easy to lash out and tell him he's crazy if he thinks that's why I want to do this, but I realize this isn't about me.

I suddenly understand it clearly.

This is about him still sitting on a ledge for what he said about locking me in the office. He's not worried about me not being ready, and he may not truly be concerned he hasn't taken me out on a date yet.

He's punishing himself.

I release his hand to bring both of mine to his face, easing myself back so I can see him as his eyes open. "That would never be my reason. It's so far from any reason I can think of to do this. But it's okay if you're not there, Nate. I get it. I told you so much tonight and I know that takes some time to process."

I stand on my tip toes and press a kiss to the corner of his mouth, lingering there for just a moment. "I'll see you in the morning. I can't wait for our date."

Then I release him and step into my bedroom, giving him a smile before I close the door, leaving him in the hallway.

CHAPTER 21

SAVANNA

I don't know if Nate had the strength to walk away tonight. I wouldn't have thought I did, but I knew I had to do it for him. As much as I want him, I want all of him, not just pieces that can be here when others are stuck in his mind, thinking things through.

I wish I'd thought of that stupid button-down while we were first kissing because I can only imagine what might have happened if he hadn't thought I was moving too fast. Maybe I could have kept him out of his mind long enough for him to be so into the moment that he couldn't have gotten out.

Then again, if he'd taken me right there in the bar, I wouldn't want him to regret it afterwards, or to think the reason we went there was because of Vincent and what happened tonight.

I sigh and squeeze my eyes shut, leaning back against the closed door, a flame of burning hot anger spiking through me. Vincent. As hard as I try to rid my life of him, he's still following me around, even if only as a memory.

The aggravation slowly dies out when I hear Nate move down the hall to his bedroom. Pushing off the door, I walk to the dresser and search for something to wear to bed, coming across my softest spaghetti strapped top and matching bottoms.

I smile to myself as I finger the beautiful forest green fabric. It's a far cry from Jordan's near see-through t-shirt, but Nate would probably find it just as alluring with the amount of skin it shows.

I don't regret telling him the things I did, but I'm disappointed that such a fun night ended on such a low note. Sure, there were a couple of bumps in my evening to begin with, but by the time dinner came, those things were forgotten, and we all had a great time.

It was so much fun getting to know Nate's friends. The way they made me feel included was a breath of fresh air. I loved them all. I loved the camaraderie they all had, the obvious love that they felt for each other. The way they'd pick on each other, and bicker with one another, and how someone would always come to another's defense.

After changing, I pad down the hallway to the bathroom to brush my teeth and wash my face, laughing at the memory of Brody's face when he realized he wasn't the only hockey fan at the table. It wasn't a surprise to me, thanks to Nate sharing that nugget of information one night, but Nate obviously hadn't shared back. Oh, how Brody had suffered when he'd jolted upright in excitement, pain from his injuries overriding enthusiasm I'd never before seen from him.

When he'd finally recovered, we entered a twenty minute conversation about our favorite teams, the blockbuster trades and signings, and the upcoming season. It was the most I'd ever seen Brody speak at one time, and it would have gone longer, but Quinn interrupted us declaring hockey to be as boring as watching paint dry. Brody had sniped back about her boring scrapbooking hobby, and thus the two began the great debate of who was more uninteresting. It was Liam who had finally stepped in, announcing they were both dull, and getting laid was by far the best pastime one could have.

They reminded me of my brothers and me. The pointless arguments in good fun, the laughter and gentle ribbing. The competition. The way this group interacted was like a family, and it warmed me all night because I felt like I was part of it. As I pat my freshly washed face and minty tasting mouth off with a towel, that warmth spreads through me again.

The longer I'm by myself, the more I realize how tired I am. Maybe Nate was right to stop things tonight so we can both get a good night's sleep. By the time I'm back in my room and plopped on my bed, my eyelids feel heavy, and I know it's not because of the alcohol. I may have had more than him—certainly more shots since he declined each of them—but I stopped drinking hours ago.

I start braiding my hair so I can finally crawl between the sheets, my eyes scouring my nightstand for my elastic. I'm two twists through the loose braid when I realize the elastic I used last night is still in the bathroom. Huffing at myself, I debate leaving it. It'll be a rats nest in the morning, but my eyes want to close.

Future me will hate present me if I don't do it, so I begrudgingly get up and march to the door, flinging it wide open. And stop with a gasp.

Nate is standing on the other side of the threshold. The sleepiness that threatened me moments ago vanishes when his eyes rake over me, mine doing the same to him. He's changed into gray sweatpants but hasn't bothered with the usual t-shirt I see him in at nighttime, standing there with a bare chest instead.

Shit. My body hums from the mere sight of him. I may orgasm from it alone.

In the week I've been here, I've yet to see him shirtless, and my god, I have been missing out. I knew from that first day the sight would be impressive, but wow, it's better than I could have imagined.

His broad shoulders were one of the first things I noticed about him, but now I'm seeing all the muscle corded along his traps to his thick neck. It leads my eyes to his chest, which I know is solid because I've run into it. But that isn't even the best part. Those abs. Oh my word, those abs. They call to me. Begging me to kiss all the indents along them, making my mouth go dry. And do not even get me started on the V that his hips make that lead straight down to his groin.

Fuck me. His groin. I suddenly realize how hard he is, his cock tenting his pajama pants. I know he hears my whimper when he shifts towards me, forcing my eyes up to his face. All I see is heat, his chest rising and falling with quick, shallow breaths.

"It would never be my reason either," he says, his voice gruff and thick with desire.

Then he's grabbing me by the hips, urging me towards the bed. I'm putty in his hands, going willingly, swiftly. My arm hooks over his shoulder at the same time the door closes with a click, and then my back is hitting the mattress, Nate's body following me down.

Before I can take a breath, his lips are on mine in a bruising kiss that makes my body tingle from the top of my head to the tips of my toes. It's frenzied, heated, our tongues grappling for position, taking us right back to where we started in the bar.

My legs part for him to rest between, and I wrap them around his waist, pulling him against me. We groan in unison as his cock presses against my center, giving us both the slightest bit of relief with the friction. Hands seem to be everywhere all at once. Mine at his back, moving over muscle, feeling them contract and relax as he moves above me. He holds himself up by his left forearm which sits near my head, but his right hand is at my breast. Finally. Finally touching me.

Cupping my breast in his hand, he feels the weight of it through my tank top before his thumb runs over a nipple. I gasp into the kiss at the sweet torture, the peak hard and aching in need.

"Need this off," Nate mutters, breaking the kiss to peel my tank top off me. Hissing in fervor, he pushes up to kneel, his eyes taking me in like he's a starving man. "So perfect."

If I ever felt my chest was too small, I'll never feel that way again after the way he looks at me, eyeing my breasts like they truly are as he describes. I squirm from the intensity of his stare, causing his eyes to dart to my face.

"I love it when you blush," he says in a deep sensual caress that washes over my skin. "But I think I might find things I love even more tonight."

Oh. Oh my. My center throbs with a fresh wave of heat, burning me from the inside out, at the promise I see in his eyes. When his fingertips move along my calves, I gasp, goosebumps rising along every inch of skin at the feather-like touch he uses along my sensitive skin.

"Mmm, yeah. Think I'll find lots of things I might love more," he murmurs mostly to himself. His fingers move deliberately, his pace making me writhe as he watches me react to his touch. By the time he gets to the bottom of my shorts, I'm out of my mind.

"Nate," I gasp. "Touch me."

His eyes dance with amusement. "I am."

To prove his point, his fingertips press harder into the flesh at the back of my thighs, kneading into my skin, nearly making me come off the bed.

"Nate," I whine, lifting my hips, searching for more of his touch as he continues to run the pads of his fingers along my bare skin at the bottom of my shorts.

Bringing both of my hands to my breasts, I pinch my nipples, pulling them taut because I need something, anything, to create the pleasure I'm seeking. My eyes roll into the back of my head, and I hear his growl before his hands gently bat mine away. Then he's over me again, his lips suctioning to one nipple, the other being rolled between his fingers.

"Mine," he mumbles around the tight peak. "Don't touch."

I don't need to. Not with him now giving me what I want. Need. But I'm glad I did it because hearing him claim me as his makes every bone in my body melt, leaving me in a more aroused state than before.

Shivers race through me as he sucks and licks at my nipple, then moves to the other, giving it the same attention as he did the first. I squirm beneath him, my fingers rooted in his hair, my hips rising into him, desperate for friction.

He knows what I want, and he's happy to oblige.

A hand slides down my ribcage, eliciting a gasp from me, and he pauses, catching the sound I made. Slowly his head lifts, his eyes glazed with desire, his smile lazy while he runs his fingers over my rib cage again.

I suck in a breath, my body shying away from the touch, but also wanting more. My ribs are so sensitive, always have been, and with him finding one of my erogenous zones so quickly, I know I'm a goner.

"Nate," I breathe out when he does it again, my hips bucking towards him this time.

The curve of his lips deepens. He does it one more time before deciding I've had enough. For now at least. Lowering his head back to my breast his hand continues its descent over my waist to the band of my shorts. When he doesn't find any panties underneath, his teeth tug at my nipple as he looks up at me with approval before cupping me with his palm.

Releasing a quivering breath, I push my hips up, silently begging him to give me more, and he does, slowly sliding a finger through my slit.

It's his turn to gasp, his lips popping off me, eyes widening as they dart down between us.

"Jesus Christ," he mutters, sitting back up. I'm blushing hard as he grabs the waistband of my shorts and yanks them down to my knees, leaving me bare for him to see. "Fuck. You're soaked." I watch him as he looks back to me, desire flaring in his eyes. "You're soaked and you're blushing. For me."

"All for you," I tell him, spreading my legs wider, moving my hands down my ribcage and over my stomach as if to entice him to stop staring and start touching.

It works. He makes quick work of my shorts, and then both of his hands start at my knees and make their way up the insides of my thighs until they reach my center. I cry out as he spreads my lips apart with his thumbs and feasts his eyes on my clit, running one thumb around it. It feels so good, I could practically come just from that simple touch.

He shifts on the bed, and then his face is between my legs, his mouth covering my clit, sucking with a gentleness I want no part of. Passion, heat, hardness. Those are the things I want right now. Crying out, my hips lift off the bed towards his face, and he groans, then sucks harder, giving me what I want. My fingers plunge into his chocolate brown hair, and my head presses roughly into the mattress when I feel a finger at my entrance.

"Yes," I moan, my eyes rolling into my head as he pushes inside of me with such slowness I think I may die before he fills me. He releases me from his mouth then, and I cry out in frustration, but he flicks my clit with his tongue as his finger slides as deep as it can go.

I want to scream at him. I want to moan for him. I want to combust into a million flames. He gives me one thing I want only to take away another. It's delicious, and frustrating, and I don't know if I should laugh or cry.

His tongue skims over my clit again. This time my hips are off the bed, and he takes the opportunity to put his free arm beneath me to keep them lifted. When he adds a second finger and covers me with his mouth again, pulling hard on my clit while his fingers work in and out, curling perfectly, I can't handle it anymore. I fall apart, my orgasm hitting me so hard I can't think with the pleasure coursing through every inch of my body.

He keeps at me until my thighs are forcing themselves shut, my body unable to handle any more of his ministrations. While he removes his fingers from inside of me to use his hand to open my legs again, he continues to lap gently at me, licking up every drop of pleasure I have to give him.

I'm still panting by the time he lifts his head and slowly ascends my body, a goofy grin on his face. He looks like he's had as big of an orgasm as I have, but I know that's not true given that I can feel his erection now pressing against my center.

"I definitely loved that," he says, making me laugh. "I also really love how fucking wet you are." His eyes shift downward for a moment, and I swear he'd bite his fist if he weren't using both hands to prop himself up. "Jesus, I didn't know a woman could get that wet."

"What do you expect when I've been in a constant state of arousal all week?" I ask. If I'd confessed this prior to his face between my legs, I may have blushed, but post-orgasm, I own it.

His eyebrows lift. "All week?"

"Give or take," I laugh softly, reaching a hand to his face, running it over the stubble on his jaw before my fingers move into his hair. "Pretty much any time you've touched or looked at me."

"Christ," he mutters, dropping his forehead to my shoulder.

His hips shift, pressing himself more firmly against me, letting me feel his length, which makes me groan. I can tell just by the few glances I've had, and now this, that he's well endowed.

"Can I make a confession?" he asks, lifting his head.

With a distracted nod, I slide my legs up his body, moving my feet around to his backside to pull him even closer. He's nestled right against my slit, his pajama pants separating us, and I rock my hips gently beneath him, but he's quick to stop me.

His voice is strained when he says, "Sav, wait."

My heart drops. While I feel a million times better than I did before he gave me that mind blowing orgasm, I want him inside of me, fucking me until he's reaching his own amazing orgasm. I want him to feel this good. "What's wrong?"

"Nothing is wrong," he says, pushing a piece of hair from my face while giving me a tentative smile that says the contrary. "It's just... been a while. I don't want this to suck for you, but I can't promise it's going to last long. I'm a little amped up."

"Oh." Not what I was expecting. It's so, so much better. I bite down on my lip, debate for one second about the question on my mind, and decide he makes me feel brave enough to ask, "Well, if it doesn't last long, can we do it again? Or is this a once a night kind of deal?"

Nate barks out a laugh and leans down to kiss me thoroughly. "We can do it as many times as you want," he murmurs, his hips lifting away from mine.

My hands are at his hips in an instant, helping him with his sweatpants. Then we're nothing but skin on skin, his lips gently caressing mine in a long, languid kiss. There's a crinkle next to my head where one of his hands is resting, keeping his body weight slightly off mine.

A condom. A man prepared.

Butterflies rush through my belly. He'd come back here knowing where this would go. Had made the decision that he wanted it. Made the decision he wanted me. Despite everything I'd told him tonight, he still wanted me.

Until this moment, until realizing that he made a choice to come back here with a condom ready, I don't know if I truly believed that he wanted me. On some level, sure. The attraction had always been there between us. But I know if I'd been left alone with my thoughts long enough, I would have convinced myself that I'd screwed everything up by telling him the truth. Relief in having someone share my secret or not, I would have been terrified to face him by morning.

His lips break away as he lifts himself, the crinkling getting louder as he tears open the condom wrapper. Even though it's been a while, he's covered quickly and then back on top of me, kissing me again like he never left.

Nate reaches between us, lining us up, and without taking his lips off mine, slowly pushes inside of me. I moan into the kiss, forcing myself to relax as he guides himself inch by pleasurable inch into my body until he's seated to the hilt.

He lifts his head, his gaze soft and warm, but full of restraint. He knows his size; knows I need the time to adjust around him. Or maybe he needs to go slow so he doesn't lose his control before we even get started. I don't know. What I do know is he fills me so completely I don't think I'll ever feel right without him inside me again.

"You okay?" he asks, his eyes intent on me.

I rock my hips beneath him, and he shudders in response. I think that's his control that I feel slipping away as I nod my head. My arm slips around his neck, and I tug him back down to me, my lips brushing across his.

"So much better than okay," I breathe against his mouth. "Now fuck me."

The discipline that always seems to grip him snaps. It's as if I can physically feel it breaking inside of him while he's inside of me. His lips claim mine as he begins to move, slowly at first, trying to retain some of that control, but I squeeze my walls around him, wanting more.

He grunts in response, tearing his lips away. Hooking an arm around my thigh, he lifts my leg as he pulls back and then surges inside of me, every speck of gentleness gone. It's exactly what I wanted. His cock is big, but I'm so wet that he glides through me easily, and I moan with the pleasure flowing through my body in waves.

It's never been easy for me to come while having sex. Before, yes. After, sure. Usually by myself. I stopped caring long ago if it happened during the act itself. My expectations have always been low on that front, but I should have known that Nate would raise the bar despite his warning.

Gasping when his finger finds my clit, I reach out and grab the blankets, twisting them in my fists as my hips buck towards him. I'm out of my mind with pleasure as his finger works me and his cock pummels me. I can feel the orgasm developing within, the tension building in my belly, anticipation filling every nerve.

Stars suddenly explode around me, and I'm in a million pieces around him, squeezing his cock. Nate wraps his arm around my other leg, pushing both towards my chest, using them as leverage as he slams into me until I hear a guttural groan escape him and his hips still while he rides out his own orgasm.

We're both breathing hard as he releases my legs a few moments later and collapses down on me, barely propping himself up with an elbow to keep from completely crushing me.

"Christ," he groans from where his face is planted against my neck.

"Uh huh," I pant, my tongue sweeping along my lips to wet them.

That was incredible. More than incredible, that was two out of this world, mind blowing orgasms in a row, incredible. I'm pretty sure every part of me is mush right now, and I don't think I'm going to be moving any time soon.

Unless he wants to do that again. I'd move for that.

Lifting his head, he plants a soft kiss to my lips. "Be right back," he says, gingerly sliding out of me. I whine at the sudden loss, hating the empty feeling he left behind.

Then he's out of bed and out the door. Good lord, I hope Jordan doesn't come walking down the hall and see her brother naked. That's the last thing she needs. Note to self, fuck in Nate's room going forward, not mine. At least he has his own bathroom.

When he's back and closing the door, I prop myself up on an elbow, raising an eyebrow. "You don't think that was a little daring? Jordan could walk out at any second."

"She's not home," he says, pausing at the side of the bed in all his naked glory, a washcloth in his hand. "Her bedroom door is open and she's not in there."

Grabbing my calves, he gives me a good tug, causing me to yelp in surprise as I move across the bed. Then he takes a few minutes to clean me up with gentle strokes of the warm, wet cloth in his hand. When he's done, I'm off the mattress and in his arms quicker than I can yelp, and just as quickly I'm back on it. It takes me a moment to realize that he pulled the covers down so we could slide beneath them, but when I figure it out, I laugh.

"Smooth."

Nate grins as he climbs in beside me, pushing me over to the middle before covering us with the comforter. "I have my moments."

"You have lots of them," I tell him, snuggling into his side, my head resting on his chest. It's easy to find the perfect spot against him. It feels like he was made for me to curl into him like this. "I happen to think you're smooth even when you're not smooth. I think it's adorable."

"Good. You're the only one whose opinion matters."

My stomach flutters, and I know my cheeks are turning pink for a reason wholly different from the physical activities from a few minutes ago. For a long time, I wasn't allowed to have an opinion. At least not one that I could voice without suffering some kind of consequence. To hear Nate say not only did mine count, but it was the only one that mattered, makes my lip tremble.

Wrapping his arm around me, I steep in his words as he aimlessly runs his fingers up and down my arm and along my shoulder. This may have been our first time, but I feel like I've done this with him forever.

"Nate?" I say after a moment of silence between us.

He's sleepy when he responds. "Yeah?"

I run a hand down his chest and over his stomach, my fingers finding the treasure trail of hair that will lead me straight to his cock. "Do we have to be anywhere at any particular time for our date?"

"Nope."

"Good, cause I really want to do that again. Soon."

"Christ." I can feel him looking at me, and I turn my head to gaze at him. He has this dopey grin on his face that makes my heart quiver because he's so adorable. "You just get better and better."

NATE

From the passenger seat of the truck, Savanna is turned towards me, staring. I'm trying my damnedest to keep the grin off my face, but I'm failing miserably. I've gotten her pout, her plea, her scowl, and even a huff since we got up this morning—afternoon—and she asked where I was taking her on our date.

It's driving her insane that I'm keeping it a surprise. I know she's not big on them, but given the fact she hasn't done a lot of things around town and the surrounding area, I really wanted to surprise her with something.

The only indication I gave her of today's plan was how to dress after she informed me she wouldn't know what to wear if I didn't tell her where we were going. I glance over at the sexy yoga pants I told her to put on and can't hold my grin back any longer. Her bottom lip jutted out when I told her to throw those on with some sneakers and to bring a sweater along.

When her initial scheme to get me to reveal our date didn't work, she resorted to another tactic—teasing the hell out of me. I'll admit, it almost worked. Until I threw her on her back and had my way with her instead.

Christ, did I ever have my way with her. If I'm not careful, I'll end up with a hard on right now, just thinking about all the ways I had her last night. And this morning.

I don't remember the last time I had sex multiple times in a night. After that first time, I had her three more times in between dozing off before we finally got out of bed and got ready for the day. We're both tired, understandably so, but I haven't felt this sated in years.

And yet, when my eyes slide in her direction once more, I know it wouldn't take much for me to be ready to be inside her again.

"Nate," she pleads once more as our eyes briefly catch.

I smile and shake my head. "I told you, it's a surprise."

I'm glad I made the decision to go back to her room last night. I know she was making it easy on me by saying goodnight and leaving me in the hall, but walking away didn't feel right. The further from her I got, the worse I felt.

As I brushed my teeth and changed into a pair of pajama pants, I knew what she'd said was right. I didn't want her because she'd told me about her ex, and it wasn't because I needed to make up for what I'd said about locking her in the office. I made that comment without ever having intentions of locking her anywhere. I was frustrated with my friends for their antics, but I'd never hide her away from them, or any other part of my life.

Did I hate that I made her remember things that are painful for her? Fuck yes. But I'm not going to kid myself and think there will never be more moments like that. There probably will be. They'll be just as shitty, and just as hard, but

I'll learn from them, and I'll be better equipped to make up for it next time.

"Nate," Savanna gripes for the fifth time since we got in the truck. "Please? I feel like we've been in the truck forever. Can't you just tell me where we're going?"

I snicker to myself. If she spent more time staring out the window instead of at me, she might have a clue where I'm taking her.

Squeezing her hand that I've been holding while driving, I shake my head. "Nope. We'll be there soon, just enjoy the scenery until we get there."

"Oh, I am."

The suggestive tone in her words has my head snapping in her direction, and she gives me a demure tilt of her lips, wiggling her eyebrows playfully at me. I'm about to have a big problem on my hands if she keeps looking at me like that.

"I meant out the window," I grit, refocusing on the driving. I need all my attention on the road with all the winding and turning of this mountain road.

We headed out of town and jumped on the freeway briefly, but it wasn't long before I was exiting it to take her up into the mountain range east of Santa Rosé. We've been steadily climbing for the past half hour, working our way through the little mountain towns along the way. When we haven't been going through one of those, the forest has closed in on us on either side, shadowing us with its dense canopy. It's one of my favorite places to drive; green and lush. The redwood trees are enormous and have an other-worldly magnificence about them.

The scenery isn't as beautiful as the woman beside me, and apparently she thinks the same of me. I can feel the heat of her gaze which she still hasn't taken off me. It's only intensified in the last thirty seconds, and my cock can feel it too because it's getting harder by the second.

"Savanna," I warn, bringing her hand up to my lips to press a kiss to it. "Look out the window before I have a problem I'll need to solve."

"I don't mind helping you solve problems," she tells me, and I can feel her body heat as she leans closer to me.

I drop our hands to my lap where her other one is now resting on my thigh.

"I will pull this truck over right now if you don't look out the window," I say, following up on the threat by slowing down.

It's enough for her to finally glance out the window away from me. I know she catches sight of the sign when she pulls her hand back and faces forward, craning her neck as we drive by.

"Are you taking me to the state park? Oh my god, is this the one with the big trees?" The excitement in her voice has me smiling from ear to ear. I knew from a few of our conversations this would be something she would enjoy.

"The redwood trees," I supply as we turn into the park. "I figured since you haven't been anywhere except the beach, you might like the change."

"I've wanted to do this since I moved here," she tells me, and now that she knows where we're going, she's completely captivated by the sights outside. "But I—"

She cuts herself off as I pull into the parking lot. The sudden silence has me glancing her way to find her staring at the trees towering in front of us, her lip caught in her mouth. Savanna looks a million miles away in that moment, but it's unlike the haunted stare from last night. It's soft. Tender.

Bringing her hand to my mouth, I press a kiss to it, and pull her attention back into the truck with me. It works, except her excitement is muted compared to where it was a few minutes ago.

She gives her head a little shake, as though shaking off the remnants of a memory, and her full smile returns. "But I never made the time."

That might be what she's telling me, and herself, but not finding the time didn't stop her. I've heard numerous tales of her adventures at the beach—or rather, the adventures she witnessed others take—but it wasn't time that stopped her from coming to these woods. For now, however, I let it go, allowing her the space to tell me when she's ready.

"Well, I'm glad you haven't," I say, pulling into a spot. The parking lot isn't overly busy today despite it being a weekend, but the tourist season is also over which makes a difference. "Now you get to enjoy it for the first time with me."

Savanna turns to me, her eyes wide with wonder and excitement. "Nate, it's perfect. I love it."

With the truck in park and her seatbelt off, she leans all the way across the console and plants a kiss on my lips. She lingers for a moment, but not long enough to suggest anything.

I wish my cock would get that message.

When she sits back, I gesture behind me. "I've got a pack full of snacks and water, but I'm not sure what you're up for. We can go for a walk, or we can hike."

"That's right, you hike," she says, a little twinkle coming into her eye. It's the same twinkle I saw when I first shared that I used to hike, and it was one sign that this might be something she liked.

"When I find the time. Grew up hiking all over these woods with my parents and Jordan," I tell her, looking out the windshield at the sprawling trees. "But don't feel obligated to go on a hike if that's not something you like. I just thought the forest and the mountain air might be enjoyable. There's a waterfall not far. Maybe an hour round trip, and it's pretty flat the whole way."

"I love hiking," she says with a laugh, but I detect an undertone of whatever it was that softened her smile earlier. She pushes her door open. "An hour is nothing, so if there's more, I want you to show me."

It's like this woman was made specifically for me. I told her last night she keeps getting better and better, and this is just one more thing to prove it. I would have been okay with a simple walk to the falls and back, but I'll admit I'm thrilled she likes hiking and not just being out in nature for a bit of a stroll. If hiking is something she likes, I've got plenty of trails, near and far, I can show her.

"Oh my god!" she exclaims, coming around to my side of the truck while I get my pack from the backseat. "This explains the pants!"

I look down at my pants and frown. I'm wearing a pair of gray quick-dry cargo pants. "What's wrong with my pants?"

"Nothing. Trust me. You look great in them," she says, leaning so she can blatantly check out my ass.

"Are you objectifying me again?"

It's nothing new, but she's always been more subtle about it. I kind of like this new, open way she has about her. I'm guessing it has everything to do with last night and cracking the lid on everything she's kept locked up so tight.

"Yes." When she straightens, she grins at me. "I've just never seen you in anything besides jeans and pajama pants. Well, and the fireman outfit, but that doesn't count. These seemed peculiar."

I laugh, conceding her point, even though these are usually a staple in my wardrobe. At least they used to be, before the bar when I had a lot more time for things like hiking and camping. Laying under the stars, listening to the wilderness roam for an entire night. I suppose it has been a while since I put them on, and probably longer since I was out hiking for a day.

Not that we have a whole day after staying in bed so late, but we've got a few hours, and if it goes well, maybe we'll come back out next weekend for a day hike.

With the pack on, we start down the trailhead. The trail is wide, large enough to fit my truck down and then some, and mostly bare of any tree roots or large stones. It twists and turns, snaking through the large trees that loom overhead, watching people and critters on the forest floor. A lot of feet trudge through these trees throughout the year, the park being an attraction for tourists and locals alike.

I'm more interested in watching her than looking at the scenery around us. She's filled with wonder at the massive redwoods that tower overhead and give us shelter from the warm sun. It's like watching a little kid experience something for the first time. Savanna marvels at everything, her eyes darting everywhere all at once like she can't take it in fast enough. As though it might disappear if she blinks too long. I might love this more than I love the way she looks when she smiles.

"Nate, this is incredible," she says after we've been walking for a few minutes. "These trees are beautiful. They're so big."

"And old," I add, then nod behind us. "We'll check out the visitor center when we get back. They've got some cool info on the trees and how old they are. I think it's something like twenty-five hundred years old."

"No way!" she exclaims, incredulous, her head whipping in my direction, eyes wider than before. "Wow."

Sliding her hand around my arm, she curls in close to me

for a moment, pressing her cheek against my bicep. "Thank you for this. I haven't been hiking in ages, and I've only ever hiked in Colorado. This is so different, but it reminds me of home."

Glancing down at her, my arm slips from hers to wrap it around her shoulders and pull her tight to my side, getting the sense that she needs the closeness as nostalgia grips her. It slows us down, but we're in no rush.

Pressing a kiss to the top of her head, I revel in the way she fits perfectly against me. "I hope the good parts of home."

Savanna slides an arm around my waist and looks up at me with the same tenderness she showed in the truck, nodding. "The best parts. Hiking was something my dad and I did together."

For a moment she's silent, looking back to our surroundings, deeply inhaling the fresh air around us. "My brothers both played hockey, and that took up a lot of his time. He carted me along with them because there was nowhere else for me to go, and I think it made him feel guilty. So he started setting time aside for just the two of us. He'd take me into the mountains, and we'd spend the day hiking together."

I can tell by the way she talks about her dad that she loves him deeply, something I noticed the night she shared more about herself. That night she sounded happy and excited to be talking about her family life, but today there's a new undertone. Longing.

"How often do you talk to him?" I ask.

Her eyes snap to me and I see the pain flash through them before she quickly looks away, slipping out of my grasp. She doesn't totally break the connection, taking my hand instead as she puts a bit of distance between us.

I don't push when she doesn't answer me right away, instead keeping quiet as we walk through the woods. Birds sing around us, and squirrels and chipmunks run along the forest floor or scurry up trees, rustling around for an acorn or two. The forest is a symphony of sounds, happier than the air that's encompassed us.

"I don't," she finally whispers, emotion thick in her voice.

I swallow hard, giving myself time to collect the disbelief before it comes out in my words. That sinking feeling is back in my stomach, and I know I'm not going to like anything more I hear if I keep pressing for answers, but I want to know. "Your brothers?"

I feel the deep sigh she releases as much as I hear it. "I told you before. I don't talk to anyone back home."

My eyes close briefly and I blow out a breath. She did mention that when she was telling me about references she didn't want to get for me. I never thought it included her family, but come to think of it, I've never seen her call home. Not that we've been together twenty-four-seven.

Christ. This woman is stronger than I ever gave her credit for, and I gave her a lot of credit. She's been completely alone these last few months, running from a man she's terrified of, with no one to turn to or confide in. That's a lot of weight to be carrying around by herself.

"How long has it been since you talked to them?" I ask quietly, giving her hand a small squeeze. I want to ask her why, but I'm certain it'll come out as accusatory. Still, the question remains: Why hasn't she talked to them? I understand why she ran from her ex, but her family?

"Three days before I left," she tells me wistfully. "It was Connor's birthday, and we all went to my dad's for dinner and birthday cake. They didn't know it, but it was also my goodbye dinner."

I stop dead in my tracks. When Savanna keeps going our

hands break apart, causing her to turn around and look at me. I'm frowning at her, and now she's frowning at me.

"They didn't know you were leaving? They don't know where you are now?" I ask, fighting to keep the critical tone out of my voice.

Wrapping her arms around herself, she looks down at the path we've been following. I'm not sure if she won't meet my eyes because she's ashamed, or because she doesn't want me to see what she's feeling.

Her head shakes. "My best friend knew. I called her before I got here and told her I went west, but I told her to tell my brothers I went east, so if they came looking for me, they'd go in the wrong direction. She also had letters for them and my dad." Lifting her eyes, sadness fills the gray depths. "I couldn't tell them I was leaving; they would have stopped me, or worse, they would have gone after Vincent."

"Which they should have!" My voice is nearly a shout, and I cringe at myself, lowering it a couple notches when I add, "I want to go after him, Sav. If I ever meet him, he's going to be sorry he ever laid a hand on you."

"Which is exactly why I didn't tell them!" she counters angrily, her hands coming to rest on her hips. "I don't need anyone ending up in jail because of him! Including you. Especially you!"

Gritting my teeth, I stare at her for a long moment. If I feel this way after knowing Savanna for a week, I can only imagine how her father and brothers would feel if they knew what she'd been through. I'm guessing she never let anyone in on the fact he was abusing her, but I'd wager a guess they had a feeling something wasn't right.

I realize in this moment I don't know a lot about the situation either, something I need rectified. "Okay, but why not call them since you've been here? You're out from under this guy, you've built a life here, why can't you talk to them now?"

"Because I know him. I know if he knew where I was he would come after me, and I don't want to put my family in that position. Guys like him don't just stop because you move away. They don't care if you call the police, or have a protective order." She throws her hands up in frustration but then they fall limp to her sides.

Defeat and exhaustion. It's all I see on her face.

"If they knew where I was, they could let it slip to the wrong person. If Vincent found out and he came here, they'd never forgive themselves." Her voice drops to a whisper as she asks, "If Jordan was in a situation and you inadvertently got her hurt, would you ever forgive yourself?"

"No," I say without hesitation. I already know I wouldn't because it's happened, and I haven't forgiven myself. I never will.

Savanna steps towards me, placing both of her hands on my chest. My hands drop to rest on her hips, dragging her closer without consciously thinking about it.

"Exactly. I will not put my family in that position," she says with conviction. "Part of me hates that you know as much as you do, because I feel like it opens you up to get hurt if he finds me."

My hands tighten on her hips. "You can't carry this burden alone, Savanna. I can handle myself, don't worry about me."

"I just don't want anyone to get hurt because of me," she says, pressing her face into my chest as her hands slide up around my neck.

I wind my arms around her and pull her flush to me, hugging her tight. "No one is going to get hurt. Not me, and definitely not you. I won't let him hurt you ever again."

I can physically feel the tension ease from her, like the weight of the world has been lifted from her shoulders and she's being set free to live her life instead of living in fear. I wonder if she realizes how much she's been carrying around with her all this time, and if she can feel it melting away as we hold each other.

I'm not sure how long we stand there, me giving her strength, her accepting it, listening to nature living around us, but I know it's a while before she finally pulls back and smiles at me. Her eyes are clearer than I've ever seen them, and I return the expression, knowing in my soul she's going to be okay.

"I know you probably have a million more questions for me, but can the rest of today be about us having a memorable first date?" she asks, looking at me earnestly.

Bringing a hand up to cup her face, I search her eyes, loving how close she is so I can see all the different colors in them. They're mesmerizing and I know how easily I could get lost in them.

"Only if it can start like this," I reply, dipping my head until our lips brush.

"Mmm," she murmurs against my lips. "Best way to start anything, I think."

After a moment, she pulls away, which is probably a good thing, even though I don't like it. Slipping her hand back into mine, she tugs me forward, and we walk in silence, taking in everything the park has to offer. It's peaceful and serene.

That's one reason I've always loved hiking. It gets me out of my head and away from the hustle and bustle of life and responsibility. It's rejuvenating to be out here, and Savanna adds to that feeling.

Before long, I'm pulling her towards a smaller secondary trail. It's half the size of the main trail with more twists and turns, but it's short and will dump us at the falls. During the height of the summer, this place can be swarming with tourists, but it doesn't seem horrible today. We've passed a few people on our journey so far, but they've been few and far between.

The falls are busier though, something that's evident even before we come around the bend in the trail that leads us there. Children's laughter and shouting are coming from that direction.

When we come around the corner, I hear Savanna's gasp at the sight before us. The waterfall isn't anything crazy, but it's stunning in its own right. It cascades over a wall of rock, coming from a stream being fed from higher in the mountain. The top of the falls is smooth, water careening over the side undisturbed until halfway down when the rock juts out, giving the sense that you could climb through it. I suppose you could if the rock face wasn't slippery, but the firefighter in me bristles at the idea.

A pool of water sits at the bottom, feeding a stream that takes the water further down the mountain, winding and twisting through the city below until it reaches the river and eventually makes its way to the ocean. Lush, beautiful greenery flanks the waterfall on either side and the pool below. With no rain for months, the water is slow and gentle, but in the winter and spring months it can be rip-roaring mad.

My eyes are fixed on Savanna taking it all in, and once again I'm taken by her wonder at experiencing something for the first time.

She's so damn beautiful it makes my chest ache. Her hair is braided today, and as usual, she's only wearing mascara, the rest of her face bare of any makeup that I can see. I like that, despite this being our first official date, she didn't try to doll up or change anything about herself. It makes her even more stunning, in my opinion.

"Nate, it's gorgeous," she says, her steps quickening.

There's an entire lookout to view the waterfall, though that's as close as we can get because there are no paths that lead to the pool below. Savanna pulls me over to an empty spot along the railing, leaning against it to take it all in.

I step up behind her, rather than beside her, and wrap my arms around her waist. When I feel her hands cover mine, I smile, her body pressing back against me.

"There's a nicer one in the park, but it's a full day trip, so it'll need to wait until we have a whole day. I mean, that's if you agree to another date," I tease with a grin.

She cranes her neck so she can peer up at me, one perfectly arched eyebrow lifted. "Are you asking me on a second date?"

"I'd say I am," I tell her, taking her by the hips to spin her around until she's facing me. I know the point of being here is to look at the waterfall, but she's far prettier than the falls, and she doesn't seem to mind as she loops her arms around my neck. "If I'm lucky, you'll agree to that and more."

"Hmm." She thinks hard, debating the topic, before finally giving a nod. "Do you think you're lucky?"

I bump my nose against hers, smirking. "I sure as hell was last night." That earns me a laugh, and I grin cheekily at her. "Hoping I'm that lucky again tonight."

"It's a sure bet," she murmurs, pulling me down until our lips meet.

It isn't the same sweet kiss we shared back on the trail. This time her mouth is hungry, and I'm instantly hard as thoughts flash through my mind of what this kind of kiss led to last night. Her arms tighten around my neck, and I know she can feel the bulge in my pants when she presses herself firmly against me, not leaving any space between our bodies.

Christ. I'd really love to find a private spot where I could have my way with her right now, but we don't need someone to come along and catch us. Hell, the people around us now probably don't need this much of a show.

Regretfully, I slowly pull my lips from hers, both of us panting slightly as we look at one another. "We're going to be standing here for a while thanks to that."

Savanna giggles, biting down on her bottom lip. She doesn't look the least bit repentant about it. "Which way would you like me to stand? Like this, or would you prefer my ass?"

"Jesus Christ," I groan, my hard-on pulsing at the image she's putting into my mind. I'm thinking neither is going to help my problem now.

Releasing my arms from around her, I spin her back towards the waterfall and then step to the side, though I angle towards her so no one sees the evidence. As casually as I can, I reach into my pocket and adjust myself, gritting my teeth as the thought crosses my mind that I wish it were Savanna touching me, not my own damn hand.

I need a distraction that doesn't involve sex.

"Do you want kids?" she wonders aloud.

My brain comes to a screeching halt. While I suppose kids do involve sex, the topic change throws me for a loop. It's exactly what I needed for my situation.

For a second I think it's completely random and out of the blue until I follow where she's looking. There's a pair of kids who are obviously siblings, running around, having the time of their lives playing as their parents watch from a bench, enjoying a snack and drink of water.

When I cast a look down to her, Savanna blushes. "That's probably not first date material, is it?"

My lips curve upward. "Doesn't seem like a first date, does it? Considering we've spent the last week living under the same roof, sharing a couch at the end of the day."

"Not even a little. Part of me feels like I should already know the answer to this, but then I remember we've only known each other for a little more than a week."

"It boggles my mind too," I tell her, then glance back at the kids running around. Even as a teenager I knew I wanted kids one day. Now, ask my aunts if they thought I'd even considered it, and they'd flat out tell you no. If I had, I'd be married with a couple of them by now at my age. Considering I'm only thirty-two, I always roll my eyes at them.

"Yeah," I tell her thoughtfully, still watching the family. "I'd like them one day. At least two. Growing up I always had Jordan, and even though she annoyed the hell out of me most of the time, I couldn't imagine not having her."

Savanna wiggles her way into my side, wrapping an arm around my waist as she goes back to looking at the waterfall, a soft smile on her face. "Same with my brothers, though I think I was the one doing the annoying." Lifting her eyes to me, she adds in a shy voice, "Same about the kids too."

Though it seems like a dangerous idea, I bow my head and press a soft, chaste kiss to her lips. Another thing we seem to be on the same page about, and I once again feel like this woman was made for me.

I'm in awe of not just her beauty, but her strength. To live what she went through, get away from it, start fresh in some place foreign to her, and stand on her own two feet without any help or support, amazes me. To let me inside her world, to trust me with the burden that she's been carrying alone, and to give me a chance after everything she's been through, I feel honored.

I know as I gaze down at this incredible woman, I'm quickly giving my heart to her, and I don't think there's a damn thing I can do about it.

"Speaking of families," I say, clearing my throat as I glance away and look out to the waterfall. I've been thinking about the best way to bring this up. "Tomorrow is Sunday."

"Your mom's birthday barbecue," she states, and I look down at her in surprise. She remembered. "Don't look at me like that, of course I remember. Your mom was very firm that she didn't want you there unless I came with you, and you made it clear that you'd get the third degree from the aunts since she'd be telling them all about our breakfast together."

I already know my mom has told them. I woke up after a nap that day to a bunch of text messages from a couple of my aunts inquiring about the "beautiful woman" I had taken to breakfast. I'm certain they must have a group text going strictly for gossip.

"Right. Well, I was wondering if maybe you wanted to join me. It doesn't need to be a date," I add quickly. "We can show up as friends, and I can tell everyone to mind their own business."

I run a hand through my hair, suddenly feeling just as nervous as I did asking her out on this date. "I know it's a lot really quick. I don't want you to feel any pressure because meeting the family is a big deal, but you have the day off, and the food will be better than anything you've had since you got to Santa Rosé. I promise you that."

Savanna turns towards me, her gray eyes intent. "Do you want me to meet your family?"

I swallow hard to keep from rambling again, giving her a firm nod.

"Would you prefer not touching me all day?"

I blanch, not having considered that previously. If we tell everyone we're only friends, whether they believe us or not, I'll need to remember to keep my hands completely to myself. We both will. I'm not really keen on that idea.

I give her a firm shake of my head.

"Then I guess you got your answer." When I eye her, perplexed, she grins at me, and it sends my heart into a gallop. "Sex tonight isn't the only sure bet. That second date is, and it looks like it's tomorrow."

Christ. Just when I'd stopped thinking about sex long enough to get rid of my hard-on, she makes a promise like that.

I'm about to say screw the rest of the hike so I can get her back to the truck where we can find a quiet road and I can fuck her senseless. Because if I don't? This could turn out to be one of the longest afternoons of my life.

CHAPTER 23

"I AM UNCOMFORTABLY FULL," I SAY, SAGGING BACK IN MY seat, resting a hand over my belly. "Why was that so good? I couldn't stop eating any of it."

We've just finished eating at a hole in the wall taqueria Nate insisted I didn't judge until I'd tried. I know from personal experience back home that some of the best things come out of these kinds of places, so I didn't judge it at all.

The food was phenomenal. Even now, being as full as I am, I'm a little sad it's all gone. Though, if they brought out more churros, I don't think I'd be able to resist. They were melt in your mouth to die for.

"Best place in Santa Rosé for Mexican. Don't bother with anything else because it'll never be as good," Nate says, nodding over his glass of water.

I believe it. This has been the perfect end to a perfect day.

Not that it's over yet, but I can't imagine he has anything else planned for us besides going home and crawling into bed. If it's anything like last night, sleep will be elusive. Even if we could both use it.

"I'm going to run to the restroom," I tell him, sliding out of the booth. He gives me a nod, and as I'm walking away, I can feel his eyes on my ass, which makes me giggle. If the restaurant wasn't so crowded, I might have given it a little shake.

I feel giddy. I don't know the last time I felt this way. Maybe never. I know for certain I didn't feel like this with Preston, and I definitely didn't feel this airy and happy with Vincent, even when we first started dating. I'm floating on air. Finally I understand what people mean when they say someone is on cloud nine.

Nate makes me feel free. I think that's the best way to describe it. He doesn't want to tie me down and keep me there, he wants me to fly on my own, and be there to support me. I know it's only been one date, and only a week that I've known him, but something deep inside of me tells me this is who Nate is.

I'm washing my hands when a woman with fiery red hair twisted up in a bun comes in to use the facilities, but stops just behind me, catching my eye in the mirror. "Aren't you that girl?"

"I'm sorry?" I reply, my eyebrows lifting high in surprise as unease pools in my stomach.

"The woman from the fire. The one that was in her underwear."

"Oh." The knot in my belly loosens its grip, but doesn't vanish completely for reasons I can't explain. Embarrassment for losing my cool in my underwear that night? Or maybe I'm just feeling sympathy towards this woman if she was also affected by the fire. "Do you live there too? Was your place okay?"

"No, no," she says, waving a hand with a small laugh that quickly disappears when she realizes how apathetic she sounds. "Sorry. I don't mean to sound rude. If what you said to that guy is true, you went through some horrible shit. I'm glad you lived."

I flick my wet hands in the sink, blinking at her in confusion. Turning to grab some paper towel from the dispenser, I look over to find her watching me curiously. "Thanks. I'm glad too. Were you there?"

Her head jerks back in surprise. It's her turn to look confused. "God no. I didn't need to be."

The same foreboding feeling I used to get when something was going to happen between Vincent and me is rearing its ugly head. I can never tell if it turns my blood to ice, or if it feels so hot that the rest of me feels cold, but I know it's the worst feeling I've ever felt.

The instinct to run grows stronger by the second, and my pulse quickens as my heart gallops in my chest. "If I sound obtuse I apologize, but what exactly do you mean? How could you know what I said if you weren't there?"

The woman looks dumbfounded as she stares at me. "Girl, you're viral. Do you live under a rock? How do you not know this?"

"Vi-viral?"

I'm going to need to sit down. Dizziness makes my head swim, the room moving in circles. This woman must be mistaken. I cannot be viral. What happened at the fire scene cannot be viral. Grabbing onto the counter, I lean against it, trying to force the room to stop spinning.

"Are you okay?" she asks.

"How viral?

"I'm not sure," she says, now sounding a little worried. I wonder if she's second guessing talking to me. "I saw it on the news first, but then it came across all my feeds, and I've seen it a few times, so…"

"Does that seem like a lot?" I cringe at the sound of my own voice. It sounds winded, hoarse. Unfamiliar to me.

I've completely ditched social media since leaving Colorado. My profiles still exist, but they've all been blocked on my phone. I've made sure to avoid it since I left. I didn't want Vincent to have any way of tracking me. It might have been a little extreme, but I thought it was better to play it safe than be sorry.

"Well, I mean, yeah? But maybe it's because it happened in Santa Rosé that it kept showing up for me. It might not be that viral," she says, trying to placate me.

Nodding my head, I push off the counter. I need to get out of here. The walls are closing in and it's getting harder to breathe. There's a crushing pressure in my chest, like someone is sitting on it, refusing to allow oxygen into my lungs. I need the feeling gone, but I don't know how to get rid of it. All I can think of is to get outside. Maybe fresh air will help.

There's a small tunnel of light from the bathroom to the door of the restaurant. It's a beacon of hope and I race for it, seeing nothing but the door. Pushing it open, I step into the warm evening, gasping for air as the sound of pumping blood thunders in my ears.

The outside air doesn't help. In fact, I think it feels more suffocating than the air in the bathroom. It's stifling and hot. So hot it may choke me. My throat closes with each breath I take.

When something grabs my wrist, I scream bloody murder. Spinning around, I go to hit whatever it is, but the world sways, and I'm pretty sure I'm going to hit the ground. Something stops me before I can.

It's the weirdest sensation. A second ago, there was nothing, but now I hear cars on the road, and Nate's voice trying to get me to respond to him. The tunnel of light has opened to Nate's handsome face hovering over me, concern etched into every hard line in his skin and rooted deep into his brilliant blue eyes.

I hope if we ever have kids, they get his eyes. Where that thought comes from, I'm not sure, but I don't think I'm completely coherent at the moment.

"Breathe, Sav. Deeper breaths, babe. In, one, two, three, four. Out, four, three, two, one," he says, soft but urgent, and I swear there's fear in his voice.

That's not like him. He's always calm, cool, and collected. Except when he's asking me out, which is so adorable it makes me melt.

"That's it," he nods his approval. Then he repeats as slowly as the first time, "In, one, two, three, four. Out, four, three, two, one."

Oh, he's good. I didn't even realize I was following his breaths, but the weight on my chest is easing, making breathing a lot easier.

Feeling better is a double edged sword, though. It's making me realize the gravity of what I just learned, which I think my subconscious comprehended the second that woman told me I was viral. If she's right and there's a video of me screaming at my landlord in my underwear, and it's gone viral, I'm a sitting duck for Vincent to find.

"Thanks," Nate says to someone out of my viewing range, then looks back to me, bringing the back of his hand to my forehead, then my cheek. "You back with me?"

My face flushes with embarrassment, but I nod. He's got me propped up from the sidewalk with an arm behind my neck, but it can't be comfortable for him. I push to sit up, ignoring him when he tries to get me to lay back. As I come to a sitting position, I wish I hadn't as I see the crowd of people gathered around us, my face heating with further mortification.

Nate must sense my discomfort. "Thanks for the concern everyone, but I think she's okay."

He waits a beat or two as people disperse, then I feel his fingers at my neck, and I glance at him, wondering what he's doing. It takes a moment to realize he's checking my pulse, his eyes glued to his watch, lips moving without making a sound.

"Am I gonna live?" I ask when he finishes.

His lips quirk, but I see the worry still written deep in his eyes. "It was touch and go for a second, but I think so." There's a hint of humor in his words, but it mostly falls flat. "Take a drink and then we'll see if we can get you to the truck."

He hands me a glass of water from the taqueria, and I sip at it before drinking it down like I'm totally parched. When I'm done, I hand the glass back to him.

Watching me like a hawk, he nods again in approval. "Good, but don't you dare think I'll let you back in that restroom if you have to pee now."

I try to laugh at his second attempt at humor, but I don't have it in me. "Do you have social media?"

Nate frowns, setting the glass down on the sidewalk beside us. "Sure, not that I use it. But I'm more concerned about you than social media right now. You want to tell me what happened while we're sitting here, or you want to go to the truck and tell me?"

I ignore his question. "I need to see something. Is it on your phone?"

His frown deepens. His concerns aren't the same as mine,

but when he realizes I'm not going to budge on this, he reluctantly pulls his phone out of his pocket. After bringing up an account, he hands me the device. "You gonna tell me what this is all about?"

I ignore him again, scrolling through his feed. It takes me all of three seconds to find what I'm looking for, the color draining from my face. "Fuck."

"What?" The worry in his voice ratchets up a couple notches.

Swallowing around the lump that's forming in my throat, I turn the phone around so we can both watch the video.

There I am, screaming at my landlord, the camera zooming in on me in my underwear. The camera person lingers on me for a moment before zooming back out. That's when Nate shows up in all his gear, wrapping his arms around me to pull me away before I commit murder. Saving me from myself.

"Okay," he says carefully, but I can hear the relief in his voice. I wish I felt any of it, but my inside fear slinks into every nook and cranny, filling me with icy cold. "It could be worse. I get that it's embarrassing you were in your underwear, and while I'm not overly keen on the fact people have seen you in it, it's no worse than a bathing suit. It probably covers more than some bathing suits out there."

I wish this was because I was in my underwear. I wish my underwear was the biggest worry.

Nate looks up from the phone to me, confusion in his expression. "You ran out of the bathroom like the place was on fire, Sav. Why?"

My voice shakes as I answer, "Look how many people have seen it, Nate."

He glances down at his phone, doing a double take, his eyes bouncing between his phone and me a few times before he runs a hand through his hair. "Is that five hundred thousand? Like half a million? Jesus. That's…"

"Really bad. And not because of the underwear." Sighing, I give him his phone back and go to stand, but I'm feeling a little wobbly still. When I sway, Nate's there to grab me around the waist.

"Easy. Go slow."

Pulling me into his side, he supports a lot of my weight as we walk back to the truck. I think I could probably walk on my own, but I have a feeling he wouldn't allow me to, so I don't bother fighting him on it. Besides, it feels nice to be pressed against his body. When I'm here, with his warmth seeping into me, I don't feel like I need to look over my shoulder every two seconds, which is exactly what I want to do given this new information. With Nate, I know I'm safe.

I let him help me into the truck and then take a moment to survey the parking lot. A shiver runs through me. Vincent could be out there right now, watching and waiting for me.

I know there's a chance the video hasn't ended up in Colorado. I'm not sure what the chances are, but with the video out there it's probably only a matter of time before someone recognizes me, if they haven't already. I could log into my own social media and see if I've been tagged, but I don't want to open that door. That door scares the shit out of me.

Nate climbs in the truck and cranks the engine. The AC is on full blast a moment later and he directs some of the middle vents in my direction. It feels good on my clammy skin.

"What happened? Between leaving the table and rushing out of the bathroom like it was on fire—what happened?" he implores, angling towards me.

When he lifts a hand to my cheek and then my forehead, I bat it away. "Stop, I'm fine."

I meet his gaze and my heart sinks. His eyes are intensely dark, brow furrowed, lips set in a hard line. Instant regret for my words sets in.

"You scared the shit out of me, Savanna. You wouldn't respond when I called your name, you didn't look like you knew where you were, and when I touched you?" His frown deepens. "You turned around to hit me."

I cringe hard at that because I can't deny it. I remember wanting to fight whoever had grabbed me. But Nate's eyes don't convey anger. Or blame. Only worry.

With gentle, slow fingers I don't bat away, he cups my chin, eyes searching mine. "Tell me what happened. Help me understand."

Starting from when the woman came into the bathroom, I tell him about the conversation we had, and what I went through when leaving. I can feel his eyes watching, assessing, taking all of me in, but I can't look at him when I admit that I did want to hit whatever had a hold of me. That fear had gripped me so tightly, all I knew was that I needed to swing. That I needed to fight.

Something I'd never done before.

"And then suddenly you were there, and things weren't so bad anymore." I close my eyes and breathe out heavily before opening them. "I'm sorry I almost hit you. If I'd realized it was you, I never would have tried."

"You were in fight or flight mode. I shouldn't have grabbed you, but you wouldn't stop. I wasn't about to let you walk into traffic," he says, stroking his thumb along my cheek. "Would have been worth the black eye if you'd nailed me."

His attempt at humor does little more than make the

corner of my mouth twitch. He looks as tired as I feel, and I wonder how much I took out of him with my incident.

"Savanna," he adds, his tone serious. "I will not let him hurt you again. Even if he sees that video and tracks you down, he's not getting through me to get to you. You understand?"

"I don't want you to get hurt," I whisper, my voice thick with emotion. Tears are pooling in my eyes even though I don't want them to, and one spills over as I admit, "I'm scared. Scared that he'll hurt you to get to me. Scared he'll use you to control me. It's why…"

I trail off, turning my head so Nate's hand falls away, the words strangling my throat as I look down at my fingernails. I'm picking again. Shredding my cuticles to nothing as my thoughts drift to my brothers. My dad. Maddie. Vincent never made a threat against them, never held them over my head to make me behave or toe the line. But it was something that always crept into my mind. Usually when I was locked in the pitch black with only my thoughts to keep me company.

It was the only thing that scared me more than the basement. Vincent didn't even need to utter the words. Perhaps he saw it written on my face.

"It's why…" I try again, but the words catch once more.

Nate slides a hand over the center console, holding his palm open to me. Fresh tears fill my eyes at the gesture. He says nothing, but I can practically hear the words coming in that soothing voice of his, "It's okay. You're not alone. You can trust me."

I stare at his outstretched hand for a long moment, my fingers stilling in my lap. A lifeline. To something real and tangible. Comfort and safety. Things that, until I'd met him, I hadn't felt in so very long.

My hand slides into his as my gaze rises slowly. His eyes say the words I can hear in my mind. I take the strength he offers me and try once more.

"It's why I left the way I did," I say on a breath, barely audible against the whooshing of the AC. "It wasn't just because I didn't want Vincent coming after me, or my family to go after him. I was so scared that if he didn't believe they knew absolutely nothing about where I'd gone, he'd go after them. I needed their reactions to be authentic."

Nate's thumb runs over the back of my hand in soothing strokes. "Sav…"

I shake my head, choking out the last of the words I've never said out loud, "It would kill me if he hurt anyone because of me."

Nate's upper body is over the console and on my side of the truck before I can blink, both hands cupping my face as his lips press to mine in a hard, emotion-filled kiss. The way his lips mold against mine, slow but urgent, I know he's once again telling me it's okay. I'm safe. Even though I'm scared, he's there for me.

I take everything he's giving to me, letting his strength seep into my bones. Finding comfort from every part of him that he gives me.

We're both slow to end the kiss, going in for softer, sweeter kisses as we break away.

"Don't worry," he whispers when we finally part for good. "I got this."

It makes me laugh. Full on belly laugh. The remaining tension melts away with the power of those few words. I love that he's using my own words to ease the fears in my heart.

"Thank you," I tell him, placing another kiss to his lips. "For so much, but especially for making me feel safe."

"I can't think of anything I'd rather do," he says, then

amends with a grin, "Well, that's not entirely true. I can think of something I like equally as much." He doesn't need to elaborate further. I grin back, feeling my cheeks tinge pink. "Mmm, love that blush. Gonna bring that out again later. For now, though, we have matters to attend to."

"What matters?" I ask, frowning after he gives me one last kiss before sliding back into his own seat.

"Well, when we're out on a call, we always want as much information as possible. It helps us figure out the best course of action. I think we need to treat this the same way."

He puts the truck into gear and starts navigating out of the parking lot and onto the road. I'm not sure where he's going with this, but he seems to have a plan, and for once, I don't question him. I'm too spent after the panic attack to do much of anything but hold his hand and watch out the window as Santa Rosé goes by.

I never imagined he'd pull into the parking lot of another park. This time a city park with lots of grass; soccer fields at one end, baseball diamonds at the other. Large trees surround the park and are dotted around the sports fields, providing shade from the hot California sun.

The lot he pulled into is quiet, though there is a baseball game going on across the field. There's another parking lot over there which explains why this one isn't busy. It's lovely, but I'm not sure what we're doing here, or what information can be gained from it.

Nate gets out without a word, goes into the backseat for something, and then disappears from my view. I follow him to the back of the truck where he's pulling the tailgate down and laying a blanket on it. He backed into this spot, and I glance across the field at the view from here, the ball diamonds straight across from where we are.

"I thought we were getting information?" I ask, perplexed.

"We are. Or you are. Come here." He reaches for me, and I yelp in surprise when he lifts me up and sets me down on the tailgate of his truck. Pulling his phone out of his pocket, he unlocks it, fiddles around for a minute, then hands it to me. "My number is blocked so no one will see it come up. Find out what everyone knows."

Imploring blue eyes meet mine. "Call home, Sav."

CHAPTER 24

SAVANNA

"What?" My eyes widen to saucers. Horror rushes over me. He can't be serious. Call home? I... I can't! "No! Nate, I can't."

"You can. You need to, especially with that video out there now." His hands are running up and down my thighs in a comforting gesture as he stands between them. "If they've seen it, they're probably worried sick. Can you imagine if one of your brothers disappeared and six months later you saw a video like that?"

My heart sinks and I bite my bottom lip, picking at a nail on one hand as I hold Nate's phone in the other. I hadn't thought of that, but of course he did. While I've been consumed by fear of Vincent, Nate's been putting himself into other people's shoes to see how they would feel.

My number one priority has been everyone I love, which sounds ridiculous because I know I hurt them by disappearing. With the secret of where I am out in the world as public knowledge, however, there's no reason I shouldn't call home. If the roles were reversed as Nate suggested, I would be sick with worry. And then I would be doing everything I possibly could to find him. Though, if I'm being honest, I would have been looking long before any video.

Maybe I should be glad they haven't shown up at my front door.

Not that you have one right now.

I frown at myself. It's not entirely true. I do have a door at my apartment, it's just that no one is allowed in. And the one at Nate's… well, they'd never find that one. But if they've seen the video, they might already be in Santa Rosé looking for me. My heart aches. If they were here, in this city, so close, and yet so far, because I didn't have a home they could track me down in, I would be heartbroken. As would they.

Nate sees when I put it all together, giving me a smile. "Quinn texted me earlier, reminding me of the slo-pitch game going on. She, Hailey, and Shawn are playing. Said I should bring you by to watch as part of our date."

He curls a finger around a tendril of hair and brushes it behind my ear. "Come join me when you're done, or I'll come check on you in a while if you don't feel like coming down. Take your time."

He cups my face in a gentle palm and leans in to press a soft kiss to the corner of my lips. "Then we'll go home, and I'll hold you all night if that's what you need."

"Okay," I whisper, and he steps out from between my legs, turning towards the field.

Anxiety grips me at the loss of his calming comfort, but he's only two steps away when he turns back and holds up a finger. I turn to watch as he goes to the cab of the truck before returning with a box of tissues. Giving me a wink, he places it beside me and then he's gone, leaving me to make a phone call I've thought about more times than I can count, and cried over enough to fill a swimming pool.

I watch as Nate walks across the field and reaches the baseball diamond. He slaps a guy on the back, Shawn I think, before they both turn to look my way. I lift a hand, getting a wave back from the other man. Then I see Hailey, her copper hair a tell-tale sign, and she gives me a wave as well.

I wonder what he'll tell them. I kind of hope it's something along the lines of him not allowing me to be near them after the night before. Just to get them back a little. Make them a little worried.

Taking a breath, I look at the phone and sigh. It's been six months. I never used to go longer than a few days without talking to my dad or brothers. I spoke with Maddie daily. It was a hard adjustment to make when I left, not being able to talk to my people. Something that never got easier.

Part of me believed I would never talk to them again, just so I could keep them safe, but here I am, phone in hand, about to make a call I'm unsure my heart can handle. Biting my lip, I pull up the phone app and dial the number I know by heart. I'm not halfway through typing it when it becomes hard to see through my watery eyes, but I manage to get it done and take a deep breath, pressing send before I can chicken out.

It rings twice before it's picked up and I hear my father's gruff voice full of trepidation. "Hello?"

I wonder if that's how he sounds every time he's picked up the phone since I left.

The thought or the sound of his voice, I'm not sure which, sends me over the edge. One word. One word and I have a steady stream of tears running down my cheeks. All the nights I spent thinking about this. The days I longed to hear him. To hear his thoughts, his laughter, feel his joy.

I can't help the soft sob that escapes, a tidal wave of homesickness washing over me. I need to pull it together so he doesn't hang up, but my heart is clenched so tightly in my chest, my throat feels squeezed shut. Managing words seems an impossible feat.

"Savanna?" he whispers, his voice quiet, like he doesn't dare dream it's me.

A heart wrenching sob releases from deep within. I cover my mouth and pull the phone away from my face for just a second so he's not more concerned than I'm sure he already is. I suck in the deepest breath I possibly can and let it out slowly before bringing the phone back to my ear.

"Hi dad," I say, trying to sound as collected as I can muster but the wobble in my voice is apparent.

"Savanna. Oh god. My Savanna." I hear the emotion in his voice, and I know he's trying not to cry, but there's a choking sound on the other end of the line as he loses his battle. "Savanna," he repeats, "My Savanna."

Nate was smart to bring me the tissues because I can't stop crying. Listening to my dad is tearing my heart out, probably like his has been torn out over the last few months.

I hate that I've done this to him. I truly do. Even if I had the best intentions, I hate that he's gone through this. I tried to explain as much as I could without going into serious detail in my letter to him, but I know it was little consolation.

Above the sound of my father's sobs, I hear, "Dad? Dad, what's wrong?" There's a fumbling sound, and then I hear Connor, "Hello? Who is this?"

I choke back a new wave of emotion, forcing a deep breath into my lungs. "Hey bro."

"Savvy? Holy shit." A short pause. "Is it really you?"

"It's me," I tell him, the corners of my lips beginning to

lift, though the tears don't stop. Talking to Connor seems less emotional than listening to my father, who I can't hear anymore. Either he's walked away, or Connor has, but I'd bet it's the former if I know my dad. "How you doing?"

"I'm not sure how to unpack that," he says in a tone only reserved for a sibling. I can practically see him leaning back against the kitchen counter, casual and cool, one ankle crossed over the other, while having this conversation. "Should I start with I'm glad you called so I don't need to go on a wild goose chase with Dev and Dad to the west coast looking for you? Or the fact that I've now seen my sister in her underwear?"

I wince, a deep frown replacing the smile. Obviously the video found its way to Colorado. I suppose I expected that, given the internet these days. All it would take is one person to recognize me and then tag my brothers, friends, or Vincent in it. "You saw that, huh?"

"I think everyone here has seen it," he says with a frustrated sigh.

"Fuck."

The tears have stopped, and I bring my fingers to the bridge of my nose and pinch, squeezing my eyes shut. I have zero doubt now that Vincent has seen it. That doesn't mean he knows how to find me, though. Staying at Nate's could be my saving grace. But I will need to be more careful.

I use my shoulder to hold the phone to my ear while I pick at my fingernails. They're red and bleeding, and they're going to hurt tomorrow. They hurt now. "How's dad?"

Another frustrated sigh. "How do you think he is, Savvy? Fucking heartbroken, like the rest of us. You took off without a word or goodbye, and you haven't even called."

"I had my reasons, Con," I say quietly, but I know I deserve every tongue lashing I get.

"Yeah. I know," he bites the words out like he's saying them through clenched teeth.

Grabbing the phone, I lift my head from my shoulder and frown. "You…know?"

"I made Maddie tell me what she knew. Why didn't you tell me?" he snarls, and in my mind I can see the look on his face. Anger pulling his lips taut. The hard set of his jaw. The crease above and between his brow. "You could have come to me. I would have helped you. I would have gotten you out of there."

"And then beaten Vincent until he was a bloody pulp?" I counter, trying to contain the sudden surge of anger that comes out of nowhere. "You don't think I didn't think of that? I ran every scenario through my head, Con, and this one made the most sense to me."

"It would have been nice to be given the benefit of the doubt that I wouldn't kill him. He's still alive now, you know."

The thing Connor doesn't know is Maddie wasn't aware of it all. She had no idea how bad it really was. I have no doubt if I'd told my brother certain parts, he would have gotten the entire story out of me. Connor is good at pulling information out of people. Especially me. If he knew everything that went on, I know he wouldn't have been able to stop himself from going after Vincent. Which is why I never told a soul, including Maddie.

Not until Nate.

I glance at the baseball diamond now, focusing on the bodies there, and it's easy for me to find him. We're across a large field from each other, but I can feel his eyes on me from here. My heart reaches out to him, wishing he were here to pull me in his arms and tell me it's going to be okay.

"Do you know if he knows about the video?" I ask, my voice as quiet as it's been since I got on the phone.

"He was tagged in it," Connor tells me, and I can hear the hard edge in his words. My heart sinks, and I expel a breath. Before I can say a word, I hear Connor say to someone else, "It's Savanna."

I expect to hear my other brother, Devin, when the phone is fumbled, but I'm shocked to my core when it's Maddie instead. "Sav? Oh my god, I have so many questions, the first being what was it like to be manhandled by a fireman?"

Oh, if she only knew.

I RAN NATE'S PHONE RIGHT OUT OF BATTERY. AS IT TURNED out, Maddie, my brothers, and my dad were all getting together to devise a plan to come find me. Devin showed up ten minutes into my conversation with Maddie and demanded to talk to me, during which time he proceeded to first ream me out, and then tell me how much he'd missed me.

Neither of my brothers had listened to my letter. Both of them had gone straight to Vincent to demand what he'd done to make me leave. When that hadn't yielded results, they'd gone to the police, but with my letters there wasn't much they could do. Or would do.

Maddie had done her job as my best friend perfectly. She'd led my brothers to the east coast where they'd contacted police agency after police agency, spreading my picture around. When Devin had finally packed his bags to go looking up and down the coast over the summer, Maddie had finally confessed the truth. My brothers had been furious with her. I never did find out how that got patched up, but I'm sure one of my subsequent phone calls with her will tell me.

The phone was constantly passed around, each of them taking the time to chastise me about not calling. I was mildly surprised none of them were upset I had left, just that I hadn't called to keep them updated on my wellbeing. Even my dad seemed okay I had taken off to spread my wings and fly, something I'd said in my letter to each of them.

When I talked to Connor the second time, I asked if he'd told our dad, or Devin, what he knew about Vincent. He informed me he hadn't said a word, but that they both speculated I left because of Vincent. I'm not surprised he kept my secret; Connor and I were always close, and he's kept more than a couple of my secrets over the years.

Each of them asked when I was coming home, but I told them it wasn't happening. For starters, I'm still scared of running into Vincent, not that I told my brothers or dad that. I did tell Maddie, though, swearing her to secrecy. I have this feeling she'll tell Connor, but given he knows certain details, I'm okay with that. I got the impression something more was going on there, but I decided not to ask just yet. I promised her I would call again, and we'd have a longer best friend chat where we could divulge the things we didn't want to say with my family there.

I may have mentioned a certain firefighter, though.

Nate was right to push me to do this, and I'm grateful he did. I don't think anything would have made me feel as good as calling home and speaking to all my family. Even though I'm exhausted, I feel refreshed and rejuvenated after talking to them. It feels like a piece of my soul was restored, and I plan on showing Nate my gratitude as soon as we get to his place.

He's sitting in the grass, legs outstretched, arms propping

him up, watching the ball game. I'm nearly to him when he looks up and sees me, a smile spreading across that handsome face.

"They're still playing," I nod towards the ball diamond.

Nate's eyes remain fixed on me. "Double header."

My eyes are bright as I step one leg over his, dropping down to straddle him. My arms wrap around his neck, and I curl myself into his warm body, pressing my face into his neck. The essence of him wraps around me like a cloak, and I inhale deeply, the scent of woods and whiskey filling me. It's as though the bar has penetrated his skin and become a part of him. It's not foul like alcohol, but spicy, with a hint of sweetness.

He pushes himself up a bit to slide his arms around me, squeezing me to him. A hand rubs at my back and his head turns, his lips pressing a kiss to my hair. He says nothing, waiting until I'm ready, knowing I'll tell him in my own time. I don't know how he's figured it out already. To wait patiently, even though questions must run rampant in his mind. Perhaps years on the job have taught him that wisdom and he's just extended it to me. In any case, I'm grateful for it.

"Thank you," I finally murmur into his ear.

I can feel his smile grow, hear it in his response. "I take it that went well?"

Nodding, I let out a content sigh before easing back. Running my fingers along the back of his neck, my mouth curves up. "My whole family was there. They were making plans to come out here and find me after they saw the video. You were right to make me call them."

Nate shakes his head. "I didn't make you do anything. You had a choice whether to do it or not, and you chose to do it. That's all on you, babe."

My heart swells for this man. A choice. I hadn't thought

of it like that, but looking back, he's right. It's been like that since the day we met on the elevator. Always the choice. The elevator, the hospital, the ride. Staying with him, working for him. Even the other night with his friends at the bar, when I could see so clearly how much he wanted me to come. Everything had always been a choice, right down to calling home.

I'm reminded of the feeling of freedom he evokes in me, how he wants me to fly, and he's just there to support me. In this moment, I know that despite not knowing each other for long, I'm falling for him. Hard and fast.

The thought is scary. But also…exhilarating. Fear lingers there, too, Vincent dancing in the background of my mind, but I push it away, not wanting to sully this moment with Nate.

"You're right. But I wouldn't have done anything more than dream about it if not for you," I tell him with a shy smile.

"Dreams are meant to come true," he responds.

Tilting his head, his lips brush mine in a gentle kiss. My eyes close and I savor the feel of his soft lips and the way they sweep across mine with a featherlike touch.

"Tell me one of yours," I murmur quietly into the kiss.

Nate stills, but doesn't back away. After a moment, I open my eyes, inching back a fraction. Enough to break the kiss, but still close enough I can feel his breath against my skin. His eyelids flutter open, and his gaze meets mine. As he does to me so often, I wait for him to find the words, not pushing or pressing, giving him the time to figure it out.

Finally, he responds, releasing a deep breath that comes from deep inside of him. "I dream of the bar being okay. Not for me, but for everyone around me. For my Uncle Pete and his memory. For Jordan. For everyone who works there and earns a living. And for…"

He pauses and I wonder if his arms weren't around me if he'd run a hand through his hair right now. Not born of the same nerves as asking me out, but because he's not used to voicing his own desires. His own dreams.

"For everyone who walks through the doors and finds some kind of solace there. People like Liam and Brody. Or the guys you met from the other firehouse." His lips curve upwards at the thought of the people who walk through his doors. "The ones who need an escape, even if it's just for a few hours."

My eyes are swimming with unshed tears. This beautiful, incredible, selfless man. Even his dreams are full of other people. It brings him joy when others are cared for. When he can make a difference in their lives.

I vow to make a difference in his.

"We're going to make your dreams come true, Nate," I promise him in a whisper, bringing my lips back to his to seal it. "I'm going to ensure it."

CHAPTER 25

NATE

"What the fuck?" I growl, slamming my hand against the steering wheel.

My eyes follow my sister crossing the street a few houses down, heading towards my grandparents place. It's in a swanky part of Santa Rosé with luxurious homes dotting the street with yards large enough that one doesn't feel suffocated by neighbors. My grandparents have lived in this house my entire life, with many celebrations taking place here. It's the only place big enough to host our expansive family of aunts, uncles, and cousins.

It isn't Jordan that has me angry per se, it's the man at her side that makes me want to punch a hole through something. I might not generally be a violent person, but when a guy screws with my sister, or screws with my woman, you can bet your ass I'll be out for blood. Paul and Vincent are at the top of my list.

Rolling my window down, I yell out to Jordan in a tone

that says not to ignore me before she's across the grassy front yard to the Spanish-style, creamy yellow home. "Jordan!"

Her spine stiffens as she comes to a dead stop, causing Paul to stop next to her. He looks in my direction first, lifting a hand in a greeting that I don't return. I stop the truck in the middle of the street, waiting for her to turn around and come over. She knows me well enough to know that I'd confront her at the party one way or another, and she won't want this conversation to be overheard.

She says something to Paul and finally turns, leaving him standing there as she stalks toward the truck. Even from the street I can see the firm line of her lips and the hardness in her eyes. She's not happy I caught her, or that I'm about to call her out on her date.

"What?" she says by way of greeting, and then glances around me at Savanna. "Hey Sa—whoa, you okay?"

My head snaps in Savanna's direction. It sounds bad to admit, but I nearly forgot she was there. In the passenger seat, she's white as a ghost, and my stomach drops as I realize I must have scared her with my outburst. My face instantly softens, and there's an apology written in my eyes, but she's not looking at me. Whether intentional or not, I'm not sure.

"I'm fine!" she says in a cheerful voice that sounds convincing, but I'm sure is only for Jordan's benefit. Or maybe mine. Either way, I'm not sure I believe it. "Just nervous about meeting the family, you know? It's technically only our second date."

"Please, they're going to love you," Jordan says flippantly, then holds up a finger in warning. "Just don't get stuck alone with Aunt Laura. She will talk your ear off, tell you every-one's life story, and then demand to know when you and

Nate are getting married and having babies that she can cuddle."

"Personal experience?" Savanna asks.

"Yes. Though come to think of it, that's every aunt that will be here, which is why I brought a date that everyone already knows and hates," Jordan says pointedly with a snide smile, returning her gaze to me.

"Is this where you've been the last couple of nights? With him?" I question, unable to keep the censure out of my voice.

The line of Jordan's lips flattens again. I can see her grinding her teeth before she answers. "Not that it's any of your business, but yes."

My eyes narrow at my sister. "You do recall sitting in my bar, crying and drinking over that asshole, right? Telling Liam and me how he was getting nudes, and sending them back?"

"It's *our* bar," she corrects with venom. I hold back my wince because while she's right, I'm more than a little pissed. "And they weren't exchanging nudes. She was sending underwear pictures, and he was sending shirtless ones."

I'm not sure I see the difference when the guy was supposed to be in a committed relationship with her. It's all semantics, but apparently not to Jordan.

"Okay," I grind out, correcting myself, "telling Liam and me that he was doing things he shouldn't have been doing."

"Look, I get it. You don't like him. No one fucking likes Paul. I know that. You know that. The whole damn world knows it, Nate. But I was not showing up to this barbecue alone, especially not when you're showing up with Savanna," she says, exasperated, and then looks around me to Savanna. "No offense to you. You just don't know what it's like to be single at one of these things. It's better to be here with someone than without."

"You could have brought someone else," I seethe, my tone far from calm and collected.

Jordan snorts with derision. "Like whom? Liam?"

"Sure! Yes! I don't give a shit. Anyone would have been better than Paul!" I hiss at her.

Eyes that match mine turn into slits as she glares at me, contempt coming off her in waves. "Paul's not your friend. It's not your life. So, it isn't your choice." Then she whirls around and strides away, leaving me feeling irritated and unsatisfied.

In a perfect world, she would have listened to me and ditched Paul right then. Unfortunately, the world is far from perfect, as Jordan is quick to remind me.

There's only one rule when it comes to her dating life and me as her big brother. No dating my friends. Even if I would have made an exception if she'd brought one of them with her today, Jordan never would have done it. But fuck, it would have been better than her getting back together with this douchebag.

A honk sounds behind me, and I glance in my side mirror to see one of my cousins sitting there. He sticks his head out the window and yells, "You planning on parking there for the afternoon, Nate?"

I give a wave and start down the street, pulling into the closest available spot I can find. Running a hand through my hair, I blow out a breath and close my eyes for a moment. The afternoon has barely begun, and I've already managed to upset two of my favorite women in the world. I really hope this isn't how the rest of my day is going to go, or I'm going to need some headache relief, sooner rather than later.

Savanna has been silent since her brief part in the conversation, and I'm a little worried about what I'm going to see when I look at her. I shouldn't have gotten that angry.

Shouldn't have hit my steering wheel. Seeing me react that way must bring up memories for her, and I don't want her upset. Not because of me.

Finally, I gather my balls and chance a glance in her direction.

She's sitting there watching me, a concerned smile lifting the corners of her lips, her eyes gentle and kind as she looks me over. I start, not expecting the warmth staring back at me.

"You okay?" she says softly.

"Me?" I ask, my eyes widening, incredulous she would be asking me what I should be asking her.

There's a soft chuckle from her as she reaches over and takes my hand in hers. "Yes, you. You were pretty upset with her."

"Shouldn't I be asking you that? I scared you," I frown, sliding my fingers through hers, pulling her hand towards me to press my lips to the back of it. "I'm sorry. I didn't mean to freak out like that."

She rolls her eyes good naturedly. "Nate, you need to be able to have emotions. Yes, it startled me, but so does running into someone when I come around a corner. Life happens."

Eyeing her skeptically, I don't have a chance to answer before hands slam down on the truck beside me and my cousin's head is halfway through the window, surprising both Savanna and me. "Yo, man! You brought a date? Fuck, you should have texted me. I thought for sure you'd be here single, and I wouldn't be the only one they'd come after."

"Ah, Savanna, meet Danny. Danny, this is Savanna," I introduce them.

He shoves his arm through the window and extends his hand across me to shake hers.

"Danny is one of my cousins," I tell her, and then to him, "Savanna is…"

I realize I have no idea what to call her. My date sounds kind of pathetic, like I picked her up specifically for the party, but given that it's our second date, I haven't exactly asked her to be my girlfriend. If that's something people do these days. Hell, even if they don't, I planned on it. I just figured it was too soon.

"His girlfriend," she supplies easily without missing a beat.

My head snaps in her direction, and I see a friendly smile for Danny, but her eyes turn shy as she glances at me.

"Well shit. I don't think Nate's brought a girlfriend around for five years. It's good to meet you!" Danny gives me a slug on the arm and grins at me, drawing my attention back to him. "She's a knockout, man. Good for you. But also, fuck you for leaving me hanging here."

Without an answer he shoves his hands into his pockets and walks across the street to join the party, making me feel a little remorseful leaving him high and dry.

Turning back to Savanna, I know two things. She's snickering at me, and Danny is right. She is a knockout.

Her long blonde hair is curled in waves and falls all over her shoulders and cleavage. She's got a little extra makeup on today that accentuates her high cheekbones, almond shaped eyes, and those perfectly kissable lips. I think what gets me the most, however, is her dress; a sky blue, off-the-shoulder sundress that alludes to her being braless. It hits her just above the knee to show off those perfect calves I enjoy so much.

It's cute, flirty, and the second I saw her wearing it, I wanted to get her out of it. I can't wait until later when I can do just that.

That's coming from a guy who has had two very athletically paced nights in a row. This woman drives me crazy, and I can't seem to keep my hands off her. Not that that's a bad thing, especially when she can't keep her hands to herself either.

"What's so funny?" I ask her.

She full on laughs. "Your dating life really is the center of everyone's attention."

"You mean my lack of dating life. Now I've got you, so people will soon forget about me." I smile at her, bringing her hand back to my lips as I look her up and down, amusement in my eyes. "Girlfriend, huh?"

Color blooms across her cheeks. "For the day at least. I thought it was easier than anything else, and you seemed to be at a loss."

"Maybe it shouldn't just be for the day," I say with confidence, surprising myself.

I seem to have trouble asking this woman on dates, but suggesting she be my girlfriend is no problem. Holy shit, maybe I do have game.

Savanna lifts an eyebrow at me. "Maybe?"

"Well, yeah, I mean… you know. Maybe it should be longer than that. Maybe you should just, you know, be my girlfriend. If you want. I know this is only our second date, but—" I catch myself, realizing I'm stammering my way through this like a fool. I take a steadying breath and try again. "With the way we've been living together, it just feels… longer. Feels right. You know?"

Nope. No game. And now my palms are sweaty. Unfortunate for me since I'm still holding her hand.

I can tell she's trying her best not to giggle right now. I'm fairly sure this is highly amusing for her, but she does her best to keep a straight face when she says, "Are you asking me a question? Or merely suggesting this?"

Running my free hand through my hair, I take a deep breath. I've seen this woman gloriously naked. I've made her come multiple times. I've gotten very intimate with many parts of her body. This shouldn't be that hard, but I'm nervous as hell.

"I'm asking a question," I hedge, gauging her reaction. I never want to play poker against her, because her face is remaining rather neutral while I try to gather some courage. "Will you be my girlfriend?"

I feel dazed by the smile that lights up her face with such happiness it makes my heart swell and my chest puff with pride.

She starts to lean towards me over the console. "Well, to my boss Nate, you should know I might want to take weird days off during the week."

"Oh?" I raise an eyebrow. "Why is that?"

"Because my boyfriend does long shift work, and I think I'd definitely like to spend some days off with him," she says with a grin.

"Hmm. Well, I'll have to see what I can do for you, but I'm sure we can work something out." I grin back at her, moving across the console to meet her halfway.

"Dating the boss comes with some perks, huh?" she asks, her lips almost touching mine.

"It definitely does. I'll have to show you some others later," I tell her, closing the last bit of distance between us, my lips capturing hers in a sweet, tender kiss.

~

"Where have you been? You're late!" My mother admonishes as Savanna and I walk in the front door. When she notices Savanna in the next breath she squeals with delight. "You made it!"

We could have gone through the side yard to the back, but Savanna needed the bathroom before we joined the party, so I opted for the front door thinking we'd be in and out without anyone noticing. I should have known better.

"You told him not to show up without me," Savanna teases as my mom embraces her in a hug. "Good to see you again, Elizabeth. Happy birthday."

"And you, my dear. This dress is lovely. You look beautiful," my mom says as she lets go of Savanna and turns to me. I get a smack on the shoulder instead of the warm embrace. "Where've you been?"

"Picking up your gift," I tell her smoothly, holding up the gift bag in my right hand. Inside is a beautiful white gold pendant in the shape of a heart with a rose gold rose through the center. It's a bit of a lie considering I picked it up the other day. I hold up my other hand, showing her another bag with a bottle of wine in it. "And picking this up for the collection."

My mom doesn't need to know the sweet kiss Savanna and I shared turned into a full-blown make-out session like we were a couple of teenagers. When we were finally done, I needed another five minutes to lose the raging hard-on we'd created. It took every ounce of willpower in me not to drive us to some deserted parking lot so I could be inside her. Because fuck, I wanted to be inside her. Knew how bad she wanted the same. Knew without going up the skirt of her dress she'd be dripping wet for me.

She makes me delirious with need. If I were ever to be caught in a compromising position in public, it could cost me my job, one thing I love the most in my life, and two days in a row I've considered it.

I glance at Savanna now. She's smiling brightly at my mom, but steals a look at me. The memory of the truck passes between us, and the only thing keeping my dick from going rock hard all over again is my mother standing before us, taking her gift from my hands.

"Oh Nathan, you shouldn't have! But I'm so glad you did," she says with a twinkle of laughter.

Much to my chagrin—or relief, I'm not sure—she chooses that moment to finally give me the hug I was waiting for. It's easier to control raging hormones when you're being hugged by your mother.

I give her a tight squeeze and press a kiss to the top of her head. "Happy birthday, mom."

When we release each other, Savanna doesn't meet my eyes, instead looking at my mom. "Could someone point me in the direction of the bathroom?"

"Right down here, dear!" my mom says, pointing down the hallway to our left. "First one on your right."

"I'll wait for you in the kitchen," I tell Savanna, pointing towards the back of the house. She'll have to go through the formal living room and dining room before finding the more casual areas of the house, but I have no doubt she'll be able to find it.

She gives me a smile, our eyes catching once more. My dick twitches, begging me to go after her as she heads to the bathroom. A room with a lock. Away from prying eyes. No threat to my job.

Use the other head, man. Mom's birthday. Think of mom's birthday.

Right. My mother. Who is staring at me with a bemused look on her face, like she knows exactly which head was doing the thinking. My neck burns and I know I'm turning crimson, but she remains silent, shockingly, as I hook an arm around her shoulder and start to lead her towards the kitchen.

Even more surprising is the lack of questions. I was prepared to answer them, especially with Savanna nowhere in sight, but she doesn't ask a single one.

I understand why when we walk into the warm brown kitchen and find three of my aunts working away around one of two islands in the middle of the enormous room. I cringe, realizing I should have thought about this before entering the lion's den.

"Is it true?" Aunt Laura asks, standing at the island furthest from me, washing carrots.

Aunt Rita, cutting up potatoes at the first island, waves her knife at me. "Is she here?"

"Where is she?" Aunt Shirley questions from the island with the sink, smashing a hamburger patty between her hands.

As if they planned it out, they ask the questions in succession. It's a coordinated dance between the three of them, something my cousins and I swear they've rehearsed a million times, though the questions always differ slightly. These three aunts—there're two more who are the wives of my uncles, plus my mom—are all my dad's sisters and the family resemblance runs strong.

Three pairs of lively blue eyes stare at me from where I've stopped just inside the kitchen, my mom still under my arm. Aunt Shirley with her blonde hair, and Aunts Laura and Rita with their dark brown. Their expectant looks are all the same, and I know if they were smiling, those smiles would look near identical to the one my grandmother has.

My mother steps away from me to rejoin the others,

giving me a smug look as I run a hand through my hair. The four of them look like the rainbow, each one wearing a bright color to match their outgoing, busy personalities.

"It's true, I saw her with my own eyes," my mom says, setting her gift on the far granite countertop where a few others sit for later. "She'll be right along any second now, ladies."

The questions come at me all at once, each aunt talking over the next, volleying for my attention. I put my hands up to silence them, astonished when it works. The aunts aren't known for quieting, but a second later I realize it had nothing to do with me, and everything to do with the female presence now standing beside me.

Savanna looks exquisite with the blush coating her cheeks, and I slip an arm around her shoulder, urging her into my side. Shielding her physically for what I know is coming. Not that it'll do her any good.

Aunt Rita is the first to murmur into the now quiet space, save for the laughter and chatter I can hear coming from outside. "My heavens."

"She's gorgeous," Aunt Shirley breathes to her sisters and my mom.

"Mmmhm," my mom hums her approval.

Aunt Laura's fingers are hovering near her lips, her eyes sweeping Savanna up and down like the others. They turn to me next and give me an assessing glance. "Can you imagine? The babies…"

Savanna's arm wraps around my waist and I glance down at her, an apology written in the furrow of my brow and tight line of my lips. There's nothing but ease and a twinkle of mischief in those gray eyes, though, and she turns back to look at my aunts, her smile as bright as I've seen it.

"I know," Savanna nods at them as though they've all been

the best of friends for years. "I picked him because I knew we'd have beautiful kids. Two, I hope. One boy and one girl." She lifts her hand and waves it dismissively. "But it'll be a while. We'll need to get married and settled before we think of them. Maybe two years?"

My eyebrows are as high as they'll reach on my forehead, my eyes wide. My shock has nothing to do with the plan that Savanna lays out before them. That doesn't bother me at all. Because I can see it. I want it. Whether she's being serious or not, I can picture it all.

My astonishment is how easy this is for her. How easy she made it look to come into the lion's den and meet them head on. Gave them the meal they wanted to feast on, but didn't allow them to play with their food first.

No one says a thing. No one even moves. We all just stare at the woman tucked under my arm, smiling broadly at everyone else. Not one of my cousin's partners has rendered the aunts speechless. I'm not sure if it's happened in their entire lives. But Savanna…

Her "I got this" attitude is the sexiest thing I've ever experienced.

"I'm not sure I can wait that long to knock you up," I finally say, breaking the silence. "We may need to talk about this timeline. Married in three months, pregnant in six? As long as we have no issues conceiving that is."

Beside me Savanna's shoulders shake with a silent chuckle. It's my mother, however, who catches my eye and throws down the towel she'd picked up to dry dishes before Savanna walked in.

"Oh Nathan," she calls, exasperated. "Don't tease me like that! It's my birthday!"

Savanna and I both break out in laughter, followed by each aunt, one by one, as they realize they've been duped.

After we all share in the laugh, I make the formal introductions, but the flurry of questions I expected never comes. Yeah, they fawn over how pretty Savanna is, and murmur amongst themselves, but unlike the rest of my cousins in the past, we're not subjected to an inquiry.

It makes my blood hum. A weight I hadn't known existed lifts away and I can breathe just a little easier. I'd been concerned about Savanna being able to handle this, just as I'd been concerned about her handling my friends. The worry hadn't been warranted though.

I should have known.

NATE

I FINALLY MANAGE TO PULL HER AWAY, USING THE EXCUSE THAT I need to get her a drink and show her around. They don't let us go until I promise we'll all talk again before the day is over, and as we walk away, I can hear them talking about how she'll fit right in with the whole family.

My grandparents house is built into the side of a sloping lot. A large bungalow with a walk out basement that leads to the sprawling backyard and rolling hills beyond. While I could have taken her out the patio doors off the kitchen to the large deck that overlooks the land to join everyone in the backyard, I opt to lead Savanna downstairs to give her a tour of the entire house.

At the top of the stairs, I halt, gripping Savanna's hand tightly to bring her to a stop as well. She turns to look at me, her eyes curious, and I glance towards the basement. It should have occurred to me before I decided on this route that it would potentially be triggering for Savanna. "We can go out the other way if you'd rather."

There's a furrow in Savanna's brow as she glances down the stairs, then back to me. It takes her a moment, but something she must see on my face makes recognition dawn. "I'm okay, Nate." She gives me a reassuring smile, bumping her shoulder into me. "It's open and bright, with no door."

I assess her for one more moment before giving her a nod, satisfied that I won't be putting her into a bad head space by taking her downstairs. A second later, I'm guiding her again.

The stairs leading to the basement open up to a large games room with a pool table and shuffleboard—the setting for many late night competitions between me and my cousins during family gatherings. Beyond that lies a casual family room filled with oversized couches and chairs, and a big screen TV that fills almost the entire wall beside the corner with a small wet bar.

To my surprise, the basement is empty. With a family as large as ours, it's not often you find these rooms unoccupied at one of our get-togethers.

There's a small tug on my hand when I reach the bottom of the stairs, and I pause, glancing over my shoulder to where Savanna has also stopped, one step higher. The difference makes us eye level and I move to face her. She's glancing around the open space, then casts a quick look back up the stairs. Ensuring we're alone.

When she finally looks at me, she's chewing on her bottom lip, worry in her gray eyes. "You didn't mind, did you?"

My eyebrows raise in surprise. "Mind? Mind that you shut my aunts up before they could utter a single word?"

Savanna blows out a breathy laugh then nods.

"Are you kidding?" I ask, my voice low as I step closer to her. My free hand finds her hip, my fingers sliding across the delicate fabric of her dress, the warmth of her body seeping through to me. I swear she shivers at the touch, leaning closer. Seeking more. "It was the sexiest thing I think I've ever seen. No one ever challenges them, or meets them head on. It was brilliant."

Her cheeks flush at my praise. "Spur of the moment idea while I was freshening up."

Freshening up. In a room with a lock where no eyes could pry. Because of me and what we'd done in the truck. My cock twitches at the memory, my eyes darting to her lips. Soft and pliable. She'd yielded to every brush of my lips, every stroke of my tongue.

"Nate…"

My name is a gasp of air. Her chest rises in such a way that I know she's being assaulted by the same memory. The movement draws my attention down to where her exposed skin is flushing, the blush disappearing below the neckline of her dress. I found out in the truck that there was no bra, though the way the material lays doesn't show what I'm certain is happening beneath. In the truck her nipples were taut and ripe for playing with, and the way her breath hitches, I know I'd find them the same now.

With deliberate slowness, my eyes peruse back up to her face. Every lick of heat that we tamed before coming inside has roared back to life. Her handling herself upstairs was oxygen to my fire, my intense stare the same to hers. Neither of us move, our heavy breaths the only sound beside the din of noise from the outside party, and the aunts upstairs. We're completely alone down here, just the two of us. It would be so easy… so fucking easy.

I'm a man of restraint, but fuck if I can find it now. In a

single blink, I make a decision. Slipping an arm around her waist, I haul her up against my body, and lift her off the step. She gives a soft squeal of surprise, music to my ears, and releases her hold on my other hand, grabbing onto my shoulders. My feet are already moving, taking us down a hallway off the main rooms that lead to the downstairs bathroom and a row of bedrooms. All spares for guests who spend the night.

The hallway turns to the right and the second we're out of sight from anyone who may walk through the game room, I've got Savanna pinned against the wall opposite a bedroom door. Her back is barely pressed against it when her lips are crashing into mine. Picking up where we left off in the truck.

I groan into the kiss, my hips pressing into hers, cock straining against the fly of my jeans. She lifts a leg, hitching it against my hip, and I grab hold of her thigh, my fingertips digging into the bare flesh where her dress has ridden up.

Our tongues war for position; one second I'm sweeping through the warm crevice of her mouth, tasting the mint of some gum she had earlier, the next she's flicking the roof of mine. I swallow her moan as my fingers creep up her thigh, her hips grinding into mine, both of us looking for any friction that may ease some of the fire burning inside of us.

It's no use. The only thing that will curb my desire for her will be being inside of her.

We could use the bathroom. Or one of the bedrooms. The one at my back would be perfect. Or the one further down the hall, further away if someone were to come in and use the bathroom. We'd have to make it quick, but I can work with that. I'm confident it won't take much to get her off, and I'm wound as tight as ever.

"Fuck," I hiss, wrenching my lips from hers. Fuck. I don't have a condom. I don't have a fucking condom with me.

Savanna is gasping for breath, her fingers curled through the hair at the back of my head. "What? What's wrong?"

My forehead falls to hers. I blink a few times, breathing hard, trying to think through the fog of desire and need pounding through every inch of my body. It's like a god damn drum that beats to some music only my blood can hear. It thunders in my ears.

"Nate?"

I blow out a breath, pulling my head back. "I don't have a condom with me."

"Oh."

Disappointment flashes in eyes clouded with the same need I feel. Her hips shift against mine. Not in a move to turn either of us on further, but in an effort to move away from me, to help us both.

I can still make this better for her. I'll have to wait to bury myself inside of her, but it doesn't mean she needs to be left longing the entire day.

Holding onto her thigh, I drop down to my knees in front of her. She gasps in disbelief above me, the sound making me smile.

"Nate!"

Her leg is over my shoulder before she can whisper another word, but a sound has me freezing before I make another move.

A door opens and closes. The door to the basement in the living room. Footsteps sound across the wood floor, indicating someone has come inside from the backyard. Fuck. We're at my grandparents'. Jesus Christ. In my lust filled head, I'd basically forgotten where we were.

Delirious with need. That's what she makes me.

My eyes dart to Savanna's and I put a finger to my lips.

Her eyes are wide, her chest not even moving with her breath. She heard it too. Knows we're not alone.

I cast my gaze to the side as whoever came inside approaches. When I turned the corner in the hallway, I didn't go any further, and from where we ended up, I can see the bathroom door. If anyone were to glance in this direction while headed into the bathroom, they'd see us.

Neither of us moves when the footfalls enter the hallway. Not even to breathe. Then I see who it is and nearly sag in relief. Jordan. As much as I don't want to be caught by anyone, if I had to choose, I think it would be her. Not that I need my sister seeing any of this, but she'd be the only one to keep her mouth shut about it. Plus, it's easier to explain to someone who knows both Savanna and me than someone who doesn't. I think.

But she doesn't even notice us. She goes straight into the bathroom and closes the door. I look back to Savanna who is gaping at me, the terror of being caught written with the twist of her mouth and large eyes.

I'm still uncomfortably hard in my jeans, but my problem is sorting itself out with the interruption and realization of what I was about to do—or rather, where I was about to do it. Releasing Savanna's leg, it slips from my shoulder and I'm on my feet again, pressing a chaste kiss to her lips. One to calm us both down. Reassure us that we weren't caught, and things are fine.

While Savanna fluffs her dress and straightens the top of it out, I adjust myself in my jeans. Once. Twice. Blowing out a deep breath, I close my eyes for a moment, flexing my thigh muscles to pull the blood into them instead of my cock. I may need to walk around for the entirety of the afternoon flexing muscle after muscle, willing an erection away.

A soft, warm hand touches my cheek, pulling my attention to her. She silently asks me if I'm okay. I nod, giving her a smile, my head turning to press a kiss to her palm. Then I take her hand and lead her back through the hallway to the main room.

It was stupid. Stupid to steal her away in my grandparents' house with my entire family lurking about. I don't know what I was thinking. I wasn't. There wasn't a single brain cell firing off any kind of smart thoughts. There was only need, only desire. On both our parts, apparently.

Our hands entwined, Savanna presses in close to me, perhaps sensing my thoughts. I glance down to her to find her smiling knowingly, but with a shyness that wasn't there minutes ago.

I plant a gentle kiss to her hair as we make our way through the family room. "I'm sorry," I murmur.

She shakes her head, her grin widening. "Don't be. It was…exciting. One of the most exciting things I've done in a long time." Savanna glances back towards the bathroom before adding, "It's not just you. I want you that much too, Nate."

I open the sliding glass door to the backyard, letting her step out ahead of me before shutting the door. "I shouldn't be putting you in—"

I'm interrupted by a familiar voice calling out. "Savanna?"

We both turn to look across the patio space of the backyard, finding my grandmother standing there with a glass of white wine in her hand, a stunned expression on her aging face. I'm sure I look much the same. They know each other?

"Mrs. Miller?" Savanna replies, sounding just as flabbergasted as I feel. She's quicker to recover, however, taking the few steps that separate us from my grandma. "What are you doing here?"

"Me?" My grandmother's eyes are wide, her mouth

slightly agape. She presses a hand to her chest, shaking her snow-white covered head. "Child, what on earth are you doing here?"

My grandma looks to me, then back to Savanna, things clicking into place for her. A delighted smile crosses her face that warms me to my core. I don't care how they know each other. I'm thrilled my grandma seems to already know and approve of Savanna, her delight increasing as I gather myself enough to join the two women and put an arm around Savanna.

"Nathan, I heard you brought a date with you, but I never would have guessed it would be Savanna." My grandma reaches out and touches Savanna's hand. "My goodness, dear, how are you?"

"Is that Savanna?" I hear my grandpa say from our left, and we all turn to look in his direction. "Well, I'll be damned."

He looks between us, the same way my grandmother did, connecting the dots before his grin broadens. "Nathan, my boy, you didn't tell us you had a new girlfriend!"

He claps my back in approval then turns his full attention to Savanna. "How you doin' sweetheart? You ready for preseason? What did you think of the big blockbuster trade?"

Hockey. Right. Savanna mentioned the trade to me, and I remember wondering what my grandpa would think about it, knowing he was a huge hockey fan. Cheering for the San Rocco Rampage, the team closest to us geographically, while Savanna cheered for the Colorado Blizzards, the two teams making some huge trade that I didn't understand but had seemed to irritate Savanna.

Savanna waves a hand dismissively, her eyes rolling. "You guys got the better part of the trade, in my opinion. Nicholas Austin for Bennett and Rutta? Austin was one of, if not the best forward we had. I know they had to make room on the salary cap, but my heart broke a little when I heard."

My grandpa shoots her a Cheshire cat smile. "I thought of you right away when I heard the news."

I feel like I've entered the twilight zone. My eyes dart back and forth between the two, listening to the casual conversation like they're old pals.

"He did. I was sitting in the living room with him. The first thing out of his mouth was, 'I wish we knew where Savanna was so I could gloat over this,'" my grandma interjects, causing the three of them to laugh. "I told him it was rude to gloat, but he assured me you'd understand as a hockey fan."

My grandpa smirks. "I also told her that you'd throw it right back if the situation was reversed."

It's a known fact in my family that it can take my grandparents time to warm up to someone new, but no one ever lets that stop them from bringing dates. I've always thought it took them time because all the cousins learned early to bring someone along if we didn't want to face the aunts and their swarms of questions. It probably got hard for them to keep up on the revolving door of dates that were coming and going.

For them to already know Savanna, and obviously like her—did my grandfather call her sweetheart?—I feel mindblown.

"Can someone please tell me what's going on?" I ask, scratching the back of my head as I look between the three of them. "How do you all know each other?"

They exchange glances. I know there's a story there judging by the looks that cross each of their faces, but it's Savanna who finally turns to look at me, a blush creeping into her cheeks. "You remember the day we met in the elevator?"

I nod.

She shifts where she stands, her fingers fidgeting with the skirt of her dress. "Remember how I told you I was with clients, and walked in on that thing?"

I nod again, my eyebrows pulling downwards as I frown, thinking about that asshole of a boss she had.

Savanna gestures towards my grandparents. "Meet the clients."

My mouth falls open. I stare at the three of them, putting it together. My grandparents were there, experiencing her boss fucking a woman in a boardroom?

They're a little old fashioned; they believe in getting married before having kids, not living with your partner until you're married, and if they had it their way, I'm sure no one would have sex before they'd said 'I do'. They've had to evolve over the years, though, because I know not one of us from my generation has followed all those beliefs.

For them to walk in on someone having sex, not just in a place of work, but somewhere they do business, I can only imagine the outrage they felt.

My face and neck burn thinking about the hallway from a few minutes ago. The hallway in their house. I don't even want to think about the outrage they'd feel if they knew what Savanna and I had been doing. What I'd wanted to do. What I'd been about to do if Jordan hadn't walked in.

"We tried to reach you the next day, but the receptionist told us you'd quit," my grandma says with a frown. "I was disappointed we couldn't get a hold of you, but thankful to hear you weren't working for them anymore."

"I packed my stuff right after you left," Savanna tells them, waving her hand in the air. "There was no way I could stay there after that. And, as it happens, I met Nate on my way out of the building."

She turns her smile on me. I'm still reeling from the last minute of conversation, but I manage to return the expression, despite the fact I think Savanna's lips are still red and swollen from our impromptu make-out session.

Her gaze turns perplexed, and she looks between me and my grandparents, a thought suddenly occurring to her. "But wait, how do you guys know each other?"

I gesture towards the couple opposite us. "Meet the grandparents."

Savanna's eyes move between me and them, widening. It's her turn to put everything together, and I wonder if I looked as dumbfounded as she does now. "Oh wow. What a small world."

Embarrassment aside, my heart warms as my grandparents watch us, and I watch Savanna. I squeeze her to my side, pressing a kiss to her forehead. "The smallest."

"I like her, Nathan," my mom says as she steps up beside me.

I'm standing on the upper deck, gazing down where Savanna is with my sister, and a few of my cousins and their spouses, around the large firepit in the center of the patio. Jordan came and stole her a little while ago, saying she wanted to introduce her to some of the family without me around. Savanna seemed more than happy to go with her, even though I was a little concerned what might be said without me around.

Again, I should have known better; every awkward situation I've put her in she handles with grace and ease. Her "I got this" attitude is so sexy. Watching her down there now, I can't help but feel that she fits in perfectly with all the crazy that can go on in this family.

I glance at my mom. "Me too."

"I know. I can tell." With a knowing smile, she takes a sip from her wine glass. "Been a long time since you brought a girl to one of these things."

I take a drink of my beer and nod, thinking about what Danny said earlier. He thought it was five years since the last time I brought a girl around, but I think it's been longer than that. I've never been one to bring a date just so everyone would leave me alone. There haven't been many girlfriends that I've felt serious enough about to introduce to this crazy bunch. Mostly because I didn't want any of them getting the wrong idea about where things were headed when my aunts started talking about marriage and kids.

"This one is different," I tell her, my eyes drifting back to the blonde below.

"I know," she repeats, her voice near singsong. "I can tell."

I raise an eyebrow, turning to her, amused she thinks she knows everything before I tell her. What I don't admit is she normally does. "Oh yeah? What else can you tell?"

"Oh, my beautiful baby boy," she murmurs, wrapping an arm around my waist in a side hug. I'm hardly a baby the way I tower over her. "If you don't settle down and marry that woman one day, I'll be mighty surprised. I've never seen you look at a woman that way, nor have I seen a woman look at you the way she does."

Putting my arm around her shoulders, I hug her tight to my side. My mom has always been perceptive, so I'm not totally surprised that she's figured out my feelings for Savanna.

As if Savanna can sense we're talking about her, she looks

up at the deck where we're standing at the rail, her face lighting up in a smile I know is meant for me.

I smile right back. "One day, mom. One day."

"Seeing the two of you together today is the best birthday present you could give this old woman, Nathan," she says, sighing with contentment.

I lean down and press a kiss to the top of her head, giving her an extra tight squeeze. "I love you, mom. Happy birthday."

CHAPTER 27

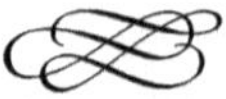

SAVANNA

I don't know if I've ever felt more accomplished, or proud of something I've worked on. Sitting behind the desk at work, staring at the USB in my hand, I could practically burst into happy tears.

I gave myself twenty-one days to finish Nate's books, but I only needed nineteen. I worked through the past weekend to get there, telling Nate that I wanted to plow through the rest of it because I was so close to being done. Unlike the weekend of our date, he let it be. I think he was starting to get anxious as the deadline loomed closer, but I wasn't stressed about it. I was on a roll and wanted to keep my momentum going.

It's also not like I haven't seen Nate. The days he hasn't been working at the firehouse, he's been at the bar, as usual, and he's very keen on me taking plenty of breaks to keep me from getting burnt out behind the computer. Or so he claims.

I think it's more like he's as insatiable as I am, and we can't get enough of each other.

We weren't three hours into our day, the day after the party, when he came waltzing into the office, closed the door, and made me come in the office chair with his face between my legs. Since that day I've been wearing a dress or skirt to work, the easy access coming in handy more than a couple of times.

I have a feeling the second he finds out I've completed everything for the accountant, he's going to be on me. I've kept him at arm's length all day, refusing to even kiss him because it only leads us to trouble.

Nate isn't out of the woods yet, though. The bar owes the government a good chunk of money, though it's not nearly as bad as it could have been. We hit middle of the pack when it comes to best-case or worst-case, which I'm considering a win. I don't know if he'll see it that way, but I've got a few ideas how we can manage the payment without the bar going belly up. But first I need to deliver the news that I'm finished.

Pushing back from the desk that Nate has been calling mine for the last week, I stretch my arms overhead and smile as I look around.

We talked about what my role would be once I finished this. He offered to make me the bookkeeper, along with the accountant, if all went well with the taxes, as well as returning to serving, and possibly managing the bar when he's working at the firehouse. He needs someone to take over for Bryn when she's done with school, and he thinks I'm a perfect fit for it.

I told him I'd think about it, but if I'm being honest, I knew the second he asked me that I would accept. I've grown to love this place in the few weeks I've been here. There's a sense of family, and that's something that feeds my soul. Plus, it allows me to do a few things I love while being around the guy that I'm falling for.

I can't believe I'm thinking that way after everything I've been through. These past couple of weeks have been nothing short of magical, even though I've been working like crazy at the bar.

Every night, except the days he's worked at the firehouse, Nate gets dinner ready, and then takes me to a new location for us to sit outside and enjoy our meal. He told me that I needed to expand my knowledge of Santa Rosé beyond the beach I frequented during the summer. What better way than to have dinner in a new place every evening.

I've seen some gorgeous sunsets because of it, and I've also learned a lot about him since we're usually too busy stuffing our faces to have our hands all over each other.

Leaving the USB on the desk, I head to the kitchen, my stomach rumbling with hunger.

Jeremy, the sous chef, catches my eye and grins. "Ready for dinner? Nate said he wasn't sure when you guys would be eating tonight."

Being in the back office for the last two weeks, I've gotten to know the kitchen staff a lot better. Nate was right when he told me they wouldn't treat me any differently if we were dating. Not a single person here has batted an eye over the fact, something for which I'm grateful.

"I'm not sure," I tell him, deciding I feel like taking Nate out to celebrate and go over things. "I think we might end up somewhere else tonight."

"Ouch, Sav!" Jeremy lays a hand over his chest. "You're breaking my heart over here. My cooking ain't good enough for you?"

"It's me, not you," I retort with a dash of sass, and he erupts into laughter.

I'm halfway through the door to the front of house, his laughter still ringing behind me, when I freeze in place. Everything disappears from around me. Adrenaline floods my body in an instant, realizing before my mind can process it, that I'm in danger. The whole world slows down, and I feel like I'm trudging through mud as I try to comprehend the sight before me.

Sitting at the bar, two seats down from where Liam and Brody are, is Vincent.

He's shaved all the dark hair on the top of his head, but his beard remains, perfectly groomed along the sharp lines of his face. There's no mistaking it's him, especially with the way my body reacts to him being this close. I can see the tattoo of a bear on his muscled upper arm peeking out from under his black t-shirt. He got it for me, even though I told him not to, saying it was his way of showing me how much he loved me.

It's only been half a second since I stepped foot into the bar, but it feels like it's been a century of me standing there, frozen, staring at the man of my nightmares.

Movement catches my eye, time normalizing as the sounds of the bar penetrate my ears. I need to move before anyone realizes I'm standing here.

Anyone other than Bryn, that is.

She's coming at me, and I use her as cover, grabbing the other half of the door to open it up towards the kitchen which changes my course and puts me back into hiding from the front.

"Thanks," she says, walking through the open door with an armful of dishes.

"No problem," I squeak, clearing my throat, hoping she didn't hear the terrified edge to my voice.

When she doesn't say anything, I breathe a sigh of relief

and force myself to walk calmly back to the office. I feel anything but calm. Terror seizes me, thrumming through my veins at a steady pace. I'm shaking like a leaf, and if I looked into a mirror right now, I know I'd be ghostly white.

I'm moving on pure instinct, grabbing my purse and my keys, thanking God I came in earlier than Nate and drove myself. I head out back, walking through the kitchen, keeping my eyes averted from the guys. From a sideways glance, I can tell they're all busy with something and paying no attention to me.

Slipping out the door, I bolt towards my car, my hands fumbling with my keys. Now that I'm outside and away from prying eyes, I allow myself to freak out just a little, but I know I can't fully lose it. I'm not safe and I need to keep my head, but at least no one will see me gulping in breath after breath as I try not to hyperventilate.

He found me. He fucking found me, and now I'm not the only one in danger. So is Nate.

If Vincent had seen me, and Nate knew Vincent was in there, all hell would break loose. Nate has told me as much. And I wouldn't put it past Vincent to do whatever necessary to hurt Nate if he knew that we were together.

I need to get away from here. As far away from Nate as I can before he gets hurt, or worse. I wouldn't be able to live with myself if something happened to him. I knew going into this with him that Vincent finding me was a possibility, one that was made greater with the video of me at the fire, and I still foolishly let myself get involved.

I've got my car door open when I hear a groan from behind me. It's hardly a sound, but it makes me shriek, none-theless. Whirling around, I find a man collapsed in front of the dumpster I'm parked next to, looking wrecked out of his mind.

This isn't a patron of the bar. This man looks roughened by the streets, and I realize I've seen him a few times wandering around near the bar. The first time I saw him, Nate told me his name was Tony, a known drug user. I had the feeling Nate and his crew have helped him a time or two.

Everything inside me tells me to get in the car and leave. Run. Everything except my heart. My brain is screaming it, my body is yelling at me, but my heart says I need to go back inside and get Nate because this man needs help.

I recall the day I told Nate I didn't know how I would ever repay him for everything he had done for me. The only thing he wanted was for me to help someone in need. Here I am, faced with a choice, and I know which one I have to make, no matter how much my instincts are telling me to make the opposite one.

Slamming my door shut, I race back into the kitchen, hopeful that Nate is back here instead of up front, but my hope is in vain.

"Jeremy!" I yell at him because he's the closest. I stop long before anyone would be able to see me from the front if the doors were to swing open. "I need you to go get Nate. Now."

He stops what he's doing, concern furrowing his eyebrows. "What's wrong?"

"Just go get Nate!" I bark.

I think it's my tone because he doesn't hesitate again, rushing through the doors to the front where I can hear him. My eyes squeeze shut and my heart drops into my stomach when I hear my name being used, but I don't have time to worry about that before Nate is slamming his way through the swinging doors into the kitchen.

The concern on his face makes me want to drop to my knees and beg him to forgive me for what my instincts are still crying for me to do.

Run. Run, run, run.

"That Tony guy is out back; something is wrong with him," I say hurriedly before my legs give out, or he can question what's wrong with me. I don't know if I would be able to stop myself from telling him, and I need to keep him from knowing about Vincent.

"Shit," Nate mutters, shifting into firefighter mode. Grabbing the first aid kit hanging on the wall, he's heading out the back within seconds of entering the kitchen.

I'm quick on his heels. There's more movement behind me, and though part of me doesn't want to look because I'm scared I'll see my ex, I glance over my shoulder, breathing a sigh of relief. Liam and Brody.

"Savanna, call 911. Tell them what's going on and that we're going to need an ambulance to the bar," Nate tells me as we go through the door. "Where is he?"

I step out, pointing towards the dumpster. Liam and Brody are right behind me, all three men converging on the man still laying there. From what I can tell, he's not groaning anymore, nor is he moving, which can't be a good sign.

Pulling my phone out like Nate said, I dial 911. I'm still shaking from the fear of seeing Vincent, never mind the wave of it from seeing the man on the ground, and I fumble my phone before I can hit send. It lands on the pavement with a clatter, causing me to wince before I bend to pick it up.

As I'm standing up straight, I catch Liam looking at me with narrowed eyes, like he knows something is up with me. Paranoia. It has to be because there's no way he could know.

Finally I hit send and with a hand at my forehead and phone to my ear, I wait until I hear an operator. "911, do you need police, fire, or ambulance?"

"I need an ambulance to the 10-42 bar. There's a man out back who's collapsed, and he needs help."

"Do you know what happened?" the voice on the other end asks calmly.

I watch as Nate and Brody work on the man. "No, but there're firefighters here, and I think they're giving him Narcan."

Confusion from the other end. "Fire is already on scene?"

"No, no," I huff, frustrated. I can't think. "I… no, I mean, there are off duty firefighters here. One of them owns the bar."

"Okay, do you know the address to the bar?"

I open my mouth to answer her, then close it. I should know this because I've been using it and seeing it everywhere for the past three weeks, but it's completely gone. The number, the street, everything is just gone. I'm drawing a complete blank.

The guys are busy with Tony, so I don't ask, instead turning to look down the alley towards the street to see if it rings a bell. I freeze when I meet the cold eyes of Vincent standing at the mouth of the lane, watching my every move. The phone slips from my hand as the whole world stops.

After more than six months of hiding, he's found me. I knew this day would come, but I wasn't ready for it. I don't know if I'd ever be ready for it.

The panic doesn't come until something touches my arm. I shriek in surprise, reflex making my feet finally move from their spot as I spin around to confront my attacker.

Except my real attacker is standing seventy-five feet away from me down the alley, and Liam is standing beside me, watching me with a sharpness I've never seen him use.

The man might be a playboy and jokester, but the way he's looking at me right now tells me he knows something is going on, and he's trying to figure out what it is. I'm guessing this is what makes him good at his job, but it sure as hell isn't helping me right now.

My phone is at his ear, and he's talking to the operator without taking his eyes off me.

I swallow hard, chancing a glance back down the alley, nearly sagging when Vincent isn't there.

No. No, no, no. If I know where he is, it's easier to stay safe. It's easier to keep Nate safe.

But now it isn't just Nate I need to worry about. I think I may need to worry about Liam and Brody too, since Vincent has seen me with all three.

"You okay?"

I look up from the computer to find Nate leaning against the door jamb of the office, observing me with keen eyes.

I love those eyes. So much. I love the way they look at me like I'm the only woman in the world, and how tender they get right after he's given me a sweet kiss, or how dark they can be when he's hungry for me. They're inquisitive and insightful, wise beyond his years.

It kills me that I'm going to leave them, and him, behind. But it's for the best. I know I need to do it, just like I needed to walk away from everything in Colorado.

"Yeah," I tell him, lying to his face. I hate myself for it, but I've got to do what needs to be done.

His eyes narrow marginally. "It's okay if you're not. That couldn't have been easy to see."

I'm perplexed that he hasn't come further into the room, but maybe I'm giving off a vibe that says I don't want him in here. It would be both true and untrue at the same time. I want him to wrap me up in his arms, but I know that I would cave and tell him everything. I can't afford that.

"It wasn't something I could do every day," I tell him honestly.

He gives me a reluctant smile. "Why don't you shut it down for the day and I'll take you home? We can grab something to eat on the way."

"No," I say quickly, cringing inwardly at myself. I hope I didn't tip him off by sounding too forceful. "I'm so close to being done, I just want to get this finished."

Nate glances at his watch, runs a hand through his hair, then nods at me. "Okay. But if you're not done in the next hour, I'm not taking no for an answer." I almost breathe a sigh of relief when he turns to leave, biting it back when he pauses. "Hey, what were you doing out in the alley in the first place?"

I don't think I will ever find something I hate more than lying to him.

I thought up my lies when I was sitting at my desk after the guys told me to go back inside. I had some time to come up with things that were plausible, but I didn't want to have to use any of them. Unfortunately, the universe seems good at not granting my wishes.

I shrug nonchalantly though I feel anything but. "My earbuds died. My charger was in my car."

"Ah." He nods like it makes perfect sense, which I know it does, but hate that he takes it at face value. The part of me that wants to tell him everything is silently pleading with him not to believe a word. "Tony's lucky you were there."

I'm glad one of us was.

"Yeah, I guess so, huh?" I wave a hand to shoo him out. "Go. Let me finish."

I've been waiting for this. Waiting for Nate, Liam, and

Brody to come back inside and go out to the bar so I could slip out the back and disappear without them knowing. I grabbed one of the knives in the kitchen to take with me in case Vincent is outside waiting, but I have a feeling he won't be. I don't think he would expect me to leave alone after seeing him. There would be no psychological thrill he's looking for. His favorite thing to do was fuck with my mind until I submitted to him and snatching me in an alley wouldn't give that to him.

I think.

I hope.

I pull out the note I hand wrote to Nate. He deserves so much more, and tears fill my eyes as I read my writing, wishing things were different. It's shitty and short. It doesn't give any kind of explanation, but it does tell him that everything is ready for the accountant, all he needs to do is hand over the USB.

I'm doing this for him. I will not let him put himself in harm's way because of me.

"Hey."

The sound of a voice startles me, the USB bouncing off the desk when I drop it. I look up to find Liam standing in the doorway, and quickly avert my eyes to the floor where the drive landed.

Shit. I thought maybe Liam and Brody would come into the office with Nate, but I didn't expect Liam to show up alone. It makes me uneasy because I'm nearly positive he saw Vincent, though I couldn't swear to it. Even if he did that doesn't mean he's realized what's going on. I know Nate hasn't shared any of my past with Liam or Brody because he told me as much. I didn't care at the time, but I'm damn thankful now.

"Hey," I say back, leaning over to grab the USB from the floor. It gives me a moment to blink the tears from my eyes.

His eyes are narrowed, much like they were in the alleyway as he assesses me from where he stands. "You wanna tell me what's going on?"

Rising back up, I bring my eyes to his, putting on my best poker face. "I'm not sure what you mean."

Liam shoves his hands into his pockets, glances over his shoulder, then takes a few steps further into the office. "Nate might have been too busy to notice, but the thing about firefighters is when one of us is busy with one thing, others are looking out at the scene. Assessing, calculating, figuring out what else might happen. Then we do what we need to in order to prevent it."

My blood runs cold. He's doing exactly what he just explained to me. Assessing, calculating, trying to figure out what's going on. He needs to stop before I cave and confess. I can't. I can't put any of them in more danger than I already have.

When he continues, he's matter of fact. "We work as a unit, which is why we're so successful at scenes. It's how we're trained, it's what we do."

It's easier to lie to Liam, but only by a small fraction. "Liam, I'm not sure what you're talking about. I get how firefighting works. Nate has explained it to me."

"Something spooked you." It's not a question.

The words send a shiver racing down my spine. He's too close to the truth, and it's making me uncomfortable. "Yeah, the fact that I saw a guy almost die."

"I know everyone thinks I'm some dumb fuck boy, but I assure you, I'm not." Liam stares at me, weighing what I'm telling him, then drops the bomb I knew was coming. "Who was that guy? He was staring at you."

"Liam, seriously!" I say, throwing my hands up in exasperation to try and get my point across. "I'm trying to finish this accounting stuff for Nate. I'm so close to being done. He gave me an hour to finish or he's cutting me off for the night. Do you know the stress that will be off his shoulders once I get this done?"

For the first time since coming into the office, Liam hesitates, looking unsure of himself. Glancing at the computer, I can see the wheels switching gears in his mind.

It was my Hail Mary to get him off my case, and to keep him from asking more questions, or expecting answers I'm not about to give. I know how much he worries about Nate. He's confessed his gratitude to me when we've sat at the bar together when Nate hasn't been around.

He sags as the confidence billows out of him, along with a deep breath. "Okay. Sorry. I just... I've never seen you freaked out like that. Not even after Nate pulled you out of a burning building." He gives me a tight smile. "Seemed like something else was going on, and Nate missed all of it, so I thought I'd ask you straight up."

I smile back at him, but inside I'm screaming that he's probably never been more right about anything in his life. "I appreciate your concern. I really do."

Just like that, the Liam I've come to know and adore is back, his expression turning debonair. "Well, you're one of us now. We take care of our own."

I wait until he's gone to let the tears fall, and even then I only allow a few of them.

Between Nate and Liam, I feel like my heart is being ripped out of my chest. I just need to keep reminding myself I'm doing this for them, to keep them as safe as I possibly can.

I wait another five minutes to see if anyone else is going

to burst through the office door before I set my note and the USB on the desk, grab my purse, and head out the back door for the second time in the last hour.

This time the coast is clear. There's nobody overdosing on drugs behind the dumpster, and like I thought, there are no signs of Vincent.

Just to be safe, I weave my way through the streets on my way back to Nate's house. There are a few things I need before I can disappear, I just need to be quick about it. The hour window that I bought myself is quickly closing, and I know the first place that Nate will look for me is home.

His home. Not mine.

CHAPTER 28

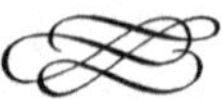

NATE

Snapping my fingers in front of Liam's face, I watch my best friend return to the present moment. He's been staring into space for the last five minutes.

I smirk as he blinks at me, then takes a long drag from his beer bottle.

"What's got you so out of sorts?" I ask curiously.

"Nothing," he mutters, but a second later he's drumming his fingers on the countertop. His eyes are glued to the doors leading to the kitchen, and I can't help but wonder if he knows something I don't.

I glance at Brody, who looks at me, an eyebrow cocked. He's noticing Liam's odd behavior as well.

Leaning against the bar, I grab my glass of water. "C'mon man, seriously. What's up?"

That makes him stop tapping, only to grab his beer bottle in both hands to still them. "Just a feeling. It's probably nothing."

I can't help my snicker.

"Dude, we knew you were capable of them," Brody says with a grin, clapping Liam on the back. "We're proud of you."

"Oh, fuck you both," he says, rolling his eyes, and pulling away from Brody's hand. He seems grouchy, which isn't normal for Liam, so while it's fun to rib him, it makes me feel a little apprehensive. Then he asks, "When's Savanna's hour up?"

That has me standing straighter, sobering completely. I'm not sure why he knows about that, the uneasiness growing in the pit of my stomach. I've been trying not to think about her, or the hour I gave her, because something seemed off when we came back inside. I just couldn't put my finger on what but decided to shrug it off as her seeing someone overdose and needing some time with it.

Glancing at my watch, I frown. "Another thirty-five minutes. Why?"

"I dunno, man," he says, drumming his fingers again.

"Liam." My voice is sharp, unable to hide my growing worry. "What the hell, man?"

"You know what I want to know?" Brody asks from beside Liam, and we both turn to look at him. "Why'd she send Jeremy out here to get you?"

The breath leaves me in one long exhale. I'd forgotten about that. At the time it had scared me half to death because I thought something had happened to Savanna in the back. A myriad of thoughts went through my mind while my heart found a new home in my throat. I know it only took me two seconds to get to the kitchen to find her standing there, but it felt like an eternity. I nearly laughed with joy when she told me what the problem was, but the firefighter in me took over and then I was in work mode.

"Did you guys see the guy in the alley?" Liam questions hesitantly.

Alarm bells louder than we've got at the station sound in my head. My hands slam down on the counter as I lean towards my two friends.

"What guy?" I demand.

Liam looks startled at my outburst. "I don't know. There was a guy at the end of the alley. It looked like he was watching her, but he could have been watching us. I was more concerned with her, so I didn't pay attention. She was spooked about something."

It's all I need. Something is wrong. I knew it in my gut, but I let her talk me out of it instead of trusting my instincts. Christ. If something happened to her, if he somehow found her, if that was him in the alley...

I'm flying through the doors to the kitchen one second, the next I'm in the office. It's empty, and there's no sign of her, but there's also no sign of a struggle. Surely if Vincent had found her and taken her from the office, one of the guys in the kitchen would have said something or would have stopped it.

I'm about to head back into the kitchen when a piece of paper on the desk grabs my attention. The USB on top of it looks like the one I gave Savanna when she asked what she could put everything onto for the accountant, so I take a second to grab the sheet of paper, seeing her flowing script on it.

Nate,

Everything is done and on this USB. The accountant will know what to do with it.

The bar will be fine with a little effort—a fundraiser, your grandparents. I think you should also have a ladies night, and a karaoke night. I was going to talk to you about that when I accepted your offer.

Don't worry about me. I got this.

Xoxo

Sav

I've hardly finished reading the words before I'm out the back door and in my truck. If she's not here, maybe she's at home. I have this sinking feeling that if she is there, she won't be for long. If my hunch is correct, I already know what's going on in her mind.

By the time I pull into the alley at home, I've come to a couple of conclusions.

First, Vincent was in the bar. Second, Savanna saw him. Third, she's doing to me what she did to her family. At least she's trying.

That's the thing when you open up to someone; they can read what you're going to do before you do it. I know I'm right when I see her car parked in the parking pad at the back, relief causing some of the tension to drain from my body. At least I haven't missed her.

I throw the truck into park behind her car, effectively blocking her in, and jump out. I'm at the back door in record time, throwing it open and striding inside.

"Savanna?" I yell, quickly making my way towards her bedroom.

Rounding the corner, I come to a halt just inside the door. She's sitting on the bed, head bowed, an old t-shirt of mine clutched in her hands and held to her face. Her suitcase is open and half packed beside her.

Under normal circumstances the sight would have gutted me, but I'm so relieved she's still here it's hard to feel anything beyond that.

I get the same sense I had the night she broke the glass at the bar. A wounded animal who will flee if I move too quickly or do the wrong thing. Moving slowly, I stop in front of her and crouch down, tentatively resting my hands on her knees. Nothing moves except for her eyes. They open and rise to meet mine, and now I am gutted. She's petrified.

I know better than to push her to talk to me, so I just gaze at her, our eyes locked, until she's ready. It takes her a minute, but then the t-shirt is coming away from her face, dropping into her lap along with her hands.

"He found me," she whispers, the sound of her voice destroying me further.

"I know," I say, then add quickly when she sits up straighter, "Liam. I put it together."

Giving me a small nod, she casts her eyes downwards. "I was going to leave."

"I know." When her eyes pop back up in surprise, I smile gently at her. "Trying to do the best thing for me, right?"

Fresh tears well in her eyes, and I reach up, brushing one away as it falls down her cheek. "I can't stand the thought of you getting hurt."

"Do you remember when you sat down in the office and told me that you could help me with the mess in there?" I ask, and she nods, confusion clouding her eyes. "You remember how I put my faith in you because you asked me for that chance?"

Another nod, this time accompanied by more tears. She knows where I'm going with this, the protest already taking shape in her mind. I can see the wheels turning, see her wanting to tell me this isn't the same, so I press ahead.

"I need you to have faith in me now, to trust I know what I'm doing, and that I won't get hurt," I tell her, squeezing her knee gently. "Even if I did, it would be my choice, Sav. I would go through anything, do anything, if it meant keeping you safe, because I care about you. So much."

The words were right there on the tip of my tongue to tell her that I love her. They almost came out. The only reason they didn't is because I don't want those words to have anything to do with Vincent. I want it to be a moment that is just us, because of us.

Just because I didn't say them out loud, however, doesn't mean she doesn't see it in my eyes. I know she does just by the way she's looking at me.

A sob bubbles up her throat before she's launching herself at me, causing me to fall back on my ass as her arms wrap around my neck. I brace myself with one arm behind me, the other snaking around her waist to pull her closer as she buries her face in my neck, the emotion bursting out of her.

"Shhh, it's okay, I got you," I murmur against her hair, rubbing my hand up and down her back. Shuffling backwards until my back hits the wall, I'm finally able to envelop her in both my arms, tethering her securely to me as she lets go of everything she's been holding in for so long.

I'm sure we could sit here all night, me rubbing her back, her letting it all out, but a noise from the front room puts me on alert. That wasn't a normal noise my house makes.

My body stills, listening intently over the quiet sounds that Savanna makes, and I hear it again. I really hate to scare her, but I'm not going to have a choice.

"Sav," I say gently but urgently, "I gotta get up and check on something. I need you to stay here."

Before she can fully lift her head, there's a louder sound that has her jumping against me, then cowering against my chest. Her eyes are wide with fear as she looks at me. "Nate…"

"You need to stay right here," I tell her, grabbing her hips to lift her off me.

I hate that I'm not giving her the comfort I know she

needs, but if that asshole, or someone else, is trying to get into the house, she needs protection before comfort.

Savanna is on her feet at the same time I am. Another noise comes from the front door, and I look around the bedroom doorway down the hall in that direction. I'm not a guy who keeps a bat around, let alone firearms, but right now I wish I were. Doesn't mean I don't know how to throw a solid punch, which is going to have to suffice.

With one more look at Savanna, I tell her to stay in the bedroom before I'm slipping down the hall. I stop just before I can see the front door, peeking around the corner to ensure it hasn't been opened yet, and then I dart across to the dining room where I grab one of the chairs.

I get back to the front door just in time for it to open and a body to walk through it. The chair is over my head and coming down towards the intruder when a second body walks through the door and catches the leg with lightning reflexes before it can smash into anyone.

"Nate!" Brody yells.

"Whoa!" Liam ducks, his arms flailing when he spots the chair looming overhead. He glowers, "What the fuck?"

If it weren't for Brody, the chair would be on the ground right now as the horror of what almost happened dawns on me. Then anger swells. "What the fuck, you guys? What the hell are you doing here?"

"Are you shitting me right now?" Liam says as Brody takes the full weight of the chair and sets it down. "You took off like a bat out of hell and didn't come back. Then we find out from Bryn you left, and Savanna was gone. You wouldn't answer your phone. What did you expect us to do?"

"So you break into my house?" I seethe at them.

Logically I know my anger is misdirected, but that isn't

stopping me from lashing out. There are too many things roiling through my body and mind to find control.

"I have a key, asshole!" Liam spits back, taking a step towards me, feeding off my energy. "And you need to get that front door fucking fixed because it's a bitch to open."

No one ever uses the front door, so I haven't bothered looking at it. "Not exactly on the top of my priority list."

"Okay, enough. Both of you," Brody says, stepping in between us, a hand coming to each of our shoulders. "We were concerned, man. That's all."

It's not like Liam and I were going to exchange blows or anything but leave it to Brody to step between us and play referee. It's not often any of us get truly snippy with each other, but emotions are running high for me, and to Liam's credit, I did just about take him out with a chair. I close my eyes and scrub my hands over my face, letting out a deep sigh of frustration. I get it. I would have done the same thing.

"I know." Dropping my hands to my sides, I look between the two of them. "Sorry. There's a lot going on."

Like they coordinated it, they both look at the chair sitting there.

"No shit," Liam says, then glances around the place. "Where's Savanna?"

She must have been standing right at the edge of the hallway because at the sound of her name, she steps around the corner, her arms wrapped around herself. My heart aches. Her face is ashen and distressed; I'd love nothing more than to see that beautiful smile of hers even for a second.

"I'm here." Her voice, meek and small, is a nail to my chest.

Brody and Liam both turn, take one look at her, then turn back to me, jaws set, eyes hard.

"Whose ass are we kicking?" Brody says, and it's so out of

character for him that I laugh. Even more than me, Brody is the guy that steps between fights, he doesn't get into them.

"Close the door," I tell them, then stride over to Savanna, wrapping my arms around her shoulders to pull her into me.

I take a moment to breathe in her scent, the fruity sweetness washing over me, filling me with strength. I feel like I've been put through the wringer tonight, between adrenaline, fear, and relief. I need a moment to collect myself.

Pressing my lips to her ear, I whisper, "It's okay. We're going to get through this." I'm not sure if it's to convince her, or myself. "I think we should tell them what's going on, though."

She stiffens in my arms, pulling back. Indecision battles in the gray pools of her eyes and I realize she hasn't fully changed her mind about leaving. My heart cracks inside my chest. I thought when she threw herself into me it meant her decision was made. That she would stay and deal with this.

"Sav," I breathe, my head shaking. I release my hold from around her, my hands coming to rest on her shoulders. "Please. Don't leave. Don't run."

"Nate…" she whispers. I've never before heard my name said with so much conflict. It guts me. More than even the terror I saw in her minutes ago.

"Please," I beg, taking her chin between my thumb and forefinger. "Stay."

"If you're going to break his heart and leave us to pick up the pieces," Liam says from behind me, his words cool and calculated, "At least explain why before you do it."

Hurt flashes in her eyes, and I throw a warning look over my shoulder at my best friend. When I turn back to her, the pain is gone, resolve meeting me instead.

She steps away from me, wrapping her arms around

herself and addresses the two men. "Let's sit in the kitchen and have a beer."

It's not confirmation that she'll stay, but it gives me more time to convince her not to go. I'll take it.

CHAPTER 29

NATE

By the time she's told them everything, I've finished one beer and I'm almost done with my second. I know I've got to stay sharp, but I needed something to take the edge off. With Liam and Brody here, I know I can relax a little more than I probably would otherwise.

I'm surprised at how much detail Savanna went into. It's nothing compared to what she's told me, but she gave them more than I thought she would.

It was tough listening to it all again, but I can't deny a weight has been lifted from my shoulders to be able to share this burden with my brothers. The more people that know, the safer I feel Savanna will be, which is my number one priority. With Vincent in town, I need as many eyes as I can get on the situation. If she stays.

Liam is the first one to move once she's finished. He and Brody opted to stand on the other side of the island while Savanna sat at it, and I stood behind her, rubbing her back to give her strength and comfort while she talked. Now Liam comes around and she turns in her seat, sliding off it when he moves in to hug her.

It moves me. My best friend is completely accepting of the woman I love, and is there to support her in whatever way she needs. I've always trusted him with my life, and I know I can trust him with hers.

Brody follows suit, engulfing Savanna in his big arms, pulling her into his massive body. She looks so tiny against him that I can't help but smile. Even though he's a gentle giant and hates to hurt even a spider, I can count on him to keep her safe as well. Brody might not be the guy that will fight someone, but he'll step in front of something and take a blow meant for another.

"You're one of us," Brody says when he releases her, and Christ, if that doesn't choke me up. "We take care of each other."

I meet his eyes over Savanna's head and nod my appreciation. Then I look at Liam, and he claps a hand on my shoulder, nodding in understanding, which I'm grateful for because I don't think I have the words right now.

Liam moves back around the island, crossing his arms over his chest. "I suppose I'll forgive you for lying to me earlier."

Savanna grimaces, returning to the chair. "I'm really sorry about that."

"You can make it up to me by shoving this bullshit of you leaving to the side," he says coolly.

While he may protect her, I know he's also trying to protect me. But there's a warning in my voice when I say, "Liam."

"Nah, man. Fuck that." He crosses an ankle over the other, his casual stance contrary to his words. "Nate might stand there and be all noble, putting what you want first, but I'm going to tell you right now, Sav, that if you left it would destroy him. And if everything I know about you is true, it'll destroy you too. You might as well stay and fight if you're both going to be miserable."

"Liam," I say again, glaring at him.

Before I can say another word, Savanna looks over her shoulder at me, shaking her head. "No, he's right. I—" She cuts herself off, catching her bottom lip between her teeth as she rotates the stool around to face me. "I could have been gone before you got here, but I couldn't... I couldn't leave. Even when every instinct keeps telling me to run, my heart says stay. Stay and fight. Stay and be with you."

"Sav..."

"I hate the thought of you—any of you—getting hurt because of me. It kills me to think about, just like it killed me with my family." Pools fill her eyes, but she takes a deep, steadying breath, one that I mirror, and continues. "I can't go through that kind of heartbreak again."

Something inside my chest stitches back together. Stepping between her legs, I slide my arms around her shoulders and pull her into my chest. Her own arms wrap around my waist, and I press my lips to the top of her head, taking in her scent. My eyes lift to my two best friends across the island, and I mouth my thanks to them. They both bow their heads in return. Maybe I could have convinced her to stay on my own, but I know having the support of my brothers made it easier.

"So what now?" Liam asks when Savanna and I have released each other and she's turned back to face him and Brody.

I slide my arm around Savanna's shoulders, pulling her into my side to press a kiss to the top of her head before I answer. "I'm not sure. We hadn't gotten that far when you two scared the shit out of us."

"You were scared?" Savanna asks, surprised.

I look down at her, perplexed. "Of course I was. I thought you were in danger and that was terrifying. But it's like running into a burning building; just because it's scary doesn't mean I'm not going to do it. I'm going to do whatever it takes to keep you safe."

"We all are," Liam adds.

When I look over at him, he's looking seriously between the two of us, and Brody is standing beside him nodding his agreement.

Giving them both a nod, I pull in a deep breath and let it out slowly, looking back to Savanna. "I don't want you alone. Someone needs to be with you at all times, okay?"

I'm surprised when she doesn't put up any fight, but then again, I know how scared she is of Vincent.

"We're on shift in the morning," Brody says quietly, reminding us that the three of us all have to work tomorrow.

I'd basically forgotten at this point, and I curse now.

"Why doesn't Savanna just come with us?" Liam suggests. "You could talk to Cap, tell him what's going on."

"What? No, I can't come with you guys to the firehouse!" she says, shaking her head vehemently. "I can just go hang out at the bar."

"No," I tell her, my voice firm. "It's the one place he's seen you. I don't want you there without one of us." Maybe not at all, but I keep that to myself for now.

I look at Liam, thinking about his idea. He, Brody, and I all exchange looks. They're thinking the same thing I am. It's a short term solution to a bigger problem, but it's a good one. With the administration offices, there would always be someone around if we were out on a call, and when we're not on a call, I can keep a close eye on her.

She'd also have a lot of emotional support and a constant distraction, which I think she could use more than she realizes at this point.

"Sav," I say, twisting her towards me, my hands coming to rest on her upper arms. "It's a good plan, at least for tomorrow. We don't have time tonight to figure something else out. The only other thing I can think of is that I take tomorrow off."

"No!" she nearly shouts. "No, I won't let you do that. I don't want this affecting your work."

Clenching her jaw, she gives a frustrated cry, pulling out of my grasp to get up from the stool. I let her go, watching as she walks around the kitchen, pushing her hands through her hair. I'd be surprised if her fingers weren't picked to pieces at this point.

"I hate this. I hate that this is putting you all out and that you're having to worry about me like this," she vents, pacing the floor.

"It would be worse if we didn't know what happened to you, Savanna," Brody says, sorrow laced in his words. "When I lost Heather, the worst part was not knowing what was happening. The unknown is worse to live through than a little disruption."

Liam and I exchange a look. Brody doesn't talk about Heather. He doesn't talk about what happened to her, or how he feels, or what he went through during the whole thing. We were there for him as much as he let us, but it was something he made himself go through mostly alone. I haven't told Savanna a lot about it, but she does know Brody lost his wife a couple years ago, and she's quick to go to him, her arms squeezing around his waist.

"You're right," she tells him, nodding firmly when she releases him, glancing around at the three of us. "Okay. I guess I'm coming to work with you guys tomorrow."

For the first time since Jeremy came rushing through the kitchen doors earlier saying Savanna needed me pronto, I relax. Tonight and tomorrow Savanna will be safe. The rest we can figure out later when emotions aren't running quite as high, and we've all had something to eat and a little sleep.

"Anyone up for some pizza?" I ask, getting a chorus of yeses in response.

I meet Savanna's eyes and she smiles at me. There isn't just gratitude swimming in the gray depths, there's love. Things might be a little screwed up and messy right now, but the look she's giving me will carry me through. It'll get me through whatever the next few days hold for us.

"Since we're sharing and caring," Savanna says while I pull my phone out to order pizza through an app. "I finished the books today."

My thumb stills over my screen, my eyes darting up to meet hers. She only catches them for a second before she glances at Liam and Brody, both of whom are watching her, interest piqued.

"We can talk about that tomorrow," I tell her, recalling the note she left on my desk. Dealing with the bar is the furthest thing from my mind right now, even though I'm relieved she's got her part done.

She shakes her head, putting her hands on her hips. "I think right now is a good time. Since I know you have a problem accepting help from people, I think it may be wise to share while we're standing around brainstorming anyway."

Liam looks pointedly at me, a smirk on his face. Brody snorts. Both amused that Savanna knows me that well already, and is willing to call me out on it, just like they do. Another person to add to their ranks.

I cross my arms over my chest and lean a hip against the kitchen island. Despite being called out, or maybe in spite of it, I grumble, "I can handle it."

Savanna's eyes roll in my direction. "That's what I thought." She addresses Liam and Brody. "The bar owes the government. There's some money it can pull from, but not all of it. Given Nate's resistance to help, I doubt he'll ask his grandparents for—"

"Absolutely not," I vehemently disagree.

She continues like I didn't utter a word. "I was thinking a fundraiser. Maybe a silent auction or something. I hadn't gotten that far in my thoughts."

Just the thought makes me uncomfortable. I don't want to take anyone's charity. "No."

"Silent auction?" Liam muses as though I haven't said a word. Like I'm not even there. I grit my teeth, but he continues, "What about a firefighter auction?"

Brody chokes on the beer he was taking a swig out of, coughing the liquid down. My mouth gapes open at Liam and Savanna, the former with a devilish smirk, the latter with an excited gleam in her eye.

"Yes!" Savanna nods with enthusiasm. "It would be so much faster than a silent auction. We wouldn't have to try and find prizes because you guys would be the prize. Do you know other firefighters who might be willing to participate?"

Liam doesn't even take a second to think about it. "Definitely."

"No," I snarl through clenched teeth. My tone must say enough because they both finally look at me. "No to my grandparents, no to an auction. No to it all. I'll figure it out. I can take out a personal loan and cover it."

"Fucking hell," Liam mutters, grabbing his beer to take a swig.

Savanna's arms fold over her chest. "Why? Why won't you let anyone else help you? Why would you take out a loan when you might not need to? Why put yourself in the hole like that?"

"Because I…" My eyes move from each of their three faces. The faces of three people I care a lot about. Three people I can trust in this world.

All they want to do is help—it's all they've ever wanted to do. But for two of them, I'm their leader, and the third, I'm her man. And sure, maybe that sounds like something a disgusting, filthy pig would say, but fuck it, I grew up in a household where the man took care of things.

Savanna can take care of herself; she's shown me that time and again in the few short weeks we've known each other. I don't doubt her capability or competence. The woman is brilliant. But that doesn't mean I don't want to take care of her. I want to show her that I'm also capable. Competent.

I don't want her to see weakness.

My hands grip the edge of the island and I bow my head, closing my eyes. Accepting help isn't something I do in my life. I took it when Savanna offered to help me with the accounting because I was helpless. I had no idea what I was doing.

And look at the stress it relieved.

I blow out a long breath. There's no denying it took an enormous weight off my shoulders. It's made a huge difference in my life. Savanna has made a huge difference. And now she wants to make another difference, and I'm resisting the idea.

A soft, warm hand touches my cheek, turning my face to

the side. Opening my eyes, I find Savanna at my side, a tentative smile touching the corners of her lips.

"Vulnerability doesn't need to have shame attached to it," she whispers to me. "No one will think less of you for needing help."

Standing upright, I angle my body towards her. Emotion that I'm unable to hide sounds thick in my voice when I ask, "What if I'll think less of me?"

"Then we'll remind you that you wouldn't think less of us, so you shouldn't think it of yourself," she says with a tenderness I've not yet heard from her.

"I have no problem smacking you upside the head if you start spouting shit like that," Liam remarks with a smirk from across the counter.

Savanna sucks her lips into her mouth to keep from giggling while I shoot him a glare. The asshole blows me a kiss, daring me to come over there. Brody stands there, beer bottle in one hand, watching it all unfold. To his credit, he doesn't laugh, but I can see the amusement lurking across his tanned skin.

All they want to do is help. They care about me enough to want to help. For once, maybe I should allow them. Show them that sometimes I can't do it all by myself.

Show myself that it's okay.

I slip my arm around Savanna's shoulder and pull her into my side, pressing a kiss to the top of her head. "What do you think?" I ask, and she looks up at me, eyebrow raised. "Out of these two boneheads, who'd fetch the bigger amount?"

Savanna tosses her head back and laughs, throwing her arms around me in the process. She knows what my question truly means. I'm accepting their help. Allowing them all to come in and rescue me for once.

She gazes up at me, the terror and worry of earlier gone, replaced with a joy I had a hand in creating. "Brody," she answers with conviction, garnering an uproar from Liam. "No question, hands down, Brody."

And thus began the great debate.

CHAPTER 30

I'M STARTING MY FOURTH SHIFT AT THE FIREHOUSE, AND BY now I know the routine. Nate drops me off in the rec area where I wait while everyone changes and gets ready for shift before their morning meeting. The first day he didn't let me out of his sight, which worked out because I ended up joining the meeting so he and Captain Bernard could explain to the rest of the crew what I was doing there, and what was going on.

It had been intimidating telling the Captain my story, mostly because I'd never met the man before, but Nate did a good job explaining most of it, holding my hand when his boss asked me a few questions. He had no problem with me being at the firehouse as long as Nate, and everyone else, still performed their duties. He even called one of his friends at the police station who came down and had a chat with me.

The shitty thing was they couldn't do anything about Vincent, which I'd already assumed. The cop said he would create a file including everything I'd told him. This way there would be documentation if something were to happen. It didn't make me feel better, and I know it didn't help Nate either, but I think we were both in the frame of mind the cops wouldn't be able to do much at this point.

It'll be two weeks tomorrow since I saw Vincent at the bar. Two long, stressful weeks.

I haven't stopped looking over my shoulder, expecting him to show up. When Nate and I haven't been at the firehouse, we've mostly been at home, or at the bar. Every time the door to the bar opens, my heart stops, and I quit breathing until I see who walks in.

I knew Vincent would do something like this, keeping me on edge, but I honestly didn't expect him to vanish for this long. It's starting to wear me down. The only time I ever seem to be alone is when I'm using the bathroom, and while I love Nate for keeping me safe, I'm starting to feel a bit smothered.

I'll take it over leaving him, though. I still can't believe I was ready to walk away. I know why I was doing it, and I really did have the best intentions, but thinking back, I'm not sure how I thought I'd be able to do it.

Leaving my family was one thing, but leaving this man I've fallen in love with is entirely different. I realized that once I got home and started to pack. It was his damn t-shirt that did me in.

He'd been wearing it a few days before when he came into my room while I was folding laundry, attacking me from behind with a myriad of kisses, tickling me until I couldn't take it anymore. Then he'd spun me around, kissed me breathless, and looked into my eyes the entire time he made love to me. I think I knew before then he felt the same way I did, but gazing at him while he moved inside of me, tender and sweet, solidified it for me.

So when I found that damn shirt, I knew I couldn't leave.

"Damn it," I mutter to myself, digging through my bag to look for the smaller bag that houses my chargers and earbuds.

I've been through it twice and can't find it, but I know I packed it before we left this morning. In my haste to be ready on time, I dumped my bag in the back of the truck, though, and I'll bet I missed it when I picked everything up when we got to the firehouse.

I drop my bag to the ground with a thunk, letting out a grumbling breath. There's no way I can go without them. The one good thing about being stuck at the firehouse all day is the time it's provided to plan the firefighter auction at the bar, which has meant being on the phone. A lot. We didn't wait for the accountant to confirm what I'd already figured out, though he did two days after he got the USB Nate dropped off to him, to start planning. Liam and I set to work immediately.

Tomorrow night we'll throw the doors of the bar open for the first ever 10-42 Firefighter Auction. The support for it has been overwhelming. Nate has helped so many people over the years without asking for anything in return, that once word spread, the offers came pouring in.

I think everyone besides Nate knew it would happen. It's been heartwarming to watch his surprise and awe every time Liam—who has been instrumental in finding candidates for dates—or I tell him of someone new reaching out. Firefighters and community alike.

Frustrated and grumpy, I grab Nate's keys and push away from the table I'm sitting at. He argued over leaving them with me the first day, saying I wouldn't need them, and he didn't want me outside by myself. Once I'd pointed out that if something happened while he was on a call and I wouldn't have any way out I'd be screwed, he relented. Now I'm thankful he did. I can run out there and be back before he even knows I've left.

Swinging the keys around my finger, I make my way out the side door that dumps me into the parking lot. Unless someone with a code is going in or coming out when I return, I realize I'll have to go through the front door to get back in, but it's not a big deal. Sure, it leaves me a little more exposed, but even if Vincent knew I was here, I don't see him trying anything at the firehouse. Too many people, too big a chance of getting caught.

Opening the back driver's side door, my eyes scan the bench and then the floor for the little case, but I don't have a chance to look for long. Something grabs my hair and forces me face first onto the floor of the truck, and I screech, my body folding in half at the pressure. Fighting to turn and see what the hell is happening, a body presses up against me from behind, pinning me in place.

Adrenaline floods me, causing me to struggle before I force myself to stop, knowing it's futile in this moment. I should conserve my energy even though every instinct is telling me to fight back.

"Hi bear," Vincent coos into my ear, the scent of his cologne so close making me nauseous. "God, I've missed you."

Bone crushing fear turns my blood cold. I don't respond. I know he's trying to get a rise out of me, but he got enough when he pushed me down. I don't want to give him anything more.

Though it makes me feel physically ill, I let him cover me with his body, sniff my hair, nuzzle my ear. I let him take his fill of what he wants because I have no idea what Vincent's plan is. All I know is he isn't going to let me go anytime soon, so the longer I can remain in this parking lot, the better chance I have of Nate realizing I'm not inside.

Nate.

God, I wish I'd listened to him. I should have known better than to come outside alone.

Without warning I'm being yanked up by my hair and I cry out at the sharp pain radiating from my scalp. Vincent is looking for a reaction from me, and not giving him one is infuriating to him.

It's a double-edged sword. If I give him what he wants, it eggs him on, but if I don't, he gets more violent.

His breath is hot against my ear. "Did you miss me too, bear?"

Now that I'm upright, I struggle against him again, trying to wrench my body away from his. With his hand tight in my hair and a leg between mine, hips pressed against me, he's got me mostly under control. Reaching back, I go for his face with my nails, but I feel him duck out of my way and then something cold and hard presses into the bottom of my chin causing me to freeze.

"I wouldn't do that, baby bear," he says coldly. "Don't make this harder than it needs to be."

Panic is grabbing hold of me, my chest heaving with each breath I take. There's a gun aimed at me, and I have zero doubt that it's loaded. It takes every bit of fight out of me.

Closing my eyes, tears well in them, defeat surging within me. Not once in all our time together did Vincent pull a gun and threaten me. Apparently he knew that I wouldn't be easy to manage this time around.

A gun changes everything. A gun means that if Nate, or

any of the other guys, came out and found us, they'd be in imminent danger.

"Okay. Okay, I won't. I promise." My mouth is dry as dust. I try wetting my lips to make my words less hoarse, infusing them with as much happiness as possible. It's fake, but I'm hoping he doesn't notice. "There's a little café down the street. Why don't we go there and have a coffee and talk?"

I feel the gun sliding up my jaw and cringe, squeezing my eyes closed as it brushes my hair away from my face. Then Vincent's lips are at my ear and I can feel him smiling.

"Oh, baby bear, I have something different planned for us." He nuzzles me again, making my skin crawl. If I could, I would knee him in the balls. "You're a hard woman to get alone, you know that? It's been driving me insane to see you with all these different guys."

A tear slips down my cheek. "They're just friends."

Vincent pushes the gun into the side of my head, and I swallow a yelp.

"Don't lie to me. I've seen the way the one looks at you," he growls at me, and I can hear the hate and jealousy he has towards Nate. "I've seen the two of you in and out of the car together. Here. At that bar. Into that house."

Fear claws at me, threatening to shred my heart and lungs to pieces. Breathing is difficult and my heart shrieks. He knows where Nate lives. He's been there. He's seen it. He knows we're together.

I've never known true fear before now. The basement, the beatings, the gun… they were all walks in the park compared to the bone chilling terror that seizes me.

Before I have a chance to respond, the sound of a vehicle coming into the parking lot has us both looking through the windows to see a large red truck with a surfboard in the back.

Brody.

Oh god. Part of me is grateful that he's there, someone I know and trust, who could help. But another part, the part that I know will override anything else, dies a little inside as he parks a few spots down. I can't let him see Vincent. I can't put him in any more danger than I already have.

It might be your last chance at being saved...

But to what end? I wouldn't be able to forgive myself if something happened to him because of me.

Will he be able to live with himself if he knew he could have done something to save me?

I think of him losing his wife, and what he said to me that night in the kitchen. The unknown is the worst part.

I'm about to plunge them all into the unknown, and I already hate myself for it.

The hand in my hair tightens, yanking my head back. Vincent snarls, "Get rid of him."

He releases his hold on me, and I feel him drop down into a crouch behind me. He isn't a fool, however. Before I can think of kicking him so I can run, he's got the barrel of the gun pressed against my lower spine, effectively forcing me to comply.

"Hey Sav," Brody calls from near his truck. I look through the window on the other side of Nate's truck and lift a hand in greeting, but it isn't enough to placate him. He heads in my direction. "What are you doing out here?"

I step out from the back door of the truck, shielded partially from view by the bed of it. If I can keep Vincent hidden, and Brody on the opposite side, I might have a shot at this not ending badly.

Forcing a smile on my face, I gesture towards the back seat. "Looking for my headphone case. I dumped my bag this morning by accident."

"Oh." Brody nods because it's a plausible story, glances at his watch, then looks back to me. "I'll wait for you."

"What? No. You don't need to do that, I'll be inside in a second." I hope my voice doesn't sound as high as I think it does. "I don't want you to be late."

Brody shrugs, adjusting the bag he's got slung over his shoulder. "All good. I've got a few minutes. Plus, I think Nate would understand if I was late under these circumstances."

I feel Vincent pressing the gun harder into my back, and I know it's a warning. I need to get Brody out of here.

"Right. The thing is, I just…" I trail off, giving a sigh. Trying to look as sheepish as I possibly can, I lower my eyes and bow my head. "I just need a moment to myself." When I chance my next glance, I frown, trying to look pained. It's not hard considering the circumstances. "I feel like the only time I've been alone the last two weeks is when I'm peeing. I know it's for the best, but I'm feeling a little smothered."

"Ah," Brody says, nodding in understanding. "I can sympathize. When I lost Heather, that's how I felt."

Fuck my life. I'm going to hurl. Here I am, lying to Brody, and it's bringing up memories of his late wife. I feel like such an asshole right now. I just have to remember it's for the greater good. "So you understand I just need a minute."

"Totally." He glances over his shoulder towards the building, then back to me. "Not too long. Nate will have a heart attack if he knows I left you out here by yourself."

"Oh!" Reaching into the backseat, I grab Nate's jacket and toss it to Brody from where I'm standing. "Nate was looking for that. I found it under the seat while I was looking for my headphones."

Brody easily catches it and nods. "If you're not inside by the time I'm changed, I'm coming back out for you."

I give him as much of a smile as I can muster. "I'm sure Nate will be out before that happens."

He shoots me a knowing grin then turns and heads towards the side door. After one last look over his shoulder he disappears inside.

"What the fuck was that shit with the jacket?" Vincent hisses at me, hauling me towards the back door where the cab of the truck provides more coverage from view.

I wince at how tight he's holding my wrist but manage to hold back any sound of pain.

"I was buying us more time," I tell him, though the opposite is true. "If Brody hadn't taken that inside, Nate would come out looking for it. Is that what you want?"

Vincent growls but doesn't argue with me. "Come on. Let's go. Too many eyes around here."

Every instinct is screaming not to go with him. If I go, I'm a goner. The problem is my heart. My heart is telling me if I stay, someone else is going to get hurt, and it'll be my fault. It's telling me it won't be able to handle that, and I know it's right.

I force my feet to move as Vincent jerks me away from the truck and shoves me towards the front of it.

"Where are we going?" I ask as he keeps me moving along the front of the cars in the parking lot, probably using them as protection from the building on the other side in case anyone comes out.

"So many questions, bear. You know I love to surprise you. You'll see when we get there."

When we reach the street, he directs me down a few cars to a blue car. I curse under my breath. It's not Vincent's so it must be a rental, which means tracking me down is going to be harder. Fresh tears well in my eyes as we reach the vehicle.

This could be the end for me.

Kissing Nate before he went to get changed might have been the last time I got to kiss him. It wasn't even a good kiss. It was just a simple peck on the lips along with a "see you after your meeting". I might never see his gorgeous smile, or those brilliant blue eyes staring at me with love, ever again.

Oh god.

I haven't even told him I love him. I might never see him again, and he won't know how I feel. I should have told him. I should have kissed him like I meant it. I should have done so many things I didn't, and now I might never be able to.

The sound of a motorcycle engine coming down the road in the opposite direction catches my attention before Vincent shoves me through the driver's door. My heart leaps into my throat.

Liam.

As I climb to the passenger side, with Vincent getting in as soon as I vacate the driver's side, my eyes are glued to Liam pulling into the firehouse parking lot. Vincent starts the car and I glance at the clock while putting my seatbelt on.

Liam's running late. All he has is five minutes to get changed and get to roll call or he'll be suffering the wrath of Nate. I need him to take his time. I need him to be slow enough that I can get his attention so he knows I'm in this car and he can get the description to the police. Vincent needs to be the one to hurry the hell up and pull out.

In the next second, he does.

My eyes dart to where the gun is lying in his lap, to the button for the window, and then back to Liam in the parking lot. My heart is beating ferociously, my pulse thundering in my ears. This is the second time I'm throwing a Hail Mary with Liam. It worked the first time; I pray it works a second.

All I need is a fraction of space where the window is low enough he can hear me shriek.

Things move in slow motion as I watch Liam's helmet come off just before we're driving by the mouth of the parking lot. Hitting the down button on the window, I draw in a deep breath, and scream his name at the top of my lungs.

"Liam!"

For one brief moment, our eyes meet. I see the confusion, the surprise, then the horror. I know he understands. I know he knows.

Relief surges through me knowing someone has seen me, has seen the car, and knows for certain I'm in danger. The relief is short-lived, however, as my world speeds back up to normal again.

"What the fuck are you doing?" Vincent bellows.

I turn to look at him. The last thing I see before my world goes black is the butt of the gun coming straight for me.

CHAPTER 31

NATE

Placing my street shoes in my locker, I grab my phone and shut the door, throwing the lock onto it. It's been almost two weeks since Savanna saw Vincent at the bar, and there's been no sign of him since.

We're both starting to go a little stir crazy. Being locked up in the house, or stuck at the bar, isn't the best way to start a relationship, but I haven't felt comfortable enough having her out somewhere that makes her readily available to him. It's why I've decided to ask Liam and Brody to stand watch while I take Savanna on a date so we can both let our guards down and enjoy our time together. I hate that we need to resort to that, but I don't know what else to do.

I just want this to be over.

I want to be able to take my girl out without feeling like I have to check around every corner or look over my shoulder to see if he's there. Everyone I know has been put on alert for him, including some cop friends beyond what Captain Bernard called in for us. So far, no one has seen a thing.

After having a taste of what Savanna has gone through the last six months, two weeks of it has been enough to last me a lifetime. Every day that goes by I'm left further in awe of her strength and resilience to keep moving forward. All I want to do is find the asshole and kick his ass into next week and out of our lives.

I glance at my watch as I walk out of the locker room. I've got a couple minutes before morning roll call, and I debate going back to check on Savanna, or going straight to the conference room to get myself prepared. I should probably do the latter, but the former seems a lot more enticing.

"Hey man."

I look up to see Brody heading straight towards me. "Running behind?"

"Caught a good wave," he grins at me. "Not as behind as Liam, though."

"Yeah, well, he caught something else last night," I tell him, rolling my eyes.

Liam was doing as Liam does last night. I watched from behind the bar as he picked up a pretty little blonde that was there with some friends. Savanna got a firsthand account of the way he works his magic, and she couldn't stop giggling at all the corny lines she imagined he was using.

Brody stops in front of me, stopping me as well, and holds an article of clothing out to me. "Here."

"What's this?" I ask, taking it from him.

His head cocks to the side. "Uh, your jacket."

I'm perplexed as I look at it, then back to him. "I can see that. Why do you have it?"

"Savanna gave it to me," he responds, looking and sounding as baffled as I feel.

My stomach tightens in a knot. "When?"

Reaching up, Brody scratches his temple, refusing to meet my eyes. "Man, she told me you were looking for it."

The knot grows into a leaden weight in my gut. Every alarm bell is going off in my head as I ask, urgency in my voice, "Where Brody? Where did you see her?"

"Outside," he tells me, glancing over his shoulder at the door. "I know I shouldn't have left her out there, but she said she needed a minute alone."

I'm running before the last words are out of his mouth, alarms and sirens going off with blaring agony in my head. I was never looking for my jacket. I never said a word about it. I knew where it was all along.

Savanna giving it to Brody was a message. Something is wrong.

I can hear Brody following me, yelling down the hall at Mac to get Captain Bernard as I throw the side door open and spill into the parking lot. I'm just in time to see Liam shoot off like a rocket out of the parking lot, taking a right at the street.

My stomach bottoms out. I know without talking to him he saw something, and he's going after whatever he saw. I need to follow, but when I reach into my pocket for my keys, I come up empty handed. Fuck. Savanna has them.

Cursing again, I turn towards Brody. "Give me your keys!" I snarl at him.

"What's going on?" Captain Bernard asks with the commanding authority only a Captain can possess as he and Mac come out the side door.

"He's got her," I tell him. "Liam went after them." I look at Brody again, my hand outstretched. I need to get going if I'm going to catch up. "Give me your fucking keys."

"Dude, you're not driving," Brody says, then looks at the Captain.

I'm about to lose my fucking mind on all of them.

Captain Bernard nods at him. "I'll handle things here. Go."

Christ. The last thing I give a shit about is work, but Brody's right about one thing. I can't drive. I'm trained to stay calm and collected in high pressure situations, but I've realized when it comes to someone you love, all the training in the world can't prepare you for how you'll feel, or what you'll go through.

My phone vibrates in my pocket as I get into the passenger side of Brody's truck. I pull it out, hoping to God it's Savanna, but it isn't. It's the next best thing. Liam.

"Talk to me," I say by way of greeting, grateful he's got Bluetooth in his helmet.

"He's got her. She screamed my name. They were in a blue Charger heading north on Crenshaw," he says, and I can hear the bike whizzing through traffic. "When I came to that T in the road, I went left thinking they're headed towards the interstate, but I can't see them."

"Fuck." I pinch the bridge of my nose, squeezing my eyes shut as Brody puts the truck on the road. "Go right at the T," I tell him.

If Liam went left, we'll go right; divide and conquer.

"Fuck!" Liam shouts, echoing me, but more fervently. "Fuck!"

The sound of the bike has practically died, and my heart is pounding in my chest. I hear my own desperation as I yell into the phone. "What? What?"

"They were right ahead of me. I fucking saw them, and this fucking idiot cut me off. I missed the light," he says angrily. "I can't run this red. I'm at ninety-sixth."

I slam my hand against the dash. It's one of the busiest

intersections in town, a spot we're called to more often than we'd like to be for crashes.

"No," I say even though I want to scream at him to keep going. "Don't even think about it. You can't help us find her if you're dead."

Just as Brody is about to take a right at the T, I flail a hand to the left. "Left! Left! They went left."

I cringe as he navigates the truck left at the last second, causing a horn to blare behind us as he cuts someone off. This is exactly why I shouldn't be driving.

The whir of the motorcycle is back, and I know Liam is through the light, doing his best to catch up. What neither of us has acknowledged is that once you're through the lights where he was stopped, you're on the interstate. If Vincent is driving a Charger, Liam may have his work cut out to catch up.

If anyone can do it, it's him.

Brody hits me with a hand. "Where's Liam?"

"The interstate," I say automatically, then into the phone. "You're on the interstate, right? Do you see them?"

"Not yet," he answers, then falls silent again, hopefully to concentrate on the road.

I nod at Brody, and that's when I clue in he's on the phone with someone via the truck Bluetooth. I don't recall him dialing, let alone talking, but the screen on the truck says he's connected to 911.

Fuck. Of course.

I want to hit something for how stupid I feel right now. I'm a fucking firefighter and it didn't even cross my mind to call the police. This isn't how I normally operate, but I can't seem to get my brain to make sense of anything except the fact that Vincent has Savanna, and there's nothing I can do about it.

I'm fucking helpless. I promised her I would take care of her. That I wouldn't let anything happen to her, and still this happened on my watch.

"There!" Liam yells into the phone. The sound shocks me, and I lean forward to look out the window like they'll magically appear in front of me. "I got them. I got… no, no, no. Mother fucker!" There's a frustrated growl and I can hear the bike slowing and then revving up again. "He cut over to the fourteen, but I've got him."

"They're on the fourteen," I tell Brody and the operator still on the line. "They're headed around the mountain. Someone needs to find them and get them pulled the fuck over." My other line beeps and I glance at my phone, my heart lodging in my throat.

Savanna.

I don't even tell Liam to hold on before I'm swiping right on "answer and merge call". "Savanna? Where are you? Are you okay?"

I pause, listening intently. There's the sound of a male voice that must belong to Vincent chattering in the background, but I can only make out every few words. It makes my blood boil, but it's nothing compared to the sound of him suddenly screaming at Savanna.

There's a fumbling sound, like something is rubbing over the mouthpiece, then a shriek, followed by the sound of the phone being dropped.

"Stop! Stop! I'm not doing anything! You're hurting me!"

The sound of Savanna being more petrified than I've ever heard her dials me in. Everything comes into clear focus for me, and I grind my teeth together, my breath coming in harsh, heavy pants.

I might be helpless right now, but when I find this fucker, and I will, I'm going to commit murder.

CHAPTER 32

I'm not sure how long I'm out, but when I open my eyes, we're on the interstate.

My head is pounding, and dizziness threatens to swallow me, sending my stomach roiling. I know I'm bleeding before I reach up and touch the spot just above my temple where the gun hit me. Sure enough, my fingers are red and sticky when I pull them away.

I'm so screwed. I should have done something more when I had the chance. I should have alerted Brody in some other way. I should have stayed inside in the first place.

Most of all, though, I should have told Nate I love him.

"There she is," Vincent says from beside me. It's apparent from his tone that he's calmed down since I screamed at Liam. Fingers brush across my forehead, moving through my hair a second later so he can push it out of my face. "You have a nice nap, bear?"

The fact he thinks what I had was a nap is disgusting and

delusional. I wish I could tell him he hit me so hard I blacked out, but I'm pretty sure it won't help my case.

Shifting in my seat to get as far away from him as I can, I press myself against the door, watching the outside speed by. "Where are we going?"

"Baby bear, I told you," he coos at me as though nothing has happened. As though I haven't been gone for six months. It was always the same after he hurt me. The period of sweetness, the soothing, the lull of a promise he wouldn't do it again. "It's a surprise."

I don't look at him. I'm frozen in my spot by a glimmer of hope. When I shifted, I realized my phone was in my back right pocket. If I can get it out, there's a chance I can call for help.

Nate will know by now I'm gone. Liam would have made sure of that. They'll have the police searching for me. If Nate answers his phone, maybe I can get Vincent talking and he'll tell me where we're going.

I chance a glance his way. His eyes are focused on the road, his fingers tapping the wheel to the tune of whatever rap song he has playing in the background. I always hated listening to his music, but the way he's bopping his head to the beat has me feeling a surge of gratitude for it.

Keeping my eyes semi focused in his direction, I slowly shift my arm behind me, craning my wrist so I can grab my phone and pull it out with the tips of my fingers. I nearly lose it when it suddenly comes free, but I wriggle my entire body in a feigned shiver in order to keep my hold on it.

"Can we turn the AC down? I'm freezing."

Vincent's eyes flash to me and he grins, turning the AC down a notch. "California girl now, huh? Can't stand the cold. I'll admit, bear, the place has grown on me the last couple of weeks." He nods appreciatively. "I heard they got snow in the mountains back home the other day, meanwhile I've been sweating my balls off. I could get used to it out here."

I use his ramblings as cover to shift in my seat, making enough room on the edge that I can set the phone down for balance while I hold it and maneuver it with one hand. Another look in his direction tells me he's watching the road, not what I'm doing.

I'm about to answer him to keep him distracted from what I'm doing when he suddenly swerves sharply to the right. I yelp in surprise, narrowly managing to hold on to my phone.

"Sorry bear. Almost missed our turn." He chuckles sheepishly. "That would have been a shame. I can't wait for you to see where I'm taking you. It's gorgeous."

"Great. I'm excited," I say distractedly, swiping through my phone to get to my contacts.

"Me too, baby bear. You know, I was so damn happy to see that video." He glances my way and I'm quick to look at him, trying my best to smile, though it isn't easy given the circumstances.

"I forgive you, you know. For everything. Leaving without a word, not calling for the last six months, letting the internet see you in your underwear." Vincent sighs, but it's not entirely unhappy. "That one was a little harder to forgive than the rest, but it led me to you, so I can't stay too mad."

I swear he wasn't always this delusional. I mean, looking back, he wasn't well, and there were some definite psychopathic tendencies, but I wonder if leaving him made him snap in a way I didn't realize he could.

Glancing out the front window, I fight the sick feeling in

my stomach. "I appreciate that. So now that you've found me, what are we going to do?"

"Don't you want to know how I found you?" he asks, smiling proudly.

I nod when he looks in my direction. Does it matter? No. But I need to keep him talking. The longer he talks, the safer I think I am.

"It was genius. I went by your apartment building, and there was a neighbor outside looking at the construction. The woman couldn't stop chatting my ear off and was more than happy to tell me about the firefighters that saved the day." He's grinning wildly, and while his eyes are focused on the road, there's a sinister glint in them that has a true shiver sliding down my spine.

I steal a glance down to my phone, finding my contacts and scrolling through. With Vincent this distracted, I feel safe enough to find Nate's number, hitting the call button. I see it come up dialing, and suck in my bottom lip, praying it connects. A second later it does, and I know he's picked up. On this secondary highway, however, and this close to the mountains, I worry that I may lose the connection at the worst possible moment.

"She told me about this place that firefighters hang out. Said if she were fifty years younger, she would frequent it daily, and pointed me in the right direction," Vincent continues, his fingers tapping the steering wheel. "I went that night, thinking I'd strike up a conversation with some guys at the bar, see if they knew anything. Imagine my surprise when I heard your name not fifteen minutes after I sat down."

I close my eyes and take a deep breath, letting one tear slip down my cheek. I know the catalyst for him being here was the video, but to know if some neighbor of mine had just kept her mouth shut, he might never have found me, causes a lump to form in my stomach.

In that moment, I hear a quiet beep, and without thinking, open my eyes to look down at my phone. I must have tightened my hand around it and bumped the keypad button because it's on the screen along with Nate's name.

"What are you doing??" Vincent bellows, a hand suddenly gripping my other wrist, jerking me towards the driver's side.

I shriek in surprise, dropping my phone between my seat and the door.

"Stop!" I cry out, twisting towards him because he's giving me no choice with the way he's turning my arm. "Stop! I'm not doing anything! You're hurting me!"

"You were doing something," he growls, releasing my wrist.

He only lets go of it so he can reach over me and pat the seat beside me before he grabs my other wrist, pulling it towards him. As he does so, he's all over the road, paying more attention to me than it.

"Hands over here where I can see them, bear. Why don't you put them right here?" he suggests, placing the hand he's holding over his crotch. "Fuck yeah, baby, right there suits me just fine."

I swallow the bile that comes up my throat. I can feel him getting hard beneath my hand, but it doesn't surprise me. Control always turned him on. Maybe I can use that to my advantage, though. It makes me sick, but if I'm going to survive, I need to do what I have to.

"You know, Vin, if you tell me where we're going, I might be inclined to have a little fun while we're on the road," I purr to him, using the sexiest voice that I can muster. My stomach churns at the thought of it.

"Bear," he whines, but his hips lift in response to me. "I wanna surprise you."

I lean closer to him. "You still can. I won't know what it looks like until we're there. I just want to know where it is that we're going."

Running my hand down the length of his thigh to entice him, but also so I don't need to touch the growing bulge in his pants any longer, I look around for the gun. It hasn't been in his lap since I came to, and I'm not sure where he put it. Apparently he doesn't think I'll put up much of a fight while we're in the car.

Glancing in the backseat to see if he ditched it there, the vehicle behind us catches my eye. But it isn't actually a vehicle.

It's a crotch rocket.

My breath catches in my throat. I would bet my life it's Liam. A bet I realize I'm going to need to make.

"Okay, fine, we're going up there," Vincent says, nodding to the mountain beside us.

There's a large pasture between it and us, and I'm guessing there's a road that will lead us to the other side before we start climbing. I need to do something before we get off this highway and onto some back mountain road.

"I've been staying there. I know you'll love it, bear." His hips lift again, eager for me to do what I told him I would. "Now touch me, baby. I wanna feel your hands on me."

I'm not sure if it's that I know Liam is behind us, the prospect of heading into the mountains with this psycho, or the thought of touching this disgusting piece of shit that has me feeling strong enough to rebel.

"Fuck you, Vincent."

I'm about to punch him in the dick, but he sees the move coming and grabs my wrist, twisting it so hard that I'm screeching. Blinding white pain shoots through my arm, hot enough to make me want to vomit. Somewhere in the deep recesses of my mind, beyond the pain, I know it's broken. It's a warning from him. To bend to his will and stay in line.

"Does he make you scream like that? Huh? Does he know what you like? That you like being punished? Does he make you beg for it, Savanna?" Vincent spits at me in a tone that chills me to the bone, releasing his hold on me.

Despite knowing it will only spur him on, I whimper as I drag my arm away, another stab of pain, worse than before, shuddering through me.

"I hope you enjoyed him while you had him because you're never going to see him again," he rages, the nice guy façade vanishing. "I'm going to make you scream and beg until you can't take anymore, and then I'm going to do it all over again until you are completely broken, destroyed, and on death's door."

With each word that comes from his mouth, I get angrier and angrier. I hate this man. He controlled every aspect of my life for so long, and I let him, but I won't let him control me any longer. If death is what he wants for me, it's going to be on my terms, not his.

He sounds inhuman when he snarls, "I'm going to make you beg for me to end it, Savanna."

"No," I seethe, my chest rising and falling heavily, clarity as clear as a sunny summer day easing the brutal throb in my head as my body prepares for what I'm about to do. "You don't get to hurt me anymore."

Grabbing the wheel with both hands, my one arm rippling with pain, I pull hard to the right.

I know Vincent doesn't see it coming when he yells, slamming on the brakes, but it's too late, the damage is done. We're sent careening into the ditch and pasture beyond. As the car starts its first flip, I hope my phone is still connected, and Nate can hear me because I don't know if I'll ever get another chance to tell him.

"I love you, Nate."

It's all I can manage before I start screaming as the car flips, and everything in it gets thrown around. There's a loud pop, and white dances in my vision as the airbags go off. Then something large smashes through the windshield, but I can't tell if it was coming in or going out. I know the roof is caving in more and more every time we land on it, but I stay rooted in place thanks to my seatbelt.

That doesn't mean I don't feel like a rag doll being tossed around in a washing machine.

The sound is something from a horror movie. Metal scraping, crunching, cracking, grating on every nerve I have left. It feels like it takes forever, but also happens in the blink of an eye, time feeling like a strange, unruly concept.

Then it's over. The car stops, the ride is done, and the only sound I can hear is someone shrieking. It won't stop, and I need it to stop, because it's horrifying to listen to.

I turn my head to the left to see if it's Vincent, but he isn't there. The only person in the car is me.

I'm the one screaming.

Sucking in a breath, I contemplate doing it again because I know I'm on the verge of a major meltdown, but find some scrap of strength left to swallow the urge.

I need to get out of the car. Before it catches on fire, or Vincent comes back with the gun, or something comes down from the mountain to eat me because I'm a sitting duck and the scent of blood is all over me.

I look around the car, trying to figure out why everything looks so weird when it hits me. I'm upside down.

"Oh God," I gasp, hating the thought of being upside

down even more than the thought of something coming to eat me.

I'm stuck in this small, tight space. It hurts to breathe. It feels like someone is sitting on my chest, making it impossible to pull air into my lungs.

No. No, I need to breathe. I can't melt down right now.

Closing my eyes, I focus on trying to breathe to a count of four, but I only make it to two. My chest is on fire. Hanging upside down is doing nothing to help. In fact, I'm starting to feel a little woozy and lightheaded.

"Savanna!"

Nate. Oh, sweet, wonderful Nate. The man I love. I need to hold on, I need to tell him that I love him. I need to make sure he heard me.

"Savanna!"

Turning my head towards my window, or what's left of it, I blink slowly at the face that drops in.

Not Nate. Liam.

"Liam," I say, but my voice doesn't sound right.

"Yeah, it's me. Listen, don't move, okay? We're going to get you out as quick as we can," he says urgently. "Can you tell me what hurts?"

I can't hold my head the way I need to in order to see him, so I stop trying to crane it. I do, however, see movement come through the small sliver of window that's left and then feel his fingers at my neck.

I whimper. "Chest. Arm. Head. Maybe everything. Liam?"

"I'm here," he says, but I already know that because he hasn't taken his hand away.

My stomach lurches with fear. "Vincent?"

There's a pause before he answers. "He won't be able to hurt you ever again, Sav."

"How do you know?" I ask hoarsely. Though it hurts to

do so, I turn my head again, trying to peer at him, then beyond him. There's hardly any space for me to see through, but if Vincent is out there, if he's close, he could hurt Liam while he's on the ground trying to help me. "I don't want him to hurt you. Liam, he has a gun—"

"Sav," he interrupts in such a way it demands my entire attention, pulling me back into the moment. "He went through the windshield. He isn't going to hurt anyone. Ever again."

For one heartbeat I stare at Liam, unable to comprehend his words. My body understands before my mind, a breath of relief whooshing out. Safe. My family, my friends, my love. All of them are safe.

The motion sends a flurry of pain through me so severely I become nauseated. I stop craning my neck, my eyes closing as I manage to say, "Liam?"

"Yeah?"

"Tell Nate I love him, okay?" I whisper.

I'm pretty sure if I could cry right now, I would, but there are no tears. There's nothing but pain. Even the relief was short-lived. I think I might be teetering on the edge of death. Which scares me. More than being scared of dying, I'm scared that I won't be able to live. To live and experience all that life may have had to offer with Nate. With the friends I've met, and the ones I haven't seen in too long. With my family.

"He heard you, Sav. But you're going to tell him yourself as soon as he gets here, okay? He's almost here." I can hear fear in his voice, and it makes me think that whatever he sees can't be good.

"Liam?" I say, the dizziness beginning to make the whole world spin. I don't know if I can take it much longer.

"Yeah?"

My mouth feels like I've eaten sand. I lick my lips, tasting blood. "How bad is it?"

He blows out a big breath. "I've seen worse, but it's not good. You need to get to a hospital." That makes me smile. Leave it to Liam to give it to me straight. "But you're a survivor. You're going to be fine."

That's the last thing I hear before I succumb to the darkness.

CHAPTER 33

NATE

IT'S BEEN TWELVE HOURS OF HELL.

I'm not used to being on this side of things. Normally I get to help a person in a car accident, get them in an ambulance, and then I'm done. It's the end of the road for my relationship with that person. Sometimes Quinn and Hailey tell us about the trip to the hospital, but nine times out of ten, we know nothing.

I realize now how much I take that for granted. I wouldn't be able to do my job if I were emotionally invested in every single person I helped, but this gives me a different outlook on those I help, and their loved ones.

It's hell. I am living in a waking nightmare.

By the time I got to the scene, Savanna had blacked out. If it hadn't been for Liam and Brody, I probably would have lost my damn mind. Those two kept me levelheaded. With the three of us working together, we managed to get the door open on the driver's side so we could at least get in there to assess her properly.

When I say we, I mean Brody got in there. Liam was in firefighter mode so he was keeping it together, but Brody could see he was right on the precipice of losing it after witnessing the crash. I was a write off.

There was no compartmentalizing my feelings, or what I was seeing. Once we got the door open, I knew the things we had to do, but I couldn't make any part of my body function. It was like I had stepped outside of myself to watch everything going on. My fingers and toes went numb, I felt sick, and at one point when I looked down at my hands, I realized they were shaking as badly as Savanna's had the night she broke the glass at the bar. The night she first told me about the scumbag who put her in this position.

This wasn't my first time at a scene of someone I knew, but it was the first time the woman I love was involved. I've never been so happy to see another rescue crew show up so they could get her pulled from the wreckage. When a hand clapped me on the shoulder, it took me a moment to realize that it was Tyson. The same Tyson who had stared at her like he'd wanted more than just a meal, or her number.

"We'll take good care of her," he'd said to me.

They had. It felt like it'd taken all day to free her, but that wasn't the logical part of my brain talking. The firefighter in me knew they'd worked efficiently, yet carefully, extricating her in the safest and quickest way possible. It had been hard to watch, but harder to look away. Especially when I had looked away, it was to see a couple of other guys looking at Vincent who lay in the field.

Dead.

Some dark part of me wishes it'd been me to end his life.

The rational part of me knows it's better this way. No longer a threat and will never be one again. At least not physically.

Savanna spent most of the day in surgery. There was internal bleeding, which was the most critical, but they managed to get it under control after they removed her spleen. At least that's what the doctor told me.

Then there was everything else.

Her left forearm was fractured, her right collarbone had to be repaired along with a dislocated shoulder, and she'd sustained major blows on both sides of her head. That was the most concerning right now; the doctors were worried about the swelling in her brain, but they wouldn't know the full damage until she woke up.

They're keeping her pretty heavily medicated, which I know is the best thing, but Christ, what I wouldn't give to see those gray eyes of hers.

Movement out of the corner of my eye catches my attention and I expect to see a nurse coming into the room. Instead, it's Brody.

He gives me a nod before glancing at Savanna. "How is she?"

Sitting up in my chair, I release a breath, running a hand through my hair. "No change."

Savanna was airlifted to the trauma center in San Jose which is a little more than an hour from Santa Rosé, so Brody drove us to the hospital once she was loaded in the helicopter. Liam followed on his bike, not wanting to leave it on the side of the highway even though we both tried to convince him not to ride after being so shaken up. Damn asshole wouldn't listen to us.

They both left once she got out of surgery, and only after I insisted they go home and get changed. They both had her blood all over their clothes. I still do.

"Stopped by your place," he says, reading my mind. He holds up a bag. "Brought you this. Figured you weren't leaving anytime soon."

My chin juts out, jaw set. "I'm not."

"You get a hold of her dad?" Brody asks, taking a seat opposite me on the other side of her bed.

Leaning back in my chair again, I clasp my hands together and rest them on my stomach, letting my eyes settle back on Savanna where they've been for the majority of the time I've been sitting here. She's breathing on her own, so she doesn't have a bunch of tubes and wires coming out of her face, but I feel like they're all over the rest of her.

I hate that her dad and brothers are going to have to see her like this. Sighing, I nod. "Yeah. Her family is flying in first thing tomorrow."

For a while we sit in silence, listening to the machines monitoring Savanna.

It guts me to look at her, to see all the bruising and swelling on her face, the cuts and scrapes. It's partially why I keep staring at her. I need to punish myself for everything that's happened, for everything I couldn't stop, and this is the best way.

I should have done a better job protecting her. I should have kept my promise of protecting her. I don't know what more I could have done, short of handcuffing her to me, but Jesus, there must have been something.

"Stop it," Brody says.

I look up at him in surprise. "Stop what?"

His lips pinch together, exasperated. "I can hear you from here. You're beating yourself up."

"I didn't say anything," I scoff, shifting guiltily.

Keen brown eyes watch me over Savanna's bed. "You didn't need to."

Breathing out a sigh, I scrub my hands over my face. Sometimes it's easier when it's Liam instead of Brody. Sure, Liam picks up on things, but he doesn't call me out in the same manner Brody does. Brody has this quiet way of throwing things at you that make you stop and think, and I really don't have the capacity to do that right now.

"I should have done more," I tell him, leaning forward to rest my elbows on my knees, looking down at the floor. "I should have been there for her."

Closing my eyes, I take a shaky breath, hating myself for the thoughts running through my head, but I need to tell someone, and it might as well be Brody.

"I love Liam, and I'm grateful as fuck he was there for her, but it should have been me," I choke out, pushing a finger and thumb into the corners of my eyes. "I wish it had been me talking to her, holding her hand, telling her it was going to be okay. She must have been so scared, and I couldn't even comfort her."

Brody scratches at his chin for a moment, letting the silence weigh down on us, digesting what I've said before responding. Finally, he says, "When Heather died, I wished the same thing. I felt guilty I wasn't there to hold her hand. I wasn't there in her last moments."

When I look at him, his eyes are planted on Savanna, and I wonder if he sees her, or if he's seeing Heather. "I didn't think I would survive the guilt of it. I let it consume me, and fuck man," he pauses, grimacing. "I wanted it to consume me. I didn't think I deserved anything more."

My heart goes out to him. Brody never really talked about what he went through after Heather died, choosing to freeze us all out as he worked through it himself. And he did, to a point, though he's never been the same.

"Feels like if you'd just been able to protect her, keep her safe, everything would be okay," I say quietly, running a hand through my hair. "That's how I feel. If I'd been better, she'd be okay. She wouldn't be stuck in a hospital bed. I just keep coming back to the same damn thing, man. This is all my fault."

"Let's get one thing straight," Brody says sternly. His eyes are trained on me, hard and unwavering. "There is only one person to blame for all of this, and that son of a bitch is dead. This wasn't your fault, and it wasn't Savanna's. This is all on him."

I breathe out a sigh. "I wish believing that was as easy as saying it."

"You can't let the guilt destroy you. You've just got to be happy she's still alive."

I look at him, contemplating what he's said, what he shared about Heather, and how he felt afterwards. "How did you get over the guilt?"

Brody laughs, but there's no humor in it. "Who said I did?"

"Heather dying wasn't your fault," I say, frowning. "You weren't driving the car."

He gives me a pained smile, and I can see then that he still lives with guilt every day of his life. It's not something I normally see in him, but maybe that's because he hides it so well none of us see it.

"But I should have been." He rubs his hands together for a moment then leans forward, elbows on his knees, his fingers tented in front of his lips. "Do you think she'd want you to be sitting here beating yourself up for what happened?"

I bark out a surprised laugh. "No." I sigh, reaching my hand out to run my fingers over hers as I gaze at the cast she's in. "She'd probably give me shit if she knew the things I was thinking."

Then she'd make me forget all about it.

"Then maybe you should give her what she wants without her having to tell you," he suggests.

I wave a finger at him. "You're a wise man, Mr. James. A very wise man."

He smiles in acknowledgement, and we lapse into another silence.

Brody, to my surprise, is the first one to break it. "What do you want to do about the auction?"

I curse under my breath, scrubbing my free hand over my face. The auction is the lowest thing on my priority list right now. It shouldn't be, because the bar is screwed without the money that will potentially come from it, but I don't know if I can deal with it. Don't know if my heart has the strength. The auction was Savanna's baby. Sure, she asked for my approval on this or that while she planned, but she was the one with all the knowledge of it.

My answer might be different if I could just see her eyes, but in the dreary hospital room with the machines beeping, the cords strung all over, and the distant sound of voices down the hall, I tell him, "Cancel it."

While I hated that it was Brody with his perceptive eyes, keen sense, and wise words, I'm grateful it's him now, rather than Liam. The latter would have fought me on it, but Brody just nods his acquiescence and lets me be.

I know he's letting me soak it all in, to stew in his words about guilt and the auction, but my thoughts drift from what happened today to what Brody's gone through, and after a few minutes I say, "It wasn't your fault man. No matter what you might think, it wasn't your fault."

Rather than agree with me, he just gives me a smile, this time a placating one. I know he doesn't believe me. "Thanks man. Appreciate that."

THE NEXT DAY, I STAY AWAY AS LONG AS I CAN, BUT I CAN'T BE away from her any longer. With a coffee in hand, I'm headed back to Savanna's room after leaving her bedside when her family got into town.

It was awkward at best to begin with, them not knowing me, me not knowing them. I could tell they were a little hesitant about me, and who could blame them, with everything she'd been through. They all but threw me out within the first half hour they'd been there, telling me to go home and get some sleep since I'd been at her side since she'd gotten out of surgery the day before.

Out of respect, I conceded without much of a fight. It wasn't that I wanted to leave her, but I know they needed some time to be with her after all this time, and after everything that had happened.

Jordan and Bryn had brought my truck up to the hospital in San Jose the night before, along with some dinner, so I made the trek back to my place in Santa Rosé where I slept for a couple of hours. I did more tossing and turning than sleeping, though. I laid there for ages, thinking about how cold the bed was without Savanna beside me, lonely without her pressing against my chest, and devoid of any laughter and happiness without her smiling face.

I think under normal circumstances, being without her would have been tolerable, but given what we'd gone through the last thirty-six hours, and few weeks as a whole, it was my own personal hell. I don't want to live without this woman. Today, tomorrow, the rest of my life.

I half wish she was in the hospital in Santa Rosé. At least then I'd know people who I could hang out with, sort of, without being in Savanna's room. Close enough I could check in every once in a while and still give her family the space they needed.

Then again, she wouldn't have gotten the same treatment in Santa Rosé as she got in a trauma center in the big city. I'm grateful for that treatment. Grateful to the surgeons that put her back together, and the nurses taking care of her. I'm grateful to my family and friends who have reached out with an outpouring of love and support, offering to bring me food, help with the bar, and look after anything that either of us might need.

I've always known I have an amazing circle around me, a second family within the firehouse, but the last day and a half of my life have really shown me how special everyone is, and how lucky I truly am.

The great thing about the hours I keep at the bar, and at the firehouse, is that I won't have a problem taking the night shift with Savanna. It's not quite dinnertime, but now that I'm back at the hospital, I'm here to stay until at least the morning, hence the coffee in my hand.

I nod at the nurses as I walk by and then head into Savanna's room, hoping to find the woman I love sitting up and laughing with her brothers and her father. Disappointment assails me when I see her still laying there, the tubes and wires still connected, the sound of the machines still monitoring her.

One brother sits in a chair at her side, head bowed as he looks at his phone that's plugged into the wall. Connor.

Sensing my presence, he looks up, dirty blonde hair, a few shades darker than Savanna's, tousled like he's been running his hands through it all day. He gives me a nod when he recognizes me.

I nod back, taking the chair opposite him, on the other side of Savanna's bed. "Any change?"

He shakes his head. "No. I would have let you know."

I nod with appreciation. Connor swore he'd let me know if there were any changes in her condition, and I'm glad he mentions it now. Meeting the family with Savanna being out cold might have been awkward, but I like him. Out of the three of them, Connor seemed the most welcoming of me.

"You the only one around?" I ask.

"Yeah. Dev took Dad back to the hotel for a bit. This has all been a lot for him." Setting his phone down on the arm of his chair, he regards me thoughtfully. "It's been a lot for all of us. Especially her. I'm glad she had you looking out for her."

I wave my hand, brushing off the comment. My eyes drop to where her arm with the fractured collarbone and dislocated shoulder is in a sling, the other in a cast. "Nothing to be glad for when she still ended up like this."

I can feel Connor's eyes burning a hole into me, but I don't give in to the need to look at him. I don't need to see the reprehensible look in his eyes. Or maybe worse—pity.

"She told me you were the one that got her to call home. That true?"

My eyes flash up to him, eyebrows raised in surprise. I didn't realize she'd shared that with her family. I made it clear to her it wasn't me that got her to do anything. "She made a choice to call."

Connor laughs like I've told him something absurd, shaking his head at me. "Man, she told me you were smart," he says like he doesn't believe it, and I'm not sure if I should be offended.

"Savanna didn't realize she had a choice. In her mind, the only choice was keeping herself away from us. You made her open her eyes." Connor leans forward in his chair, resting his elbows on his knees as he keeps his gaze on me. "If it weren't for you, we still wouldn't know where she was, or what she was doing. Besides being in Santa Rosé, anyway, thanks to that video."

I drop my head backwards and look up at the ceiling. "That fuckin' video."

"As much as I never wanted to see my sister in her underwear, that fuckin' video got her in touch with us, so I don't view it as a bad thing," he says gratefully.

I can't agree with him. That video is what ultimately led Vincent to her, of that, I'm sure. It was the catalyst in putting her into this hospital bed.

I only found out the day of the video she hadn't talked to her family since before she left, but I'm convinced I could have gotten her to call them if I'd had a little time. I know I could have made her feel comfortable enough she would have called them. Or we could have taken a weekend trip to Nevada, or Washington, and called them from there.

So I can't feel good about the video. Not when she's lying in a hospital bed with injuries I can't fix with a first aid kit.

Connor must take my silence as a disagreement. "I get it, man. The video brought Vincent here. We all think it, even if we don't know it for sure. But have you thought maybe it's better this way? That piece of shit is dead now. He can't hurt Savanna."

Reaching for a water bottle on the bedside table, he opens the cap to take a sip, but first adds, "If that means she's a little worse for wear for a bit, I gotta say, I'll take it. Not trying to be a dick, but I'd rather this," he gestures towards her, "than him still being out there hunting her down."

Everything he said makes me want to lurch out of my chair, get in his face, and demand he take it back. My fingers curl around the arms of my chair until my knuckles turn white. It's hard to see it that way. Every instinct tells me protecting Savanna, keeping every hair on her head injury free, is the way things need to work for me to be okay in life. It tears me apart inside to see her laying in this bed, hooked up to monitors, in a cast, in a sling, her face beat up and bruised all to hell.

But maybe, just maybe, Connor has a point. One I hadn't considered before.

I think of the times Savanna was triggered around me, the look on her face, and in her eyes. She was petrified. And then there was the day at the taqueria where she passed out in my arms from the panic attack, caused because she thought Vincent would be able to find her with the video out there.

That's what she was living with. Every day she had to deal with the fear he would turn up. She always had to look over her shoulder. That isn't any way to live. I experienced it for a fraction of what she did, and I hated to see how it affected her. Going through weeks, months, or years, would have been impossible.

"I might be able to agree after she wakes up, but until then..." I trail off, releasing a breath that says it all, running a hand through my hair.

"Yeah," he sighs heavily, sounding as tired as I feel. "I hear you."

We're both silent for a while, lost in our own thoughts, before Connor says, "She told me everything you did for her. For the record, I like you. We all do."

Giving him a brief smile, I nod in acknowledgement. "That's a good thing, because I'd really like to be a big part of her life if she'll continue to have me."

Connor laughs, takes a sip of his water, then puts it back on the table. "Man, if you heard her talk about you, you'd know she'd have you for as long as you'll have her. And as much as we'd all like to see her come home, I think we all feel pretty good about her staying here if you're around."

That warms me from the inside out. It also lifts a weight that's been sitting on my chest I didn't realize I was carrying around. I feel it leave almost instantly, and despite everything, I'm grinning from ear to ear. "I'll do everything in my power to keep her safe."

"Good," he says, settling back into his chair with a smile. "I'd prefer not to beat your ass, but don't think I won't if you hurt her."

"I'd let you," I tell him, and mean it.

CHAPTER 34

NATE

My phone buzzes in my pocket, and I lean back to fish it out.

Savanna's dad and other brother, Devin, came by half an hour ago, but since I was there, the three of them decided to head out for a bite to eat. They'd planned on Devin sticking around, but I assured them they could all go out as a group and I'd keep my ass planted in the chair, promising to call if there was any change.

Connor whispered something to Devin when he looked like he was going to argue, and whatever it was made Devin agree to go without a fight. If I were to wager a guess, the conversation Connor and I had went a long way in him feeling comfortable leaving Savanna without one of them here.

I glance down at my phone's lock screen and see I have a message from my mom. Pulling it up, I smile.

Mom: How's my boy holding up?

Me: I'm okay.

Mom: How are you really?

I sigh. Leave it to my mom to know even over a text that my initial answer was bullshit.

Me: Tired.

Mom: How's Savanna?

Me: No change.

I frown, glancing at Savanna's still form on the bed. A groan here and there, but I gave up hoping a while ago it would lead to anything else. Besides those little sounds, nothing.

My phone buzzes again.

Mom: Are you at the hospital?

Me: Yep.

Mom: Have you had dinner?

Me: Nope. I'll grab something when her dad and brothers are back.

Mom: Don't you dare. I'm on my way with dinner for you.

Me: Mom, don't. That's over an hour's drive for you.

Her reply is instant, as though she knew what I would say and had it typed out already.

Mom: Too late, I'm in the car. See you soon. Love you.

Me: You're the best. Love you too.

I'm chuckling lightly at my mom as I stare at the conversation on my phone. My attempt to stop her from coming was half assed because it would be nice to have her here, even if it's a brief visit before she has to head back home.

I'm not a momma's boy by any means, but there's something comforting about having your mom around when times are tough, and I'm man enough to admit that.

Hell, it's nice to have support, period. Liam, Brody, and Jordan have all stepped up to help take care of the bar while

Savanna's in the hospital and I want to be by her side. I think Liam is doing it because he's feeling a little screwed up after witnessing the accident, not that he's told me as much. I just got the sense after talking to him today that he needed a distraction. I can't blame him. I'd love one right now.

As if someone heard my thoughts, there's a groan from the bed, causing my head to snap up.

I suppose I do still have a little hope with every sound that comes from her. Each of them has me looking, balancing on the edge of my seat, wishing her eyes open next. So far, I've been left disappointed every time.

Another groan, followed by a sigh has me sitting up a little straighter.

The sigh is new. So is the head movement.

I watch as she turns her head towards me, groans again, stops, takes a deeper breath than before, and turns it back. The hope that always comes, and usually dissipates quickly, is rising by the second, my heart leaping into my throat with optimism.

"Sav?" I say softly, standing from my chair to get closer to the bed.

Running my thumb over the back of her fingers on her cast-covered arm, I swear I feel them wiggle against mine. The movement is so small I might be imagining it, but when it happens again, I know I'm not.

My breath catches in my throat. For a second I forget how to speak, how to form words, how to communicate, but then the words come in a rush, "Sav? Baby, can you hear me?"

Her eyes part to slits, and in that moment, I swear I could fall to my knees and cry with relief. I know she can't help it when they close a moment later, her lips separating and moving instead. Trying to say something though no words are forming on the breath she lets out.

"Shh, hey, don't worry about talking, okay? You sound like you're in pain. I'll get a nurse," I tell her, but before I can reach over and hit the call button, her fingers are curling around mine.

Her eyes are open, glassy, but wider this time. She's forcing herself to look, to focus. I'm sure the medication is trying to pull her back under, but she's fighting it. Then she looks away, taking in her surroundings before she finds me again, confused. Again she tries to say something, but nothing comes out.

"You're okay. You're safe," I whisper, fearing my voice may break. "Banged up a bit, but nothing that won't heal. You don't need to worry about anything, okay? He's never going to hurt you again, Sav. He's gone for good."

I can see relief shine briefly in her eyes before she loses the battle, and they close on her. Still fighting the medication, though, she forces them open a moment later. It's taking everything out of her, I can see it in her eyes, but before I can tell her to close them and go back to sleep, her lips are moving again. This time I realize she's asking for water.

An orderly just brought a fresh cup of water for her in case she woke up. I grab it and bring the straw to her lips, helping by keeping it steady as she takes a small sip. When she's done, her eyes close again and I pull the cup away, setting it back on the tray.

"Nate," she croaks, her voice hoarse, hardly loud enough to be considered a whisper.

"Yeah, babe, I'm right here. But don't talk. I know you're tired. Just go back to sleep, sweetheart," I tell her, squeezing her fingers gently.

Again she forces her eyes open, peering up at me with intense focus that I didn't expect to see.

"Nate… I love you," she breathes before her eyes close again.

My mouth opens, then closes. Inside my chest, my heart feels like it cracks wide open at her declaration. I heard her yell it through the phone, knew she meant it then, just like she does now. What I didn't know until this moment was how terrified I was that I'd never get to hear it in person. I've allowed the guilt and self-loathing to rule my thoughts the past thirty-six hours because I couldn't bear, or dwell, on the thought I may never hear her tell me in person. Or worse… she wouldn't hear me say it back.

"I love you too, Sav," I choke out. There's the faintest squeeze on my fingers in return.

It's only a few seconds before I know she's succumbed to the exhaustion and medication she was fighting against so desperately. That's when I bend over her bed, pressing my face against her arm above her cast and let the tears fall, yielding to every emotion I've felt for the past two days.

Over an hour later, I'm back in the hospital chair, staring numbly at my phone. I'm exhausted. Seeing Savanna's eyes, hearing her voice, and what she had to say, destroyed the little thread that was keeping me together. Everything I'd refused to feel since the day before, plus everything I'd allowed myself to feel, bore down on me like a torrential rainfall. There was no compartmentalizing this.

I managed to pull myself together after a while. Managed a phone call to Connor to let him, Devin, and Savanna's dad know she'd opened her eyes. It had sounded like the three of them were on their feet to rush back before the words were out of my mouth, but I got them to relax and settle down when I explained she had slipped back into unconsciousness, and being awake even for a couple of minutes had taken everything out of her. They agreed to at least finish their meal before heading back, but I expect them soon.

When I hear footsteps entering the room, I switch my phone off. It's not the three large men—the footsteps are too dainty for that—but my mom who walks in, holding a glass bowl of whatever she made for dinner. Her eyes sweep over Savanna first, then move to take me in. A frown as deep as any I've ever seen my mother wear creases her forehead and tugs her mouth down.

"My sweet boy," she sighs with sadness, moving further in the room with outstretched arms.

Christ. A wave of emotion tugs at my heart. It's unlike the one from earlier, less intense and heavy. More relief and comfort. I get up from my chair, taking the couple strides across the room, and allow her arms to engulf me in a hug only my mother can give. It makes me feel like a boy again, warm and safe, and wholly protected.

But I'm not a boy. I tower over my mom these days, and as I hug her back, I can't help the smile that tugs my lips upwards.

"I'm okay," I tell her quietly, rubbing her back in an effort to convince and comfort her.

She hums her disapproval, releasing me. "You're exhausted. Have you had any sleep?"

I shrug, taking the container of food still in her hands. A welcome distraction so I don't need to meet her eyes as I move to set it down on Savanna's bedside tray. "Some. Thank you for dinner."

My mom says nothing more about it, but I can feel her displeasure radiating through the room. She knows there's nothing she can do. Instead, she changes topics, moving closer to the bed on the same side as me. "How is she?"

"She opened her eyes since I talked to you," I tell her with a small, thankful smile.

My mom's hand comes to her chest, her eyes glowing with hope. "Oh, honey, that's wonderful. It's a good sign, isn't it?"

I nod, my fingers brushing over Savanna's knuckles as I gaze down at her, thinking of the clear focus that had been in her eyes as she managed to tell me the words in her heart. She fought so hard to get them out. Fought the medication, the pain, the drowsiness. For me.

"If you plan on running off to marry the girl the second she's out of here, could you at least invite your mother?" There's a teasing tone to her words, but I think I also detect a level of seriousness.

Stepping sideways so we're shoulder to shoulder, I sling my arm around her and pull her to my side. The thought of Savanna standing before me, in a dress she chooses with me in mind, chases every wretched emotion from my veins, and I smile, warming from the inside out. "If that day comes, mom, I promise you'll be there."

"When Nathan. Not if."

My smile grows and I bend enough to place a kiss atop my mother's head. I amend, "When."

A moment later music begins to play, the sound coming from my mom's purse. She rifles around in it, throwing me an apologetic look, probably for not having it on vibrate.

"Oh, it's your sister," she says when she pulls it out and reads the screen. It's not a phone call, I realize, but a video call. My mom swipes right on "accept".

Jordan's face fills the screen. I blink. Red lipstick. Dark make-up lined eyes. Her hair down and in waves from what I can tell in the picture. It's the way she looks when she's headed out for a night on the town, not a night serving at the bar.

"Hi sweetie," my mom greets Jordan.

My sister smiles and waves, but says nothing. Possibly because she couldn't hear my mom with the noise of an obvious party going on around her. Behind her, the lights of wherever she is are dimmed, music blasting through the speakers. Suddenly, the phone erupts with a new sound, this of an entire crowd erupting in cheers and screams.

"Where the hell are you? Aren't you working the bar?" I question, irritation creeping into my veins. It isn't Jordan's fault Savanna is in the hospital and I'm not there looking after the bar, but I can't help feeling aggravated that she isn't helping after she told me she would.

Not that it matters. I'm—we—are going to lose the thing anyway. Maybe Jordan's already figured that out and decided to say the hell with it. I can't blame her. She's not attached to it like I always have been.

My mom pats my arm, and I'm not sure if it's to soothe me, or quiet me. She says, "Just watch."

With a frown, I glance down at her. Her own eyes are focused on her phone, refusing to meet mine, and when she suddenly smiles, I look back to the device.

And can't breathe.

Jordan has turned her camera around, revealing her location. It's 10-42, but it's...so different. The place has transformed since I was there the night before Savanna was taken. Though I can't see the entirety of it, I can see enough.

Tables have been shifted, moved out of the way to make room for a stage. A stage, I realize, that Liam had been working to construct for the last two weeks. It no longer looks like a barren piece of lumber against the far wall of the bar. Black fabric hangs from the front of it, garlands of streamers hung from it. Three large vases of flowers I don't know the names of sit perched on the floor while bunches of balloons line the side of the stage. Hanging from the wall is a banner that looks all too familiar.

10-42
Save A Fire Truck, Date A Firefighter AUCTION

Liam stands on the stage in a suit—a fucking suit—grinning devilishly at the audience, a mic in his hand. The music quiets and I can hear Liam's voice over the speakers like I'm standing in the bar with them. "Next up, we've got Station Nine's very own Brody James. Personally, ladies, he's my favorite. Besides myself, of course."

Brody. The same Brody that I told to cancel the entire auction. The same Brody who said "over my dead body" would he participate in this. Brody who is striding up the stairs, and across the stage like he owns the whole fucking thing. Completely shirtless with jeans hanging low on his hips. Full of more confidence than Liam has on a daily basis.

Jesus. How many drinks did Liam feed him before this? It's the only explanation.

"What the hell is happening?" I breathe into the room, to my mom, to Savanna, to whoever wants to answer the question. No one does.

The auction was supposed to be canceled. Everyone knew it. Once I gave my answer to Brody, everyone knew. Liam confirmed it this afternoon when I talked to him. And yet…

"Brody may look like a beast, but let me tell you, he's a gentle giant. Quiet and reserved, this man enjoys surfing and long walks on the beach, ladies." Liam pats our friend on the shoulder. "Let's start the bidding off at one hundred dollars. Do I have a hundred?"

I can hear several cheers through the crowd, a couple of signs lifting in the air, and then like he was born to be an auctioneer, Liam begins working the crowd, the bids going higher and higher. With each new offer that comes in, Liam races around the stage pointing out what I can only assume are the different bidders. Brody stands in the middle, flexing a muscle in his arm or showing off his abs, and again I wonder how many drinks must be in him for the man to let go of so many inhibitions.

"Nine-thousand-nine-hundred-and-ninety-nine dollars," says a woman's voice so loudly that there's no doubt it came from someone at Jordan's side.

A silence falls over the crowd. Even Liam pauses, mid-point, his eyes scanning over everyone. Brody smiles. My breath catches in my throat. My mom, beside me, hums in appreciation. As though she knew it was coming. I'd look at her, but I can't take my eyes off the phone. Not when Jordan is turning the angle, showing me the person beside her.

My grandmother stands there with an auction paddle raised high in the air and repeats herself, "Nine-thousand-nine-hundred-and-ninety-nine dollars."

Finally I look at my mom, my mouth gaping, trying to wrap my head around what's going on. The auction... Without my knowledge, they went ahead and did it anyway, even though I told them not to. Because they knew. Knew I needed it to happen, but knew I couldn't deal with it myself.

My chest fills with emotion thicker than mud. My throat closes with the same feeling. For the second time tonight, I find my eyes wet, but with witnesses this time, I press my thumb and forefinger into the corner of my eyes to try and pinch it away.

"For him?" Liam's astonished voice booms through the speaker, causing both my mom and me to laugh. I'm grateful for the comedic relief.

I'm positive I hear Brody faintly say, "Asshole." When there are immediately a few laughs within the crowd I know I'm correct.

"Yes, Liam," my grandmother says, exasperation showing in her tone and the way her paddle holding hand finds her hip. "For Brody. I prefer the quiet ones."

"It's always the quiet ones!" Liam exclaims.

Jordan moves the camera back to the stage. Liam is shaking his head in disbelief, but Brody... Brody is standing there like a proud peacock with a fanned out tail. It clicks into place for me then. He agreed to get on stage because he already knew who would bid on him and there would be no chance of being outbid. My eyes slowly turn back to my mom, narrowing slightly as I work it all out in my mind.

"You knew," I accuse her. Not in malice but in awe. I'm in awe of it all.

My mom waves a dismissive hand in my direction, then points back to the phone. "Shhh."

The video is bouncing all around, making it obvious that Jordan is on the move through the crowd. It's mostly dark then suddenly gets a lot brighter and I realize she's climbing onto the stage, the camera pointed at Liam and Brody, both standing in the middle.

"The beautiful Jordan Miller, everyone," Liam croons to the crowd through the mic, waving a hand graciously towards her. "Sorry gentlemen, she's not the next one up for auction. And if she was, you'd need to get in line behind me."

Jordan laughs, and I see her hand come out to swat Liam playfully in the arm. I can imagine the massive eye-roll she's giving him right now. "Flirt."

Liam grins at her, handing the microphone over while he takes the phone. Planned. This was all fucking planned. From my mom being here to answer her phone, to Jordan walking on stage. I'm gobsmacked.

The video angle switches then, and Liam's face fills the screen while Jordan talks to the crowd in the background. He's still wearing a shit eating grin, and when Brody shows up over his shoulder, the latter is sporting a matching one. All I can do is shake my head at them, but I'm also smiling. A real, genuine smile. The first in a couple of days.

These two fools. My brothers. I wouldn't trade them for a single thing in this world.

"You ready, man?" Liam asks, wiggling his eyebrows at the camera.

My brow furrows. "For what?"

I swear the grins on both their faces get wider before they disappear. In their place is Jordan standing on the stage, but beyond her is the bar. Liam slowly pans from one side to the other, showing my mom and me the crowd.

A choking noise bubbles up my throat. The wave of emotion that enveloped me earlier is back, tenfold. The place is absolutely packed. So packed the firefighter in me worries about the fire code. In my wildest dreams, I never imagined it could be that full.

"Everyone say hi to Nate," Jordan says from somewhere out of the camera's view.

The entire place erupts in a chorus of hello's, cheers, and whoops. At the overwhelming sound, my knees give out and I sink into the chair behind me. My mom follows me down, perching in a second chair that one of Savanna's brothers brought in this morning, still holding the phone for me to watch.

I run one hand through my hair, the other rubbing my

chin, completely speechless as I take in the sight. Words escape me. Thoughts evade me. There's nothing but disbelief. And gratitude. That slams into me so hard I have to bow my head to take a deep breath that's shaky at best.

The comforting touch of my mom lands on my back as she rubs up and down in a soothing motion. "I know, baby boy. I know."

"Nate," Liam says, and I lift my head to find the video back on him and Brody, Jordan having joined them. "We love you, man."

All I can do is nod at him and press my fist to my chest because even if I had the words, they wouldn't do this moment justice. Nothing I could say would convey how I'm feeling. Even telling them that I love them back seems dismal in comparison to what is happening in my heart. After facing some of the darkest days of my life, to have the love and support of my friends and family means the world to me.

It's not easy to be vulnerable. And had a pretty little blonde not walked into an elevator and declared men disgusting, filthy pigs, I may never have learned how to become vulnerable. How to feel safe showing what I always considered a weakness.

I reach over to her now, taking her hand in mine, my eyes sweeping over her. Things aren't perfect. Neither of us is okay. I'm not delusional enough to think we'll magically be okay the second her eyes open for good. There are going to be a lot of things that Savanna needs to work through, and I've got my own shit to deal with. But together? Together we can conquer it all.

I locate my sister and brothers' faces in the phone and smile. With Savanna's hand in mine, I finally find the calmness needed to say, "I love you guys, too. Thank you."

CHAPTER 35

NATE

"Is anyone else hungry?" Connor asks the next day, and there's an eruption of laughter around the room.

Even Savanna is giggling, the sound music to my ears, though I can tell she's exhausted. "Some things never change, huh, Con?"

"I'm a growing boy!" he tells her, puffing his chest with pride.

Devin rolls his eyes. "You realize you're a grown ass man, right?"

"Whatever. Who's hungry? I'm starving. Dad? Dev? Let's go get some lunch."

I'm perched on a chair next to Savanna's bed, my hand covering hers. Our fingers have been brushing each other's for the last half an hour when she woke up, this time a lot more perky than the night before. Still exhausted, still medicated, but she's done well for being this awake for so long.

I'm surprised Connor is trying to get everyone to go for lunch, but then maybe he realizes how tired she is.

"What?" Savanna's dad, Byron, says. "No, I'm not hungry. You go ahead."

"Dad," Connor responds firmly. Byron turns to look at his son, and Connor nods towards the door, using a tone that implies he shouldn't argue. "Let's go get some lunch."

"What's gotten into you? Savanna's awake, and you want to leave?" Devin asks, frowning, before Byron has a chance to reply.

Connor throws his hands up in the air, the frustration evident. "Yes, Savanna is finally awake, and we've said hi. Now we can go so that our sister and her boyfriend can have a minute alone." He glances my way and shoots me a wink. "Pretty sure Nate doesn't want to be kissing her with the three of us around, so why don't we make ourselves scarce for a while?"

I can feel the heat climbing up my neck and into my face. He's not wrong, but Christ, way to throw me to the wolves. "No, it's okay, you don't need to leave."

"Yes, please go. I'd really like a kiss," Savanna says at the same time.

The two of us look at each other and laugh, though I'm the first to sober, clearing my throat as I remember our audience.

"Really, you don't need to leave," I tell them, shaking my head. "You've all traveled so far to be here with her."

"Dad," Savanna says, ignoring my remark. "I promise later on I'll kick everyone out, including Nate, and you and I can sit together and talk alone." She glances up at her brothers next, adding, "I'm getting tired anyway. I don't think it'll be long before I'm passing out again. Go for lunch, and when you get back, I'll be good as new."

It doesn't take much more convincing after that. The three men shuffle out after they each give Savanna a kiss on the forehead, offering to bring both of us back something. Connor makes sure I also hear him say I owe him one. I can't deny it. The guy is looking out for me.

I've been dying to kiss her for days, especially after her declaration last night, and then her waking up this morning. It wasn't how I wanted to hear her say it for the first time, but I know why she did it. She didn't know if she was going to survive, and she wanted me to know before she went. It killed me she couldn't hear me say it back to her.

I never should have waited to tell her how I felt. I should have told her as soon as I realized, but I didn't want to scare her away. She'd already been through so much, could spook so easily, I thought holding onto the words would be better. Plus, I didn't want it to have anything to do with Vincent. After the last couple of days, however, I've come to the realization that it doesn't matter what's going on in our lives, if I love her, and I do, she needs to know it.

With her family gone, it'll be a lot easier to tell her everything that's been sitting in my heart, waiting for this chance.

Connor is hardly out the door when she tugs on my hand to pull my attention to her. I turn to find her smiling at me, waiting expectantly for the kiss we both want. Need. I surpassed want the second I knew she was gone from the firehouse.

Still holding her hand, I stand from the chair and move to the edge of the bed, lowering myself to it beside her. I take note of those gray eyes, tired but shining with happiness that she's here, awake, alive, and I know that mine mirror hers.

Lifting my hand to her face, I brush my fingers along her jawline, then tuck a piece of hair behind her ear. I didn't know it was possible for my heart to feel like it's grown immeasurably because of another human, but here I am. So fucking in love with this woman, the last couple of days have nearly killed me. Just seeing her eyes open has me on cloud nine.

I honestly don't know what I would have done if I'd lost her.

"I know, but I'm okay," she whispers, squeezing my fingers. I wonder if I said the words out loud, or if the emotion is just conveyed by the look I'm giving her. "I'm sorry for putting you through that."

"Shh," I murmur, shaking my head before the words are out of her mouth. "Don't be sorry. This isn't your fault. I'm just glad you're okay."

Now Savanna is shaking her head at me. "But I'm not. I won't be until you kiss me."

That makes me chuckle.

Leaning in, I bring both hands to her face to cup it, my lips tenderly brushing across hers. It's soft and sweet. I don't intend to turn it into anything else, but Savanna has different ideas, the gentle kiss not enough for her.

Moving towards me, she groans so I gently push her back to the bed, my lips becoming harder against hers. When I tilt her head she complies easily, opening to me, sighing into my mouth as my tongue sweeps into the warm crevice of hers. She tastes like mint from the mouthwash she used after she first woke up, and I wonder if she was thinking ahead to this inevitable moment.

It's a long, languid kiss, one I'm sure we'll repeat a few times before she falls asleep, but I finally ease back, breaking our lips apart. I smile at the dreamy appearance on her face, her eyes opening to reveal a dazed look. I'm not sure if it's from the kiss or the medication, but I'm going to choose to believe it was the former.

"You okay now?" I question with amusement.

"Feeling much better, but you should probably do that a few more times, just to be on the safe side," she says, grinning. I can tell it hurts when she winces, her expression falling. "How bad is it?"

I frown. "How bad is what?"

She shifts uncomfortably, her gaze dropping. Quietly, she clarifies, "My face."

I rub my thumbs gently along her cheekbones, my fingertips dancing along her jawline. I take in the clear parts of her skin, the bruises that mar the skin beneath her eyes, and the angry red lines from the gashes on either side of her head. There's one above her temple, the other below her hairline, glue holding both wounds together.

Sighing contentedly, my lips crook upward as I take in all the different parts of her. "You're more beautiful than the day I saw you checking me out in that elevator ."

Her eyes roll, but at least they lift back to mine. "Nate, seriously."

"I am being serious," I tell her, my tone earnest. I search her eyes, imploring her to believe me. "I thought you were stunning then, but that was before I knew you. Before I knew your strength, your smarts, your willingness to put other's safety above your own. Before I knew your laugh, and your smile, or how your eyes sparkle when you're excited or happy."

A blush creeps into her cheeks, and my smile deepens. I can tell she wants to look away from me out of shyness, but she doesn't. Her show of bravery fuels me, spurring me forward.

"You are one of the most courageous women I've ever met, and I am so damn proud to call you mine. Don't ever doubt I find you more beautiful today than I did that day," I say sincerely, watching her cheeks redden by the second. "Tomorrow I will find you more beautiful than today, because every day I learn something more about you, and each new thing adds to your beauty."

"Nate…"

I put a thumb over her lips, gently brushing it along the fullness. "I should have told you this when I first realized it, but I didn't want to taint it. I wanted a perfect moment without anything hanging over our heads, but I know now that doesn't matter. Perfection is what we make it, and there's no more perfect moment than now."

I can see the hope in her eyes, and I slide one hand into her hair, leaning close enough I can feel her breath on my lips but pausing to still see her eyes. "Savanna, I love you. So much. I didn't realize I could love someone as much as I love you."

Tears are shining in her eyes, making them sparkle in the most brilliant way. "I love you too, Nate. So, so much. I wish I'd told you sooner too, but we're not going to live in the past with any regrets, okay?" Fisting my shirt in her fingers that are poking out of her cast, she tugs me forward until our lips are barely brushing. "Promise me?"

I still, pulling back enough to look at her. I can hear the implication in her words; more than not telling her I loved her, she doesn't want me to feel guilty, or blame myself for what happened. She already knows me well enough to know that's exactly where my thoughts have taken me. It makes me feel naked and vulnerable in front of her, but I face it, face her, being brave like she's been for me.

"Sav…"

"It wasn't your fault, Nate. You did everything you possibly could to protect me. I made a choice. More than one of them." A tear falls from her eye as she runs her fingers along the stubble on my face. I haven't shaved in a few days and her fingers running over the thick whiskers feels nice.

"You still saved me. You got me to trust you, to tell you what was going on. You kept me safe this entire time. You got me to love your friends and trust them too, and when I needed you all the most, you were there," she says with conviction. "If it hadn't been for you, no one would have been following me. Liam wouldn't have been there to help me as quickly as he did."

Her fingers curl into my jaw, ensuring I'm paying attention, though I don't think I could tear my eyes off her if I wanted to. "If I didn't love you, I might not have had the will to survive, or the courage to crash the car. Loving you got me through this. So promise me—no regrets."

I have to take a few shaky breaths, swallow a lump of emotion in my throat, and sniff twice before I can find the strength to speak. I never would have looked at it like that if it weren't for her. I'd have spent day after day beating myself up, even after the talk with Brody.

Savanna's declaration releases me, sets me free of my own guilt, though I'm sure I'll still need to work through some of it. Finally, I nod. "I promise. No regrets. No living in the past."

The smile I get in return lights up her eyes, and though I'm sure it still hurts, she doesn't flinch this time. "Good. Now kiss me until I'm so tired I have no option but to sleep. And when I wake up, I want you to tell me the full story of the auction."

Warmth blooms in the center of my chest and moves outward until it fills every inch of me. The auction was a success. Jordan said we'd have enough money to cover the bill with the money the bar already had. Everyone rallied together to help. Even when I didn't want to take it, even when I'd lost the ability to care.

"Just wait until you hear about Liam's outrage at earning far, far less than Brody," I tell her with a chuckle, my lips hovering right above hers.

Her closed eyes pop open with surprise, which quickly transforms into amusement. "Don't tempt me out of a quick make-out session."

My lips brush across hers with the same gentleness of our first kiss. I murmur against her lips, "Wouldn't dream of it."

Then I kiss her and kiss her. Until she's so tired she has to sleep.

EPILOGUE

SAVANNA

FIVE MONTHS LATER...

"Hey Sav?"

I look up from the computer to see Bryn standing in the doorway of the office, her chin length hair looking exceptionally cute all barrel curled. Nate calls it my office, but I roll my eyes when he does; it's our office.

I officially accepted his offer when I went back to work a month after getting out of the hospital. He wouldn't let me back any sooner than that. Now, after getting certified in California, I do all the accounting and bookkeeping for the bar. Nate let his old accountant go after he got confirmation everything I did was perfect, and in working order. I wasn't surprised, but I had to prove it to Nate, for myself at least, before he did anything drastic.

The bookkeeping doesn't keep me busy enough, though,

so I spend my other time serving, and when Nate isn't around, I manage the bar. That's not all. Nate's grandparents, Bob and Mildred, asked me to consult for them when they found a new firm to join after leaving Prescott and Wesley. They said before me, they'd never met someone they felt comfortable enough with at the firm, which was why they changed consultants every time they came in. I asked them why they hadn't left years earlier, and they amused me greatly when they admitted they enjoyed making everyone there uncomfortable.

"What are you doing here?" I ask, raising an eyebrow.

Bryn and I have grown close since I started, and given that I do the scheduling these days, I know she's not on it. I'm surprised she'd be here for dinner without telling me beforehand. Maybe she has a date.

Waving a hand casually, she rolls her eyes. "I left a jacket here last weekend and I need it for tonight. It completes the outfit."

I give her a once over. Black jeans, sheer black, long-sleeved blouse with a lace camisole underneath, and her leather jacket in her hands.

"You look hot," I fan my face. "Hot date?"

"I am too busy for dates between work, Gran, and serving," she laughs, shaking her head. "A friend has a party tonight."

I snap my fingers. "Too bad. I was looking forward to some juicy gossip about a man."

She waves me off. "On my way back here, Martin asked me to let you know there's a guy asking for you at the bar."

"Oh." I check my watch. It's almost six.

At one time, hearing the words someone was asking for me would send me into a tailspin, but these days it does little more than make me curious. Therapy, and my worst nightmare being dead, probably have something to do with that.

I have no idea who it might be. I met with a vendor earlier today, but the next meeting I have scheduled isn't until the following week. Maybe a vendor dropped by unexpectedly. I've learned they do that sometimes.

Nate should be here soon too. He worked at the firehouse yesterday, so I only saw him briefly this morning when I was getting ready for work, when he'd told me to dress up a little so he could take me for dinner tonight. When I chose an off-white cable knit sweater dress with a scooped neck that flares a bit at mid-thigh, he grinned at me, called me perfect, then threw me on the bed before I could finish getting ready. I didn't object.

"I don't want to know what you're thinking right now," Bryn laughs, and my cheeks heat. "I gotta go, though. I'll see you tomorrow. Don't keep the guy at the bar waiting with whatever you're daydreaming about."

"I'm not daydreaming about anything!" I call out after she spins and leaves.

Whoever it is, I want to get rid of them before Nate shows up. I've been looking forward to our date night all day, and while I may have denied my daydreaming to Bryn, I've been fantasizing a lot after this morning.

I really thought our appetite would have curbed by now, and I guess it has slowed a bit. We can be in bed together without ending up tangled between the sheets, but I still constantly want the man.

I suppose we did go six weeks after the hospital where we didn't have sex. Nate was way too concerned he'd hurt me, and he has the willpower of a saint. We were a grouchy household by the time I said fuck his rules and got him so worked up he couldn't fight it any longer. I learned more than a few things that night about what drives him wildest.

Pushing away from the desk, I make my way into the kitchen, pausing for a moment when I don't hear the usual sounds of the guys. Looking around, I realize no one is in here.

That's weird.

A small knot forms in my stomach as I think worst case scenario. They wouldn't all quit at the same time, with no notice, would they? I've gotten to know all these guys and they're all a great bunch. Happy, goofy, here to do a good job while having a good time doing it. No one has come to Nate expressing unhappiness, so I'm not sure why no one is in the kitchen. An emergency?

I glance towards the back door and bite my lip, thinking of the night Tony overdosed. Would they all have rushed out there if it happened again?

A loud commotion from the front of house catches my attention, my frown deepening as I twist back to the swinging doors. I can see a bunch of people standing around out there, which is just as unusual as no one in the kitchen, especially on a Tuesday evening.

Deciding I'll leave the issue with the kitchen staff for a moment to investigate what's going on in the bar, I head towards the doors, pushing my way through them only to come to an immediate halt.

I blink once, twice, a third time, trying to understand what I'm looking at. The entire bar staff is out front, along with the firehouse crew. There are other faces I recognize as well, but I'm so caught off guard that everyone is turned to face the door I just came through, that I'm having trouble placing them.

Until I recognize one couple.

"Mildred? Bob?" I ask, shaking my head in confusion. Then I realize Elizabeth, Nate's mom, is standing there along with his dad. Jordan is next to them. "What's going on?"

No one speaks. The only indication I get from any of them is when Mildred nods her head to the side, indicating a spot I can't see from my vantage point. With just as much uncertainty as before, I take a few tentative steps forward, my heart galloping in my chest with anticipation.

I'm not prepared for what I see when I turn the corner at the edge of the bar, both hands coming up to cover my mouth as I gasp loudly and stop.

Down on one knee is Nate, holding a black velvet box in his hand, his other held out to me.

It takes me a moment to move my feet because I'm so overwhelmed by the sight and what I think is about to happen. Tears sting my eyes, but I manage to move closer to him, taking his outstretched hand.

The man is beaming at me like I've never seen. Enthusiasm lights up his bright blue eyes, and there's pride in his smile. Someone who didn't know him may mistake his reddening neck and face as excitement, but I know it's nervousness.

He's so damn handsome I can hardly stand it, and I have to hold myself back from screaming "Yes!" before he has a chance to ask me.

"Hi," he says, eyes dancing.

"Hi," I respond, swiping a finger under my eye to catch a tear. "You're making me cry."

His grin ratchets up a notch. "These are the kind of tears I don't mind, but I could stop what I'm about to do if you'd rather."

"No!" I cry, and there's laughter all around us. I think the whole room had fallen away until that moment, but now I remember everyone we know seems to be here. Nate must feel rather sure of my answer for him to invite everyone. He'd be right, and I love that he's included his family and our friends. "Please continue."

Nate chuckles, giving me a short nod before he takes a deep breath. He gazes up at me with so much love shining in his eyes that I think I might melt into a puddle.

"I know we've only been together for six months, so this might seem sudden, but Savanna, I love you," he says, his hand squeezing mine. "I think maybe I've loved you since the first day I saw you in that elevator and you called me a disgusting, filthy pig."

I can't help it; I throw my head back and laugh. I am never going to live that down.

"Christ, I love that sound. I love it more when I know I'm the cause of it," he beams, a sense of pride mingling with the love in his eyes. "I know I want to hear you laugh for the rest of my life. I want to spend every day getting you to laugh, and smile, on good days, and especially on bad ones."

He brings my hand to his lips, kissing the back of it before he continues, and yep, I'm a puddle of goo because of this man.

"I want to hold you every night, grow with you every day, have a family with you when we're ready, then get old with you and chase grandkids around." I swear his eyes are shining with his own tears, but I can't be sure because mine are filled with moisture.

"Will you make me the luckiest guy out there, and marry me?"

I could easily scream my yes, jump into his arms, and kiss him until we're both breathless. And I will. But I'm really impressed with how composed he's been through this entire proposal. It's completely different from when he asked me on a date, and it might be a little devious, but I kind of want to make him sweat a little.

I suck in my bottom lip, releasing it a moment later. "You want me to be your wife?"

Confusion clouds his eyes, and I have to bite back a laugh. "That's generally what happens when a guy marries a woman…"

"Like you're asking me to be yours forever?" I raise an eyebrow.

He's going to give me hell later. I can see the panic creep into his eyes, like he isn't sure this was the right move, something I remember fondly from when he asked me on our first date. It's adorable he hasn't clued in yet.

"I am," he says hesitantly. His Adam's apple bobs as he swallows hard.

Biting down on my bottom lip, I know he can see the amusement in my eyes because his start to narrow at me. I think it's dawning on him that I'm toying with him.

I give him the most innocent smile I can muster. "You're my boss."

There it is. The recognition of the first time he asked me out. "If that's a problem, you're fired."

Laughter spills out of me as I throw myself into his arms, shouting what has been in my heart since the second I saw him down on one knee. "Yes! Of course I'll marry you!"

Nate's arms wrap around me, his lips capturing mine, and for a moment we stay right there. Then he's standing up, spinning me around as we kiss each other until we're both gasping for air and he's setting me back on my feet.

I'm not sure if the cheers and claps were happening the whole time we kissed, or if they only start as we finally part because the whole world seemed to have disappeared for a time, and it was just the two of us, sharing the moment together.

Though I want nothing more than to stare at this incredible man for the rest of the night, I glance to my side, my smile glowing as I look at our friends and family.

Then do a double take as one face catches my attention.

"Connor?" I shriek at my brother. I realize that Devin is beside him, and my dad is behind them. "Dad? Dev?"

My head snaps back to Nate, my eyes wide, and he grins at me, giving me a nod to go. His eyes convey an ease and happiness that says he knew this would happen when I saw them. He anticipated it.

I'm halfway to them when I recognize one more familiar face standing beside Connor, and I scream so loud I'm sure I scare half the people in here. "Maddie!"

I'm overwhelmed at the sight of my best friend and my family, the four of them enveloping me in a hug that seems like it's one giant embrace. I think I actually go from one to the next, but the tangle of arms all seems to be the same. When I get to Maddie, she squeals and I shriek while we hug fiercely.

I can't believe she got time off to come out here. We saw each other at Christmas when Nate and I went to Colorado, but she wasn't able to get out here to visit.

"Let me see the ring in person!" she says, letting me go.

My eyes widen to saucers, and I spin around, looking for Nate, who is right behind me, chuckling.

"The ring!" I gasp, horrified. "I didn't even let you put it on!"

"It's not going anywhere, beautiful," he says, laughter erupting around us. "At least I know you didn't say yes for the merchandise."

When I thrust my hand in front of him, he takes it, smirking, and slips the ring on my finger. It's the perfect size. I don't know how he knew, but he did, and I love him even more for it.

"Oh, wow," I murmur, looking down as it sparkles on my finger. It's white gold, and has a larger diamond in the middle, with little diamonds spread sporadically through the metal that is cut into an intricate pattern down each side of the band. It's breathtaking with all the character woven through it. "Nate, it's beautiful."

Tilting my chin up with a finger, he smiles at me. "Not as beautiful as you," he murmurs, leaning in to brush his lips to mine, eliciting a sigh from me. "I love you."

I smile, wrapping my arms around his waist, pressing my cheek against his chest. "I love you too."

Hours later, in the comfort of our bed, I'm blissed out, draped over Nate's chest, cuddling after the best orgasm of my life. I should probably be exhausted after all the excitement, and then the amazing sex, but I'm wide awake.

The way he's running his fingers up and down my back with one hand, and playing with the ring on my finger with the other, tells me he's feeling the same. Perhaps he'll spin the ring for hours and hours until he's ready to give into sleep. I have a feeling he's going to play with the band a lot if the pride radiating from him is any indication.

Claimed me as his own for life. Happiness spreads through my chest and I smile against his. I can't wait to start that life together with him. We're well on our way, I suppose. Maybe getting engaged after six months seems fast, but for us it seems like it's right on par considering I basically moved in with Nate the day I officially met him and haven't left, having given up my apartment before it was even livable again.

"Let's go to Vegas," I say, smiling when he stops all movement. Not even his chest rises with breath.

He clears his surprise with a cough. "You want to elope?"

Lifting myself up, I rest my arm on his chest and gaze at him, shaking my head. "No. I want us to plan something, but I think we should do it in Vegas. I don't want to make your family travel to Colorado, or mine travel to California. Let's go to Vegas, and whoever wants to come can come."

There's a long pause as he regards me thoughtfully, then quirks an eyebrow. "But no Elvis, right?"

I laugh, giving my head another shake. "No Elvis. A real wedding in a real venue, not some chapel on the corner. We could go a few days early with some of our friends, hang out at the pool, maybe catch a show, or go to a club." I run a fingertip along his chest. "We can do our own thing, and if people want to join us, they do, but they could do their own thing too. We just make it a fun few days and cap it off with you becoming my husband."

I can see the gears turning in his head as he thinks about it, envisioning it as I lay it out for him. A soft smile plays on his lips, and I wonder if he's picturing me walking down the aisle towards him in some beautiful white wedding dress, our friends and family surrounding us. My stomach does a somersault at the thought of it.

"You mean, you becoming my wife," he says after a moment, winking at me.

I lean closer to him, my lips just barely brushing his. "I really love the sound of that."

"Me too," he murmurs, his fingers tangling in my hair as he pulls me down so our lips fully connect. He adds against my lips, "Okay. Let's do Vegas."

Sliding a leg across his body, I straddle his waist, nipping at his bottom lip. This man. He changed my entire world, opened me up and showed me exactly what love truly was. Now I'm lucky enough to call him mine for the rest of my life. "I love you so much."

"Show me," he requests.

So I do.

MEMORIES WITH FIRE EXCERPT

Climbing out of my car at the firehouse before shift, after hanging up from a conversation with my mother about the blind dates she's been setting me up on, I lose my grip on my coffee mug. Reflexes are great, but they can be a bitch when you're wearing white. Somehow I manage to save the mug from the ground while everything else in my hands goes flying, and not before I wear half my coffee.

Deep breath, count to five, release.

"Good morning, sunshine! I love what you've done with your sweater! Brown is a good color on you."

Quinn Kelly. My partner in crime. My other half at work. My best friend. She's wearing her shaggy, jet-black hair up in a high ponytail, a pair of aviator sunglasses covering her eyes. I wonder what color they are today. Every day is different, and they could be any color of the rainbow. The girl loves her contacts.

I glare at her, close my door, sling my bag over my shoulder, and grab my phone and keys from the ground. "I'm glad one of us is in a good mood."

Quinn grins at me as I join her in our walk across the parking lot to the side door of the building. "Is this freaky Friday? Have we switched roles? Normally I'm the surly one."

Rolling my eyes, I punch my code into the door and let us inside. "You are not."

Quinn pretends to be a hard ass, but five minutes after meeting her, you realize that she's nothing but a flirt. She just doesn't care about doing things the conventional way or what most people would consider the proper way. Unless we're on the job. On the job, she's professional but to the point, and she doesn't take crap from patients that are being difficult. It's one reason I love being her partner.

"Am too. Ask Tony, he'll tell you." One of our frequent flyers. He loves trying to get a rise out of Quinn; sometimes she lets him, others she doesn't. When I don't respond, she nudges me on our way to the locker rooms. "Seriously. Was last night that bad?"

I texted her when I got home so she got a quick debriefing, demanding that I give her more details today when I told her I was tired and going to bed. I wish I could say that was the only thing making me grumpy this morning.

Without meeting her eyes, I sigh. "My mom already has another date lined up for me."

Quinn stops in her tracks, grabbing my arm to effectively stop me as well. The girl has some serious strength on her. Despite working out along with her, I'm rounder and softer where she's strong and solid.

"You're shitting me, right?" The look on my face says it all, and she bites down on her lip to keep from laughing.

"Damn. Deb works faster than I do on ladies night with a pack of studs."

Rolling my eyes again, I refuse to comment, mostly because it's true. Pulling out of her grip, I spin around to come face to face with a wall of muscle, stopping only because two hands grip my arms. We're both dangerously close to wearing what's left of my coffee. At my five feet, four inches I'm short enough to be staring at a chest. One that I recognize before I even lift my head to see a gorgeously handsome face of a man grinning down at me.

"Good morning, beautiful! How are we today?"

"Ugh."

Liam King. One hell of a looker, charming to boot, usually hilarious, and one hundred percent playboy. We're good friends and I love him to pieces, but I don't think I can stomach his bright, buoyant personality this morning. Or questions about last night. Everyone knew I was going out on another blind date. Part of the reason I woke up so cranky was because I knew I'd have to tell them all about it.

Ducking around Liam, I head towards the locker room amidst giggles from Quinn. I can hear her tell him about my mom's newest date request. She wouldn't be laughing if it were her. Then again, Quinn would never allow such a thing to happen. Nor would her mother ever do such things to her. Quinn's mom took off when she was a little girl, and essentially raised herself after that.

"Just tell your mom you're dating me!" Liam calls out as I open the door to the locker room, heading inside. "I'll pretend to be your boyfriend!"

My mother has met Liam. She's met everyone from the firehouse. There's not a chance in hell she would believe that I was dating Liam, nor would I want her to think it. As much as I adore Liam, the guy gets around. He's not exactly what I would call a safe option, in so many ways, and if I'm going to be forced into a boyfriend, it's going to be with the safe option. Someone who likes nights in, doesn't do a lot of crazy activities, hasn't had a heaping helping of women prior to me. Dull. Boring. Practical. Maybe a video game nerd or a computer whiz. Maybe someone who likes slo-pitch because that's relatively safe, and the one thing I do enjoy being a part of. A guy who can fit in with my friends on the occasional night out. I'm not sure if I can find a gamer or computer guy like that, but if I can't, I'm happy to stay single. The crazy cat lady. It's not a bad thing to be. Animals need love.

"You know what?" Quinn says, following me into the change room. I drop my stuff on the bench and open my locker as she continues, "I think it's a good thing your mom is doing this. It's good to see you going out. I know you don't necessarily want to go, but I think it's good for you."

I glance in her direction with a sneer.

"Don't look at me like that. I'm serious. You're probably worse than Nate was with the lack of dating life and look at him now. With the love of his life, getting regular ass, and it shows. You just need some regular dick." She snaps her fingers at me. "Maybe that's all you need! Maybe we should just go out and get you laid."

None of this is helping my mood. Quinn knows I'm not the girl that goes out and gets laid by some random guy. Not even by a non-random guy.

"Stop!" I tell her, throwing my sweater in her direction. We're both half stripped from our street clothes and getting into our work uniforms. "We are not going to go and—oh my god!" I screech, eyes widening in her direction.

Without realizing I'm doing it, I'm pointing at her. More importantly, I'm pointing at her chest which is still covered by her sports bra. "Did you... what did you... are those..."

"Nipple piercings!" she says excitedly. Obviously mistaking my horror for enthusiasm, she yanks the side of her sports bra over and exposes a perky breast to me. "I got it done two days ago. I wondered if you'd notice. Isn't it amazing?"

"Quinn!" I can feel my cheeks flaming, a hand coming up to cover my eyes. I love her, I really do, but I don't need to see her boobs. Not that this is the first time. Quinn has no scruples about baring it all for anyone who wants to look. Sometimes I envy that about her.

Grabbing my hand, she pulls it down from my face. "Don't be a prude. Check it out. I got them both done. They're sore and sensitive, though, so I haven't been able to really try them out. But I love them."

I inch an eye open, then the other, giving in to take a look. It's brief, mostly just to satisfy her, but in the quick look before I turn away to finish getting changed, I have to admit, they suit her. "Just keep them clean. Don't let them get infected. That would be something awful."

I catch her rubbing her boobs out of the corner of my eye, both of them firmly back in place behind the cover of her bra. I nearly snort because I can tell she doesn't want to think about it, yet I put the thought in her mind. She knows the horrors of what can happen if something gets infected. Thankfully, she knows how to take care of herself.

"Okay, back to you," she says, making me sigh. "While I think it's a good idea and I think you should go out on another date—as many as she wants to set you up on—if you truly don't want to go, you need to tell her. You've got to lay down the law. Tell her straight up—"

I cut her off. "I know, I—"

"Let me finish!" she interrupts, raising a hand to tell me to stop speaking. "Tell her straight up: Mom, I love you, but I don't want to go on anymore dates. You need to stop setting me up because I won't go on any more of them. I will find my own man, or I won't, but it's my life and I'm going to live it how I want to live it."

By the time she's done, I'm dressed for shift and I've turned to face her, my arms crossed over my chest as she finishes changing. Raising an eyebrow in question if I can now talk, she waves me on. "I already told her. I made her a deal that I would consider this date on the condition she never sets me up again."

"Oh." At least she has the decency to look a little sheepish. It only lasts for a second before she's grinning at me and tossing her stuff in her locker. "Good! When's the date?"

"I told her I would consider it. I didn't tell her I would go on it."

"Oh Hails." Slinging an arm around my shoulders after we both shut our lockers, we head towards the door. "Just say yes. One more date won't kill you."

"I'll think about it."

Quinn, Liam, and Shawn are all howling with laughter over the recount of my date. Even Brody is sitting there with a smirk on his face, and I've heard him chuckle a couple of times as I told my tale. The three men are firefighters, and all my family in this house.

"I'm telling you, Hails. Just tell your mom you're dating me. She'll leave you alone right quick," Liam says, causing everyone to burst into another round of laughter. He holds a hand up to silence everyone. "If you tell her we're dating, she'll end up so busy trying to convince you to break up with me that you won't need to worry about any more dates."

Though I laugh, he has a point. I could see my mom telling me to run for the hills if she thought I was seriously dating Liam. Maybe I'll keep the idea in my back pocket just in case she doesn't stick to her end of the bargain when it comes to this final blind date I'm considering.

"You'll be my secret weapon, Liam," I assure him. "There's no one I'd rather fake date than you."

"I don't know," Shawn disagrees. "Maybe you'd rather fake date the new guy. Your mom won't be busy doin' nothin' to you then."

The new guy. Right. Today is his first shift. I don't even know his name yet, but as we all sit around the conference room where we hold our morning briefings, I imagine Nate will be walking in with him at any moment. He's here to replace Mac, the oldest member of our crew, who retired last week.

That final shift with him nearly killed us all. Since the day I started, Mac has treated me like one of his own, and I came to love and adore him. Not having him around is weird. There's a sense of loss around the house with his departure, but none of us have talked about it. I think that makes it too real. This new guy, however, is also going to make it feel real.

"I wonder if he's cute," Quinn muses, glancing at me with a twinkle in her eye. I know for a fact that she'd never lay a hand on someone she works with, but that doesn't mean she won't flirt. Good or bad looking. Quinn doesn't discriminate. "Maybe you could get a real date, Hails."

I roll my eyes at her. As grumpy as I felt this morning, I'm feeling better since we got together for our meeting. Retelling the story of last night made me see how funny it could be if I thought of it in the right light, even if it was annoying in the moment.

Today isn't going to be so bad, I decide. Maybe this new guy won't be so bad either.

"Oh shit," Quinn whistles low. "He is cute."

My back is to the door, but she's facing it so she sees the new arrivals before I do. Everyone in the room straightens and turns their attention to the front. My head swivels in the direction of the door, and I see Nate first, his chocolate brown hair styled a little longer on top, vivid blue eyes glancing around the room, nodding a good morning to all of us.

I don't spend much time looking at Nate because my eyes are immediately drawn towards the man walking in behind him. For a second, I think I'm seeing things. There's no way. It isn't possible. I've got to be hallucinating. All this dating is bringing up crazy things in my subconscious, and now I'm imagining things that aren't there. This must be a dream and I'm about to wake up any second.

"Good morning, everyone," Nate says to the room, though I hardly hear him. I've blinked so many times that someone who didn't know me would probably think I have a tic. "I'd like to introduce you all to—"

"Luke?"

My voice sounds foreign to me. I don't even realize I'm the one who has spoken until everyone's eyes shift in my direction. Not that I'm looking at them. The only one that I'm staring at is the man at the front of the room beside Nate. The one who's light ash hair is no longer worn in a crew cut but buzzed close to his head. The one whose eyes I could never decide were blue or green because it always depended on the light. The one who had dimples that melted my heart every time he flashed me a hint of a smile.

The one gaping at me, mouth hanging open in surprise. "Hailey?"

"You two know each other?" Nate asks, sounding as surprised as I feel.

Thankfully, I don't need to answer. The alarm sounds, indicating a call. I don't dare take my eyes off Luke, nor does he look away from me as we all listen. We've both been caught by surprise, and I don't think either one of us knows what to say or do in this moment. I'm more than thankful when the call turns out to be for only Quinn and I, but I can't seem to make myself move from my spot, my eyes firmly glued to the man standing a few inches shorter than Nate.

"Hailey, let's go," Quinn mutters, giving my shoulder a push as she gets up from her seat.

It's enough to pull me out of this trance. My head snaps in her direction and then I'm out of my seat, shaking my head and the cobwebs that seemed to have formed within seconds. "Coming."

"Stop in and see me when you're back," Nate says as we head towards the door.

I don't bother looking at Luke again, but I know his eyes are focused on me as we walk by Nate and him. I know because I can feel them. The same way I can feel my entire body tingling just from being around him. The shock was so great when he first walked in that I didn't realize it was there, but dang it, it is. Just like it used to be. My body always seemed to know when he was around even when we were ten years younger.

I don't know why he's here or how he ended up in my firehouse, but I do know that my day went from bad to worse. I expected the new guy to create waves in the house with Mac leaving and all, but I didn't expect this.

Luke Reyes. The first and only man I've ever loved. The only one to ever break my heart.

ACKNOWLEDGMENTS

Wooo! We made it, fam! Know that no matter who you are, mentioned or not, if we crossed paths, I am so grateful for you.

For the record, this is in no particular order. I let fate decide the order through a name picker!

Fitting that fate would pick Biffle first. You've been there through it all. Talking me down ledge after ledge. Where would I be without you? You helped shape me into the writer I am. Into the woman I am! It took you, and the years that we wrote together, to help find myself and leave my own Vincent. The number of times you have saved me from toasters is countless. I'm so fucking thankful for you. For never judging me. For always being my sounding board. For never telling me to STFU when it came to Nate and Savanna, because we both know how much I drone on and on. And a special thanks for being willing to always tell me if I'm right or if I'm being a massive fucking idiot. Love you x pie forever!!!

Fate is kicking ass with this list. A do-run-run-run a do-run-run. Rosebuds been with me for all the twists. A do-run-run-run a do-run-run. Da-do-da-do! Yeah! She's read my whole back list. Da-do-da-do! Yeah! Got us tattooed wrists. Da-do-da-do! Yeah! She's always there with the assist! A do-run-run-run a do-run-run….! Haha. I couldn't resist reliving one of the (many) best nights of my life with you! Singing in cars, hunting for Montana. I know not a single soul will understand a word I've said except for you. The Cowgirly to my Cowgrrl. The JC to my JT. You my Day One. The only one that's been there since the very first story I ever wrote about five guys we both love. I love you something fierce. Always. Isn't that something?

Jen. Soul sister. I'm not sure if words can truly convey what I want to express. Even as a writer, you leave me speechless. After thirty-four years of friendship, we both know that's hard AF to do haha. But honestly, do I need to tell you the words? Because let's face it, you already know them. Thanks for sticking with me through all the ups and downs, rollercoasters and smooth sailings. Thanks for putting up with me even when I didn't know how to put up with myself. And for listening to the endless talk about characters, stories, and books. To my chosen sister: I love you.

Mia, Mia, Mia. You put up with soooo much with this freaking book. Not only cause you had to listen to me constantly talk about it, but because you were the one who had eyes on it first with edits. You made it so much stronger before I had even reread it. Honestly, you made it possible for me to gather the courage and read it. I love you!

Q&C Sisterhood! Yaaaaa'll. Ya'll. Words won't do this justice because I can't put the feelings inside of my heart onto the paper. The late nights and early mornings at the kitchen table, surrounded by one or a bunch of you. You are all so integral to this book. I would not be here without you. You've helped me believe in myself. And on the days that I didn't believe, you believed for me. Ania, AJ, Allison, Feya, and so many others… I love you all so very much.

Midnight Crew… ya'll I would not be here without you. You guys got me through countless ups and even more downs. You were there with me when I needed to cry, when I needed to laugh, and all the in-betweens. I love each and every one of you!

My Busy McBeavers, Mandy & Jen. Damn ladies. You are so flipping amazing. You both have the patience of a Saint, helping me through this process, answering all of my questions, listening to me squeal and freak out and everything in between. I remember when I found out I would get both of you and holy hell, the fright I had with being paired with TWO powerhouses? Despite knowing I'd hit the jackpot of all jackpots, I was intimidated as all hell. You both showed me I didn't need to be—of you or of this industry. I never feel alone these days with you two around. I love you both.

FAB FOUR! Becky, Jen, and Catie. How can I possibly express my gratitude towards you? Dance parties, shenanigans, midnights—the good times are endless! You three are a piece of my puzzle I didn't realize was missing until it was found. I can't wait to see what the future holds for all of us, and all the crazy adventures we'll find along the way. Thank you for reading and commenting and making this story a million times better than it was. Thank you for being there through all my mental breakdowns, the tears of happiness, pain, anguish, frustration, joy, and love. I wouldn't be where I am today without you guys. I love you, my sisters!

Michelle! The ultimate hype woman! The one who doesn't just push me out of my comfort zone, you shove me out of it. Thank you for making me take the flying leap to do so many things that I wouldn't have otherwise done without you. Thank you for trusting me. Thank you for everything. I can't wait to see all the crazy shenanigans we get up to!!! Love you!

Bestie… where would I be without our midnight chats, cries, and laughs? You ground me in a way I didn't know I could be grounded. You are always there, just a text away, even though you're an entire world away. Thank you for being my partner in crime at the midnights, and teaching me SO MUCH – especially about timing on reels. Haha. I love and adore you.

Kaaaaaaatie… Cousin. Partner in crime. The one who actually knows all the answers to all the things. Thanks for being on this wild ride with me. Thanks for giving me space to be embarrassed to read the first draft of this book in front of you. And for laughing at me when I realized it was pretty good. Thanks for being a huge cheerleader and keeping me on track. Love you so much!

My whole team that helped make this the best possible… Brenda, Kristin, Sarah, Lemmy – THANK YOU! You all are Goddesses who often made the impossible, possible. I promise next time I'll be better prepared!

Tyneal… I know we may not talk these days, and you may never see this, but thank you for everything you did while I wrote Nate and Savanna. You were the perfect hype girl when I needed it the most. I miss you. I love you.

Uncle Neil… thank you for supporting me. Because of you, this book got the attention it deserved, and I am so utterly grateful. All my love to you!

Mom… thanks for reading and loving this story as much as I do. For all the late night chats about it and helping me make decisions I didn't know I could. I love you.

Dad… thanks for not reading and loving my story anyway. Thanks for all the hours you spent with River while I worked diligently. I appreciate and love you.

Grandma… You may have hated it, you may have wanted to burn it, but you gave me the best freaking tagline because of it. Despite your brusque words, I love you, and I'm glad you read it.

To my own version of Vincent… thank you for the

lessons along the way. I'm a motherfucking badass despite all that you put me through.

To my future Nate, Liam, or Brody… I can't wait for our own love story.

To all my readers, thank you. I love you. I'm so fucking grateful for you.

To all the women with a Vincent… I see you. You are strong. You are a badass. You can do this. You deserve so much more than you are getting, and my hope for you is that one day you will walk away. Maybe not today. Maybe not tomorrow. But one day. And if you ever need to talk, know that I'll answer.

ABOUT THE AUTHOR

Tamara lives with her cocker spaniel, River, in the beautiful city of Calgary, Alberta. When she's not busy writing the stories of sexy firemen, she can be found with River at the river, writing in her journal, biking, doing yoga, or collecting butterflies and unicorns. She's a poptart, through and through (think classic Britney, Christina, and NSYNC), a Swiftie, and enjoys country, rock, and a little piano instrumental when she's trying to focus. Give her a hot man to look at, a book boyfriend to swoon over, and friends to laugh with and she's set.

9 781068 904721